# Forever Fallen

*"Awake, arise or be forever fallen"*

— *John Milton, Paradise Lost*

## JOHN GRASHAM

ISBN: 0989870707
ISBN-13: 978-0989870702

# DEDICATION

To my wife Judy who encouraged me to finish it.

# CONTENTS

| | Acknowledgments | i |
|---|---|---|
| Chapter 1 | Prologue: Destruction | 1 |
| Chapter 2 | Competition | 7 |
| Chapter 3 | Collector | 13 |
| Chapter 4 | Burned Out | 20 |
| Chapter 5 | Hearing Things | 26 |
| Chapter 6 | The Headhunter's Call | 35 |
| Chapter 7 | Lunch in Manhattan | 42 |
| Chapter 8 | Remembering | 51 |
| Chapter 9 | Deciding | 61 |
| Chapter 10 | Change of Heart | 69 |
| Chapter 11 | Birth of Evil | 73 |
| Chapter 12 | On the Fortuna | 82 |
| Chapter 13 | Skeletons of the Past | 89 |
| Chapter 14 | To the Target | 100 |
| Chapter 15 | The Deluge | 107 |
| Chapter 16 | Finding the Prize | 118 |
| Chapter 17 | Looking at Death | 129 |
| Chapter 18 | The Blood Forge | 139 |
| Chapter 19 | Recovery | 147 |
| Chapter 20 | The Monolith | 162 |
| Chapter 21 | Blind Spot | 170 |
| Chapter 22 | Inside | 178 |
| Chapter 23 | Awakening | 188 |
| Chapter 24 | Siege | 196 |
| Chapter 25 | Demon | 206 |
| Chapter 26 | Command Word | 215 |
| Chapter 27 | Followers | 225 |
| Chapter 28 | Priest of Darkness | 235 |
| Chapter 29 | Child of Darkness | 244 |
| Chapter 30 | Throne Room | 252 |
| Chapter 31 | Capture | 263 |
| Chapter 32 | Elemental Trial | 268 |
| Chapter 33 | Sacrifice | 276 |
| Chapter 34 | Epilogue: Death and Birth | 291 |

# ACKNOWLEDGMENTS

To all of my proof-readers Judy, Elizabeth, Eric, Linda and Leslee:
I never imagined there would be so many corrections to make.

To my editor Arwen who gave me some tough advice:
your patience and persistence made a difference.

To Morgan for her cover painting:
you captured the atmospherics of the book so amazingly.

To all of you: Thank you.

# CHAPTER 1 - PROLOGUE: DESTRUCTION

*"Bring to my remembrance from what state I fell"*
*— John Milton, Paradise Lost*

5600 BC

She felt a sharp nip and jerked awake. Disoriented for a moment, she couldn't remember where she was or what had just happened. Then, in the dim moonlight, she saw that her arm had pinched her right breast as she slept. Her dream came back to her. She had been holding a baby in the dream, but what had happened then? She felt the images evaporating even as she tried to hold onto them. The baby in her dream had done something, what was it? Oh yes, it had bitten her on the nipple, the little devil. *Babies had to be cured of that during nursing*, she thought and a pleased grin came to her face as she lay in the dark. She woke a little more and shifted her weight. *Oh, that hurt.* She was far along in her pregnancy and was ready for it to be over. She turned and couldn't get comfortable. Her baby had not been born yet, but it would be soon. *Just not soon enough.* She shifted again, unable to find a position that was comfortable and allowed her to breathe.

So, Chalara turned her thoughts elsewhere. *If something is unpleasant, then deal with it or distract yourself.* She chose distraction and thought about the baby's future. This baby would be the King's second child, both through her. None of the other wives had been able to bring a child to term. *Only I've been able to give him a live child.* A smug smile crossed her face. She was still lean and strong. Her honey-colored hair was still the envy of every other woman in the harem. *I know how to please him.* She might be his oldest wife, but she was still his best wife.

The King said that the baby would be a girl. He said that he could tell. He said he could hear the baby's tiny thoughts. The king was a living god, able to read minds. How could anyone understand him? Still, he was her lord, and she was close to bearing him a second child. The first child, his son, had grown tall now and was away on a mission for his sire. She hoped he made it back in time to be here when his sister was born. The boy was so strong and powerful, almost as much as his father, but no one, not even his son, was as capable as the King. The King could do anything.

He had certainly proved it again tonight. She smiled as she turned to look at his huge frame lying next to her. The King had been very active in the harem last night. She was large with child and hadn't been able to participate as she liked to when the King visited the women's house by the sea, so she had satisfied herself with instructing the younger women in how best to please him. He had found that amusing and the other wives hadn't dared object when the king was obviously enjoying it all. Yes, it irritated her to have to share the King with the other wives, but truthfully, the King's appetites were far beyond the ability of any one woman. Truly, a dozen women would not be able to satisfy him. She looked again at his sleeping face. What did he dream of? Armies? Conquest? Death? Other women? That last thought made her chuckle. Looking around at the other fifty sleeping women, she smiled. *If he thinks of other women, after receiving the full attention of these fifty, then he could not be satisfied by any number!*

Chalara shifted once more, trying to get comfortable. This close to her time, she knew that very little could be done to ease her aches. She moved again and finally gave up and rose from his side, taking care to be silent. The King was a light sleeper and she did not want to wake him. She pulled on a loose robe and moved closer to his face. She mouthed silently, "Sleep, mighty king. All is well." She stepped quietly toward his feet and noticed a large ring on the floor near his massive hand. She reached down and picked it up and realized it was one of his golden trophy rings engraved with his seal, the bull. This would be the large hoop ring that the queen of Katal had worn in her nose. When the King had conquered her army and taken her prisoner, he took the ring from her. Then he had taken her, not as a wife or concubine, but as a kitchen slave. Chalara and the other wives had been fiercely proud of their Lord that day. He had refused to marry the Queen of Katal and sent her to work as a servant. He had said to the woman that he had plenty of wives and besides, who puts a snake into his own bed? He took the large nose ring and had it stamped with his seal and wore it as a trophy on his little finger. It was the only finger small enough to fit the large ring. The ring must have come off sometime during last night's more athletic events. She smiled again. Some of these girls were extremely limber.

She remembered those days when she was as supple. It seemed long ago, and in fact it was. It had been eighteen years ago, half her life and before some of these new wives had been born. She felt sad at the years gone but comforted herself. No other woman had ever born him a living child. Many had miscarried and some had delivered dead children. Some had died in childbirth along with their babies. A few had given birth to dead and deformed monsters. Those women had been burned in the daily sacrificial offerings to the king. The king's fires never died, and no day went by without a human sacrifice. The offerings kept him strong. When the king was strong, no one could hope to defeat him.

She slid the ring into a pocket in her robe so she wouldn't lose it. She decided she'd give it to him as soon as he woke, and thought she'd go for a walk by the shore while he slept. The sky had started to lighten with the predawn. She loved the cool of the sand and the breeze down by the sea. The guard outside the harem entrance nodded drowsily at her as she walked by.

The long corridor was lit by a few dim torches. She walked past a row of columns and then down a path to the sea. The breeze picked up immediately and she could smell the wind over the fresh water. The sand felt smooth under her bare feet and the breeze ruffled her hair. She felt the baby give a very strong, sudden kick. The baby turned and she felt what must have been an elbow jamming up against her ribs from the inside. She massaged her belly near the rib and after a while, the infant subsided. She resumed walking and noticed that dawn was breaking. She stared off into the distance over the sea, to catch the first light of the sun. A sudden thunderous horn blast sounded behind her from the fortress and the women's house.

She heard a rumbling crash after the horn blast and then the sound of screams. The baby kicked even harder. She winced and her heart started pounding. *What had happened?* She looked up the slope to the women's quarters.

A cloud of dust was rising from the center of the partially collapsed building. Her throat clenched tight at the sight of giant winged creatures descending from the sky, some landing on the ruins, others hovering or circling over the destruction. Some had already gone to ground. Four of the winged monsters flapped ponderously as they approached the ground, a burden suspended between them. *They were gigantic!* Their bodies looked greater than the largest vessels that rode on the sea. Their wings were larger than sails and they had bodies like bulls, though many times larger. Their heads were like those of bearded men, their extended wings fully four times as long as their massive bodies. Wings flapped ponderously under the weight of immense chains looped through huge rings attached to a silvery rectangular ... something. *Was it a chest? A case? No, it was too large.* Whatever it was, they labored to lower it to the ground between them. The silvery box looked to be as large as one of the rooms of the fortress, though it was more than twice as long as high.

The ground trembled under her. Beyond the carnage at the king's fortress and the women's quarters, in the distance to the southwest, she saw

3

a column of white like a vertical cloud rising to the sky. The billowing white mass towered up like a tree branching to cover the sky. Her mouth went dry and a sick knot formed in her gut. The earth shook, the clouds darkened, the fortress lay broken. *How could this happen?* Then she remembered the King had been there where the roof and columns had collapsed. *Was he hurt?* A strong wind began blowing from the southwest and the clouds sped toward her, darkening deeply in the center. The ground jerked sharply. She lost her balance and fell awkwardly, barely catching herself on her hands. She climbed back to her feet and ran over the shaking ground to a pile of boulders near the shore. She climbed the boulders and was able to see between the fallen walls and into the fortress. The wind continued strengthening and her hair flew back toward the sea. The rocks under her shifted and shook.

In the direction of the harem, she saw the giant winged shapes landing with their heavy burden. They set the silvery rectangular box set down in an area mostly clear of rubble, except for some pale shapes with spreading pools of red beneath them. She heard a loud bellowing voice that seemed to be shouting out commands or curses, or maybe both. It sounded like the King. She saw him and her heart sped up, but he was surrounded by winged figures as tall as himself. He shouted as they held him tightly, and she heard a curse here and there. The largest of the winged figures was wearing a helmet with glistening armor, carrying a bright shield and a huge sword. He strode up to the King and thrust his face inches from his chained prisoner. He shouted at the King and pointed with the sword at the gathering cloud in the southwest. He swept his sword backward at the fortress as if laying waste to it. The King bellowed and strained forward to reach his enemy but the other winged figures held the King and he was unable to break free.

The armored general of the King's captors stepped back and motioned for some of the others to come forward. Between them, they dragged the limp form of another large being that was contorted and bent almost double. Her breath caught in her throat. It was the King's brother! The armored enemy leader grabbed the King's brother and lifted him with one hand. He shook the limp form in the King's face. She gasped. This enemy general had unbelievable strength. It might be even greater than her Lord's. It was like seeing a rabbit being shaken in the jaws of a wolf.

The King cursed viciously and surged forward, tearing loose from several of his captors. He strained to reach his giant enemy, but the general stepped forward, slamming his shield into the King's face. Stunned, the King staggered back, but the armored monster stepped forward and struck a terrific blow with the flat of his sword against the side of the King's head. He went limp and a cry of terror tore from her mouth.

"My Lord!" She shouted. His attacker turned at her scream and saw her across the distance. The enemy general seemed to lock eyes with her. His long pale hair blew in the screaming winds, and he stared at her for a moment longer, paused and then nodded as if agreeing to a command only he could hear. He motioned at her with his shield hand as if he were brushing away an insect. Instantly, she felt herself lifted up and away, tumbling backward, the wind carrying her like a leaf until she suddenly splashed into deep water. Somehow the monster had thrown her a great distance without touching her! Frantically, she struggled back to the surface of the water. She paddled desperately as she tried to make for the shore, but the wind was lashing her furiously. Waves kept hitting her and flooding her eyes. She caught narrow glimpses of the beach but then waves crashed around her and she lost sight of the shore. She bobbed up and down between waves, unable to see the rubble of the palace.

The dawning sky was covered in dark clouds and distant winged figures. All of the creatures including the gigantic ones were airborne again, but this time without the giant silvery object between them. The full strength of the storm broke around her and she couldn't see anything beyond the driving, salty rain. *Salty rain? How could that be? Rain was never salty!* She struggled to stay afloat and paddled to keep her head above the surface. How long could she do this? A rumble sounded, deeper than the thunder of the storm that surrounded and submerged her. She seemed to feel the water itself vibrating.

She fought against the wind and tried to remember where the shore was. She decided the wind had been in her face when she was thrown into the water, so if she faced into the wind, the shore would be in front of her. She swam in the direction of the shore, but the wind seemed to push her further back with each stroke. She realized that her situation was rapidly becoming desperate.

Fear rose in her throat and she felt screams trying to force their way out. A wave surged over her and she tumbled again under the water. In the darkness beneath the waves she felt a sharp pain as something slammed into her shoulder from behind. Gasping to the surface, she saw that she'd been rammed by a floating timber. She grabbed it and pulled her head clear of the surging sea. Gulping large breaths, another wave crashed over her and she swallowed still more salty water. *There it is again, salty water. But the King's Sea is fresh water! What has happened?* She clung to the timber as a huge wave carried her to its crest. From the top of the wave, she saw the remains of the palace, water flooding into the ruins. It was as if the King and all of his works were sinking into the sea. Over the increasing rumble she saw something that nearly stopped her heart; a titanic foaming wave in the distance, rushing from the base of the storm. The wave swelled toward her and she knew she was doomed. Her baby would never be born.

Suddenly, she felt something grab her by the shoulder and felt herself pulled up and out of the water. A huge, muscled arm deposited her into a boat. A giant dark face loomed over her, water streaming from his hair. The giant yelled into her face through the screaming wind, "Mother! What has happened?" He held her head in his huge hand, a ring on the third finger. She looked past his face, saw a wave as large as a mountain hanging over them and fainted. As she passed into unconsciousness, there were shouts and screams and the roaring of endless water. The baby kicked her in the ribs again. All went dark around her.

# CHAPTER 2 - COMPETITION

*"When night darkens the streets, then wander forth the sons of Belial"*
*— John Milton, Paradise Lost*

The Present
It was a terrible night for a landing. Wind roared past the ships in their docks and lightning flashed almost continuously. The landing pad was lit with vertical search lights, but the rain was heavy and the air between the Russian's perch and the helipad seemed murky, like something already submerged. Through binoculars he saw storm-dimmed lights approaching from offshore. The lights flickered above the violent waves, seeming to slip and twist in the air as the helicopter fought closer to the shore.

The Russian continued to watch through his binoculars. The helicopter was barely visible but could still be seen moving spasmodically up and down and side to side in the treacherous blasts of the storm. *That pilot must be a nervous wreck. Only an order from the top would justify flying on a night like this. This has to be the one I'm waiting for.*

He felt the hair on his head and arms lift. A strobe-flash of lightning struck the bridge of a freighter docked two hundred meters from the approaching helicopter. The bolt blinded the Russian momentarily. A split-second later, an explosive thunderclap slammed into him with a shock wave that rocked him back and shook the floor beneath his feet. He blinked away the after-image and tried to find the helicopter again in his binoculars. He watched the craft buck as more sheets of rain lashed it. It finally settled to the pad, still seeming to rock from side to side in the wind as the blades rapidly wound down. The blades stopped their spinning motion, twitching up and down like the nervous hands of a frightened child.

*The engine is off. The pilot is probably slumped over the controls, exhausted. He's just glad to be alive after that landing. He isn't going to fly this bird anywhere until the*

7

*storm passes.*

The Russian watched patiently as a large limousine pulled up to the edge of the helipad. The driver got out, uselessly unfurled a large umbrella and ran to the side of the helicopter. A single passenger stepped out and under the umbrella, shielding something with his body. The drenched driver and passenger ran the short distance to the car and scrambled inside the waiting vehicle. A moment later, the car pulled away.

The Russian pulled out a phone and placed a call.

A voice answered at the other end and asked, "Yes?"

The Russian said, "The courier has landed and been picked up. The limousine is leaving the helipad at Dock Nine. Alert the men near the PetroRomania headquarters building that they are to be ready. I will join them soon." He ended the call without waiting for acknowledgment. He left the rooftop, descended the stairs to the street, mounted an expensive Ducati motorcycle and rode off into the pouring rain, unfazed by the downpour.

Inside the car, the courier sat dripping and trembling with the after-effects of too much adrenaline. He spoke rapidly in Romanian, "I can't believe we made it to shore. Twice I thought we would crash into the sea. Then when we came in to land, I thought we'd been hit by lightning! I am still shaking. Look at my hands!" He thrust his hands forward, palms-up toward the driver. Drops of water sprayed from his fingertips onto the back of the driver's neck. The driver did not flinch and said only, "Yes sir," as he pushed the accelerator pedal down and drove the car quickly away from Dock Nine.

Rain lashed the windows of the car. The wipers on the front windows seemed to have almost no effect, but the driver didn't seem bothered. The passenger slumped back into the seat and tried to calm himself. He wiped the water from his still trembling fingers and tried to dry his face with his sleeve. He breathed deeply three times and then reached for an inner front pocket in his overcoat. He removed a cell-phone and pressed a speed-dial code.

The ringing at the other end stopped. No voice spoke, but the courier knew that the answerer was waiting for him to speak. "I have the item and have arrived at Constanta. I'm on my way to the drop point right now."

The voice at the other end rumbled, "Did you look in the package?"

"No, sir. I was told not to."

"Good." The line clicked. The call was over.

The courier didn't know if that last word had been intended to mean that it was good that he'd been <u>told</u> not to look at the contents of the package, or that it was good that he'd not looked. Either way, he was glad he hadn't looked. That voice sounded like it belonged to someone that would not put up with disobedience to orders.

The trip from the Constanta port to Bucharest was a full two hundred thirty kilometers. The rain continued to pour down onto the car, but oddly, a motorcycle sped past them in the downpour. The courier shook his head. *What kind of a crazy man would be out in this kind of weather on a motorcycle?* He settled back in his seat and closed his eyes. He had several hours to rest and he intended to catch up on a little sleep if it was the last thing he ever did.

"Sir. We are in the city and arriving at your destination."

The courier sat up straight. *What? Hours gone by already?* He looked at his phone and saw that the time was very late. He stretched and yawned and with a sudden fright, checked for the package at his side. *Ah. There it is, nothing to worry about.* He looked out the window and saw the rain had stopped. Bucharest was a strange mixture of architecture, mostly old and gray, left over from its Communist past, but there were newer buildings. The driver turned the car down a side street that lead to the entrance of a modern building's parking garage.

In front of them, a car pulled from an alleyway. The courier's driver slammed his brakes. The doors of the blocking car opened and men jumped out, reaching inside their coats. The chauffeur frantically threw the car in reverse and stomped the gas pedal. He looked into the rear view mirror. His eyes grew momentarily huge and he flinched in advance of what was about to happen.

The tail-end of the courier's car was smashed by the front of an old delivery truck that had moved in behind them and sealed the entrance to the street. The driver's neck snapped against the headrest and he bounced forward. The airbag deployed and prevented him from being crushed face-first against the steering wheel. He bounced back against his seat and sat, senseless. In the rear seat, the courier was thrown backward and then rebounded forward, striking the back of the front seat. He slumped over in a daze, his lip bleeding.

The driver of the pickup and the men from the blocking car walked quickly to the courier's vehicle. Striding in the lead, the Russian went to the driver's door, opened it and leveled a silenced nine millimeter against the mumbling driver's temple. He pulled the trigger and a sound like a freed champagne cork echoed down the side street from one building to the next. The front passenger seat and the deflated air bag were covered in a splash of red. The corpse of the driver slumped bonelessly over into the bloody spray that coated the passenger side of the car.

The Russian grabbed the door handle to the rear seat, opened it, leaned in, grabbed the insensate courier by his collar and hauled him out the door. Pushing him against the car and seeing that the man could not stand, he held him up and motioned to one of his men. "Smelling salts," he said.

Handed the tiny packet, he held the man up while he cracked the little tube under the courier's nose. Flinching, he tried to move away but the

Russian held the pungent packet under his nose. Sputtering bloody saliva, the courier gasped and cursed incoherently.

One of the Russian's men handed him the package that had fallen down to the floor of the back seat section of the car. "Open it _very_ carefully," he said to the man.

The accomplice gingerly sliced along the brown paper wrapping, exposing the thick bubble wrap underneath. Piece by piece, he methodically cut through the remaining tape binding the bubble wrap and exposed a brownish-black, gnarled mass. The Russian momentarily mistook the object for a bundle of jumbled, polished wooden branches, each one and a half inches thick. When his eye landed on the silvery ring encircling one of the blackened pieces, his vision seemed to blur. With a sudden rush of comprehension he realized he was looking at a huge blackened skeletal left hand with a ring still on the third finger. The fingers were each about seven inches long. The breadth of the grasp from outstretched little finger to thumb would have been about fourteen inches. He took in a quick breath of surprise and then chuckled quietly to himself. _This giant was married?_ He also noted that the ring had a carved emblem of a bull on it. He motioned his man to re-wrap the skeletal hand. The Russian turned back to his captive and shifted his grip to the man's throat.

The courier had regained enough of his senses to understand some of his situation. He inhaled, perhaps to shout for help, but was cut short in a strangling gurgle as the Russian effortlessly cut off his wind with a vice-like tightening of his fingers on the man's throat.

The captive's hands shot to his neck to try to pry the fingers loose, but no amount of twisting could lessen their grip on him. Unmoved, the Russian held the courier until the man's face began to darken, his eyes bulging.

"Make sure you listen. One chance is all you will get. I will ask you questions. You will answer completely and truthfully. If you do not obey these instructions exactly, that will be the end for you."

The Russian raised his eyebrows significantly and stared at the courier's purpling face. The man nodded desperately and yet feebly. The Russian lessened his grip just enough to allow a small stream of air through the man's windpipe.

The courier's trapped breath whistled out his constricted throat and then he inhaled.

"Did you know what was in the package?"

The man swallowed with difficulty and spoke in a whispered rasp, "No!"

"What ship did the package come from?"

"The _Fortuna_."

"How do you know its name?"

"I was sent by helicopter to receive and carry a package to a drop point."

"Who was to receive the package?"

"I don't know. I don't even know where the drop point is. Only the driver knew."

"No. I knew as well. Now tell me what you know about who hired you. How much were you paid?"

"I do jobs for a friend who runs a casino for tourists. He gave my name to someone. I was going to get five hundred dollars American for this. I don't know who hired me. My friend never told me."

"You chose your friends poorly and now you've sold your life cheaply. You obviously know nothing, but I can't leave a loose end. Even one as pathetic as you."

The courier opened his mouth to plead, but the Russian pulled a knife from its sheath at his side and held its point to the man's neck just below his jaw line near the right ear. With the practiced precision of many such efforts, the Russian pushed the knife into the man's neck, through the skin, muscles and throat and out the left side of the neck. With a jerk, he pulled the entire blade out the front, severing veins, arteries and windpipe.

Now holding the dying but still gurgling man by the back collar, the Russian heaved the courier's body up and onto the hood of the car. He positioned the body on its back so that the nearly severed head lolled off the edge of the hood of the car in a way that would grab the attention of any onlooker. The Russian held out his hand and was handed a long pointed steel rod. The Russian took the rod and hefted it once to get its measure. Holding it firmly, he swung it over head, ramming the pointed end through the dead courier's body and puncturing the metal of the car's hood. The splayed, nearly decapitated corpse was pinned like a beetle in a display case.

The Russian held out his hand again and the man gave him the still open bubble-wrapped package. Looking at it to be certain of its contents, he nodded and handed it back. The man resealed the package and the men followed him out of the side-street and to a waiting van just around the corner. They got in and drove away. The Russian placed a call on his phone.

The click of the receiver at the other end sounded. "Yes?"

"I have it. The driver is done. The item came from the ship you named and the courier knew nothing else. I left the body of the courier in the way you specified. It is a big mess for someone to clean up," said the Russian.

"Good. Let him digest that message for a while. He should remember me now. Meet me at the airport and give me the package. You'll receive payment for this work and I have a quick job for you in North America. I have some associates there that need to learn to be more discreet." The phone line went dead.

He spoke to the driver. "The airport."

The driver said, "Otopeni or Băneasa?"

"Otopeni."

The Russian looked idly out the window at the business district as they drove. *I assume Dmitri meant the international airport and not the charter airport.* It was still quiet in the downtown streets. *No flashing lights. Still no police. I suppose the kinds of crimes that happen in this part of town don't often get reported to the police. Not in these posh skyscrapers.* He listened for sirens, shouts, anything. All was quiet. Not for long.

# CHAPTER 3 - COLLECTOR

*"What in me is dark illumine"*
*— John Milton, Paradise Lost*

Janos Parasca sat in his penthouse corner office overlooking the city of Bucharest. His eyes swept the city, calculating and weighing the ancient metropolis as if it were a puzzle to be solved. A man at the end of middle age, his face was weathered and tanned a deep brown with many wrinkles, but mainly on the right side. That side showed his age and several parallel scars, the remains of an old confrontation. The left was his better side. No scars and fewer wrinkles. He toyed with one of the small statues from his collection. It was a mass of gold crudely shaped into the form of a bull, complete with horns on the head and a phallus underneath.

Parasca smiled as he held the statue. It was one of his lesser possessions, but even at that, in a typical museum he would never be allowed to touch the priceless objects, especially with his bare hands. However, here in his own world, with his own collection, he could and did touch everything. Museum curators would have never allowed it, but in his own museum he did what he liked. In fact, he never bought any item for his collection until he touched it first with his own hands.

Somehow the touch of an ancient object spoke to him: he knew when something was old and could feel the years that hung over an artifact. He could thus uncover fakes, and anyone that tried to sell him a fake never tried again. Holding an object in his hands, he could not only determine if it were from an earlier age, he could sometimes feel the use to which the item had been put, especially if spilled blood had been part of its past.

He set the golden bull paper-weight down on his desk and walked to a framed shadow box that hung on the wall near a bookcase. It was the first item he had ever chosen for his collection. He stretched out his hand and touched the unprotected object resting against the black velvet backing. His fingers slid along the blade and he closed his eyes, feeling the story of the crude knife.

Dreamlike images swept across his inner vision. Countless years and hands covered in blood, hands rising and falling with this rough stone knife dripping red: first with animal sacrifices and then human sacrifices. Adults, men and women, sometimes children: they all expired at its touch. It was very old and had killed so many! Somehow those victims had left their twinges of departing life energy embedded in the stone of the blade. He felt as if he swam through an ancient river of blood, the stolen lives that still echoed in the knife energizing him.

"Sir?"

Parasca pulled his mind back to the present and slowly withdrew his hand from the stone blade. He turned and faced his lieutenant who stood in the doorway. He raised an eyebrow but did not speak.

"Sir, the delivery that you have been awaiting... here it is." The man carried a tray with a cloth covering. He held the tray toward the older man and waited. Parasca motioned him toward the desk.

"Place it there."

"Yes sir."

After the man had gone, Parasca stepped to the desk, lifted the cloth from the tray and looked at the tiny item. His eyes glinted and widened. It appeared to be a small stiletto, the size of a small letter opener. *Perhaps it had been made for a child?* The blade was a smoky, sparkling metal of some kind, but the handle was of dark wood. A symbol was engraved on the base of the blade just above the handle. The etched symbol looked like a bull. His hopes rose. The bull often meant blood in the item's background. He carefully grazed his index finger along the wood of the handle.

Images swirled in his mind of a fierce, pale-skinned but shockingly beautiful blonde-haired woman who held the stiletto. A gigantic, hazy dark figure loomed behind her and she seemed to stand on the pinnacle of a great mountain of years, so many more years than he'd ever experienced. This dagger was so old that the years seemed to make it heavy in his hand. Yet, this blade had drunk only small amounts of blood. This blood was very different, and along with it he glimpsed a scene of unique terror. Huge with child, the woman was caught in a torrential rain. Wracked with labor pains, she was delivering the child with no other hands to help her. She wielded the blade herself, cutting the umbilical cord, flinging it aside, blood sluicing, knife spinning, falling ... *and the blood seemed to splash over Parasca with a jolt of energy.*

He snapped his hand away from the artifact and his eyes grew large. He looked at it in awe. What was that surge? He had almost felt burned. He looked at his hand as if expecting scorch marks. There was no visible damage, but surely there must be.

Parasca inhaled sharply. His hand did look a trifle different, but how? He held both hands up side by side to compare and then noticed the difference. His right hand wasn't quite as gaunt as the other. Did it look smoother? His left hand appeared as it always had. It showed the spots, marks and wrinkles typical of a man in his late sixties, but the right hand looked less wrinkled. This was a change from just a few minutes ago. He looked more closely at the tiny blade on the tray.

This dagger had arrived several days before at Headquarters, but he had been in Athens closing some deals and had not been able to see the stiletto until just now. It had been recovered by the crew of his new exploratory ship, the *Fortuna*. While going through some shakedown tests in the Black Sea, they had come across a tar deposit on the sea bottom. When one of the ship's submersibles had been sent down, the small blade had been found embedded in tar from the underwater seep. Parasca had been told of the find and ordered it sent here, to his headquarters in Bucharest. It had been dispatched immediately on the next helicopter going ashore and had remained here at his offices awaiting his return.

Back out at the ship, two days after the first discovery, a second item had also been found at the same site near the ocean floor oil seep where the stiletto had been found. It had been preserved in another glob of tar, just like the tiny blade, but it was a different type of item. It was a huge, mummified hand. Parasca had sent word from Athens to have the hand also brought to Bucharest. It should have arrived last night. He should have been able to see both items today. It had never completed its trip. Early this morning, it had been intercepted by a team that could only have been headed up by assassins. They'd killed the driver and taken the mummified hand, leaving the body of the courier impaled to the hood of the car with his throat cut. *How had the assassin (or whoever employed him) found out about the artifacts? What else did they know?*

Also, the method of the killing was unmistakable. An impaled body spiked to the hood of a car with its throat cut. *That was just as I killed in my younger days.* Only someone who knew Parasca as a young officer in the Romanian Securitate would have known about his penchant for leaving dead enemies pinned like bugs to the hoods of their cars. And only someone as strong as Parasca was in his youth would have been able to do it. That meant that one of his old rivals in the Securitate had taken his artifact and was sending him a message: "I have what was yours. I killed your people. I know your past. Try to stop me."

This operation would have been expensive. He started to mentally narrow down the list of possible rivals that were capable of financing such a venture. *Maybe it's Dmitri. He's the only one left from the old days powerful enough to get in my way. Hmmm. I'm sure he never forgot about Tresa.*

But even with that loss, he still had the dagger. *It is such an exquisite, tiny thing. What kind of metal was this?* His technical people would find out. Parasca knew that it was old and beautifully made. So old, but the power of life blood on it was still new and shockingly strong: strong enough that just the memory of it could change the aged skin of his hand. Parasca had to find out more. He must have his crew look harder.

But something nagged at him. Something seemed familiar about that jolt, that shock he'd felt. What was it? Had there been a knife like this before? *No. I would remember that. Then what? What would cause that kind of electric shock and this smooth skin on my hand...?*

His breath caught and he moved his left hand to his face. The smooth side. The left side. Suddenly he had an idea of what had just happened. He remembered someone else's blood. *Was it twenty years ago?*

*She did this to me first. She is connected to this somehow. I've got to find her, get her here.*

He picked up the phone and dialed, waited for the satellite link to kick in and then waited again. The phone rang twice and then a relaxed male voice answered, "This is Jack."

Parasca's expression shifted from fierce, his features smoothed out and he assumed a friendly, collegial air like an actor putting on a different role. "Jack, this is Janos. How are you?"

There was a moment of silence. The voice at the other end of the line shifted immediately to a much more formal mode and said, "Janos ... Mr. Parasca ... so good to hear from you. How can I help you?"

"Jack, no need to worry. I'm calling you with good news."

After a pause, Jack said hesitantly, "That's great, Mr. Parasca. What would that good news be?"

"Our new exploratory ship in the Black Sea has found something astounding and unexpected. I will send all of the information to you in an e-mail. But first, I need you to wrap up your North Sea work in Aberdeen within a week. Can you do that?"

"I beg your pardon, Mr. Parasca?"

"Jack! You must always call me Janos. The contracts you've been working for our stake in the new North Sea development drilling: wrap them up. I need you on the *Fortuna* and I need you to put together an expert team. We have oil and gas find possibilities, but there is also something that only you and a specialized team can handle. At our test site in the Black Sea, we've found some archaeological artifacts near a tar seep that we want to explore. I need you to wrap up the work in Aberdeen and put together the team that can handle both the geological side and the archaeological difficulties that come with some of these undersea finds."

There was a pause on the other side and then, "Sir, the negotiations are at a somewhat delicate stage right now. The majors are all pushing for larger shares for too little cash up front. The independents are trying for larger shares based on only operating the development sites. We are poised to grab operating rights from the independents, but only if we make a better offer. I don't know that I can get it done in a week."

"You can, Jack. What will it take to get the majors to agree with us being the operator?"

"Worst case, I think we can get operator status by taking on ten percent of the capital investment and twenty-five percent of the operating costs."

"What kind of share will that get us in production?"

"Fifteen, maybe eighteen percent."

"Agreed. Don't worry about this anymore, Jack. I will make a phone call to one of my friends who happens to be the CEO of one of these very same major oil companies. After that, the lawyers can handle the rest. You've done well, Jack."

Jack's voice displayed some irritation. "Now wait a minute, Janos, I've been working on this for quite a while now. This whole situation could go belly-up with the wrong touch..."

"Not to worry, Jack. I know you've done well. You'll see a sizable bonus in your next paycheck. Now I need you to head up the Black Sea effort." Parasca added a stern tone to his voice, "Are you with me?"

"Well, yes." Jack audibly tried to squelch his reluctance. "Sure ... Janos." Parasca heard Jack swallow and take a deep breath. "What's my first step?"

Janos said, "Good, Jack. I knew you were the right choice for this job. First, look for an e-mail from me over our secure network. Then, based on what I specify, you start building your team. In the e-mail I will have several suggestions for the secondary roles that need filling. You will see. The primary role, the Geologist / Archaeologist, must be a specific person. You will see in my e-mail. Remember, Jack. It must be the person I specify. Do not hire anyone else and do not take 'no' for an answer. You will understand my reasons later."

"Well, okay, boss. I'll look for your e-mail. Anything else?'"

"No. You just continue to do well for me and I will not forget you. Remember, Jack."

"I'll remember."

Janos Parasca hung up from the call and stroked the stiletto again. No powerful surge came from it again. Parasca wondered. *Did the surge come because the knife had been used during a birth? Was there something about umbilical cord blood? Or was it the child?* He knew from the images that the scene with the baby had happened many hundreds or thousands of years ago, but somehow it was also connected with <u>her</u>. What was it about that specific child that had caused the jolt of energy and the changes in his hand? And what was it about <u>her</u>? He looked again at his right hand. It seemed even smoother and less discolored. The hair on the back of the hand was darker.

It looked ten, maybe twenty years younger than the other hand.

"Sir?"

His concentration broken again by an interruption, he turned a glare at the huge man standing in the door to his office.

"What. Is. It?" Parasca said, emphasizing each word with his annoyance.

"Sir, I think we've found the source of the information leak that resulted in the second artifact being stolen and our men killed," the man said. His voice seemed too low in pitch even for his large bulk, almost like the echoes from a deep cavern.

Parasca dropped his note of impatience and put on a conciliatory tone. "Rakslav. Forgive me, old friend. What is it you've found?" He motioned him in and Rakslav closed the door behind him.

"We reviewed the records and surveillance video in the building for the previous twenty-four hours. We found nothing until we rechecked video showing one of the cleaning staff removing trash from your secretary's office. Nothing seemed wrong until we tracked his movements through the building after leaving your office. In the basement he fed all of the paper trash into the industrial shredder. While waiting for a shredder cycle to complete he read a small note from your trash, then tossed it too into the hopper to shred. Then he sent a text message to someone."

"The security team managed to track the text message with the phone company through some of our people there and got the text of the message. It said, 'Midnight Constanta Dock Nine helipad.'"

Parasca sucked in his breath with a hiss through clenched teeth, "That is exactly what I called and told my secretary while I was in Athens! Where is this man that goes through my secretary's trash? And where is my secretary?"

Rakslav said, "She didn't come to work this morning. We sent two men to her apartment to check on her. When the landlady let them in, they found your secretary dead."

Rakslav stepped to the door, opened it and motioned to someone out in the reception area. Two large men in flawless suits frog-marched a man to the center of the room and held him by the arms in front of Janos Parasca.

Rakslav said, "I sent some men to his home and we caught him trying to leave with packed suitcases."

The janitor's face was puffy and bruised. His eyes seemed to be nearly swollen shut. A bandage covered a swelling bump on the man's forehead. A trickle of blood dripped from his flattened nose and ran down his chin. One of the men noticed the blood forming a droplet and hastily stuffed a handkerchief to the man's face, to Parasca's approval. *Good, he knows not to let anything soil my office.*

While keeping his stare on the captive, Parasca asked, "Who did the text message go to?"

Rakslav swore in disgust. "A disposable prepaid phone. No contract. The phone is probably already at the bottom of the Danube."

Parasca said to the janitor, "But not before it did its job. Isn't that right?" He turned back to Rakslav, "What did you find out from him, anything?"

Rakslav said, "He's been working here for eighteen months. How much else he's divulged to your adversaries, we don't know yet. If he worked with your secretary, perhaps they revealed some of the negotiation details behind the purchase of the *Fortuna*. That might explain why it took so long to get that ship and at such unfavorable terms."

Parasca's eyesight seemed to go red. His heart raced and he clenched his fist in front of the captive. "Pig!" He spat a large mass of saliva into the man's face. "We need to find out a lot of information from you now. If you want to live, talk. If you want to die, stop talking. Perhaps it will take days for you to die. It depends on how much you can tell us. I've always been curious about how long a person can will themselves to live." Parasca smiled at the bruised man. "Of course, I suppose everyone would be different in this respect. With you at least I'll have another data point."

Parasca turned to the desk and seemed to consider the small dagger there. He shook his head and walked to the shadowbox on the wall. He removed the old, crude stone knife. He heard distant screams of pain sound from the past as he held it. He smiled and walked back to the janitor.

# CHAPTER 4 - BURNED OUT

*"To be weak is miserable, doing or suffering"*
*— John Milton, Paradise Lost*

The baby across the aisle and two rows up from her screamed while the mother tried uselessly to calm it. Mercy gritted her teeth. *How long is this going to take?*

"Lady! Can't you shut that brat up?" It was the jerk behind her complaining again. Most of the people around them either frowned, nodded their heads in agreement, or murmured. Mercy couldn't tell if the murmuring was agreement or disapproval. Mercy noticed a man across the aisle looking at her. At least he wasn't agreeing with the jerk. He just looked at her with a questioning expression on his face as if to ask, 'Are you going to do something about this?'

The young mom said to no one in particular, "I'm sorry! I've tried everything. He won't eat or sleep and he doesn't need to be changed. I don't know what to do." Tears of frustration welled in her eyes. Her hair was in disarray and her clothes were rumpled. She patted the baby who continued shrieking with a voice that could have shattered glass.

The jerk shouted, "Bad enough the airline leaves us stranded here for hours on the tarmac. No, we have to put up with this too! Hey! You listening to me? SHUT THE KID UP!"

*That's it.* Mercy undid her seat belt and stood up, stepping into the aisle. She stood over the jerk and glared at him. He was overweight, sweaty and red-faced. His eyes were deep set and small. His brows knitted as he glared up at her.

He said, "What's your problem?"

She spoke forcefully, "You're not helping. Yelling at her is not going to calm the baby. Besides, the mother is doing all she can." She pointed at the jerk and said, "You should keep your mouth shut. One crying baby is all we can take. If you don't lay off her, you'll deal with me. Got it?"

His mouth opened and shut like a fish gasping in air. Before he could respond, she had turned and walked to the front of the cabin and found a crew member.

The flight attendant said, "Ma'am, you'll need to return to your seat. The lavatories are no longer usable, so there's no reason to be up and about. Please return to your seat."

"I just want an update on our situation. Why can't we taxi to the gate? We've been on the tarmac for two-and-a-half hours. You know if you don't do something in the next half-hour, the fines will start kicking in."

"Ma'am. It's the weather in the Midwest that's slowing everything down. Thunderstorms in Chicago have shut down O'Hare and that causes cascading problems everywhere. The pilot will get us to the gate as soon as possible. Believe me, we don't want to be here anymore than you do. It's misery for all of us. Please return to your seat."

"I can understand that. We've already landed at DFW though. We just need to roll a few hundred yards to a gate. What's the delay?"

"All the taxi ways are full with planes waiting to take off, so the planes at gates can't pull away. We can't get to a gate until there's one open, and there isn't a single open gate right now because no-one can get clearance to take off. These delays ripple through the system. I'm very sorry."

Mercy sighed visibly, nodded, thanked the attendant and turned back toward her seat. The baby was still crying and some people glared at the young mother, while others stared numbly into space or just sat in misery with their eyes closed. The athletic fellow across from her seat who had been looking at her earlier nodded as if acknowledging her. The jerk studied Mercy as she walked up the aisle, his little eyes darting over her, up and down.

She looked at the mother of the weeping child and said. "It won't be long now. They can't leave us out here more than twenty-five minutes more or they'd have to pay huge fines. Either we move soon or they'll offload us to a bus." The young woman smiled back wanly and mouthed a silent, 'Thank You'. The baby cried. A line of drool ran from his chin to his soggy shirt. Mercy smiled in spite of herself. *Slimy and crying! Still somehow, I want to hold the poor little guy.*

Mercy sat down and immediately heard a whisper behind her. "You'll deal with me? What're you gonna do to me, sister? You picked the wrong guy to mess with." The whisper went silent. Mercy closed her eyes and tried to unclench her teeth. *Got to calm down. Can't let a fool like that upset me. Besides, he's the one in danger if he tries to pull anything.*

The jerk didn't say anything else and a few minutes later, the plane started moving again. The passengers applauded half-halfheartedly. At the gate, they deplaned and Mercy slung her backpack over one shoulder and pulled her suitcase behind her through the airport. Usually at this time of night, there would be few passengers competing for walking space with the janitorial crew polishing the floors and emptying trash bins. Tonight however, the late and cancelled flights had backed up throughout the system. Weary travelers sat dozing in the waiting areas for connections that might or might not fly tonight. Others knew they were stranded at least until morning and were stretched out on the dreary carpet, eyes closed and hands protectively resting on luggage or other possessions. In spite of the number of people, there was little noise and the terminal had a strange, detached feel to it. There was an ever present low hum from the lighting and it felt too bright for the late hour. The motors in the maintenance machines sounded like the rumbles of a distant storm. *No matter where they are, airports all sound like this after midnight. What lonely, god-forsaken hell-holes these can be. It's not like the place is asleep. It's more like it's on life-support.*

She took the train to the A terminal and walked to the last gate with an exit to baggage claim. She went past a closed up security checkpoint. *Huh. This one still has one of those strip-search x-ray machines. What will these guys do when they can't ogle the departing passengers anymore?* She took the escalator down to the bottom garage level and headed to section A4A where she always parked her car.

She heard steps behind and stopped. A stranger jogged up carrying a small suitcase. Not a stranger. It was the jerk from the plane. She frowned and narrowed her eyes. She said, "What do you want?"

"I thought I'd give you a chance to apologize to me," he smirked.

She laughed bitterly, "You've got nerve, I'll say that. You get tired of scaring helpless babies and decide to try your luck with me?"

His face darkened. "No, sister. I have some powerful friends and thought you should know before you decide to ruin your life picking a fight with me. I work for the Chevreau family. You know who they are?"

"Hmmm. Wait, aren't they the rich folks in Highland Park who are always in the celebrity news and can't seem to keep their mouths shut or their legs closed? Are they the ones? Am I supposed to be impressed? What are you, the guy that walks their dogs?"

His lips pressed together so tightly they became white and bloodless slits. He spat, "You're dead, you bitch!" He lunged at her, grabbing for her arms.

Instead of trying to back away as he expected, she stepped toward him and between his reaching arms. She punched her right fist into his belly, following through with the blow, pounding deep inward and upward. His foul breath whooshed out and his eyes bulged as if about to pop out of their sockets. His legs gave out and he collapsed backward. Mercy caught one of his arms and lowered him to the parking garage's concrete floor, keeping him from cracking his head open. He lay on his side, purple faced and vomiting, choking and gasping for air.

Mercy studied him for a moment, then reached down and checking his pockets, pulled out a phone. She studied it for a moment and dialed a number. To the operator that answered, she said, "I'm at DFW airport, parking garage A4A. There's a man lying on the ground here having a seizure. He needs help." She took the phone from her ear and turned it off. She wiped it clean and dropped it on the gasping man's chest. She turned and walked to her car, got in and drove away.

After her car had left the garage, the tall athletic man from Mercy's flight stepped out from behind one of the concrete pillars that had been shielding him. He walked to the wretched man lying on the concrete floor, still gasping in pain. He shook his head in disbelief. He knelt down and grabbed the man's hair and pulled his head up toward him. The prone man whimpered. The tall man spoke with a Russian accent and asked, "Now why would the Chevreau family hire a fool like you to work for them? You should have spent more time observing the woman on the plane than complaining about the child. If you had, you'd have seen she was not someone to annoy. She moves like a panther. And her strength? Well, you still feel the punch. When the ambulance arrives, tell them to check for internal bleeding. She may have damaged you permanently, though I doubt she meant to."

A distant siren cried out and grew slowly louder. The Russian took the wallet and looked at an ID card.

"Don't worry. I'll tell our mutual employer about your 'seizure'. No need to call in sick." He stood up to walk away and turned back. "One more thing. I'd suggest you not go after her again. She might kill you the next time. She'd probably be sorry afterward, but you'd still be dead." He left as the ambulance's cry continued rising in volume.

* * *

Mercy opened the door to her apartment wearily and fumbled to find the light switch. *I'll never get those hours of my life back. At least I took out the jerk and stood up for that woman and baby on the plane.*

She set her backpack down and took her roller-board straight to the laundry room. *Every trip I take, week after week, seems to get worse. What am I doing? Where did I go wrong? I am so sick of it all.*

She opened the luggage and dumped the dirty and wrinkled clothes onto the floor of the room. *I'll wash these things tomorrow.* She wrinkled her nose and almost gagged. *I hate that dirty-clothes-ripened-in-a-suitcase smell.* She fished out her toiletry kit and a few things that could still be used and went to the shower and turned it on as hot as she would be able to stand. *I can't go to bed smelling like this, even if I fall asleep in the shower.*

She took her clothes off and glanced in the mirror. She felt run down, but mostly it didn't show. Tall and long-waisted, at five-foot-eleven she would have been the envy of most women. Mercy hadn't gained weight since she entered college, but no one else knew what she went through to keep her weight stable. Some asked about her diet, but she always changed the subject or said, 'high metabolism'. They wouldn't believe the truth anyway.

Mercy felt her pale blond, pony-tailed hair. *What an oily mess. Got to wash this.* Her hair was so blond it was nearly white. Each strand was very strong, but not coarse. It had no curl at all, but at least there were no split ends. She took the tie out and shook her hair free.

Her stomach was tight and her waist narrowed without being painfully thin. *I'm no Vivian Leigh, but who'd want a waist like that anyway? I've still got a good shape with curves where they should be. I still turn heads, even if it's just the airport security drones. At least I know that if the right guy turns up I could hold his attention. In fact, get some sleep in me and I'll be good as new. I just wish I didn't have to turn right around and fly back out again next week.*

After her shower, Mercy walked heavily toward the bedroom, towel wrapped around her head and bathrobe around the rest of her. She stopped at the bookcase in the hall and took the middle of three dark objects in her hand. It was almost spherical, shiny black with a number eight in a white circle on one side. She turned the eight-ball over and looked at the window in the bottom. Through a dark, inky liquid, words appeared, "Try Again Later." She sighed, set it back on the shelf and walked into the bedroom. She started to sit on the bed, but thought better of the idea. *I've got to stay awake long enough for my hair to dry.* She sat down on the small divan beside her bed and tried to think through the haze of her exhaustion.

*Glad this job's almost over. Very touchy, very high pressure. Ever since that gigantic screw-up in the Gulf of Mexico, all of our offshore projects get micro-managed. Yeah, we worked it out in the end, but there's always something going wrong no matter how well you prepare for it. But I don't have to worry about that. We're all done, and safely. Now, I just go back next week and wrap it up ... and ... what? Go on to another project and start all over again? Why not? It's not like there's anyone waiting for me when I come home.* She stared across the bedroom and looked back down the hall at the bookshelf. *When was the last time I actually used the books on the bookshelf instead of the eight-balls? When have I sat down and read a book for fun? All I do is work. I go from one assignment to another. Why do I do it? Why can't I have a normal life?* She closed her eyes. She felt very tired and very low.

Mercy's head nodded forward suddenly. She jerked it back up and stood. *Almost fell asleep with my hair still wet.* She didn't want to have to soak it again tomorrow to get the tangles out. She walked to the refrigerator and looked around on the shelves for a minute, but ended up where she knew she would. She opened the freezer compartment and looked past the frozen dinners to the ice cream containers. There were six half-gallons of different flavors. She settled on chocolate and took it out of the freezer. She got her favorite long-handled spoon and started eating straight from the carton. *This is so good.*

She ate the ice cream slowly and carefully, with precise, practiced movements. She started at one side and took spoonfuls all around the rim, working inward until a layer a spoon-bowl deep had been removed. Then she repeated the process and ate another layer and then another until the half gallon was gone. She still felt slightly hungry at the end. *This is so wrong, but hey? What do I care? My health is good, I never gain weight, my cholesterol and blood work are always good. What can I say? I've got high metabolism.*

*High Metabolism?* She laughed out loud. *How many calories did that half gallon have, three or four thousand? And how much fat? How many hundreds or thousands of grams? And I eat like that all of the time. Not where anyone can see me of course. And I never gain weight. I guess I could tell my doctor the next time I go and see her. Yeah, that'd be hilarious. "Doctor, there's something I want to tell you. I know it will sound strange, but please hear me out. You see, I'm thirty-eight years old, stand almost six feet tall, weigh one-hundred and sixty pounds and I routinely eat twelve thousand calories a day. If I try to eat less, I lose weight until I'm like a skeleton. Is there something wrong with me?" Yeah, that would be a great conversation starter. They'd probably dissect me so they could turn my genetics into a cure for obesity. Just one more thing people don't know about me, one more thing that I can't tell. Why can't I have a normal life? Because I'm a freak.*

Mercy walked back to the bathroom and began to blow-dry her hair. *What is it about me and work? Do I just expect too much from it? I'm never satisfied for long. A few years in one job and I get so I can't stand it. Is the problem me, or is it the work? Come to think of it, there is no good answer to that question. What if the root problem is me? How does a person go about changing themselves? Entire religions have grown up around that question. Change yourself. Right. Impossible.*

*But what if the problem is the work? Then I've wasted my adult life doing the wrong things. At thirty-eight, I'm basically half-way through my life. I'm half used up. Do I really want to go back and start all over again? Learn another profession? And how could I be sure that I'd be any happier? What makes me think that would be the right choice either?*

Mercy walked back to the bedroom and sat on the divan again. She picked up another eight-ball from the night stand beside her bed and twirled it idly. She laid her head back and closed her eyes again.

*Shouldn't I just make the best of it and go on? And then what? Spend another thirty-years doing something I'm good at but don't enjoy? Do I want to get to the end of my life and say, "I made a good living but wished I'd done something else?"*

Mercy's exhaustion finally took over and she drifted into sleep. She curled up on the couch and snored quietly, the eight-ball still in her hand.

# CHAPTER 5 - HEARING THINGS

*"What hath night to do with sleep?"*
— *John Milton, Paradise Lost*

She became aware that she was marching. It was cold and snow fell lightly. Others were marching alongside her. They all looked young. Someone squeezed her right hand. She looked and saw Stefan. He was excited, his cheeks rosy in the cold air. His smile flashed at her, he winked his left eye and turned back to face forward. He held up his fist, shook it toward the sky and shouted, "Down with the Dictator!" He seemed to glow with some inner radiance. Others echoed his shout and the pace of the march picked up. Ahead lay the city square. The cobblestone streets echoed with the tread of their boots and the sounds of their shouts. *Stefan! I knew I'd see you again. I knew it.*

They burst into the square and were met with blasts of icy water. Fire hoses had been turned on them. The front rank faltered and fell in the freezing, high pressure streams. Guns started firing into the front ranks, and the crowd changed. It became like a wild animal and the sound of it was deafening. The rear rank surged across, around and over the fallen. Screaming in rage and with arms lifted high, the crowd dashed across the short distance straight into the gun fire and streams of water. People fell.

Finally, the mob surged against the police wielding the water cannons, beat the policemen down, tore the hoses from them and ripped them from the hydrants. The water spouted into the streets like blood from severed arteries, flowing over the filthy cobblestones, washing away the soil of decades.

More gunfire rang out and people fell by the dozens from one edge of the crowd. The mob rippled back from the bullets, then struck back reflexively. Missiles made from anything at hand flew through the air: rocks, loose bricks torn from the pavement, shards of glass from broken windows, chunks of concrete fallen from decaying buildings all rained down on the gunmen. The shooters fell from the hail and if they could, ran away. The mob surged over the fallen, took the guns from their broken hands and flowed after those that fled.

There were thousands of people, angry from decades of hunger, deprivation and fear. They marched through the streets, breaking windows, overturning cars, setting buildings ablaze. The mob moved on, still hungry, flowing like a raging river torn free from its banks. The torrent surged by and left her behind. She was kneeling on the ground, crying for help. She held Stefan, his head cradled in her lap

He'd been shot. She shouted for help from someone, anyone, but the crowd flowed on. The young man's hand gripped hers, strength fading, but his eyes held her gaze. Words choked in her throat. An instant before, she had cried for help. Now, however, when she wanted to speak to him more than anything, no words would come.

*I have to tell him one last time. He has to hear me say it. I can't let him die without my voice in his ears telling him how I feel!* She could not speak. Her tongue clogged her throat, gagging her, yet still he held her eyes. He was weakening by the second, but his eyes said he was holding on. Waiting. For her to speak.

She gripped his hand more tightly. Her tongue felt dry and wooden. From the corner of her eye, she saw the pool of his blood spreading and the snow falling lightly. For a second she realized that flakes were falling into his blood, their white tracery disappearing into the darkness of it, their structure collapsing in an instant at the touch of its warmth.

A boot came into view, moved up beside the bloody pool and stepped into it. The splash sprayed her with red droplets. She looked up at the man standing over them both, fearing what she would see. He loomed over her. She looked, but could not make out his face. He was hidden in shadow and swirling snow. Only his mouth was visible. The blood pooled larger. Stefan grew weaker. Terror built in her.

Barely able to see lips moving in the shadowy face, she recoiled with a sudden thought. They might not be lips at all, but something rubbery and fleshy, twitching with grub-like life. Not part of the face, but wriggling on the face! Panic rose inside her. He raised his hand and pointed a gun at Stefan. His limbs moved jerkily as if commanded by a distant intelligence. The grub lips twitched. The face remained hidden. Gorge rose in her throat.

The threatening figure seemed to be whispering but she couldn't make out the words. She looked past the pointed gun and studied the thing's mouth. Somehow she knew that it was saying something that could mean life or death to Stefan. Her sight telescoped in on its lips and they had changed. There was no mouth or lips, only a torn hole of flesh. It whispered harshly through the ragged, bloody tear and she saw movement in that blackened cave of a mouth. She realized its tongue was made of dozens of twining worms.

A wave of overwhelming terror shot through her and her voice suddenly broke free of its paralysis.

She cried out, "Leave us alone! Why can't you let us be?"

Whispered words came from its maw, "You didn't listen. If you'd listened, this wouldn't have happened. The next time, you'll <u>have</u> to listen."

His free hand ran up her neck and cupped her face, turning it up toward him. She should have been able to see his face at this distance, but all she saw was the creature's decaying mouth. Snow fell thickly into her eyes. She heard a click and felt the pressure of a gun muzzle at her neck. An explosion rocked her and her ears rang. Everything seemed muffled and silent. *It's the end of me.* Her consciousness faded slowly, yet somehow she felt her heart still pounding, harder and harder. She saw herself from above as her blood splashed from her neck onto the pavement stones, mingling with Stefan's. The stranger stood over them, a wisp of smoke rising from the gun. A church bell rang in the distance, tolling continuously, unceasingly.

The clanging of the bell seemed to echo inside her dying brain. She saw the two bodies, Stefan's and hers, receding from her, now far below.

She heard a distant voice. "Listen. Now wake up."

The voice rose in volume, "Wake up."

\* \* \*

The voice shouted, "Wake up. He's almost here."

Mercy flailed her arms and fell off the divan. She hit the hardwood floor and landed on her shoulder. Her elbow struck the floor and went partially numb. She was suddenly and painfully wide awake.

She cursed in near-agony and then hissed through clenched teeth, "Who's there?" No one answered. She hugged her elbow to her. *How come something that's numb still hurts like it's on fire?*

She got to her knees and then stood, waiting for her head to clear. No voice. She sighed. *Must have dreamt it. Dreamt. Oh God, another dream about Stefan and Timisoara. No, no, no…*

"Get ready. He's coming." the voice said firmly.

Mercy spun around and looked. *No one by the front door. No one in the living room.* She stumbled to the bedroom and then looked into the bathroom. *No one. Where did that voice come from?* Her head finally cleared and then it hit her. **Voice? Oh. No.** *I forgot my medicine last night when I was on that flight!*

Mercy dashed to the bedroom. *Where's the roller board? My pills are in there.*

The voice shifted and changed. It became a low-pitched grunting. "Nuh.

Nuh. Nuh. Nuh." *Oh my God. Not this!*

She couldn't find the suitcase. She couldn't remember where she'd left it. She was trembling. *They aren't real. They don't exist. There is no sound. It's just chemicals in my brain. I can stop them with my medicine. They aren't real. They don't exist. There is no sound. It's just chemicals in my brain. I can stop them with my medicine…* she repeated to herself.

The voice changed again into the lecturing voice of a professor. "You haven't been listening. You know it's much easier on you if you listen. I'm only telling you these things for your own good. You've been trying to ignore me and that's not good. Now there's so much to teach you. You're really far behind in your progress. I don't know how I'm going to get you ready in time …" the voice went on and on.

She stood still and gritted her teeth. She shook. *They aren't real. They don't exist. There is no sound… Oh how could I be so stupid! I knew I should have taken the pills before that long flight. Stupid! Stupid.*

A shriek stopped her cold. She stared, eyes open and dilated. Three more blood-curdling screams sounded. She trembled. A low, rumbling growl spoke. "You don't need those things. You know they don't make me go away. Now listen, here's how you should kill them …" the voice insisted.

*My back-up stash! It's in my laptop carry case!* She ran to the front door, grabbed the shoulder bag and opened the side pocket. Her hands shook as she pulled out the pill bottle. *This is what I need.*

A child's voice pleaded and begged. It wept in bubbling terror and then screamed as if being eaten alive. Mercy choked down the pill. An angry parental voice scolded her and warned her. A growling voice hissed. No words, just hissing. Mercy's skin crawled. *Oh, God no! Not the hungry ones.*

"Nuh. Nuh. Nuh," The grunts repeated. The hissing sounded again, and then Mercy could hear a distant voice rumbling, "Tear. Shred. Slice. Rend." The voice became louder as if rushing toward her. Now it sounded as if three voices were speaking in unison. "Kill. Eat." Mercy's heart pounded and her panic rose higher.

She dug frantically through her backpack and pulled out her MP3 player, plugged in the headphones, turned the music up to high and dashed into her bedroom. She threw on some workouts and laced up her running shoes. She left her apartment moments later. *I need loud music and strenuous exercise.* The medicine might take hours before it kicked in. Hard workouts and loud music were her only other weapons once the Voices got going.

Out on the street, she ran at a rapid pace. The music blasted in her head. Though she could hear the occasional clot of words from the Voices during pauses between the heavy metal tracks, the panic started receding. With the continuity gone, the insane sounds lost most of their power. She did feel calmer, but the snatches of words still made her cringe.

29

"Mercy is insane ... this won't help you know ... hiss ... now the next thing you need to do is ... and you mustn't go there anymore ... cut yourself deeply ... he's simply a waste ... come here ... kill her ... choke ... choke ..." A long, trailing scream sounded twice.

She completed her one-mile sprint and then stepped up the pace. She had to keep running until the Voices faded to a whisper. She ran by a pedestrian who looked at her with sudden alarm. She realized she'd said something out loud but didn't know what. *I must have said something crazy.* She tried to ignore the thought of the man staring after her and ran faster, humming along with the music. Eventually, with the rhythmic pounding of feet and soundtrack, her mind relaxed ... the voices faded some more ... her thoughts drifted into memories.

\* \* \*

The voices first came to her at age sixteen. She and her parents never knew what had happened to cause it, but it had come on suddenly and alarmingly. At first she heard talking and thought the sounds were coming from other rooms and would go to investigate. After the first few mistakes like this, she stopped asking others if they had heard sounds. She tried to hide the problem, but the voices were always there. At first the voices were merely conversational. Over time, they became more varied and frightening.

Her parents took her to doctors. The first psychiatrist asked relatively simple questions. "When did the voices start?"

"When I turned sixteen."

"Is there one voice or many?"

"Many."

"Is there one main voice?"

"No."

"Are the voices soft like whispers or loud like shouting?"

"Some whispers, some shouts, some regular."

"Are they men's or women's voices?

"Some of both. Some sound like children."

"What kind of things do the voices say?"

"Lots of things. They talk about what I do, or what they want me to do. Sometimes they just grunt or scream. Sometimes they sound like they're eating something."

"Do they talk to you or about you?"

"Some of both."

"Give me an example of when they were talking about you. What exactly did they say? Try to use their exact words."

"They say things like, 'She never listens. She shouldn't go there. She is a very bad girl. She must be punished until she obeys.'"

That psychiatrist referred her to a specialist, one who dealt with psychoses. "Mr. and Mrs. Teller, she needs help from someone who specializes in schizophrenia. What she has are some of the classic characteristics of the schizophrenic mind: voices that speak in the third person, voices that narrate the person's activities; voices that threaten or plead; voices that ..."

The memories receded for a moment. Mercy rounded a corner and continued running. The music rang in her ears. She couldn't hear anything from the voices but low mumbles as if from a distant crowd. *Almost peaceful back there. Finally.* Mercy stepped up the pace again and hummed along with the bass riff.

She remembered that her parents wanted a second opinion. They took her to another psychiatrist, one with a definite spiritualist leaning.

"Do they tell you to hurt yourself or other people?"

"Yes."

"Have you ever wanted to obey the voices?"

"No."

"Where do you think the voices come from?"

"I don't know."

"Do you think the voices come from other people?"

"What?"

"Do you think you're hearing other people's thoughts?"

"I don't think so. How could someone do that?"

"Could these voices be from spirits?"

"Spirits? Like ghosts?"

"Do angels talk to you sometimes?"

"I don't think they're angels."

"Could the voices be from devils?"

"Maybe."

"Why?"

"Because sometimes they tell me horrible things."

"What kind of horrible things?"

"Gross stuff about torturing me and cutting me open."

"Why would they tell you these things?"

"Because they're evil."

"Do you think you're possessed by an evil spirit?"

"Sometimes."

At the mention of evil spirits, her parents pulled her out of the interview. They took her for a third opinion. That doctor interviewed her and seemed all right at first, but Mercy got an increasingly creepy feeling from him.

"Do the voices make it harder and harder to concentrate?"

"Yes."

"How hard?"

"I can't do anything. The voices never stop. I can't think. I can't concentrate."

"Never? Do they speak even while you're sleeping?"

"Yes, at least I think so. I think I hear them in my dreams sometimes."

"They don't ever stop?"

"No. Sometimes they're quieter, but they never stop."

"When are they quieter?"

"When I exercise hard or listen to loud music."

"Do the voices actually get quieter or are you drowning them out?"

"I'm drowning them out, I think."

"Are they talking to you right now?"

"Yes."

"I don't hear anything. Are you sure they're talking to you right now?"

"Yes."

"What are they saying?"

"They're telling me to not listen to you."

"Is that all?"

"No."

"What else are they saying?"

"That you don't believe me and that you think I'm crazy."

"Do you think you're crazy?"

"Maybe."

"Why?"

"Because it's not exactly normal to hear things, is it?"

"Are the voices telling you anything else right now?"

"Yes."

"What is it?"

"I don't want to say."

"Why not?"

"I just don't want to."

"Are the voices telling you something bad about yourself?"

"No."

"Then what?"

"It's something bad about you."

"Oh?"

"Yes."

"What is it?"

"I don't want to say."

"You can tell me. What do they say?"

"Ok. You're not going to like this."

"I can handle it."

"All right. They're saying that you're having an affair with one of your patients, and now you want to get me alone."

Mercy's parents stopped the interview. Years later, Mercy found out that the doctor had been sued by multiple patients for malpractice involving "inappropriate behavior." Her parents searched carefully and found an older female doctor that Mercy referred to privately as "Granny". She prescribed a series of medications for Mercy but almost all had horrible side effects. There were some kinds that made her so sleepy that she couldn't move. Others made her jittery and hyper. One type made her feel as if there were a knife stabbing her in her left eye. Still other kinds had no effect at all.

Often, the medications had to be used for weeks until they could be judged as effective or not. In the meantime, the voices were persistent and disturbing. For a while, Mercy completely lost the ability to distinguish the auditory hallucinations from reality. She was especially vulnerable at night and began sleepwalking. Once she got up from bed, walked out the front door, down the block and into on-coming traffic wearing nothing but a light sleeping gown. The first car swerved away from her. Luckily for Mercy, the second car was driven by a female police officer. She stopped, got Mercy out of the road and realized she was still unconscious, though carrying on an argument with unseen and unheard people about the quickest way to get to "the deep places". The policewoman finally managed to wake her and took her home.

After the sleepwalking incident, Mercy's parents installed alarms that would sound if any door or window were opened. They did not give the disarming code to Mercy. She became isolated from friends since she couldn't go to school or be left alone. Her mother took a leave of absence from the business she and Mercy's father ran and stayed home with Mercy. Finally, after months of different types of medication, "Granny" found a kind that didn't keep her in agony or a stupor. Two weeks later, Mercy suddenly noticed that the voices sounded very low and far away. They stayed that way, as long as she remembered her medicine.

From then on, Mercy thought of it as a volume control for her brain. Years later, she switched to a still better medication, but back then the drug felt nothing short of miraculous. It allowed her to turn the voices down low enough so that most of the time, she was able to ignore the chatter. She began to get her life back. Slowly, she was allowed to add back activities. She didn't return to the same high school. She couldn't bear to face her old friends, some of whom knew what had happened to her. Her parents enrolled her in a private high school and she finished her last two years in eighteen months.

\* \* \*

Mercy finished her run and cooled down with a quick walk back to her apartment. She felt much better and had to strain to hear the voices. This was as inaudible as they ever got. She moved to her elevator, took it to her floor and noticed a business card stuck in her front door. Printed on the front, it read, "Don Carson, Maritime Resources Inc." followed by a phone number. It had a hand-written note on its back side that said, "Mid 6 figures / permanent job / call me at home:" followed by another phone number.

Carrying the card with her, Mercy opened the door. She tapped it in her hand and thought about it. *Switch jobs? Is that what I should do? I've been doing the consultant grind for quite a while now. Maybe it's time to try the employee thing again. Maybe. I'm not getting any younger or happier. I'll call him tomorrow and see what this is about.*

Exhausted, but feeling better, she cleaned up and went to bed. She was asleep in moments.

# CHAPTER 6 - THE HEADHUNTER'S CALL

*"Who first seduced them to that foul revolt?"*
*— John Milton, Paradise Lost*

She woke with a jerk and sat up. Something was ringing. She reached to silence her alarm clock, but then realized that it was her phone. She grabbed it and fumbled at the phone with sleepy hands.

"Hello?" she stammered.

A woman's voice asked, "Is this Dr. Teller?"

Momentarily confused, she remembered and said, "Yes, this is she."

"Please hold."

The line went silent. Mercy used the moment to gather her wits. *What time is it? 9:30 am. Good thing the phone woke me. Now what is this call about ...?*

A man spoke. "Dr. Teller?"

"Yes?"

"I'm Don Carson of Maritime Resources Inc. I received your name from a client that has asked us about you. I have a possible position to discuss. Are you free at the moment?"

Her mind cleared partially and she sat up straight. *The business card in the door last night. This is the guy that left it.* "Yes, of course. What can I do for you?"

"As I said, I've a client that has expressed interest in some of your past work. They've put together a large team and a brand new state-of-the-art ship and need a Geology project lead for a prospect in the Black Sea. With your background, your experience in bringing in large and difficult projects within budget, well, the head of their Exploration division would like to meet you to discuss a possible arrangement."

"What ship is it?" Her vision stopped swimming and her hand steadied. She looked at her other hand and saw it was clenched into a tight fist. She intentionally loosened her fingers.

"Beg pardon?" he said.

"I asked, 'What ship is it?' I follow these things rather closely. Most of the newer exploration ships are already out at sea. It couldn't be the *Fortuna*. That's all tangled up in a lawsuit. I don't know of any other new ships that are this close to being sea-worthy. Some deal must have fallen through and made a different ship available."

"It *is* the *Fortuna*."

"Really? Hmm. That must have taken a lot of cash, pull or both to shake that one loose. I thought it would be tied up for years."

"It would have been, but my client has both a lot of cash and a lot of pull. His head of Exploration would like to meet you for lunch, tomorrow if possible. Are you free? I understand you're located in Dallas. Is that right?"

"Yes, currently. My office is downtown."

"Could you catch a flight to New York this afternoon? Of course, we'll make all of the travel arrangements to help reduce some of the inconvenience."

Mercy closed her eyes and considered. *Well, here's the chance to take the risk, or pull back. Which will it be?*

"Could you hang on for just a moment, please? I need to consult my ... calendar." She grabbed at the eight-ball on the night stand, turned it over and waited for the answer to come up. It said, 'Signs point to yes'.

She spoke into the phone again. "I'm back. Sure, I can make it. What time and where?" she said.

"Tomorrow, 12:30 at Junior's near Broadway."

"Junior's? The delicatessen? The one down from Times Square? That's no place for a business lunch. It's so noisy there with tourists and lunch crowds, we'd have to shout to hear each other."

"The client is a little eccentric about some things. One of them is New York Cheesecake. He told me he never misses a chance to have a slice at Junior's when he is in Manhattan. He'll meet you there at 12:30 pm tomorrow if you're willing."

*This feels odd. Junior's? When was the last time I was there?* She snapped back to the present. "All right. What company is he with and how will I know him?"

"He said he would recognize you. Just sit at the bar and wait for him. As for his company ... I'm not yet allowed to release that information. Suffice it to say that the organization in question is international in scope with the highest of financial ratings. It's a vertically integrated concern whose operations run the gamut from exploration and production through refining and marketing."

"Excuse me, but that sounds strange that you won't tell me the name of the organization. I need to do some research on it in order to be prepared for my interview tomorrow. You understand, don't you? I don't want to come across as ignorant. I'll need to do my homework in order to speak knowledgeably about their situation and understand my potential part in it."

"I know, it does sound odd, but they asked that I not divulge that information. They specifically *don't* want to be investigated before the interview. They aren't interested in your knowledge of them, and they are already more than satisfied with your qualifications. Their purpose behind the interview is not to test your knowledge. It's to see if there will be a fit of personalities. Hold on. Here's the quote from the e-mail I received from them: '… We are completely satisfied with Dr. Teller's reputation and skills but we need to see if Dr. Teller's personality is a fit with that of our head of Exploration. We need to know if she can work with us and be comfortable with the project and the way we want to operate.'"

*'Curiouser and curiouser' as Alice would say.* She said out loud, "I've never heard of anything like this. I'm beginning to wonder if we're discussing a legitimate, legal employment opportunity."

"I can assure you that I am. It's legitimate, legal and potentially very lucrative as well. We'll be sending an e-mail in the next few minutes with your plane ticket, hotel and limo information. Your flight will leave DFW late this afternoon. You'll fly First Class, of course. You'll be staying tonight in a suite at the Hilton on Times Square. A limo will pick you up from La Guardia after your flight. I can make arrangements for a limo to take you to the DFW airport from either your office or your apartment. Which would you prefer?"

"My apartment. I'll need to pack a few things for the overnight stay."

"I understand. You'll receive that e-mail from me presently. Thank you, Dr. Teller, it's been a pleasure." He confirmed her e-mail address and then hung up.

*Well. That was different. The Fortuna, huh? That ship is supposed to be an awesome beast. If I remember correctly, it can handle drilling a well and completing another at the same time. But why do they need me? Plenty of groups could put a first-class project lead on a ship like that. Obviously, the client has a lot of money or he couldn't have dug the ship out of its legal tangle. I guess that all happened while I was busy and out of touch. Hmm. But why me, and why the mystery?*

Mercy was keyed up and didn't feel sleepy anymore. She went to her desk and fired up her laptop. She smiled as she started a Google search on her laptop. *I don't care if they want to keep secrets. Let's see who ended up with the Fortuna. I may find out who the client is even without his help.*

After a half-hour, she found some additional information about the *Fortuna*, including that it was currently in the Black Sea. She couldn't get the name of the new owners of the ship. That news was apparently too private to have made it out into the public networks. It was being operated by an offshore oil service company out of Romania named Oceanus, but that wasn't who owned the ship. The press release said only, "… Oceanus will be operating the new ship for an undisclosed client."

Another half-hour of work revealed that Maritime Resources had several listings on its website: exploration specialists, positions for experts in paleo-biology and engineers with years of work operating in undersea tar-sand environments. There were two really unusual spots: one for a PhD in forensic biology including five years of experience with DNA sequencing in humans and animals; and one opening for a metallurgist that called for "… expertise with cutting edge metallurgical technologies, including recent advances in crystalline matrices and nanofibers." *Maritime Resources specialized in recruiting and hiring for offshore oil and gas work. What did they need an expert, bleeding-edge metallurgist for? Very strange. What is this all about?*

She checked her e-mail and found several messages from Maritime resources. She had her confirmation information with the airline, the hotel and the limo service in Dallas and New York and noted that everything had been prepaid. *Well, they've given me two nights in the hotel. Tonight and tomorrow.* She saw the flight time and realized she better start getting ready for the trip.

She jumped in the shower. After a quick rinse she blew her hair dry, threw on minimal makeup and dressed quickly. She packed and straightened up her apartment. In the time remaining before her limo arrived, she jumped on the computer again and mentally ran through the kind of questions she might be asked at lunch tomorrow. She looked up more background on Maritime Resources. Who were some of their larger clients? Every so often, she'd stop and jot something down on a list. *'Look up the latest configuration information on the Fortuna'. 'Who has expressed interest in the ship?' 'How'd they get that lawsuit cleared anyway?'* She wanted to brush up on everything she could before the meeting. *Oh, and, 'Check on latest finds in Black Sea'.*

A few minutes later, the limo driver called to tell her he was downstairs. Mercy squared her shoulders, double-checked that she had her medicine with her, grabbed her luggage and marched out the front door. *I will be ready for this interview. I will knock them dead.*

* * *

The Russian stepped through the ornate double doors and followed the butler through marble-floored hallways decorated with statuary and ornately-framed paintings. The art work was obviously old and costly. The Russian idly wondered what prices these objects would fetch on the black market. In fact, his last client, the Chevreau family in Dallas, might have been interested in acquiring some of this art.

The butler opened a door leading into a large and beautifully appointed office, stepped through and announced simply, "Your guest, sir." The Russian followed him in.

A large, portly man in his sixties rose from behind a desk and waved him to one of the chairs arranged before the desk. The Russian sat down. The door clicked shut as the butler left.

Dmitri Slokov said with a smile, "You really must give me a name to call you by. The butler hates announcing you that way, and I hate just calling you the 'Russian.' What is your name?"

The man in front of the desk remained silent but raised his eyebrows questioningly as if asking, "Are we going to go through this again?"

Dmitri paused as if he were a man that insisted on winning at whatever game he played. He waited for the man to respond, and finally said, "If you won't give me a name, then I shall name you myself. People call you 'The Russian", so I will give you a Russian name: 'Vasiliy'. But let us not be formal. I will shorten it to the nickname, 'Vasya.' How do you like your name, Vasya?"

"I don't. I don't like names. People think they control you when they know your name. Names are used as weapons. But if you have to call me a name, that will do as well as any. I even have a false ID already with that name." He smiled briefly.

Dmitri blanked his face, hardened his eyes and looked at Vasya. "I don't control people with names. I control them by whatever means I find effective. Sometimes I use money. Sometimes I use drugs or women or sometimes threats of violence or pain. Sometimes I use actual pain. I never control people with names. Names are just labels. Your label is Vasya. How would you like me to control you?"

The Russian sat silently then said, "Money will be fine. You invited me here for a purpose of some kind?"

Dmitri said, "Vasya, I need you to work on a ship belonging to a competitor of mine. I already have a man on that ship, but he is only an informer. I need someone on board who can take action when needed."

"What kind of action?"

"Mostly watching, listening and sending reports. Industrial espionage. Possibly some rough stuff, knife or gun work if things get out of hand. Probably some demolitions."

"This is not the kind of work I like. My efforts involve my team, long planning, short execution times, short clean-up afterward and then I'm done. I don't do long-term undercover work anymore. Too much work, too little reward, too much danger, too messy. Is that all you have for me?"

"That is the job. How much?"

"Not interested. Shall I go?"

"No, Vasya. We're not done. What do you want?"

"A different job. What is this ship to you anyway? Who does it belong to? Why are you interested in it?"

"My competitor Janos Parasca owns the ship. It's called the *Fortuna*. My experts have hacked into Parasca's telecomm network and I know that Parasca's people have found some artifacts on the floor of the Black Sea offshore Romania. Parasca is very, very intent on these things. You remember the mummified hand you obtained for me? That was from the *Fortuna*. What's more, he's bringing in some experts to help. One of them is known to me by reputation. If she joins the team ... and I expect she will ... I want to know everything that happens on that ship. Plus, I want more of those artifacts."

The Russian motioned at the office, the furnishings, the art works. "You already have more than enough. Why should I help you get more?"

Dmitri said, "Whenever Janos has something, I need to take it from him. That's the way I am. To do that I will spend any amount, do anything."

Dmitri bent down, lifted a briefcase from where it had been sitting by his chair and came around the desk. He set the briefcase on the desk near his guest and opened it. Inside were stacks of five-hundred Euro notes. "That's your first payment, a million Euros. Take it."

The Russian made no move toward the briefcase. "I haven't said I'll take the job. I told you I don't like this kind of work. Besides, Euros aren't worth what they used to be."

Dmitri smiled with a very determined expression, "You'll take the job. Eventually we'll agree on a price. But think, Vasya. Every job has some unpleasant parts, doesn't it? If it were all fun, we wouldn't have to be paid, now would we?"

The Russian said, "You want me to do the job? You'd better make it more pleasant for me, and I don't mean more Euros. What else can you give me?"

"Now we negotiate. I knew we could come to some agreement. What is it you want?"

"Who is this woman that Parasca is hiring, that you know by reputation? What is she like?"

"Ah. You are interested in her maybe? She is indeed a beauty. I have a dossier on her over here..." Dmitri walked to his desk, sifted through a small pile of folders and chose one. He opened it and nodded and handed it to the man.

'Vasya' took the open folder and saw the photograph clipped to the left side. It was a three-quarter face shot of a pretty woman with pale blond hair. Dmitri studied the expression on the other man's face.

Dmitri said, "So you know this woman?" Dmitri's expression darkened and his voice became stern. "Vasya, let me dispel any illusions you have about Dr. Teller. She is not for you. Parasca thinks to get her back, but I intend to take her from him. Janos has a lot to answer for concerning this woman and I am going to see that he pays for what he did. In the bargain, I will make myself richer at his expense. You are to keep your eyes and hands off of her. She is not part of our bargain."

"Then you'd better find someone else to do the job."

"No. But I still think I can sweeten this deal enough for you. What would you say to another million Euros?"

# CHAPTER 7 - LUNCH IN MANHATTAN

*"And courage never to submit or yield"*
*— John Milton, Paradise Lost*

Mercy arrived early at Junior's, but even so, the lunch rush was in full swing. She waded into the usual crowd in the restaurant. She even had to wait to sit at the bar. She shook her head. *What kind of a deal is this? Yes, Junior's cheesecake was great, but with the swarming tourists and locals, it was so noisy! How could you have a decent interview in a place like this? Well, I'll just have to wait and see. Make the best of it. Hmm... maybe this was one of those pressure interviews where they try to take you out of your element. Try to put you off-balance, shake you up a little. Put you under stress and see if you crack up. Could be ... I don't know though. They paid for first class airfare and a top-flight hotel for two nights. They can't be too concerned with stressing me out, or worried about costs. The limo service was nice. So were the flower arrangements in the room addressed to me with the phrase, "Looking forward to our interview tomorrow." It's a mystery all right.*

The lunchroom boiled with activity. Waiters and waitresses moved quickly to and from every table. Mercy noticed that no one walked at a leisurely pace. A waitress hurried by carrying a plate with a gigantic sandwich, a Reuben that was easily six inches thick. She didn't know whether to be sick or drool. Those sandwiches were delicious, but so big! Not that her appetite wasn't huge, but she couldn't afford to scare a potential employer by eating like a horse. She had forgotten about this place. Actually, more like put it out of her mind. *How long has it been since I was here with him?*

*Twelve years. It must be twelve years since I last ate here. Wow.* She was distracted by a customer asking, "Where are my fries?" "Sir, the large hot dog doesn't come with fries. Fries are ordered separately." "Are you kidding? Back home, I order something like this and fries comes with it

…"

*Blah, blah, blah. They never read the menu. The sandwiches don't come with fries. That used to crack me up…*

"Hello, Mercy."

She jumped and almost squeaked with surprise, but managed to stifle it. She turned, but knew already from the sound of the voice who would be standing there. It was Jack. *Oh. No.*

"You busy?" he asked.

She tried to remain calm, but color flooded her face. "Yes, as a matter of fact. I'm meeting a prospective client for lunch." She straightened her jacket sleeves.

"A business lunch here? Isn't it kind of noisy?" he smiled.

"Well, yes, but we'll manage. Anyway, what are you doing here?"

"Got a business lunch too. Looking for a new employee."

She froze, suspicion rising in her. "Jack, tell me you're not here to interview me."

"No, I'm not here to interview you." Mercy relaxed visibly, and then Jack said: "I'm here to recruit you."

Mercy stood up and away from the bar. Her face went grim. "Jack, I can't do this again."

"Now wait, Mercy…"

"You know I can't be near you anymore. Not after … what I did." She took a breath, tried to steady herself, but then the words seemed to pour out of her. "I can never fix it, but I did what I did and can't change it. You have to let me go. That also means I can't be near you again. You know all of this. Why bring this up? Why are you really here?"

His face didn't look sad, just wistful. *He's thinking about what might have been. He doesn't hate me. That's what hurts the most.*

"Mercy. It's not what you think. I'm not trying to rekindle anything. This is a business offer I want to make to you. Come on. Let me buy you some lunch, we'll talk business and split some cheesecake for dessert. How about it? You can spare me an hour or two, can't you?"

*The recruiter said his client liked Junior's Cheesecake. That should have tipped me off. Jack was always a sucker for the cheesecake.* She sighed, knowing she would relent, but had to give him one last warning. She put a hand to his arm.

"All right, buy me some lunch. Just … Jack, I don't want to hurt you again. Don't box me in without a way out, okay?"

"Deal," he said and waved to the bartender. The man pointed back and to the left, leading Jack and Mercy to the opposite end of the bar to a table with a large "Reserved" sign on it. The bartender removed the sign, pulled a chair out for Mercy and waved Jack to the other.

"You owe me big time, Jack," said the barkeep. "The waitress for this section almost killed me when I told her we had to hold a table."

43

A woman in uniform swept up beside him and said in a thick Brooklyn accent, "You better believe it. I could've turned that table twice in the time it's been empty. That's two tips I'm out."

"You'll live, Sammie." He shot back at her.

"I'll live, but you may not." She sailed away as a customer waved for service.

The barkeep whispered to Jack, "Take care of Sammie, okay? I got a date with her on Saturday, and don't want her mad to start with. You understand?"

"I'll take good care of her. No worries." Jack said and palmed a folded bill to the bartender.

The bartender went back to work and Mercy studied Jack. He looked very fit, but was starting to show a little bit of gray mixed with the black hair at his temples. His clothes were business casual, but well-pressed. His face was square, his eyes twinkled and he still wore that perpetual half smile, as if there were humor in all situations that only he could see. He looked good.

The waitress came and took their order. After she had gone, Jack took a small folder from his briefcase and set it on the table between them. Mercy made no move to take it.

"What's the story, Jack? Why me of all people? If you've got a legit job you're looking to fill, then there must be a lot of people that can do the work. You know that."

"Not true. In this case, you're the only one for the job."

"If we're talking strictly job skills, I doubt that strongly."

"Mercy, just let me tell you about it first. Then you can judge." He reached for the folder and took it in hand. "I left Stanford shortly after … you did. Got a job as a field man and worked for a couple of years. Then I couldn't take it anymore and quit. Took half of my savings and took a year off. Did some things I'd always wanted to do but had never taken the time for. Traveled. Ended up in the Middle East. Volunteered on a dig in Turkey, one of the excavations they were doing at Catal Huyuk. I remember you talking about digs you'd been on during your summers and finally got to do one myself. Loved it. Anyway, it helped clear my head." He sipped some water and then continued.

"After the year was over, I felt like I could go back to work again. I did some work for one of the big majors. I ended up working for a string of jerks. Then I went to work for a company in Odessa, Texas and found out you'd been there before me. Did you know you had a great rep there? They really were sad to see you go. After some time there and moving up a few notches, I started to put some feelers out. I got a bite from PetroRomania. They were doing some exploratory work in the Black Sea. They liked my work and gave me more assignments and then more. I moved up some more steps and now I'm the new VP of Black Sea Exploration."

"So that's who this is about. PetroRomania. But why the secrecy? Why wouldn't the recruiter tell me anything? Oh, and by the way, congratulations on the promotion, Jack," she said.

Jack looked up at her quickly, as if to make sure she wasn't teasing him. She looked sincere. He smiled and relaxed. "That's simple. I didn't want you finding out the company and then googling them to find out I was working for them and figure out I wanted to interview you. And by the way, thanks, Mercy. It's good to know that you can say things like that without being bitter. You always were such a great …"

She cut him off. "Jack. Don't get flowery on me here. I _am_ glad for you. Besides, you're the one who would be justified in being bitter, not me. You didn't dump _me_ like a sack of …"

"Stop right there." He broke in. "Like you said, it's past."

Their food came and they were silent for a minute as they started eating.

She smiled and pointed her chin toward his plate. "I can't believe you still get those giant hot dogs, plus the order of fries too. How are you going to eat all of that?"

He smiled back and raised an eyebrow. "She says that and doesn't even realize that she's stealing one of my fries?" Surprised, she dropped the fry and snatched back her hand.

She looked at him, her eyes guilty. _He wants me to laugh and forget about it. I'm not ready for that._ She pulled her attention back and forced her face into serious mode. _Let's get this back on track._

"Jack, about the job?"

He seemed mildly disappointed that she hadn't reciprocated his attempt at playfulness, but got to the point. "So, I'm VP of Black Sea Exploration for PetroRomania. We've got this new ship, the _Fortuna,_ and the crew is trying to get used to it and has it out on a shakedown trip. I'm not there 'cause I'm working a deal inland. So first, they're doing survey work. It's got full instrumentation and can do seismic surveys as well as drilling. They get to this area of natural seeps, which are all over the place in the Black Sea. There's an oil or tar deposit under the ocean floor and natural cracks in the rock structure allow some to leak out. The crew is working close in to shore in shallow water, two-hundred fifty to three hundred feet deep. There are little oil slicks on the surface from where the oil naturally bubbles up from the sea bottom. They decide to test out the submersible capabilities. There are two mini-subs on the _Fortuna_ and they'll hold two divers each. They put them out and into the water and start getting reports back."

"The divers tell what they're seeing, but the crew can also see it from the mini-sub cameras. There is a seep at the ocean floor with a large tar whip trailing upward from the seep. The petroleum leak down there has solidified into tar and it has oozed out and up into the water in a long thin blob like a whip."

Mercy cut in. "Really? That I haven't seen before. Must have been pretty thick tar to produce that kind of seep."

"Yeah. It was really unique. I've heard about these kinds of things offshore of southern California, but I've never seen one before. Anyway, they had an idea; why not use some of the external tools on the mini-sub and take a sample? So one of the subs moved in close and went down to the sea floor. The other sub positioned itself above and used its gripper tool to take hold of the top end of the tar whip. The first sub used a snipper-type tool and the diver cut the tar whip right at the sand line where the seep was coming out of the ocean floor. The other sub lifted up and away, carrying the tar whip to the surface."

Mercy was engrossed. "Sounds like the mini-subs worked great."

"Absolutely perfect. They got the sample to the ship's petrology lab and found something odd right away. The whip was about four inches in diameter at the base, made of thick, cold tar with some sand mixed in. The petrologist got out a cutting saw and started to slice across the base about four inches up from the end where the mini-sub had snipped it loose from the ocean floor. Halfway through, he hit something hard. He pulled the saw out and tried a different angle of approach. About a quarter of the way through, it hit something hard again, but this time, the saw blade lost some teeth."

"He stopped trying to cut the specimen and put the chunk into an x-ray imager. That was when they started taking these pictures and sent them back to the corporate office in Bucharest along with the item they found in the tar whip. The boss called me out of my negotiations to take charge of the *Fortuna* and to do some recruiting. For you."

Mercy said, "That doesn't make sense. Why would he want you to recruit me? What was in that tar?"

He slid the folder toward her. "The thing they found in these pictures. Open it."

She took the folder and opened it. Inside was a stack of pictures. One was an x-ray image in shades of gray that she set aside for the moment. Under it was a high-resolution photograph of an object on a padded red velvet cushion. On the velvet, next to the object was a small ruler. It was a silvery stiletto-like dagger about six inches long from tip of blade to the end of its handle. It had a small handle guard made of the same metal as the blade. A symbol was engraved on the base of the blade just above the handle guard. The etched symbol looked like a bull. The handle was deep black and appeared to be some kind of wood. The handle was short, as if intended for a small hand. *This dagger belonged to a woman.*

Jack pointed at the photograph. "We ended up using steam to get this out of the tar. Notice the metal of the blade and handle guard? It's silvery, but smoky, almost translucent. Know what it is? We don't either. Oh, we know it's a type of steel. It's got iron and carbon, and we think it's got some kind of crystalline structure. We'll know more when our new equipment arrives. Needless to say, we don't want to send this to some outside lab for testing. But let me ask you this. Where do you think the saw blade hit it when we were trying to cut through the tar?"

Mercy looked carefully at the dagger in the photograph.

"I don't see any marks. What kind of blade did the cutting saw have?"

"Carborundum. Next best thing to diamond cutting blades."

"Okay, I give up. Where did you nick it?"

"We didn't. At least, we haven't been able to tell where. Believe me, we looked."

"Jack, don't jerk me around. No way a carborundum blade wouldn't cut steel. Steel just isn't hard enough."

"Well this steel is. But here's the really earthshaking thing. Look at the wooden handle."

"I see it. Looks kind of waxy, as if polished."

"That's the embedded tar. We really lucked out here, Mercy. The dagger has a wooden handle. This would have dissolved away under water long ago, but the dagger happened to be completely encased in tar and so the wood survived. We have a really good lab on the *Fortuna* for doing Paleo and micro-fossil work. We even have an automated DNA sequencer. We also have really nice equipment for doing fossil age analysis, including carbon-14 dating. The wood in that handle is approximately eight thousand years old."

Mercy stared at him silently, her brows knitting. She looked at the photograph of the little dagger in its case and then looking back at him said, "From my archaeological studies, I know for a fact that steel didn't exist eight thousand years ago. Most metal working didn't exist either. Nothing harder than gold could be worked. Well, maybe copper, though even that is far-fetched. A steel dagger eight thousand years old makes no sense."

"I know. Isn't it exciting?"

Mercy stared at him silently and bit her lip. Jack smiled triumphantly and said, "Well? What do you think?"

"So, let me summarize. You've discovered some ancient artifact that has been embedded in tar for as long as eight thousand years. Oh yes, with eight thousand year old wood in the handle. The knife blade and guard are made of a metal harder than carborundum that we don't recognize but we know isn't steel because steel wasn't invented until thousands of years later. So both the handle and the blade are wildly anachronistic? Is that it?"

"No, that's not all of it. The team later found another item embedded in the tar at the same site, but it was lost. It was a massive skeletal hand with a ring on one finger. They were so anxious to send it to headquarters that they didn't take pictures or run tests on it. They just packed it up and sent it on. I don't know the full story about that, but it was lost or stolen before it got to headquarters in Bucharest."

"Lost or stolen? Why?"

"Like I said, I don't know the whole story about that. But we have this." He waved at the photographs of the tiny blade.

"And that is it?"

"No."

"What then?"

"I also want you to help us figure it out."

"And that's it? Because there are other geologists with archeology backgrounds as well. I'm still not buying it, Jack."

"You're not?" He tried looking innocent, but she saw through it.

"No. Not that I'm not interested. We haven't even spoken about money yet so I'm assuming that it will be good. There has to be something else to answer the question of 'Why me?' You've said you're not trying to win me back, but that's the only other thing that I can think of. What is it, Jack? What's the missing piece here?"

"Well…you might be disturbed about this."

"Disturbed? What are you talking about? Tell me. I'm a big girl now and perfectly in control."

"Okay. I'll tell you. But not until after the cheesecake. I don't want to ruin it."

"You jerk! Tell me now!"

"Nope. Dessert first."

Mercy sighed. The waitress took their plates away and brought the dessert. Jack switched the subject to small talk as they alternated taking bites of the cheesecake.

"You look really good, Mercy. You must be doing something outdoorsy to stay in such good shape."

"You know me. I work out a lot. Keep up my Taekwando and backpack in the summer. Archeological digs whenever I can fit it in. Working for myself gives me a more flexible schedule so I can get away more often and don't have to worry about accruing vacation time, like when I was a corporate minion. I like it."

"Got someone in your life these days?"

She set her mouth. She tried to keep the sarcasm out, but it slipped through. "What do you think, Jack? I'm still not cut out for it. Relationship averse. Lone Ranger. You remember, don't you?"

"I do. I also remember that we almost made it work."

She softened and put her hand out to his arm. "Almost," she said. *Until I panicked.*

He took the last bite of cheesecake and squared his shoulders. "Well, let's get this over with."

"Yes, let's!"

"The other thing that makes you indispensable to this work is that my boss asked for you by name."

"Your boss? I thought you were VP of Exploration or something. Who's your boss?"

"I'm now VP of Black Sea Exploration. But seriously, the CEO asked for you."

Mercy was clearly skeptical. "I don't believe you. I don't run with those kinds of people and never have. No CEO is going to know my name."

"This one does."

"Well, who is he? You going to make me sit here all day or are you going to tell me?"

"Okay, a little bit more story first. When they found this item and ran some tests," he waved at the pictures of the dagger, "they reported in to headquarters with the news. A few hours later, they were told to send it back on the next supply helicopter to headquarters. It was taken to the CEO, who is quite a collector of ancient museum-quality artifacts. Shortly after that I received an urgent phone call from the CEO himself. I'd met him, of course, during executive meetings, but I'd had very few one-on-one conversations with him. He pulled me out of some tricky negotiations and assigned me to the *Fortuna*. He said he wanted me there personally."

"He wants to know everything about where the artifact was found. Everything. He wants to know if there are more items to be found, if this could be from some ancient ship wreck or something. He realized we'd need some specialized personnel, including some with knowledge of archeology. He had suggestions but said he would leave most of the selections to me except for one he asked for by name. You."

"That night, I went over the list of names. Hayden Travers was one. Besides his Geology background, he has some experience with ancient offshore archeology in the Mediterranean. I also needed a metallurgist and a paleo-DNA guy. I didn't know anybody with those qualifications so recommended we contract that search out. The next morning I e-mailed my reply to headquarters in Bucharest and received a message back from the CEO."

"It just said, 'Hire them, and make sure you get Mircea Teller.'"

Mercy's skin crawled. "Jack, you're scaring me. Why would he know about me? And why would he use my legal name 'Mircea'? Everyone who knows me calls me 'Mercy'. Who is your CEO? What's his name?"

"The CEO of PetroRomania is Janos Parasca. You know him?"

Mercy's skin blanched and she froze for a split second. Then, seized by a sudden fury, she cursed and jumped up from the table, rocking it back against Jack. The water glasses and silverware slid toward him splashing and clattering to the floor. She turned and stalked for the front door, dodging through the milling customers waiting to be seated. Jack struggled with the table and the mess. He barely kept himself from falling over backward as he saw her shove through the door, dash down the steps, and storm rapidly off toward Broadway. In moments, she was out of sight.

Jack righted himself and rose to his feet, blinking slowly. *What just happened?* He thought. The restaurant around him had gone deathly silent, until a man spoke out, "Well buddy, I guess the lady's answer is 'No!'" The crowd around him burst into laughter. Jack rubbed his temples. *This headache is only going to get bigger.* He reached into his wallet and pulled out enough to cover the meal plus ten times the normal tip, placed it on the table and headed out after Mercy.

# CHAPTER 8 - REMEMBERING

*"Our state cannot be severed, we are one"*
*— John Milton, Paradise Lost*

Mercy stood on the sidewalk at the entrance to the hotel, breathing heavily. *Why did I do that? Why couldn't I just sit there and say, 'Janos Parasca? Why no, I don't believe we've met.' No, instead I had to make a fool of myself and stalk out of there like I was a crazy woman ... but of course, that's exactly what I am, a crazy woman.*

Mercy's phone rang again. She looked at the number, recognized it as Jack's from the last message he'd left five minutes ago and pushed the 'Busy' button. *Let him leave another message. I need to calm down. Now think. Why hadn't I heard about Parasca as the CEO of PetroRomania? Answer: because in spite of your big talk to that recruiter, you don't always follow the international business side of the news in the oil sector. You never did like the whole 'who-is-doing-what-to-whom' side of corporate life. Sure, you might have known if he'd showed his face in the U.S. oil industry, but not Romania. Where's he been all these years? It's been what, eighteen years since I last saw him? I hadn't heard of him after the Romanian Revolution, he just disappeared. But now he's back as the CEO of the largest private oil company in Romania and he wants to hire me. I'd rather work for an axe murderer.*

The phone rang again, a different number this time. She sighed and answered. "This is Mercy Teller. Who's calling please?"

"Don Carson of Maritime Resources again. Dr. Teller, I'm glad to have reached you. Congratulations."

"I beg your pardon. Congratulations for what?"

"Why, a successful interview, of course. Mr. Truett called and said he was very impressed with you during your lunchtime meeting. He has authorized me to make you a very generous offer. I take it you are still interested in the position?"

Mercy's head felt like it was spinning. "I haven't …"

"The salary is almost double what I usually see these jobs go for and of course, the salary isn't all. There is an extremely generous benefits package complete with fully paid medical, 200 percent matching of savings contributions, eight weeks yearly vacation…"

"Mr. Carson …"

"Oh dear, I forgot to mention the signing bonus, didn't I? One of the best I've ever seen. Fifty percent of your first year's salary grossed up for taxes, so you actually get the full amount right away. It's always nice when the government doesn't take it all away in taxes, isn't it? And then there's the expense account and company paid first-class air travel for all flights, including your vacations… and of course, you get a large enough car allowance to cover the monthly lease on a very nice automobile. It's quite the comprehensive package. I can have the papers overnighted to you if that is convenient."

"Now wait, Mr. Carson …"

"I quite understand, Dr. Teller. You're a busy woman and have no time to waste. We'll have a courier bring the papers today."

"Stop! Listen to me. I have not accepted this position. In fact, I am almost certainly going to decline this offer. I was thinking about the position when you called and am not finished considering. Call me again tomorrow at this time. Do you understand?"

"But, Dr. Teller … well … perhaps I didn't explain myself clearly. You see, this position …"

"Tomorrow, Mr. Carson. Good-bye." She pulled the phone away from her ear though she could still hear his small distant voice receding until she pushed the off button. At that level, he almost sounded like the background murmur of all of her other voices. *Hmmm. If he sounds small and far away … maybe that's what my medicine is doing; giving me some distance from the voices.*

She shook her head. *I can't think about that now. Back to reality. I don't care how much he offers. I won't work for Parasca.* She walked inside the hotel and took an elevator up to her room. She paced back and forth for several minutes, thoughts swirling incoherently. She decided to exercise to clear her head, changed into some workout clothes, called the concierge desk and received instructions on using the hotel's exercise facilities. She took the elevator down, slid her room key into the electronic lock and opened the door.

Professional caliber exercise equipment lined the walls and a thick floor mat filled the center of the room. No one else was using the facility. *Perfect.* Mercy spotted a cabinet marked, "Other Equipment" and opened it. There were some small hand weights and several jump-ropes. One of them had a digital counter on one handle. She decided to go simple and begin her workout with the jump rope. She took the handled cord out of the cabinet and began slowly with a basic two-footed jump. After five minutes, she switched to the criss-cross, moving her hands back and forth as the rope twisted over her head and under her feet. Five minutes later, she switched back to the basic jump, but every fifth hop she doubled the rope speed to get two passes under her feet before she landed. Soon she added a double-under every step, then moved into alternate foot jumping. At the thirty minute mark, sweat streaming, she turned on the jump-rope handle's electronic counter. She noted the rate. *180: three jumps a second. Let's step it up.* The next minute took her to 200 jumps a minute and the one after that to 220. Minute by minute, she sped up to 290, 300, 320, 330, 350. She knew she was approaching her record and kept pushing. Her feet drummed the mat as she moved faster than a sprint, her motions a blur, the spinning rope, invisible. 360. 365. 367. 369. 372. 374. Here it comes. 375. 376. That's her record. She held it at 376 for three minutes. Time to push again. 378, 380. That's good. Now down. Minute by minute, 375, 370, 360. 350, 330. 250 for five minutes, then down to 200, 150, 100 and stopped. Almost seventy minutes of jump-rope. Good thing she had the endurance of an ox. She toweled off and moved to the weight machine. Fluid and controlled, she went through her full range and past, repeating enough to add strength. She always pushed to add strength in each workout. Done at last, she put away and wiped down the equipment, left the exercise room and went back to her room to shower. Afterward, hair wrapped up and wearing a light t-shirt and shorts, she sat in the living room of her suite with a bottle of apple juice from the room's mini-bar. Her mind felt quiet. Her heart beat steady and strong. She felt alive and at peace. *Now I can think.*

*What do I know? First, that PetroRomania has a new top-tier, world-class exploration and drilling ship. Jack Truett is the VP of Black Sea Exploration. Jack Truett, my one-time fiancé, works for the most evil person I know, Janos Parasca. But I'd bet my bonus that Jack doesn't know Janos' background, or about my history with Janos. I certainly never told him. Jack wants me to come to work for PetroRomania because they found some kind of crazy artifact in a Black Sea oil seep and thinks I'm the best person for the job with my petroleum geology and archeology background, but I don't want the job because I'd have to work for Janos' company.*

She paused and took a long drink of the apple juice. Hunger pains hit her strongly and she knew she had to eat. She called room service and ordered a large meal for two including appetizers and desserts. *That should last me until later.*

*They're offering me some crazy high-paid salary deal. With the bonus that's more than twice what I used to make as a corporate drone. But, I never intended to go back to being a full-time employee somewhere. Too restrictive. Too much politics. Maybe they'd hire me on an hourly basis.*

Mercy stopped and gaped, realizing she'd already started working out a way to take the job, even if she had to do it by the hour.

*Wait a minute! I haven't decided any such thing. I can't just go jumping into this. Look how I acted at the mention of his name, going into a rage and stalking out of a restaurant. True, Parasca probably wouldn't be around at all. Maybe I wouldn't have any contact with him. A lot of these CEO types are too busy to ever mingle with the troops in the field. No. That doesn't matter. Just remember what he did in Romania when I was there with Mom. He doesn't deserve to live, period. I shouldn't have anything to do with him or his company.*

Mercy stopped again, realizing her pulse had quickened as her mental conflict had increased. She stood, walked toward the desk and saw something out of the corner of her eye. Stopping, she looked toward the front door of her suite. A thick envelope was protruding into her hotel suite, obviously slid under the door from without. She stooped and picked it up. It was from Maritime Resources. She knew what this was about. The courier must have slid it under her door while she was in the shower. She started to open it and stopped, shaking her head. *No, not until I'm done thinking.* She set the envelope aside.

*And on top of everything else, Jack's come back and still cares. I can see it. And (idiot that I am) I still love him. Seeing him across from me was so comforting. It was almost like the last twelve years hadn't happened. I tried to act tough, but it felt so right being there with him. The sound of his voice was so nice. He still has that sense of humor that always made me feel lighter. But Parasca's back too, that monster. I need to know what to do. I could ask the Counselor.*

A faint voice said, "No, no, no." "Run, hide." "She should kill herself." "Mercy must hurt all of them." As always when she was properly medicated, they sounded like they were speaking softly from a nearby room, right at the edge of hearing.

But asking the Counselor for advice would put her out for twenty four hours. She couldn't afford that right now. *What do I do?*

She turned on the radio by her bed to get some background music going. She couldn't afford to be distracted by the voices. *Work for Janos Parasca? I can't take it. Heaven knows it's not that I'm upset about Jack. I still love him, but I can't go to him. We just can't be together. He understands that now. And it would mean working for Parasca. The man hurt mother. ... But if I speak to the Counselor and it tells me to take the job and I don't ... something horrible will happen. Something bad always goes down when I ignore the Counselor. My poor crazy mind. What am I going to do? Those voices are auditory hallucinations. I know they are, but I've always felt that the Counselor is different somehow. Isn't it? Oh, God, I am so deranged...*

Tears came to Mercy's eyes and ran down her cheeks. She didn't sob, she wasn't wracked with shudders, but her eyes welled up and overflowed. She clamped them shut and remembered.

* * *

Mercy had names for some of the voices she heard. One voice was the screaming child that she called 'Baby Benny'. It was the terrified voice of a three-year-old being eaten alive. Mercy shuddered at the thought. There was 'The Professor' who always droned on and on about things she should and shouldn't do, except the recommendations always seemed geared toward justifying or rationalizing horrible deeds. There was 'The Torturer' who always talked about ways to cause the maximum physical, mental and emotional suffering. Then 'The Jailer' who described traps and cells and pits and confinements and cages and prisons and chains and it went on and on. *How many ways have we created to contain and suffocate others?* There was the grunting demonic voice that she thought of as 'The Cannibal'. Somehow she knew that it ate other creatures *of its own kind*. Only the Counselor's voice seemed to be right somehow. The other voices were illogical, twisted, sick, perverted or tortured. They seemed to be full of animalistic urges, crazed appetites or frenzied screams.

The Counselor on the other hand, was reasonable, to the point and seemed to hear her when she spoke to it. It was very, very soft-spoken. The first time she'd spoken with the Counselor, she had been at the ragged edge of her wits. It was after the other voices had come to her and she had been struggling with them for months. No medicine yet seemed to work in a way that left her able to function even somewhat normally. She'd been in and out of hospitals and had frightened all of her friends away. She was an emotional wreck and felt trapped and terrorized by increasingly insistent urgings from the voices to kill herself and others.

One night during a particularly bad episode with the voices, her mother had been sitting and dozing beside her where she lay in her hospital room bed in the psychiatric ward. Mercy found herself staring at her mother's neck. She studied every fold and crease, every slope and edge. She thought, '*If I only put my hands just so, there and there, and squeezed, she'd be dead in minutes.*'

The Torturer instantly spoke, "Instead of that, squeeze here and there, and hold for four minutes. She won't die, but she'll be a vegetable. Her body will still be alive, but the mind, soul and spirit, will all be gone. The brain is a vessel built to hold these three, but if you rupture the container, they leak out. That's what you want. She will be gone, but the undead body will remain behind, torturing everyone that sees her and cares for her. Her still animated corpse will last for years, maybe even decades. That's the way to hurt someone, the permanent pain comes when the damage done is something that can't be helped or forgotten."

Mercy snapped back from listening and saw that her hands were stretched out toward her mother's neck, her grasping fingers only inches away. Mercy curled her hands into tight balls as she realized she had been about to strangle her mother while she dozed in the chair next to her. Even in her terror, Mercy noticed that her mother's face seemed careworn and pale, her eyelids closed tightly as if in unrelenting pain. Mercy fought off the Torturer's insistent demands and pulled her hands back and away.

Mercy wept silently. *She's exhausted because of me, and I almost killed her!* In despair, she slumped back on her bed and raged inwardly at herself, at her mental weakness, at her mind's disease. She huddled in on herself, only allowing a thin, muffled cry to escape her closed lips. Her pillow gradually became sodden with tears. Her mother slept on beside her.

After the tears stopped and her breathing slowed to normal, she began to think again. *I can't go on like this. I can't be such a danger to myself or my family. I don't know why this is happening to me, but I can't do this anymore.* She remembered the self-hypnosis she'd been taught and had an idea.

*I know hypnosis didn't help with the voices, it just makes them louder. It's almost like the voices are closer when I'm hypnotized. But since it also lets me resist them a little, maybe the hypnosis can help in a different way. People use hypnosis for other things like quitting smoking or losing weight. It's like they can strengthen their willpower with it. Maybe I can learn to strengthen my ability to resist what the voices say even when I'm not hypnotized. Maybe that could help me fight off the compulsions.*

Mercy started the exercises she'd learned. She began with consciously relaxing her toes and feet, relaxing her calf muscles and thighs. She moved through the process until all of her body had released its tension. She felt like she was floating, but as before she heard the voices even more clearly. The Professor was droning about something. It sounded like a lecture on medieval torture techniques. Every once in a while the Torturer would speak up and offer a correction to the Professor. *Strange, I never noticed them talking to each other before. What does that mean? Maybe I'm not imagining them. Maybe I'm just overhearing them.* Mercy tried to ignore them and concentrate on her relaxation techniques.

Once calmed, she went through the next mental exercise: she imagined herself walking down a long stairway, with each downward step carrying her deeper into a relaxed state. After walking down mental flight after flight of stairs and feeling more deeply relaxed at each landing, the voices had become so loud they seemed almost like rolling thunder. Her mind felt shaken by some vast storm. *Now, how can I give myself more will power? If people who smoke can stiffen their spines and kick the habit, can I resist these insane voices?*

She repeated to herself: "I will not listen to the voices."

Baby Benny's crying built gradually into a wail. The wail became a scream, then a shriek. The crying continued building to the force of a train whistle, then the screaming wind of a hurricane. The sound in her mind almost washed everything away except her desperation. She repeated phrases to herself over and over, but they had no effect. The other voices clamored and shouted back at the banshee cries of Baby Benny. She felt overwhelmed by the sounds that seemed as large as mountains in her mind.

It was as if the gods of Olympus were fighting a battle above her head and she could only cower frantically at their feet, hoping not to be crushed. She felt tossed about like a leaf in a tornado and screamed out mentally. *What should I do? What can I do? Help me!*

"There are answers, but there is a cost." The whisper carried to her and seemed to dampen out the thunder of the other voices. Though soft, still she heard it. Not understanding at first, she shouted: *What do you mean?*

The quiet voice said, "Compared to your current strength the cost will be high, but you may grow stronger yet."

*Cost? I don't care what it costs! I'll pay any price! Tell me what I should do! Help me!*

"When you awaken, remember these two: music shields you; exhaustion eases your suffering. These will give you strength until a physician aids you."

The voice stopped and Mercy felt as if a gigantic form moved quietly away, like a vastness just below the surface of sunlit waters. Her consciousness felt pulled down by the force of its passage. Her thoughts swirled away into fragments. She slept. A long time passed. She became aware of voices speaking and caught snippets of sentences.

"...we don't know ... classic schizophrenic ... auditory hallucinations ... coma ... unusual brain activity ..."

She realized she was awakening and opened her eyes. Three doctors stood at the foot of her bed. One was holding a chart and gesturing at her. He saw her open her eyes and moved to the side of her bed. He referred to her chart and spoke to her.

"... mmm ... Miss Teller, can you hear me?"

"Yes," she spoke with a raspy whisper. "Can I have some water?"

"We'll get a nurse in here to help. Don't try to get up. You've been out for a while and will probably feel light-headed if you try to move too quickly."

One of the other doctors spoke, "Miss, how do you feel? Are you in any pain at the moment? Does your head hurt?"

"No, I just feel exhausted. So ... tired, like I've been running a marathon."

"Understandable. You've been unconscious for over twenty-four hours. We've been very concerned. Your mother should be here in a few moments, but you need to sleep after that."

"Please doctor, what's wrong with me? These voices in my head! I can't think, I can hardly hear you right now. It's like I'm in the middle of a crowd with everyone talking loudly. Where are they coming from? Why is this happening to me? I must be crazy! Can't you help me?"

"A specialist is coming in tomorrow. She has dealt with cases similar to yours. She'll speak with you and your family and hopefully be able to recommend a treatment. Until then you need to rest."

Mercy's mother came in and rushed to her side. The doctors left speaking softly among themselves.

"Thank God you're awake, Mercy. I've been praying so hard. We were all so worried."

Mercy rasped, "The doctors said I'd been asleep for almost twenty-four hours. I guess they gave me too much sedative?"

"No, it wasn't that." Her mother's eyes filled with tears. "I had dozed off sitting here beside you. Suddenly, the vital signs monitor there," she motioned to the machines at the head of Mercy's bed, "it started beeping frantically. A nurse came rushing in and checked the machine and then called for help. You weren't breathing and you didn't have a pulse. I thought you were dead!"

Her mother choked up. "They were getting hoses out to get oxygen into you and then suddenly you took a long, slow breath on your own. Then your heart beat once. The monitor stopped beeping. Then, when you didn't breathe anymore, the alarm sounded again. Orderlies came in and rushed you out and the nurses sent me back to the waiting room. I waited and waited until the doctor came out and talked to me. He said that you were having some kind of episode of 'reduced cardiac and respiratory activity' and your heart rate and breathing rate were very slow."

"I asked him what he meant and I said I'd never heard of such a thing. He seemed very concerned and said they had connected a machine and were monitoring your brain waves. He said your brain's activity was unusual with periods of extreme activity followed by coma-like inactivity. He tried to brace me for the thought that you might have suffered brain damage." She wiped some tears away with a tissue.

"The nurses tried to reassure me and said every case was different. They tried to act like everything was under control, but one of them told me a few hours ago that they'd never seen anything like your brain activity or your reduced breathing and heart rates. Mercy, you were only breathing once a minute until they put you on a breathing machine. I was scared to death! Could you tell what had happened? Did you just pass out, or did you feel anything strange?"

Mercy laughed bitterly, "Strange? You mean besides the insane voices?"

Her mom flinched, but Mercy plowed on and said, "I hear voices, Mom. One of them told me right before I went unconscious that after I awakened a physician would aid me. Is that what you want to know? That now I also have delusions of being able to foretell the future? Do you want me to tell the doctors that?"

Mother said, "Well, a specialist is coming tomorrow. This woman has had experience with this kind of thing before. She's highly recommended."

"Yeah, highly recommended by my doctors and now by one of my voices!" Mercy started to cry. Her mother held her hand, unable to say anything that might comfort.

A nurse came in and administered a sedative. Her mother sat by her bed side as Mercy drifted off to sleep. She remained there all night and the nurses that came in to check on Mercy found her mother praying each time.

* * *

Mercy had found out through experience that the Counselor was real, and it always cost her a day in a coma whenever she asked its advice. After that first time, she'd been very careful to never speak to the Counselor again until she had something truly major to ask, and at a time when she wouldn't be missed for a full day.

That hardly ever happened. Really, how many decisions in life give you a day's warning? Also, people wouldn't understand that knowing the right thing to do at any crucial point is not always a blessing. Sometimes that right thing was something she wanted, but most of the time, it didn't seem to have anything to do with what she wanted. Once, knowing what the Counselor recommended made no difference at all. She still made the worst choice of her life in spite of its advice and broke up with Jack.

The few times she <u>had</u> consulted it totaled less than a dozen times in her life. She'd found it, well, strange. It wasn't evil, in fact it always seemed truthful. It wasn't cruel. It just said (cryptically) what needed to happen. That was it. It didn't tell her what to do, it just said what needed to happen. It didn't really care what you wanted, it never explained itself or showed *why* it was the right choice for her. And, she knew through bitter experience that it could be defied. Once, in her late teens, she had gone against the Counselor and the result was so horrible, that she had immediately wanted to undo the results. Of course, she couldn't. The choice was gone, and the results stayed. She thought of these choices as one-way passages to a new reality that could never be undone.

If people had known this about Mercy, that she thought this way, they would have thought her crazy even if they hadn't known about the voices. They'd also have thought her deluded and egotistical. *Well, they might be right.* It still remained a fact that at crucial turning points in life, she could know exactly the right thing to do. Of course, that didn't mean she always <u>did</u> the right thing, but she knew what she <u>should</u> do. She wasn't forced to pick the right choice.

Considering her voices, or schizophrenia (whatever they called it), belief in her destiny would have convinced most people of her craziness. Yes, some people would have considered her "gift" of knowing what to do a miraculous blessing. Some would have wished that they knew what to do, always, in every important decision in life. They might have thought, "If only I could have known the right thing to do, I wouldn't be married to this person." Or, "I wouldn't have this awful job that I hate." Or, "I could've saved that relationship."

But it didn't work that way. Knowing what to do didn't make it something you wanted to do. *We often want to do the very things we know are bad for us.*

In spite of that, when she received a letter offering her a chance to go for a summer of archaeological digs after her junior year in college, she carefully waited until a Friday night and asked the Counselor what she should do. She heard it say, "Learn of the earth and the ancients. Go as often as can be managed." When she woke up twenty-four hours later, she knew she had chosen her path.

She was interested in archeology and had gone every summer since. She had once been offered a very lucrative internship in geology that would have prevented her from her summer dig. She paid the price to reconfirm with the Counselor to see if she was still supposed to go on the dig, and the answer came to her strongly that she should go. She didn't know why, and the Counselor never said.

# CHAPTER 9 - DECIDING

*"Solitude sometimes is best society"*
*— John Milton, Paradise Lost*

At twenty-six, she had her BS, MS, and was almost finished with her PhD in geology in spite of spending every summer on archaeological digs. "Why archeology?" her PhD sponsor had asked. She always just said, "It's something I need to know about."

That statement always made Professor Silas mutter in disgust. "Mercy, I've told you a thousand times. You're the best geology student I've had in decades. You don't need to know archeology. It's not for you. You should be interning in the summers with one of the majors. Dr. Carnes at Exxon keeps asking me when I'm going to send you over to him. He needs a sharp assistant like you. You go to Exxon, stay a few years as his right-hand man ... I mean woman ... well anyway, you help him out and you'll be on your way. The sky's the limit. You could be a VP of Exploration before you're forty. He's got a great reputation and trusts me when I say you're the best!"

She always smiled gently when he went on these fatherly tirades. She knew he meant it for her own good. He just couldn't know that she had to learn as much geology <u>and</u> archeology as possible. She didn't know why she needed both subjects, she just knew the Counselor had told her she needed to learn them. She could never explain 'The Counselor' to him, would never even try. He wouldn't have believed that she knew without a shadow of a doubt some of the choices she should make in life.

Her thoughts were interrupted by a familiar voice. "Hey, beautiful, what're you so thoughtful about?" It was a man's voice from behind her. She brightened and turned to hug him. He felt good.

"Jack! Sorry. I was remembering something." She kissed him hungrily.

Professor Silas sighed. "Jack, I really wish you'd hurry up and marry her.

She is so distracted these days. I've been standing here trying to get her to respond and she was just lost in thought, staring into the distance. If you don't stop distracting her like this, it could have serious consequences for completing her PhD."

Mercy turned back to the professor. "Dr. Silas, you know that I've finished every project you've given me and only have another week of work to complete my dissertation. I'm not too distracted to be your best student. Besides, don't tease Jack like that. We're engaged, but haven't set a date yet. It might be a few more years before we get married."

"I've seen love destroy the concentration of some of my best students. You know that once a fellow gets married, his best work is usually behind him. He loses that passion for the sciences and devotes himself to … well … other passions," the professor ended lamely.

Jack spoke up in her defense. "That may be the case for 'fellows', professor, but Mercy's definitely female. I think, aside from being occasionally lost in thought, she's doing very well."

Mercy pursed her lips and poked him playfully in the ribs. "Traitor. Don't take his side in this." She then hugged Jack again.

Dr. Silas shook his head slowly from side to side. "I give up," he said, but Mercy had already lost herself in Jack's eyes. "Mercy. Mercy!" Dr. Silas said. She released Jack and blushing, turned back to the professor. "Good. I have your attention again. Day after tomorrow I want to see the next-to-the-last chapter of your dissertation. Jack, don't distract her tonight or tomorrow, all right?"

"Sure, Professor," Jack said. They left the professor and the science building and silently walked hand-in-hand. The cool evening breeze fluttered her pale blonde hair. Jack broke the silence.

"Mercy, I think the professor had a good idea there."

"Which idea?"

"The one about us getting married sooner."

"Jack, you know I want to marry you, but I also want to get established first."

"Dr. Silas has been on you to take that position with Exxon. He said that in a few years as an assistant you could move up pretty rapidly. Mercy, I don't want to wait years while you get established. We've already waited long enough. Let's get married soon."

Mercy started to reply sharply, but pulled herself back. Instead she asked, "How soon?"

"Well, you're finishing your dissertation in a week, followed by your defense to the committee, say another three weeks for that, and then you're done. I'm done with my engineering degree when I wrap up these final courses. We could be married inside of a month!" Jack's face lit up.

"Jack, I want to go through the graduation ceremony. And I've already made plans to spend the summer on a dig. And what about me getting a job before the wedding?"

"Mercy, you can be married and go through the graduation. It's not one or the other. As for the dig, I could go with you. Why not? And as for a job, you're a shoo-in for the Exxon job. Dr. Silas just has to pick up the phone. And besides ..." he drew her close and whispered, "... I want you so much. I am going crazy."

"I know. I am too. I can hardly think sometimes, aching for you. Thank you for understanding how much waiting means to me. But it's very hard. You know I want to marry you, but I just ... I can't rush into something this big."

"Mercy, how can it be rushing? We've known for months that there could never be anyone else for either of us. We've talked through everything; we are so right for each other. We really shouldn't wait any longer. I'd drag you off to a Justice of the Peace today if I didn't know you have to finish your work on the dissertation. Tell you what: I'll walk you back to your apartment, you finish the chapter and we'll talk day after tomorrow. Just promise me that you'll think about it. Think about getting married soon. Will you?"

"All right, Jack. I'll think about it. You know I love you desperately. You know it, don't you?"

"Yes. I know it."

Two days later, Mercy turned in her chapter and found Jack waiting outside of Dr. Silas's office. Jack's eyes were bloodshot.

He asked, "Have you thought about it?"

"Jack, your eyes are so red! You look so tired. What's the matter?"

"I didn't sleep. Not for a single minute last night or the night before. I couldn't stop thinking about you and your decision."

"Why, Jack?"

"Because I can't stand to live without you. Because I want to marry you today, but I'll wait until next month if I have to. Because I'm hoping so much that you'll say yes and we can set a date soon. Oh please, Mercy, say you will."

She pulled back. Her eyes were welling up. She spoke in a small voice. "Jack, I can't."

"No! Mercy, don't say that!"

"Jack, I have to. I need to wait. I want to be firmly established. It means a lot to me. And there are things about me and my ... health that I haven't told you. Please don't be angry."

"Angry! I'm not angry, I'm devastated. What is it that you can't tell me? I don't care if you have some health problem! That won't matter to me. I ..." he stopped suddenly, seeing the fire in her eyes. "What? What's wrong?"

"Jack ... we'll ... have to wait for years to get married. I can't tell you everything about me. There's just something really wrong with me and I can't tell you yet. But I can say I won't marry without some level of security in my life. You know that I was devastated by my father's death when I was a teenager. And then I lost my mother not many years later. My ... my friend at PolyTechnik in Romania ... and ... it seems everyone I've ever loved has died. I have to have something stable and constant in my life. I have to make sure, really sure, that everything is nailed down. I want everything fixed and right and permanent so that nothing can go wrong."

"Mercy, you'll <u>never</u> get that."

"Jack, please try to understand. I can't leave anything to chance. I have to arrange it all and set myself up to survive. Because who knows when you'll ..."

Jack's voice went from desperate to icy cold. "When I'll what, Mercy? Die? Or are you afraid I'll run out on you?"

"No! Not that. Oh, please try to see what I'm saying. Every person I've loved has been taken from me or died. It's something I can't stop. I'm afraid it'll happen to you too if we marry."

"Mercy, you talk like this is fate or something. You're not under a curse of some kind, as if anyone you love is doomed to die. Stop talking like that. You don't have that kind of power. You're not some tragic mythological figure that kills everyone she touches. You're Mercy, the woman I love and want to marry. You're almost finished with your PhD and then you'll be free of this academic prison. We'll marry, find jobs, establish ourselves, maybe have a family. It's going to be a great life."

*Oh, Jack. If you knew about my insanity and the voices I hear, you'd run away in a minute.* "No! I can't. I love you and won't lose you too. I've already lost everyone else and I couldn't bear it if it happened to you too. Besides if you knew everything about me, you'd understand we can't move the date up. I want you so badly, but I can't. In fact, I think we'd better separate for a while. You're already in danger from me. Just loving you as I do is making you a target."

"Mercy, you're talking like a crazy woman. There is no conspiracy to kill whoever you love! You're a wonderful woman when you're not a lunatic; don't go megalomaniacal and think everything's about you! I'm sorry your father and mother died along with your old boyfriend, Stefan. Yeah, don't act surprised. I know you still grieve about him sometimes, and I don't care. I'm sorry they died! I'm sorry all these horrible things happened, but don't victimize me because of all of the coincidences in your life."

"They weren't coincidences! They had to happen!"

"Mercy, there you go again. Talking like these people had to die when they did. That's some powerful awful future you have if you think anyone that falls in love with you is destined to die."

"Jack. I can't explain what I know or how I know it. Believe me or not, there are some things I just know. If I told you how I know, you'd just think me crazier, so I won't bother."

Mercy paused, moved her right hand over her left, removed something from a finger and held it out to him. Her engagement ring. Tears ran down her cheeks. "Take it, Jack. Maybe someday when I've worked it out … then, if you still want me, I'll be somewhere where you can find me. It's not fair to you or me to make you wait longer. Go get a real life Jack. I love you, but I can't marry you now. Find a good woman who won't do this to you and who won't get you killed either. Just go." She walked away and down the hall. Jack called after her, but she didn't stop. He decided to wait for her. He waited all night.

* * *

*The worst part of it was I knew that the Counselor had told me to marry him. The night that I finished my dissertation, I asked and it told me strongly to marry him. But when I woke up twenty-four hours later, I couldn't. I was afraid of him finding out about my schizophrenia and I knew that he'd be a dead man sooner or later because of me. The Counselor doesn't care about my happiness. It just cares about … I don't know what it cares about. And for some sick reason, I end up getting those I love killed. That was the last time I defied the Counselor and I thought I was right to do so.*

She didn't marry Jack. For a long while afterward, she was inconsolable. Her friends told her she was an idiot. They said that she should call Jack and fix things up with him. She wouldn't. None of her friends could understand what she was doing, and she couldn't tell them.

*I can't say: "There's this voice you see… it talks to me. No one else can hear it of course. All of the other voices I hear are horrible and evil, but this one is right. When it tells me something, I always know it's what I should do, and this time I'm going against it. It told me to marry Jack, but I know that's going to get him killed because everyone I love gets killed. Plus, I couldn't face the look in his eyes when I would eventually have to tell him I'm crazy. So I'm going against fate and rescuing Jack." No, I hardly believe it myself and I'm the one who thought this up. How screwed up am I?*

She left town after graduation and didn't take the job at Exxon. She had to do things her way, and for the next few years, she felt dead inside. She got work as a field geologist for a small independent oil company in Odessa, Texas and it was definitely not the most scenic place to work. On the drive there, she passed through hundreds of miles of scrub and desert. The gnarled mesquite trees were more like bushes than trees and tumbleweeds rolled across the dust-swept highway. Buildings were dingy and weathered. Gas stations were bleak and dirty.

She remembered her first time in downtown Odessa. It seemed like there were billboard signs everywhere advertising either cigarettes or the city's world-class cancer treatment centers. *Does nobody see the irony in this, cigarettes and cancer treatment?* She also remembered her first meal in Odessa. She pulled into a cafeteria and collected her food and a glass of iced tea. With her first taste of the tea, she almost gagged and set down the glass, coughing. Nobody looked at her and she took another sip. The tea was awful. She flagged down a cafeteria worker.

"Ma'am, I think there's something wrong with my tea."

"Honey, that's the same tea we always make here. I don't care for it, myself. Could I bring you something else, maybe a Coke instead?"

"Just ice water, please." The woman raised a questioning eyebrow, shrugged, then returned in a moment with the water and set it down. Mercy took a drink and choked again. She now understood the awful iced tea. It wasn't the tea: it was the horrible brackish water. *Why such awful water?* She switched into geologist mode. *This part of Texas was once an ancient ocean, the Permian sea. Responsible for all of the oil trapped under here too. I guess some of that ancient sea salt has made it into the local water supply. Note to self : buy only bottled drinks, and no ice cubes made from the local water.* Mercy ended up with a bottled Coke for the rest of the meal.

Her work at that Odessa company gave her good field experience but at a high price. Her boss was a condescending jerk and she was constantly hit upon by the men at work and in town. As one of them said, "You're the purtiest gal in the county, and what you got against a few beers and some line-dancing on a Saturday night, anyways?" She kept all of them at a distance. Some of them had to be convinced rather forcefully to keep their hands to themselves, and she earned a reputation as an ice-queen. That suited her fine. She wasn't in the mood for a relationship. She wanted to get her head together and figure out what to do next, but she came up blank. She didn't even want to acknowledge the existence of the voices and so kept up with her medicine, slept with loud music on, or a loud television going every night. Eventually, she began looking for a way out of Odessa.

At work, they were finally treating her with grudging respect. She proved she had a nose for petroleum geology and knew where to look and how much oil and natural gas they'd find. She just had a knack for this. Well, she also had to give some credit to all of the years she'd spent getting her degrees. She got raises and promotions, but never really connected emotionally with that part of the country. She knew that some people saw the desolate beauty of West Texas and loved it, she could understand it, but never shared it. Besides, she never did break into the real good-old-boy network that would lead to the executive suite. So, after five years, she left Odessa and took a job with Royal Dutch Shell.

She wanted offshore experience and got it. She worked production rigs in the North Sea, more off the coast of Africa and then transferred to

Shell's Offshore Exploration division. She sailed with seismic crews as they scouted for sub-sea rock formations that might conceal hydrocarbons. She found she loved the ocean and the freedom of it all. She got promotions until she was lead geologist and one of the most respected names in her field. She published scholarly papers several times a year and even corresponded occasionally with her old professor, Dr. Silas.

The one person she never heard from anymore was Jack. He had tried for years to contact her and then had finally stopped. Of course, she'd never left even a message for him or tried to contact him. *Why do I still think of him? It's sad, but I do. I have such feelings of guilt toward him. I hurt him so much and never was able to explain why in a way that meant anything to him. He surely thought I was insane for what I did and said. Of course, I never could tell him I was truly crazy. Better to just leave it there and hope he's forgotten me.*

During those days at sea working for Shell, she smothered the voices as best as she could with her medicine. On her time off, she would still try to get in as much archeology as possible. In six weeks a year of vacation, she would spend five at dig sites. She realized that she was happiest while doing her archeology and began thinking harder about how to make it a larger and larger part of her life.

One evening, after a very frustrating day trying to work in spite of some crazy new procedures that the people at corporate headquarters had issued, she checked e-mail and saw a note from an alumni newsletter that mentioned an old classmate who had gotten his doctorate just a semester after she had. He had gone independent and started his own geology consultancy. *Now there's a way I could spend more time doing archeology. Charge enough an hour to work only half the year and be out at dig sites most of the rest of the time.*

She began making plans for the switch over. She had saved a lot of money, but now wanted at least two years of salary in the bank before she took this leap. She knew that start-up businesses were expensive to run and made very little money during the first year, so she needed seed money. After another year and a half of offshore work and putting every dime she had into the bank, she quit Shell and went to work for herself. She had about a month off with no calls for work, then work started pouring in.

She had a hard time regulating her consulting time at first. Companies don't want to switch every six months once they've found a great contractor because it's too difficult to recruit that quality of people to want to repeat the process twice a year. But, after some time at it, she got her mind around the type of projects she'd accept on contract and the types she'd turn down. Take the short-term "get-it-done" jobs. Pass on the long-term "no-one-knows-how-to-do-this-yet" jobs, and so she was able to stay serious about archeology and make sure she was out in the dirt unearthing ancient cast-offs as near to six-months a year as possible.

Catal Huyuk in Turkey was her latest dig and a more fascinating site just didn't exist. Possibly the remains of the oldest city on earth and inhabited before 5000 BC. The people there had lived in houses built side-by-side around courtyards. The homes had pits dug in the floor of the main room where all ancestors and family members were buried. The skeletons were covered up with dirt, the floor smoothed over and the families lived their lives right over the grave. If they'd been moderns they might have had a coffee table over the top of Grandma's urn of ashes. Fascinating. She'd been sad to leave Catal Huyuk and had been back on contracting jobs for only a few months when she got the call that had led her to Junior's and her confrontation with Jack. Now what was she going to do?

# CHAPTER 10 - CHANGE OF HEART

*"Can it be a sin to know? Can it be death?"*
*— John Milton, Paradise Lost*

Her phone rang. Mercy looked at it and saw it was Jack calling. Again. She answered it.

"Jack, I won't take the job. Parasca and I have some bad history and I won't work for him."

Jack didn't respond for a moment, but then said, "Go on."

"There's nothing to go on about. I don't want the job. Find someone else."

"Mercy, this job has your name all over it. I think you were meant for this job."

*That's probably what the Counselor would say if I asked it. Now why did I think that? I don't have time to let my mind wander.*

"Jack, it's complicated. I last saw Parasca almost nineteen years ago and it was traumatic. He's a real bad apple. I can't work for him."

"I'm listening."

"It's a long story and I don't want to tell it over the phone."

"All right. Tell it to me in person."

"No. I made a big enough scene already today at Junior's." There was a knock at the door. Mercy said, "Hold on, Jack. Someone's at the door." She walked to her hotel room door as she held the phone to her ear and spoke. "Did you send your courier again with another job offer?" She opened the door.

Jack stood there with his phone to his ear. He lowered it and hung up the line.

"No courier. Got a story to tell me?"

Mercy gaped at him, chuckled and then lowered her phone. She motioned him in and said, "I'll order some coffee from room service. This will take a while."

"No time. We have to go."

"Go? Go where?"

Jack said, "We have to catch our flight. You <u>have</u> packed, haven't you?"

Mercy raised her voice. "Jack! I haven't packed anything. I'm not taking this job."

"Sure you are. It's you, Mercy. You're the one to do this."

"You haven't been listening. I can't work for Parasca. He's a monster."

"You keep saying that, but you won't be working for him. You'll work for me. He never comes out to ships like ours."

"Jack, I can't tell you the whole thing right now. It would take too long. So I'll tell you this, years ago Parasca worked for the government of Romania before the revolution of December '89. I know this because I was there traveling with my mom. He was an official in the Securitate ... that's the Romanian secret police, and he had my mother interrogated when we were there. Later, when I was a student there, he was in charge of the Securitate thugs that attacked the students during the riots in Timisoara. After the Revolution was over and Ceausescu and his wife ended up on the wrong end of a firing squad, there was a change of government and mother and I eventually got out. She never would talk about what had happened to her, but that only convinced me that she'd been traumatized. And in Timisoara, Parasca's Securitate criminals killed ..." she stopped, breathed deeply and said, "...Stefan".

"Mercy, I'm so sorry." He reached to take her hand.

She pulled back. "Don't, Jack."

"I didn't know any of this, obviously."

She tightened her jaw. "I know. I just thought ... hoped ... all these years later that Parasca had been caught, or maybe jailed, or maybe even killed. But instead..." she growled, "...he lands on his feet after the Revolution and years later now, he surfaces as the CEO of one of the largest Romanian oil companies. Unbelievable! I'd heard about how a lot of those corrupt Securitate-types had done well after the Revolution, but it just never occurred to me that Parasca would come out smelling like a rose."

"Mercy, again, I'm sorry. You're right, this job isn't for you. I'll go. It's just that ... I'm very sorry it turned out this way. I admit I'd hoped that we might at least be friends again, working together and all. I apologize. Obviously, you're right." Jack frowned, looked down at the floor, sighed and turned toward the door. He reached for the doorknob as thoughts spun through Mercy's head.

*Parasca is a bad one and his men hurt Mom terribly and probably were the ones that killed Stefan, but do I really want to run away from the man every time I hear his name? I'm older and tougher. I've been through a lot. I shouldn't let myself be spooked by the thought of him. If I'm not strong enough to take him on now, then when will I be?*

Mercy's hand was on his, tightening gently. "Wait." She tilted her head to one side, her gray eyes shining bright with emotion. "I've changed my mind."

"What?"

"I'll take that job."

Jack looked at her, unblinking and then his lips moved to ask the question, "Why?" but she interrupted before the sounds escaped from him.

"I'll take the job. I've hated Parasca for the last twenty years, but maybe I can finally do something about the way he traumatized me. I never even thought I'd have the chance to see him again, but now, I may even have a chance to confront him. I'm different in a lot of ways. I think I'm tougher and stronger now. I'm going to take the job, but on one condition."

"What's that?"

"That if I do get the chance to speak to him you won't try to stop me. You mustn't get between Parasca and me or try to prevent us from meeting. You have to promise me that you'll allow me the chance to deal with the situation. Whether I confront him or punch him in the face, you have to stay out of it. Agreed?"

"You're going to take the job on the off chance that you'll eventually get some payback for what Parasca did?"

"Something like that. Besides, there's this guy on board the *Fortuna* that I've heard about. I want to check him out." Mercy was smiling again.

"Really?" Jack said skeptically.

"Really. I've heard he has a thing for geologists with archeology hobbies."

"Oh, that guy," said Jack, playing along. "I seem to remember something about a guy like that. Might want to watch out for him, though. He seems to get in trouble a lot."

"That's the one. I think he's the kind of guy that wouldn't be afraid to defy his boss if that was the right thing to do."

"Yeah, he probably doesn't have too much of a future with an attitude like that. You might want to stay out of his reach."

"I can take care of myself. Besides, I think someone like that could have a lot of potential, especially since he doesn't seem to be intimidated by outdoorsy tomboy-type women."

"You kidding? That's the best kind of woman."

She arched an eyebrow. "Oh yeah? Why?"

He paused, breaking into a broad grin. "Let's just say that outdoorsy tomboy-women are rugged, durable, determined and self-maintaining. How's that?"

"How romantic. You make me sound like a car battery."

"And did I say, 'with plenty of spark?'"

After an appalled silence, Mercy hit him on the arm, probably a little too hard. Jack winced in pain. Mercy felt a small flicker of hope in her heart and hid a smile.

# CHAPTER 11 - BIRTH OF EVIL

*"The mind is its own place, and in itself can make*
*a heaven of hell, a hell of heaven."*
— John Milton, *Paradise Lost*

Parasca asked, "Did you take care of the janitor's body?"

Rakslav said, "It's at the bottom of the Danube and is slowly making its way to the Black Sea."

"Good. How did he get in here? Have you dealt with the ones that hired him?"

"I won't until after it becomes obvious he has disappeared. We can't make it known that we objected to him and then have him go missing. It's tricky. An unskilled and uneducated person gets hired to scrub toilets and then somewhere along the line, they get approached by the competition. They get promised extra money to save a paper here and there out of the trash. It's difficult to completely prevent. Now we will have security people watch the janitorial staff destroy and shred all trash on-site. The cleaning crew will be searched before entering and exiting. It's time-consuming and costly."

Janos Parasca glared at Rakslav and said, "Don't complain to me about costly! Tell me why you haven't located the mummified hand!"

Rakslav sighed and said, "We haven't because we are up against professionals and they don't make mistakes very often. I do have confirmation that the Russian is in Bucharest. Two people of ours spotted him in the city and word also has it that the large contract offer that your old rival Dmitri put out has been assigned. I think the Russian is working for Dmitri's group now. No one else with the money and influence to hire him also has the desire and guts to defy you so openly."

"Dmitri is after my artifacts? Why? He has no interest in such things.

Prove to me Dmitri has done this. Why would he oppose me this way? He and I haven't been at odds for years now."

"He probably remembers the government work you stole from him by painting him as a low quality under-cutter. He still hates you for that."

"Huh. Idiot. He <u>was</u> undercutting me with inferior petrol. Trying to pass that heavy Caspian Sea slop as light Romanian? He deserved to lose the bid. I make no apologies for delivering better product to big customers."

"I know. Everyone knows this, especially Dmitri. But he still hates you. You exposed his scam and now everyone knows what a liar he is. Anyway, I think he sent the Russian after the artifacts. He may not be interested in the artifacts the way you are, but he knows you want them now. I think he wants to be offering them to you, highly marked up."

"I've cut him too much slack because of our past friendship, but I'll destroy him for this. Get out there and track this Russian down. First we take him out, then we go after Dmitri."

Rakslav nodded and left. Parasca stood and paced the floor of his large office. He felt extremely energetic today, as he always did after a session such as last night's. This one had ended in the death of that traitor they'd caught sneaking papers out of his office, but he knew the energy wouldn't last. It never lasted for more than a day or two.

He looked at his left hand, the one that had touched the tiny dagger charged with the memory of the woman in childbirth. The hand still looked better and the skin was tighter with no age spots. He held both hands together and stared. The left was definitely younger looking. He'd never seen this happen before. Sure, the blood of a dying victim gave him a temporary boost. It would wear off by tomorrow like it always did, but he'd never seen blood cause a physical change like the one in his hand. *And remember, it was only the <u>memory</u> of blood that caused this. The vision I had of that woman giving birth was what did it. It was the memory of the umbilical blood. Why? What was so special about that mother and baby? And it only worked once. I tried to use the blade with my other hand and it didn't do anything. I've got to find out if there are more artifacts like this. If only regular blood could do this or could have the same effect!*

He thought back to his earliest memories as a child, just after the end of the Second World War. When North Africa was lost to the Allies, Romania had become the Nazi's main petrol supply. Toward the end of the war the Germans abandoned Romania. The power vacuum left by the Nazi retreat, coupled with the destruction of the war, left the population in desperate conditions: disorder, chaos and starvation with no end in sight. Unknown to the people of Romania, the Allies ceded Eastern Europe to the Soviets and Romania along with it.

Of course, Janos hadn't known any of the history, causes or reasons until later. What he remembered was the painful, gnawing hunger in his belly. He was only a small child at the end of the war, living in alleys and doorways. He didn't remember what had happened to his parents. He had no memory of them.

His most vivid memory from that time was of his first Blood Day. That was how he thought of it. Other orphans had said that there might be food, because a train had come in last night and they'd heard the sounds of cattle from inside the train cars. The train went to the factory where they killed the cattle and packed the meat to be sent to troops fighting in the war, but now the war was over and the Germans were gone. Still, a supply train full of cattle had arrived and no one knew why. It was probably one of those mistakes that happen like mail coming for a person who was long dead. But then, maybe the meat went to the Russians now. It certainly didn't go to the Romanians. No one had seen a scrap of meat for months. Still, though they wouldn't get 'the good stuff' as the older boys said, there might be something left over. You just had to know where to look. And you couldn't mind getting dirty.

He had followed the older orphans to the outskirts of town, followed them down the train tracks, and then when they approached the factory, the children split off toward the river and the oily water where a huge drainage pipe emptied into the sluggish river. In single file, the children waded through sludge and up the drainage pipe that seemed as large as a cavern to young Janos. The oldest of the children motioned for the rest to be silent and wait. Janos remembered the flies and the stink. He saw large rats run by the boy in front of him and wondered what rat tasted like. He'd never eaten anything as large as a rat. Maybe they tasted good too.

Echoes from ahead ran down the pipe. It was the sound of large metal doors opening and heavy equipment in motion. The oldest boy held his hand up, kept the crowd of children back for a minute and then motioned them forward.

They crept to the end of the drainage pipe and looked out on a pit filled with blood, entrails, hide and bones. Dark water ran out of the pit and down through the pipe by which they had come. Above them from the top edge of the pit, a bulldozer pushed a pile of offal down into the drainage pit, intestines spraying wide like a giant, dead, tentacled thing. The machine backed away from the edge and into a corrugated metal building. The fall of the pile sent a wave of reddish water washing past them into the pipe and down to the river.

More rats swam by and he followed them with his eyes. They headed straight for the largest mound of blood and bone and his eyes suddenly got large. The rats were already crawling over the meat, fighting over it. The mound was covered in swarming, gorging rats. All of this should have horrified him, but all he could think of was the meat. *Look at all the meat! And the rats are getting it all!*

He screamed in fury and sloshed to the nearest pile. Other boys were scrambling with him and the rats hissed as they closed in. The boy next to him grabbed a bone and swung it at a rat like a club. The rat dodged and several snapped at the boy. Two leapt at the boy's legs. Janos ignored him. He had to grab some meat. He couldn't let these rats take it all. Right in front of him, above the foul soup, was a rib cage. Still clinging between two ribs, untouched by the butcher, was a beautiful ribbon of untainted red meat. His heart pounded. It was better meat than he'd ever seen. He reached for the ribs, but three rats swarmed up the ribs and headed for the tender flesh. He screamed at them and lunged.

He heard shouts around him and thought it was from boys fighting the rats for scraps. He was almost to the ribs, when something grabbed his leg and pulled him back and away. He screamed as rats swarmed over the rib meat. He looked back to shriek at whoever had him by the leg. He saw a larger boy frantically hauling him back in the direction of the pipe. The boy had his terror-filled eyes fixed on the upper lip of the pit. Janos followed the boy's eyes and screamed in terror. Just then, the bulldozer pushed another mountain of blood down on them both.

Pressure. Darkness. Silence. Suffocation. Screams tried to force their way out, but his opened mouth was filled with the tastes of death and disease, of garbage and excrement. He gagged, and tried to take in a breath but couldn't. He thrashed in the trap of bones and slop. He tried twisting free, tried to climb out, even kicked as if to swim, but the weight of a mountain seemed to crush him downward, further into the pit.

He tried again to breathe but couldn't. Flashing sparks of light shot through his sightless eyes. Somehow he knew the lights meant something terrible. *No! No! Not me!*

Then a burning surge of energy lanced into him. The lights in his field of vision transformed into a solid field of bloody red. His tiny frame felt as if it were on fire and so strong that nothing could contain him. He thrust his legs behind him and grabbed onto whatever he felt in front of him, pulling himself forward and upward as if climbing up a slope. He crawled through the muck and pulled himself upward and outward and finally his head cleared the mangled carcasses. He gasped one breath and then another, and fought until he was completely out. He heard boys nearby screaming and realized they must be screaming at him.

He turned back and saw them pointing at him in horror. Two ran to him to help him. Others were pulling at a body that was still buried to its armpits in meat and blood. The face was the boy that had tried to save him from the bulldozer's load of waste. He saw that the boy's mouth was full of bloody pulp and Janos knew. *This boy is dead. He was buried with me. He died just when I began climbing up and out to the air.*

Janos turned away from the dead boy and grabbed a bone with plenty of meat still on it and tore it free from the pile. He sloshed through the bloody pit and never looked back, starting to gnaw absently on the raw meat as he went. He ignored the calls and shouts of the other boys. *Let them shout. I have my food and no one can take it away from me.*

He never forgot that day or what it had taken to survive. He never felt pity or remorse when he took from those that were weaker. His determination grew and he not only survived but learned to excel. He was only marked with two fears: of confined spaces and darkness, but he took care to avoid both. Nothing terrorized him like memories of the choking darkness of that bloody pit.

Much later, he puzzled out that the boy that had tried to save him at the refuse pit had suffocated while they were both buried under the pile of entrails and bone. Janos somehow knew that when the other boy had died, his departing life had somehow energized Janos and had given him the boost of strength he needed to free himself. He eventually tested and confirmed that theory by trapping and killing another orphan and receiving the ghoulish burst of power from his dying victim.

As he grew older, he rose in power in the street gangs of his youth, graduating to the gangs of the government's Securitate forces under Ceausescu. The cruelty of the regime gave him many chances to exercise his need for death, and he had personally attended to the end of many prisoners and spies.

After the ends of the idiot dictator and his wife, Janos had seen some lean times, but had survived and eventually prospered from the treasure he'd either taken or extorted from victims. He also had made connections and took advantage of them to survive the cleansing pogroms that followed Ceausescu's fall. He never dropped his ties with the underworld and that gave him the access he needed when there were enemies that needed to die untimely deaths.

Janos Parasca snapped back to the present and found that he was still staring at his youthful-appearing hand.

*The death of a victim always gives me some temporary strength, but never before have I gone through such a transformation as this. My hands and inner sight give me visions of ancient deaths when I touch the tools that caused the deaths, but I've never been physically altered by those visions before. This is new and powerful. It has already restored my hand. What could more of these artifacts, or some of the actual blood do for me? Could it restore me, rejuvenate me? I must get more of these artifacts if it costs everything I have.*

He reached for his desk phone and dialed a number. He growled into the receiver, "Where is the *Fortuna*? I want to know now!"

\* \* \*

After Mercy accepted the job, Jack rescheduled their flights and Mercy tended to preparations for relocating. She decided to keep her apartment in Dallas but returned there to pack and send ahead some of the things she would need. She wrapped up her last project and said goodbye to the team. She also visited her doctor to get a prescription for a two year supply of her medicine. The physician was very pleased with how well she continued to react to the medication, but cautioned her.

"Mercy, some people begin to see reduced effectiveness with this drug after continued usage. I'm happy that it's still working for you, but you must let me know if you notice changes in your symptoms. As you know, consistent, recurring auditory hallucinations such as the kinds you experience can be very disturbing to many people. Not everyone who has them can deal with them as well as you. In fact, yours is the most severe case I've seen in quite some time. As you yourself have told me, if it weren't for the dampening effect of the drug, you'd be unable to function normally in society."

She said, "I'll be sure to let you know if things change."

"You do that. I also wish that you would look into the support groups that I've mentioned to you in the past. Hearing voices is a phenomenon that happens to more people than you might think. Some reports indicate that up to four percent of the population suffers from auditory hallucinations at one time or other. There are groups of people that may be able to help you deal with facets of this."

Mercy nodded and said, "I've been meaning to look into those support groups, but my travel schedule makes it very difficult to be part of something like that."

"I understand. Still, I want to stress again to you the seriousness of your diagnosis. The varied types of voices you hear, and especially the ones that narrate your actions and try to command you to perform violent behaviors, make your condition extreme. If it weren't for the effectiveness of this drug regimen in your case, you would likely have been institutionalized by now. There are many patients with less severe symptoms that are dysfunctional and severely schizophrenic. Let me know if your condition changes. I want to keep you as one of our success cases."

After getting the prescription filled, she flew to Paris to meet Jack. They caught a flight to Bucharest where they began getting Mercy enrolled at PetroRomania's corporate headquarters. Janos Parasca, the CEO, was unavailable. Some of the other executives thought he was "Out of the country." He was probably at one of his hideaways, or maybe that place he owned in the Greek isles. Jack breathed a sigh of relief at Parasca's absence. He didn't want to see the encounter between Mercy and Parasca just yet.

In the meantime, Jack was astounded by how good Mercy's Romanian was as she quickly navigated through her start-up trials. She took direction from the corporate drones when appropriate, but she also stood her ground with them too. Nobody pushed Mercy around and she caught on very quickly. She also picked up on some of the Romanian idioms that had gone out of style since her time there twenty years ago and she adapted quickly to fit the new speaking styles.

She told Jack, "One thing I notice is how much more optimistic the people are. When I was here before, it was during the last years of the Ceausescu's reign. Everything had been going downhill for so long that the economy was in a perpetual state of shortage. Everything seemed gray and the people acted beaten down by life. Now, there is an openness and optimism that I thought I'd never experience in Romania. It's great to see. One turn of phrase I've noticed: people don't like to speak of Ceausescu's firing squad death or the fall of Communism here. I've heard more than one person call it 'the regime change' like it was nothing more than an election for mayor. I know how brutal it was in Timisoara where it all started. It wasn't anything so simple as a minor election that the Dictator lost. He and his wife were cut down in a hail of bullets and their philosophy was forever discredited. But today the people call it 'the regime change.' Okay, then."

After navigating the maze of on-boarding as a new employee, Jack took her to one of the best hotels in Bucharest which was also near PetroRomania's headquarters.

"Where are you staying?" she asked as they stood in the lobby.

"I've got an apartment." There was an awkward silence as she looked at him. She arched an eyebrow and tilted her head slightly. An unspoken question seemed to hang in the air between them. He breathed out in exasperation. "What?"

"Nothing, Jack. Just ... well ... thanks for not expecting me to ask you up to my room for drinks, or offering me an awkward invitation to stay with you at your apartment. It really is better this way. Just because we were engaged years ago, doesn't change the fact that we're both much different people now, does it?" Jack didn't know what to say. Then she surprised him by stepping in close and kissing him on the cheek.

"Thanks, Jack. I really do appreciate all of the help, and the job. I even appreciate how you're not pressuring me into anything. You know how jumpy I get. Thanks for the space." She showed a brilliant smile that made his heart skip a beat, then turned and walked around the corner to the elevators.

Jack didn't take a taxi. He decided to get some air and think. He couldn't get Mercy out of his mind. Her pale hair and long slender legs ... Jack shook himself. The hair on his arms was standing up. Whew. She had a hold on him, no doubt. He kept walking. Getting close to his apartment, he decided he wasn't ready yet and went around the block and headed to the shopping district. People were coming out for the evening. He tried to imagine what it had been like when Mercy had been here before. Drab, depressing and paranoid, he decided.

Jack had learned about the local history after arriving and had become a little obsessed with it. Romania had been one of the last Soviet bloc countries to fall after the Berlin wall came down. Ceausescu and his wife strangled the country for years, selling off everything the economy could produce in order to pay back the loans the government had taken out from foreign banks. The dictator had pushed industrialization onto the country. Really, he'd shoved it down the country's unwilling throat. Farmers were forced off their land and into the cities and factories by the tens of thousands. Ceausescu was determined to modernize and control Romania, no matter what it cost the people. He never had been a fool about the Soviets and tried to steer clear of their total control, but he wasn't above taking and using ideas like Stalin's collectivization programs. And that's why he'd used the Securitate so heavily. He'd thought his people were ignorant peasants. He believed he had to force them to do what was needed. He had them herded like sheep, prodded, spied upon, threatened, investigated, tortured and killed. It was all the same to him. It needed to be done.

The Securitate was Romania's version of the KGB and had been Ceausescu's lever that allowed him to move the country in his direction. But when the protests, riots and revolt started happening in December of 1989, some said that the Securitate had been behind it. Some said that the Soviets had inside men in the Securitate and they didn't want Ceausescu running the show anymore. Those same people said that the Securitate considered the Dictator and his wife to be parasites and so they held back at crucial points, letting the tyrant fall. Who really knew? Maybe there were those that were happy to leave the history books ambiguous and vague.

But Mercy said Parasca had been in the Securitate. Wow. If that was true, and Jack would bet his life that Mercy wasn't lying, Parasca had come out of the revolution smelling like a rose. Company legend said he was a self-made man; a brilliant investor who'd built upon brilliant success after success to create an empire. Then he had taken over PetroRomania and the success arc was still trending upward. Sure, he was mostly reclusive. He showed up maybe twice a month at corporate for a day or two, but mainly spent his time at his place in the Greek isles admiring his collection.

That was another interesting thing about Parasca. Word in the company was that he had one of the largest private museums in the world attached to his villa. It was said he had ancient artwork, archeological exhibits, statues, even a completely intact house and all its goods from the city of Pompeii. Supposedly, his people had found a newly unearthed site from the volcanic-ash covered ancient city and he had paid to have the house and its contents moved stone by stone and piece by piece to his private museum and reassembled. If that was true, then the man had incredible pull. Enough to get around the Italian government's Antiquities Ministry. But then, Jack already knew Parasca had pull. Look how he'd gotten the *Fortuna* out of its legal deadlock. That must have required a virtual fountain of money to shake loose, and maybe some other kinds of pressure. And then again, maybe that was how he'd also gotten the Italian authorities to look the other way and let him make off with an archeological treasure, through using a combination of money and pressure. Yes, Parasca was a person that got his way and was an absolute fanatic about his hobby. And that lead him back to Mercy.

Parasca wanted Mercy leading the team. Originally, Jack had thought that Mercy's reputation as geologist and archeologist had put Parasca on her trail. But Jack hadn't told Mercy of all his suspicions … that Parasca had seemed to be *personally* interested in Mercy. It was almost like he'd known her. Now, Jack knew Mercy had a wild grudge against the man dating back to his Securitate days. This had the potential to get really, really bad.

Jack had been lost in thought during his rambling walk and then pulled up short. Was that tall woman … no, it wasn't Mercy. The woman and a man walked by while carrying on an animated conversation. She laughed and smiled at the man and he parried back with a comment that Jack couldn't quite hear. She impulsively threw her arms around his neck and kissed him. The man kissed her back passionately. Jack felt himself getting hot and his collar felt too tight. Jack's thoughts turned back to Mercy.

If it was possible, she was even more striking than when they'd been in grad school together. She was so fit. Lean, but still curved in the right places, in spite of the way she ate. He had never seen anyone that could pack food away like her. She ate huge meals <u>with</u> desserts and had snacks all day long. At one time he'd wondered if she was bulimic, but that wasn't her, definitely. She was the only woman Jack had ever seen that drank real Coke, not diet. She ate sweets, had a thing for chocolate too, and drank real beers like Guinness, not one of those light dishwater beers. How could she pack away the calories like that and never show it? She must have a freak metabolism. Of course, she was very active. She used to work out every day and it looked like she still had that habit. She had made a point of verifying that her hotel here in Bucharest had a gym.

She did seem more distant than she used to be when they were engaged, but it had, after all, been years. "Give it time, Jack," he told himself. Maybe this time, years later, he would have learned his lesson and not pressure her and scare her off. Jack was determined that this time he wouldn't screw it up.

# CHAPTER 12 - ON THE FORTUNA

*"Here at least we shall be free"*
*— John Milton, Paradise Lost*

The next day, Jack picked Mercy up from the hotel and they rode in the company limo back to PetroRomania headquarters. They took the elevator to the rooftop helipad and boarded the waiting helicopter with a dozen other passengers, all with as much gear as Jack and Mercy. Mercy was the only woman aboard, and no one recognized her, but all of the other passengers knew Jack and greeted him warmly.

The helicopter flew over Bucharest and followed along the Danube, the old city passing beneath them. This far up, all of the activity below seemed like furious insects swarming the streets with unknown purpose. The river teemed with traffic as well, and the chopper swept above and out toward the mouth of the Danube where it emptied into the Black Sea. The helicopter landed in a warehouse district, took on some additional cargo, refueled and then was quickly airborne again and headed out to sea. Two hours later, they saw the *Fortuna* on the horizon.

The ship was large. Not as big as a luxury cruise ship, but at least nine hundred feet long. Even from a distance, it was obviously an industrial vessel, seemingly all pipes and girders. It had a double-derrick structure at midship and four cranes: two fore and two aft of the double-derrick. The ship's helipad was at the aft end of the ship above the eight-story tower containing the bridge, the exploration operations control room, executive offices for the company men, office space, laboratories, crew living quarters, kitchen and cafeteria. The helicopter set down and the blades slowed to a stop.

Mercy stepped out onto the deck and breathed deeply and sighed. She loved the smell of ocean air with that hint of metal, grease and sweat. It meant there was the chance of discovery in the air. This time, she hoped it meant not just the discovery of oil, but maybe some new chapter of her life.

After checking to make sure that the new equipment was being unloaded properly, Jack showed her down to the crew quarters and her cabin. After dropping off her luggage, he took her and introduced her around to a few who were in their offices. Jack took her back up to the ship's exploration operations control room. Looking out the window overlooking the rest of the ship, he pointed out the locations of the major ship sections.

Closest to them were the racks of thirty-one foot long pipe used for drilling oil and gas wells. The racks of tubulars were stacked in such an orderly arrangement that it could only mean automation. When under full drilling operations, the system would unrack the pipes and convey them to the center of the ship. There they were connected into two or three piece sections, mounted into the drill and added to the length of pipe that was being punched down through the sea and into the sea bed beneath. The derricks at midship towered over the moon pool. It was a twenty-five foot by seventy-five foot door into the deep. When drilling was underway and the moon pool doors were open, the ship had an intentional hole open to the sea.

Mercy had seen many similar ships and so needed no more than a look to grasp the layout and any differences from previous ships. A few minutes later, they went to the large conference room on deck seven to introduce her to the group as the new project lead. All of her department heads were there and a briefing was held over lunch to start bringing Mercy up to speed.

The meeting was directed by Hayden Travers, a man in his early sixties with short-cut gray hair, a wiry build and a British accent. Mercy knew him and respected him from a past project they had worked on together. He quickly summarized their situation and preparations for the next day's work. With the discovery of the ancient knife freed from the tar whip and new directives from Corporate (Mercy took that to mean Parasca), the task for the ship had changed from one of discovery of oil and gas deposits to one of finding out what else might lie at the bottom of this section of sea. If they found commercial deposits of oil or gas that would be gravy, but that was no longer their first priority.

To that end, the ship had been using its instrumentation and exploratory capabilities to search as delicately as possible until Jack had returned with Mercy. Hayden had joined the expedition two days earlier. So far, using the ship's two submersibles and high capacity water pumps, divers had cleared away a large patch of ocean-bottom silt to expose the extent of the tar seep from which the whip containing the dagger had come. Pictures from the submersibles showed that the seep, silt washed away, looked like an asphalt-colored volcano, with a new tar whip trailing away from its pinnacle.

"What's the scale of this mound?" she asked, referring to the pictures.

"Sixteen meters tall from the base and about twenty-eight meters wide at the bottom of the cone. Not too different in size from that sub-sea mud volcano discovered recently over in the Caspian Sea. Unlike that one however, this is a much less active site. That mud volcano has a lot of methane out-gassing and is spewing oil-soaked mud. This one's activity is more like a submerged tar-pit. It's a very slow, thick petrol leak. We've had divers and the submersibles working for days washing away the ocean bottom silt at this spot," Travers said.

"So, Hayden, what's the plan? How do we get possible artifacts out of this asphalt without damaging them? We can't drill. There's too much chance of destroying the very things we're after. Also, if we hit more metal like in that little dagger, we might just break our drill bits. Do we steam them out?" She asked.

Hayden smiled. "That's exactly what we recommend. We want to set up a large oil recovery fabric cone that will fit relatively tightly over the mound and go close with the submersibles and hoses from the ship with very hot, high pressure steam. We fill the dome area with the steam to heat the water quickly inside the cone. This way, we flash melt the tar and when it liquefies and floats upward, we catch it in the cone and remove it from the top with hoses and pumps from the ship."

Mercy said, "That cone design sounds similar to the setup at Coal Oil Point offshore California."

Hayden said, "Right, except they don't need to melt asphalt to get the oil. They don't use steam because the oil is still liquid when it seeps out of the ocean floor there. If I remember my figures right, they catch up to twenty-three cubic meters of oil and twenty-eight thousand cubic meters of gas every day with a cone similar to the one we'll be using. The teams have been working this approach for days now hoping you'd approve the design. We'll be ready to run with it tomorrow if you give the go ahead, boss."

Mercy said, "I hear you, but first tell me more about the risks. I know from the geologic and seismic work already done that this isn't a likely spot for a large find. Sure, there's enough of an oil trap to create this seep, but it's not big enough to be a commercially viable deposit. I know that we're not drilling yet and so we don't face a potential blowout situation like BP did in the Gulf of Mexico that caused such a huge mess. However, we still need to have plans to deal with any possible problem scenarios." She turned to the other department heads. "What are we facing that we might have to deal with?"

A thin, grizzled man named Yani spoke up. He headed the submersible crews. He began, "Dr. Teller, as you say, no drilling yet. So, no problems with the oil, gas or drilling mud. The biggest problem I see is containing the tar when we melt it with the steam. We don't want tar balls getting loose and ending up on some beach. Bad publicity. We'll be using high pressure steam close to the asphalt mound and it's possible that some of the tar will get away from us if we don't take precautions."

Mercy answered, "Great points, but first, please. Everyone, call me Mercy, not Dr. Teller. All of us should be on a first-name basis. We can call each other by name and still maintain our chain of command. So how do we deal with Yani's concerns about the tar? How do we contain it?" They discussed various ways of dealing with the situation. Mercy knew that the concern was relatively minor, but she was glad to see that they took it seriously. She also wanted to see how they would deal with the discussion. She observed the men and sorted and classified them mentally. Some, like Yani, were very careful and cautious. That came with the territory of working as an industrial diver and submersible operator. In that line of work, you were careful and methodical or you died. Others were more shoot-from-the-hip types with creative approaches to problem solving. You needed all personality types to get things done well with a team. This team looked to be well-balanced.

After the discussion ended and Mercy was satisfied that they had worked through the problem, she summarized the approach, got agreement from everyone and gave the formal go-ahead for tomorrow's operation. In the aftermath of BP's disastrous well blow-out in the Gulf of Mexico, many companies had put in place policies that required well design, drilling and operation decision meetings to be recorded, so she verified that the meeting had been captured digitally.

Jack, Mercy and Hayden remained in the conference room after the meeting ended and the department heads returned to their teams to issue instructions about tomorrow's operations. Mercy considered the schedule ahead of them. Some of the groups would be working through the night to be ready for the steam ops the next day. *It could be very exciting, or deadly dull. We'll see.*

They wrapped up the rest of the day's details and then Hayden and Jack walked Mercy to the crew's quarters. After arranging to meet in the morning over breakfast to discuss the day's schedule, Hayden left Mercy and Jack standing outside her cabin.

Jack said, "You have a nice touch with command situations."

She said, "Thanks, Jack. It helped to have you in the room to establish the line of authority to me. We'll see how things go tomorrow."

"We can go back and grab some coffee if you want to talk."

"Let me have a rain check on that for tomorrow night, could you Jack? I need to get settled in, get in a workout and then get some sleep. Busy day tomorrow." *I also need to go extra hard on the work out. The voices are getting louder and it's nowhere near time to take my next dose. Got to use the old-fashioned method or*

*I'll be a basket case by morning.*

"You know, at the hotel last night, you put me off too. If I was the kind of guy that discouraged easily, I'd start taking this personally. But, no problem. I'll take you up on that rain check for tomorrow. See you at the department lead meeting in the morning." Jack said.

"If you were the kind of guy that discouraged easily, I wouldn't be here." Mercy surprised him again with a kiss to his cheek. Then she disappeared into her cabin. Jack shook his head and walked down the hall to his room.

By 9:00 am the next morning, the dome was in place over the submerged tar mound, tightly weighted down and sealed at the ocean floor. At 10:00 am, a test showed that no leaks were present at the anticipated pressures. By noon, all of the steam connections were in place to the dome. At 1:00 pm, Mercy gave the go-ahead and the steam injection started. It would take a while to get the temperature inside the dome high enough to begin to liquefy the tar, and the management team would be notified when significant amounts began to be extracted through the top of the containment dome.

Now it was a waiting game. There was some time to kill and all of her teams were busy. At this point she would be in their way, so she sat in the control room, monitoring the video feed from the ocean bottom. Mercy sat at a desk but her mind eventually wandered to the dagger. *What do I know about that thing? What can I infer? First, assume their science was good and the handle on the dagger was from wood that grew around eight thousand years ago. They used carbon dating on the handle but that can have a wide error bar due to a number of factors. Still, readings from preserved wood were often reliable as long as you understood the limitations of the method.*

She paused in her thoughts and looked back at the monitor. No change yet. *So how about in this case? What could be the influencing factors? Well, the carbon in this wood had certainly been polluted with carbon from the tar it had been soaking in for ages. But, the carbon in the tar should have very little carbon-14. It would have gone through nuclear decay long before and that could be compensated for. Another influencing factor could be that the amount of carbon-14 in the atmosphere where the wood was formed inside a growing tree was not known. Volcanic eruptions could drastically mess up the amount of carbon in the air and there might have been those kinds of events back when this wood grew. So what does all that tell me? It tells me that the wood, but not necessarily the blade, was fashioned sometime around 6000 BC plus or minus maybe one thousand years. That means that the wood in this handle probably predates the invention of written language. So how old is the blade? Don't know. The handle could have been made at a completely different time period than the blade. The blade might be very old or very recent. This might not be the original blade for one thing. Maybe the original blade was a carved bone knife that had been stuck into this wooden hilt. Then over the years, more durable materials were found and replaced the original bone knife blade. Maybe even only a few years ago, this crystalline blade was fashioned and used to complete this blade. Any of those things are possible.*

The speakerphone on the desk squawked. "Boss, we've started getting oil flow through the valve at the top of the containment dome. Not a lot, but it's increasing."

"Good. Report again in fifteen minutes unless something unusual happens."

"Will do. Out."

Mercy went back to her train of thought. *An eight thousand-year old wooden dagger handle and a blade with a bull symbol etched in it. How would they have made the etching in a metal that hard? It wasn't just some crude scratching either, but a beautiful and intricate cutting that made the bull's head look almost lifelike.* It reminded her of the larger and beautifully detailed bull-shaped vase found on the island of Crete in the Palace of Knossos. Mercy had spent a long weekend poking around those ruins with a group of visiting students during one of those golden summers during her grad school years. She'd spent most of her time on archeological digs, but the trip to Crete had been purely sightseeing. The ruins of the Palace of Knossos had more than thirteen hundred rooms and so many statues of bulls and paintings of bulls that it may have been the original source of the myth of the Minotaur's Labyrinth. Mercy remembered too that Knossos had contained a very unusual find. One of those things that experts discussed all of the time, but the general public knew nothing about. Knossos had contained numerous examples of one of the world's undeciphered ancient languages: Linear-A.

No one knew exactly how many modern languages there were, let alone how many dead languages had existed. Of those languages no longer spoken, there were dozens of languages that had never been deciphered. Scholars had worked on them like puzzles for decades. Some languages had been studied for more than a hundred years, but some had proved un-crackable. Not only did no one know <u>what</u> they meant, no one even had a clue <u>how</u> to know what they meant. One of those that had never been deciphered was Linear-A from Knossos.

Written languages could be indecipherable for many reasons: maybe there weren't enough samples of it; or there was no similar language that had been deciphered and could be compared to it; perhaps there were no consistent matches with other symbols from known languages; or maybe there were no translations found of it to another known language, like had been the case with the Rosetta Stone. How strange. People used to think and write and speak in languages that no one knew today and that no one would ever know. People whose voices were unheard and even worse: un-hearable. Their words could not be understood and it was as if they were now eternally mute. *What must it be like to speak words that no one can hear?*

Mercy's mind jerked as if it had jumped a track. *Was it anything like hearing words that no one was speaking? Like what I do every day of my life?*

Mercy shivered. She had to stop these thoughts. *How was the steam injection going?* She looked at the monitor and watched the minutes tick away. The tar was melting quickly now. The pumps had brought in a substantial fraction of the melted tar to the ship's holding tanks.

"Mercy," Hayden called in, "we're going to have to stop for a while. We've almost exhausted our steam tanks. We need to go through another heating cycle to build up pressure again in the steam injectors."

She said, "Power down the operation and call the men back for a break. After things cool down a bit, I want us to pull the lid off and check the site."

"If we do that, we're done for the day. You sure you want to?"

"Yes. Besides, we're here for archeology now, not solely for oil. Let's do some site work. First thing in the morning, I want to take a ride in one of those subs."

# CHAPTER 13 - SKELETONS OF THE PAST

*"Our cure, to be no more; sad cure!"*
— *John Milton, Paradise Lost*

"This mini-sub will keep us safe and dry for up to twelve hours at depths of three hundred meters," the sub operator said.

It was morning and Mercy saw they were diving toward the sea bottom, only a couple of hundred feet below. Mercy was surprised at how quickly the dark closed in over them. The sunny Black Sea above became a twilit gloom very quickly, it seemed. As if he'd heard her thoughts, he switched on the outer high-intensity beams. The area ahead of the sub brightened as they descended.

"It only takes about seventy meters of water to totally block out the sun. Down below that, it's always night," he said in a thick, Greek accent.

She switched to his language and said to him, "I can speak some Greek, if you feel more comfortable that way."

He shook his head, smiled and continued in English, "No, boss. You know how it is in these kinds of crews. We have so many different nations and languages on a ship like this that the only thing we have in common is our second language, English. Let me stick to English if it's okay with you. I need the practice."

She laughed and switched back. "Your English is excellent. You don't need practice. You just need to tone down that Athenian accent." He looked at her in pretend shock, his right hand pointing to his chest, as if to say, 'Me?' She smiled broadly, and pointed out the window. "Yani, aren't we almost there?"

"Sure, boss. There she is. Our beautiful dome."

Outside the window of the mini-sub, activity was just finishing up. Divers were removing the last of the weights holding down the dome. The steam-injection hoses had already been disconnected and were lying on the sand, away from the dome. The first mini-sub had been assisting with the release of the collection hose at the apex of the dome. The hose had been withdrawn and cables from the dome stretched up to the surface. Two minutes later, the first sub came back into view and floated over next to them. Jack waved from the other sub's cabin and smiled. Mercy chuckled and waved back.

She grabbed the microphone and pressed the talk button. "Jack, how'd you talk your way onto that sub?"

"It was easy. I just asked Antonio here if he liked his job. He said, 'Yes sir, and I want to keep it, too.' So he didn't mind if I came along." Antonio laughed heartily. Jack continued, "Mercy, I couldn't let you be the most senior person down here. What if you needed some management to blame for things that went wrong?"

Mercy shook her head and said with mock sweetness, "I don't need something to go wrong before I blame you, Jack."

The sub's radio sounded with a third voice. Hayden spoke, "Sub One, we're ready to lift the dome for visual inspection. What is your position?"

Antonio took the mike from Jack and answered with the exact location and added, "About twenty meters west of the bottom of the dome. We're ready."

Hayden said, "Sub Two, what is your position?"

Yani answered with their location and said, "About ten meters southeast of Sub One. We're ready."

Hayden said, "Mercy, should we go ahead and raise the dome?"

"Do it." Mercy said.

"Confirmed. Raise the dome." said Hayden.

Mercy watched. First, the cables were hauled up from above and grew taut. Under the headlamps of Mercy's and Jack's subs, the dome began to rise. It lifted and four beams from the two subs' headlamps shot through to the mound. *The mound doesn't look like it's changed at all.* Then she noticed differences from the pictures she'd seen at first. It looked jagged. The subs moved forward side-by-side. The headlamps revealed more and more as they got closer.

*Its looks like the tangled remains of a collapsed building.* There were piled rocks, petrified branches and what looked like entire trees. They got closer and lit up the tangled mess with their combined headlights. The high pressure, high temperature steam had melted the tar from large sections of the mound and its removal had uncovered a vast, tangled chaos of collected, compacted and tar-soaked refuse. Mercy said, "Let's slowly spiral up to the top of this pile." The subs moved higher toward the apex of the mound on a slow upward trajectory.

They circled the mound and finally came within a few feet of the top.

*Some of those branches look strange.* "Move in closer there," she pointed. Yani slowed and guided the sub in to just a few feet from the pile.

"What are we looking at?" Jack said through the radio.

Mercy said, "I don't know. I'm trying to make some sense out of this jumble at the top of the pile. That piece there almost looks like a ribcage, don't you think, Jack?"

His voice sounded through the speaker, "I don't see it."

Yani took a pen-shaped object from his work overalls and said, "Use this laser pointer and show him where you're looking."

Mercy took the pointer, aimed the red dot through the window of the sub, through the water and waved a circle around an area of the rubble about three feet across. "See here and here. Those look like ribs."

Jack said, "I see it. You're right. If I'm correct about the scale here, a ribcage that big must have belonged to something bigger than a horse."

"Could be, but look. It's all compressed and twisted, but … if those are the ribs, they keep going back and around here, getting narrower and narrower. Good grief, how long is this thing? Oh. It narrows down to a long tail, maybe? Let's go up the other direction. Back to the ribs, they keep getting larger and there it looks like a branch or something is sticking through the ribs and then, shoulders, maybe? Oh. What is that?" Mercy's voice trailed off.

Jack said, "Looks like jaws, maybe. Yes. An alligator or crocodile. The jaws are closed around, another branch, is that it?"

Mercy silently moved the laser pointer over the tableau. Her eyes opened wider with each tracing. She moved the pointer more and more quickly as she gradually understood what she was seeing.

Jack's voice came through the radio. "What is it Mercy? What do you see?"

Her forehead wrinkled as if solving a puzzle. "Probably a crocodile. I think alligators are limited to the western hemisphere." She paused and spoke more clearly. "It was a battle, Jack, and both sides lost."

"What do you mean?"

"Look here at these bones," she motioned with the bright red dot of the laser pointer. "The flesh is all gone, but the tar preserved the bones just like it did with those fossils in the La Brea tar pits in California. The difference is, this tar pit has been submerged. There: look at those bones, the ones that look like ribs and jaws. It's a gigantic crocodile. Here, it's twisted and compressed from the weight of the tar and hundreds of feet of water. Look at this," she said. "The crocodile was in a fight. Look here," she motioned with the pointer, "this looks like an intact human skeleton inside the ribcage. It had swallowed one victim. But this thing … a spear maybe … is stuck down right through its ribs. I'll come back to that. Now up here, attached to the thing sticking through the ribs, is this connected piece. Look

91

closely there. It's still mostly covered in tar, but I think it's a skeletal hand, holding onto this sword or spear that's penetrating the ribs of this crocodile."

"What are you saying?" said Jack.

"This was a fight, between men and a giant croc. One man was eaten whole and is still inside the croc. There's another man's arm caught in the jaws of the croc. That one's left hand is missing, maybe bitten off by the croc? Back to his sword arm, the hand is holding the hilt or handle of this sword where he'd just stabbed the croc through the chest, and there's the sword, still sticking through the ribcage. That circular thing over there looks like a shield possibly. It's still caked with tar in spots." She moved the pointer, searching.

"There's the man's chest, and there's his skull. His head is tipped back from this angle, so you can only see the underside of his chin. His rib cage is broken in several places, maybe during the fight with the beast. Wait. Hold on. Something is wrong here …"

"What is it?" Jack said.

"I need just a minute…"

"What …?"

"Quiet!" she said.

Jack voice stopped sounding through the radio speaker. He seemed to be waiting for Mercy to gather her thoughts.

Mercy's face held an intense gaze and she stared at the site of the sword and the shield. Finally, a dawning comprehension came over her.

"Okay, I think I see it, but the scale is wrong. Some of the remains are out of proportion with each other." She turned to her sub-driver. "Yani, extend the tool arm from the sub."

"Sure, boss." A few moments later, the tool arm was moving toward the skeletal remains.

"That's it. Yani, how long is that extendable vise grip assembly?"

"Oh, about one-half meter."

"Good, in fact, perfect. Now hold it near the hilt of the sword." Yani extended the tool further until it was near the penetrated ribcage. "Now move it closer to the ribcage. I want to compare it to the skull inside the monster skeleton.

Mercy studied for a moment and then nodded as if now certain of something she had suspected before. Jack waited. He knew that Mercy would tell him when she was ready.

"Jack, here it is. I was right about the size of this crocodile or whatever it was. It would have been about fifty or sixty feet long in life. I think that's far larger than any crocodiles today. I think I can make out the rest of the man including his grip on the hilt of the sword." She outlined the dead warrior's remains with the laser pointer. "Here is his other arm, trapped in the croc's mouth. His left leg has been broken as well. His right hand is still gripping the hilt of this sword that has stabbed through the beast. The thing that had me confused was the size of the sword and the hand. With the vise grip tool beside his hand, do you notice anything?"

Through the radio, Jack said, "Sure. If that tool's a half meter: eighteen or nineteen inches, then he's got pretty big hands."

Mercy laughed. "To say the least, Jack. The typical man's arm today measures about eighteen inches from the tip of his fingers to the elbow. This fellow is a meter from fingertip to elbow and this hand is proportioned correctly to the arm length. From what I can see, the rest of him is just as big."

"So he was basketball-player-tall." Jack sounded unimpressed.

"Not just tall, Jack. Gigantic. This guy would make a pro-basketball player look like he was in grade school. This fellow was eleven, maybe twelve feet tall. Yet the other man's skeleton inside the croc is normal human size."

Jack whistled. "That's got to be unusual. How many skeletons this large have been found before?"

Mercy reacted instantly, "Jack you're kidding me, right? The answer is none. There's never been a verified, documented, human skeleton found of this size. Never. This is unprecedented. This will completely rock the scientific world. This could rewrite our history books as well. No fossilized remains have ever been found of an actual human giant. The tallest known modern humans are freaks at eight or eight and a half feet tall. Nothing has ever been found of this size before. This is a first."

"So what do we do now?"

"We get human divers down to finish the job and carefully free 'Goliath' here. Then we start running tests. We can check the skeletal remains for usable DNA, checking the man and the croc and the normal-sized man too. We can do carbon-dating and see how old this tableau is. I'm guessing it will be around the same age as that dagger. That sword and shield look like they might be made from the same metal as the blade of that dagger you showed me back in Manhattan." She paused, her eyes wide. "This is stunning. Wait. Before anything else, we need to get high-resolution underwater cameras down here and document everything. I want pictures of every square inch of this site in the highest quality available. Jack, this is the best news ever!"

Hayden interrupted, "Subs One and Two. Please reply at once."

Mercy answered, "Yes, Hayden, what's up?"

Jack responded as well, "Yes, what's going on?"

"Just received word from the captain. We have an incoming visitor via helicopter." Hayden said.

"Huh?" said Jack. "The supply helicopter only makes one trip a week.

What happened?"

"It's not the supply helicopter, Jack. It's the 'Gypsy'."

From her radio, Mercy asked, "The 'Gypsy'? What's that?"

Jack responded, "It's one of the corporate copters, Mercy. One of those the VIPs use."

"…and…?" Mercy asked, waiting for Jack to finish his thought.

Jack's voice sounded pained, as if he were grimacing from a broken tooth. "It's the one Janos Parasca uses. It's his personal helicopter."

\* \* \*

Mercy's heart thumped heavily as if she suddenly needed twice the volume of blood as usual. *Not Parasca, not so soon! What am I going to do?* She heard a distant murmur from corners of her mind that whispered and muttered, like a crowd, just behind a building, muffled and nearly mute. *No, I'm not going to give way to fury! I need to be calm. Icy.*

Jack had already returned his sub and boarded the *Fortuna*. He said he was on his way to his quarters to change and then get up to the helipad to meet Parasca. Mercy told Yani to hang back and let Jack dock first. She needed the time to compose herself. Mercy put Hayden on the task of getting the diving teams ready to deploy and get hi-res photographs of the mound and its contents. A few minutes later, her mini-sub docked at the ship's side, and she boarded the *Fortuna*, still lost in thought. She walked rapidly to her cabin. Once there, she closed the door and lay on her bed, eyes staring at the ceiling.

*Think! You were so sure you could take this on when Jack was at your hotel room in Manhattan. Now, Parasca's almost here and you're in a panic.* Her heart rate shot up and she remembered the first time she'd seen Parasca in Bucharest, Romania, in the summer of 1988.

Mercy was a very rare individual in Romania that summer, a westerner who had been allowed in on a visitor's visa. She and her mother had been traveling together. Her mother was representing the farm equipment company that her husband, Mercy's father, had built before his death. Their company manufactured a type of simple, inexpensive but rugged tractor that was no longer in high demand in the United States with its large-scale farming, but in which Eastern-bloc countries were increasingly interested. Mercy's mother saw this as a chance to revitalize the company her husband had built and so joined a Federal pilot program that allowed limited low-technology equipment sales to Iron Curtain countries.

Romania seemed interested in purchasing some of the tractors for its smaller collective farms and so after months of red tape the trip was finalized. Mercy accompanied her mother, as a graduation present. During negotiations between her mother and the state officials, something had gone horribly wrong and her mother had not returned to their hotel. For two weeks, Mercy waited. She was not allowed to leave the hotel and had to endure constant interrogations. Those weeks at that run-down hotel in Bucharest still brought memories of helplessness and a burning hot anger.

Mercy had no idea what had happened to her mother. She could only guess and piece together bits here and there from the questions the interrogating officers asked. They had fingerprinted Mercy the first day. Then the second day, they had come back and done it again, only the second time, they took foot and toe prints as well. But they never tied her up. Obviously they didn't think her either a danger to themselves or a danger to escape. Once each day, a plain faced man, never the same one, would enter her room without knocking. These men all seemed to wear the same style of worn suit. The door to the hotel room had opened day after day and remained open just long enough for Mercy to see that a second man stood guard in the hallway. Her questioner would move through the doorway, walk across the worn carpet and would sit on the worn upholstered chair and question her. Always the same questions each day: Why did your mother really come here? What is your mother's real name? Did you know you were an adopted child? Have you ever seen this, your birth certificate? Do you know why your birth certificate is in Romanian instead of English? Why did you accompany your adopted mother on this trip? How much money were you paid by United States government authorities to take this trip? Who was to be your contact here in Bucharest? Where is your drop point? When did you actually finish high school in America? Why were you removed from the public high school? What have you done for the last two years since you haven't attended public school? What medical condition do you claim to have? What are these pills for? What will really happen if you don't take these pills? How did your father die? Did you see his body? Who is your contact in the CIA? The questions went on and on, and the questioning men didn't even seem to care what her answers were.

The hotel room had seemed to decay before her eyes. She saw every peeling curl of paint, every unnameable stain in the carpet and every smudge on the wall as evidence that entropy was accelerating visibly all around. The room seemed to shrink, but worst of all, since they'd found her medication on the first day, she'd been without it. No amount of pleading shook them. They simply kept the pills and observed her reaction to being denied them. Perhaps they thought she'd admit to something if they withheld her medicine.

Without the drug to dampen the voices, they'd grown beyond whispers and had become conversational and brazen. The voices were so distracting that she had to force herself to hear normal sounds. Two of the voices stood out among all the others: the Torturer and the Jailor.

Mercy had named these two particular voices early on. They never referred to each other by those names of course, but she recognized them. The Torturer said, "These fools have no idea who they're trifling with. She'll take them all on and kill them where they stand. These Securitate, what idiots. What children. They think they're vicious, but I'll show her how to kill many at once with fire or flood …"

The Jailor said, "Better than killing them, is trapping them. Confining is where the real pain lies. Not in binding tight so all movement is prevented, it's all in tying knots that are loose enough to flex, but not give way. That way the victim struggles, thinks for a long time that if only they try still harder, they'll make progress, but they can't. It's the feeling of futility and being totally exhausted and trapped not only by a prison cell, but trapped by your own body that sends them over the edge. Not many understand the art of it…"

The Torturer said, "Prison! No. It's the pain that leads to something else, something feared but not yet certain, that's what does it. The physical pain is important but the mental pain is the amplifier. Physical pain can be dealt with and shut out, because eventually the body grows exhausted. But not if the mind is amplifying the physical pain. When something is feared, such as even greater suffering or death, but there is still some uncertainty about it: that is when the mind amplifier kicks in. The pain is doubled, tripled or more because the subject doesn't know. They think, 'How long will this last?' or 'Will I ever be released?' or 'Is this my last day?' or 'Will it be worse today than yesterday?' The questions in their minds keep the physical pain fresh and keep the mind from shutting it out."

The door to her hotel room opened again. The voices distracted her so much that she didn't see him at first. Then she noticed that the Torturer and the Jailor had stopped their oblique argument. Her head almost rang in the sudden inner silence. This man seemed interchangeable with those that had come before, except for his stare. He looked at her with a disappointed, angry glare, as if he were a man about to punish a horrible child.

She heard a whispering, insinuating voice in her skull say, "It's the clothes. They're not real clothes. They're skin. These 'men' molt it every night and the other 'men' that question you put this skin on before they come in here. That's why they look the same and talk and act the same. The skin is what controls them, thinks for them, mouths their words. They always ask the same questions because it's always *the same skin* asking you."

Mercy shuddered and an insane image floated through her imagination: a mannequin wriggling out of his suit-skin each night, shedding it and then another pasty mannequin writhing into the suit-skin. It was the skin that animated the men. The men weren't really interrogating her, the men were simply the mannequins that carried the suit. It was the suit that was actually questioning her, detaining her, keeping her from her mother.

"I am Officer Janos Parasca of the Securitate. You, my child, are in a lot of trouble."

Her mind snapped back to the officer that had just entered. The inner voices mumbled in a swirling surge through her head.

"Where is my mother?" She said to the man. She studied him, looking for the seams where the skin left off and the mannequin started. Her eyes were large and the pupils were dilated with horror.

He ignored her question and manic gaze. "You haven't been telling us the truth."

"I have been telling the truth. Every question you've … they asked me … I told the truth."

He shook his head slowly, "Unfortunately, you are lying even now. Why did you come here with this woman, Mrs. Martha Teller?"

"I came with mother as a graduation present. She brought me along because she had to come anyway to try to sell farm equipment from Daddy's business."

"That is a lie. Mrs. Teller has been lying to us as well. Your 'Daddy's' farm equipment business is nothing but a sham operation for smuggling supplies into Romania and into the hands of counter-revolutionaries. Your mother was a spy and tried to pass information to her contact in the Ministry of Agriculture. She was caught. The Romanian traitor that was in receipt of Mrs. Taylor's message has been interrogated and executed." He stepped closer. "I killed the traitor myself. I can kill your mother and I can kill you. Do you understand me?"

Mercy's head spun with fear and from the man's incredible claims about her mother. The inner voices had risen again into a cacophony of noise. Mercy felt like she was in the center of a vast crowd, all of them screaming.

She shouted at Parasca, "I don't know what you're talking about! My mother is nothing like that. It's insane!"

A voice from within her shouted, "No, you're insane!" The voice changed to a gurgling, bubbling strangle. Her face twitched.

He spoke slowly and through clenched teeth. "Mrs. Teller is not your mother."

Mercy's inner voices increased. Many of them seemed to be shouting, "…not your mother!"

Parasca pulled out a yellowed form. It bore an official seal and was printed in Romanian.

"My men have shown you this form before. This is your birth certificate. You were born in Romania. You were fostered to a Romanian orphanage. The Teller woman was not your mother. Years ago, while Mr. Teller was still alive, he and his wife came to Romania and through their corrupt connections, bribed their way into adopting you. Teller had been here many times on trips, always spying on Romania for the Americans, but that was one of the few times your mother came with him. Now, years later and with her husband dead, she made the mistake of returning with you. The only reason she was allowed into Romania was so that we could break this spy ring. Now we have her, and you too."

A low rumbling voice inside her said, "They have you! We have you!"

"That's a lie! My mother can't be what you say. I'm not Romanian. I was born in America. I went to school there. I didn't grow up in an orphanage. That can't be my birth certificate. Let me go!"

He narrowed his eyes. Through the nearly closed lids they looked like slits of reflective obsidian. "It is your birth certificate. The baby footprints on this document match your footprints today. You aren't Mercy Teller. You are Mircea Rodica. Your real mother was a criminal named Tresa Rodica who was arrested in 1970 while trying to get an illegal abortion. She gave birth to you in jail and then committed suicide."

Mercy heard the inner voices shouting, "Suicide! Follow her in death!" Mercy held her hands to her ears and shook her head.

Mercy said, "I don't believe any of this."

"It doesn't matter what you believe. Your so-called 'mother' is in jail and you will be staying in Romania. Your adoption by the Tellers was fraudulent and so you are now to be repatriated. We are moving you to Timisoara. From the orphanage's records, we've located a relative: your maternal grandmother. She is a biology instructor at the Polytechnic University in Timisoara. You will live with her and attend university as a student."

Mercy looked at him in horror. A stabbing pain cut through her stomach. Her life was being torn to ribbons. The violence to her future was so brutal and monstrous that she was speechless. She knew only that this man, Janos Parasca, was the most evil man alive. She jumped out of her chair, hands outstretched and curled into claws, reaching for his eyes. Parasca was taken by surprise but managed to pull his face back. Her fingernails sliced into his cheeks just below his eyes and gouged deep bloody grooves down his face. He howled in pain and lashed back, first with a cupped right hand followed by his left. She fell heavily backward and landed on her back, her breath momentarily gone, a coppery metallic taste in her mouth and her vision darkened to a small circle in the center of which lay Parasca's face, blood streaming down cuts in his cheeks. Her inner voices were silent but the real world was also strangely muffled.

Parasca staggered to a dresser and looked into the mirror above the drawers. He cursed the gashes on his face. Grim-faced, he strode back, leaned over her and grabbed her jaw in his left hand. He tightened his grip and pulled her face up and close to his. Blood welled in her mouth from a split lip. His voice sounded like he was speaking through a thick mattress.

"Stupid child! Listen to me. You can't stop this! You'll go to Timisoara now, and you won't get away!"

From a long distance away, she summoned her strength and feeble breath and tried to spit at him. A single, small drop of bloody saliva was all that cleared her mouth, sailing as if in slow motion from her lips, across the distance between them and landing languidly in a small, ineffectual splash right on one of the cuts left by her fingernails on the left side of his face.

Parasca jumped like he'd been struck by lightning. He released his grip on her and dropped her, staggered back and leaned against the wall, gasping for breath. Mercy climbed to her knees and swayed, trying to right herself. Parasca shook his head and lurched for the door. He shouted in a stutter to the man in the hallway. "She's ... she's moving out now. Get her on that trans...transport to Timisoara." He took a long shuddering breath and said, "And give her back her medicine. Make sure the doctors keep her supplied with it. She's unbalanced. She's ... hallucinating. Can't have her losing her mind, not yet."

The other men came and grabbed her where she still stood swaying. They hauled her toward the door and on the way out, she saw Parasca staring at her with a very strange expression in his eyes. What seized her attention though, was his face: blood still streamed down from the fingernail gashes on his right side, but there were no gashes or blood on the left side. A moment before, she'd raked him and opened up bloody gashes on both cheeks. Then she'd spit at him and a drop had reached the cuts on his left side. Now there were no cuts on the left. *What happened? Did I imagine the cuts?*

She never forgot what she saw him do in those last moments before she lost sight of him. He touched both sides of his face, drew both hands back to examine and then touched his left hand to his unmarked left cheek. She hadn't imagined the cuts. He couldn't believe the left side was uninjured either. As they drug her into the hallway, she caught a last glimpse of him staring in wonder into the mirror, his left hand to his undamaged left cheek.

* * *

She snapped back to the present. *This won't help. I only have minutes. I have to calm down. Take deep breaths. Deep breaths.* She forced herself to breathe slowly, in and then out. She concentrated on a single thought as she breathed, the picture of a clenched fist, tight and trembling. As she took slow breaths she visualized the fist relaxing bit by bit, the muscles slackening, the fingers slowly releasing their tension. Finally, in her mind, the hand opened, relaxed. Her breathing was slow and deep. She sighed.

*You know what to do. Just stand up to him. He's just a man. He'll see that you've changed.*

# CHAPTER 14 - TO THE TARGET

*"Seest thou yon dreary plain, forlorn and wild
the seat of desolation, void of light?"*
— *John Milton, Paradise Lost*

Janos stepped out of the helicopter and down the stairs to the receiving area below the landing platform. Mercy stood near Jack and Hayden and looked straight at Parasca. He looked like a man in his sixties with a receding hairline, though the hair that remained was still dark. His face had a set of vertical scars on his right cheek, but no matching scars on the left. He was six feet two in height and carried an extra forty pounds on his frame from the last time she'd seen him. His hands were large and his lips were thin. He seemed to measure her, to weigh her and size her up. If he'd had a jeweler's eyepiece, Mercy might have felt like a gemstone being evaluated for flaws. His face stayed expressionless for three seconds, and then he shifted into a broad smile. He walked directly toward her, his hands outstretched.

"Mircea! It is so good to see you again. The last time we met, you were but a teenager." His English was only lightly accented. Obviously, the man had been through expensive language schools at some time during the last twenty years. He stepped forward to take her hands as if to draw them to his lips for a kiss.

She stepped back, pulled her arms away and though her heart pounded with adrenaline, her voice held a steady tone. "Mr. Parasca, in my place of employment, I prefer to be addressed formally, as Dr. Teller, if you don't mind."

Jack cut his eyes sidelong toward her. Just that morning, she'd stopped the men from calling her "Doctor". Now she was trying to force Parasca to address her by her title. Jack sighed. This was not going to be a smooth reunion. He saw Hayden wince at the awkward scene that seemed to be developing between Parasca and Mercy.

Parasca looked up at the sky, shrugged and said with a tightening smile, "Dr. Teller? Well, of course you're proud about your education. That's your grandmother in you. And like your real mother, you've grown up to be a flawless Romanian beauty. But I run the show here. You work for me now."

Mercy said with an edge of ice in her voice, "I can see we need to get a few things straight, Mr. Parasca. First, even though my legal name is 'Mircea', my friends call me 'Mercy'. All others, including you, should call me 'Dr. Teller'. Second, you and I have … shall we say … a difficult history between the two of us. I work for your organization now, and so you'll have my professional respect. But that is all. Please do not take liberties with my name or my person." She nodded toward her hands which she had withdrawn from his grasp. "Further, that does not give you the right to intrude in my personal life or family history. Therefore, please don't bring my biological grandmother into the conversation. She was an inspiration to me and many others. Because of her, I pursued my education in Romania through a very difficult period of my life. Third, my adoptive mother was never considered a beauty. She was a plain woman of unusual strength, to whom I owe everything. I would appreciate it if you didn't mention my mother or grandmother again."

Parasca had been listening to Mercy with a growing frown and a raising eyebrow. Now, his face was dark with suppressed rage and his brows lowered. He held her gaze, looked over at Jack, smiled darkly, looked back at her, locked eyes again, and said in an extremely irritated tone: "Jack, your new employee doesn't know how to behave. She apparently doesn't understand normal social interactions and courtesy. I hold you responsible for her misbehavior. Jack, fix this. Do you understand?"

Jack almost stumbled over his words, but instead gathered himself and said, "Mr. Parasca, I'll take care of it."

"Good." Parasca's eyes never left Mercy's. He said to her, "I wasn't claiming your *adoptive* mother was a beauty." He turned to face Jack and said, "Now, tell me about today's results. What did you find after the steam injection?"

Jack looked from Parasca to Mercy, to Hayden and then back to Parasca. He sighed visibly when Mercy did not reply and then he said to the CEO, "We found remarkable remains. We're sending down divers to photograph them and then recover them by hand. Which reminds me. Hayden, would you go back to the control room and check on progress?" Hayden nodded and left them.

Parasca watched Hayden leave and asked, "What kind of remains were found?"

Mercy spoke, with a tone of voice that said she was all business. "We found a gigantic human skeleton that was missing a hand and another skeleton of a huge crocodile-like reptile that had apparently been locked in mortal combat with the giant. The human must have stabbed the beast but the croc had broken the man's leg and still held onto the man's other hand in its jaws."

Parasca noted the mention of the missing hand. It was likely the one that had been recovered and stolen by his rival. His interest outweighed his earlier anger and he asked, "How could they have been caught in such a position at the moment of death? Were they fighting at the bottom of the Black Sea? I don't understand why the remains would indicate what you say."

Mercy paused for half a second, and then spoke. "I have a theory to explain this fully, but I need to double-check some references after we finish here. I will say this: I believe the remains we saw below had been caught like insects in amber. I believe the last stages of the fight took place as they were sinking into a tar pit."

Parasca frowned, "Then how did you find their remains at the bottom of the Black Sea? This is not sensible."

Jack nodded his head, but not in agreement with Parasca. He looked admiringly at Mercy. "I think I see where you're going with this."

Parasca was irritated. "I do not. Mircea, what is it you are thinking?"

She stifled irritation at Parasca using her proper name and said, "I still need to verify a hunch. I don't want to jump to conclusions, but I will state that a scene like this would have taken place on dry land. The depth at which we found it though, indicates that some elevation change took place afterward. Perhaps rising water levels could explain it."

Jack jumped in, "The man fought the giant croc on land, they became mired in a tar pit and both died in the tar. Sometime later, the tar pit was covered over with the Black Sea. The original dagger that we found in the tar whip might have belonged to the man. Perhaps it came loose in the fight. Regardless, it flowed upward from the sea bottom inside the tar whip that we found in our previous survey."

Janos Parasca seemed to be satisfied but curious. "All right. When can we see some of these remains?"

Mercy said, "It will probably take a few hours at least. I would think sometime this afternoon."

Parasca said, "Then we will wait. Jack, please show me around the rest of the ship. I'm sure 'Doctor' Teller has some work to attend to. You and I need to talk." The CEO looked at Mercy with a challenging glance. Jack's face showed resignation.

*He is sooooo in trouble, and all because of me. Poor Jack.*

Parasca and Jack walked toward the control room. Mercy tried to push down her giddy feeling. *I stood up to him! I didn't let him terrorize me! I did it!*

*But what did Parasca mean when he said that about my adoptive mother not being a beauty? But how would he know what my birth mother looked like? Did he know my birth mother at some time?* She looked in Jack's direction and saw his shoulders slump as Parasca spoke furiously at him. Mercy felt guilty, but shrugged. *I warned him.*

\* \* \*

Mercy pushed back from the computer. *Oh, boy, I just might be right after all. This is going to be a wild ride.*

Mercy's phone buzzed. She'd almost forgotten about it. The ship had a wireless network for computers and cellular devices, phones included. She took the device from her belt and checked her mail. A new message was waiting from Hayden.

"Parasca still with Jack? You free? Text me," It said.

She texted back: "He's not with me. Probably still reaming Jack after I stood up for myself. I don't care. He needs to know I won't be bullied."

"Jack will get over it." The message returned. "First package of remains are coming up through the moon pool. You want to be there when they arrive?"

"Sure, wouldn't miss it. See you there. How soon?"

"How about five minutes?"

"On my way."

Mercy clipped the phone at her hip, stood up and looked around the rest of the command center. Six other techs were busy at various consoles, fully engaged in monitoring the ship's activities. She started walking. Hayden was on the "Pool" deck which was where the ship was open to the sea below. Ships like this were made for exploratory drilling and had derricks that drilled right through the bottom of the ship, in a manner of speaking. The drill-bits and pipe were suspended from the derricks above and lowered through the moon pool down into the sea below. Sea water filled the pool up to the level of the ship's outside water line. It always looked strange to see the moon pool, because it seemed like a ship with a hole in the bottom should sink. Mercy knew the principles involved, however. Of course, the crew put a cover in place over the moon pool when the ship was moving, but now the cover was open. The moon pool was no more a danger to the ship than the center hole in a lifepreserver was a danger to someone clinging to it.

Halfway down the stairs, Mercy caught herself thinking about a warm fall weekend she and Jack had spent floating down a winding river back when they were engaged. She shook her head. *I'm not going there right now. Besides, after Parasca finishes with Jack, there likely won't be any tube rafting trips in our future. He'll probably avoid me for the rest of my life.*

Mercy arrived at the moon pool. It was similar to the last drill ship she'd been on, just a lot bigger. This one had retractable cranes and other equipment that was presently out of the way. This moon pool was over twenty feet across and Mercy remembered the ship's specs: *Twin derricks. It can do two wells at once. This baby is huge. I should have remembered.*

Bobbing in the center of the moon pool were several divers in wet suits. The drill string lift had a hook attached and it was slowly pulling a net out of the water. Mercy guessed that the net had been filled by the divers at the sea bottom and then the sub had lifted the net up to where the divers had attached it to the lift hook. The net was gingerly brought to the edge. Hayden was there and motioned to Mercy.

"You want to open it here?"

Even though she felt strangely energized she said, "Absolutely not. It goes straight to the Paleo lab. We've got a lot of work to do and we don't want to damage anything." She looked down at the net full of wrapped objects. "Good. All labeled and packaged. Hayden, see you at the lab when you finish up here. You'll have these men rotated off duty and get the next crew down there?"

"All under control Mercy. I've been around this block a few times."

"You have. But you know Hayden, you don't look it."

"I'll tell that to my grandchildren the next time I see them."

Mercy laughed, "You do that. But first, when you wrap up here, come up to the Paleo Lab. I've got a theory to run by you. I did some search engine time while you were playing down here and I think I've got enough data now to take a stab at the 'how' of what we've found."

"Good," Hayden said. "Because I've got another puzzle for you. Wait until you see some of the photographs the divers got from the site before they started bringing things up. Then check out the pictures of the shield right before it was detached from the rest of the mess. They're ... unusual. You can check out the photographs from the link I e-mailed to you. We'll have the shield up in the next net full of recoveries. I'll come to the lab when we have those ready."

"Thanks, Hayden."

"Not a problem."

The net had been opened and the contents moved to a large cart. Mercy followed, feeling unusually cheerful and excited as the cart was pushed by the lab team to the freight elevator. Two floors up, they moved out of the elevator and down the hallway to the lab. The double doors opened and Mercy walked in behind the cart. Large flat screen displays were everywhere in the lab. A few large cabinets, storage lockers and refrigeration units stood here and there amongst the screens. Specialized instruments stood in a row at the far end of the room. A long row of metal work tables stood in the center of the room and the cart was pulled up alongside the end-most table.

The technicians were gingerly lifting and placing the bubble-wrapped items on the table. The head of the Paleo lab supervised. Everyone seemed to know what they were doing.

Mercy felt light on her feet. This discovery was the kind of thing she lived for, but this instance was even more important. This time, big things were at stake. These discoveries could change the way history was understood. It could overturn theories that had stood for decades. She took a deep breath and felt brilliantly alive.

Mercy moved over to a large six foot by four foot screen. It showed a live video feed from the site below. Divers were still swarming over the cone, photographing, labeling and removing pieces using small steam jets that they applied to loosen the tar that still held the stubborn artifacts in place. Mercy stepped to a computer and logged in to pick up her company e-mail. She found Hayden's latest message and clicked on the link he'd sent. In a moment she had a series of photographs open.

The pictures were of a shield-like object, still covered in tar and separated by a few feet from the skeletal remains of the giant human and the massive crocodile. *It's almost as if the giant dropped the shield, or maybe it was knocked away in the fight. What must the fight have been like? I can imagine the two of them struggling and the beast biting the man's arm and locking on. As they fought, they sank further and became hopelessly mired in the tar. In a last effort, the giant stabbed the monster through the body with his sword and held it in as the animal thrashed and died. The man would have tried to get loose and get free of the tar pit, but the creature's jaws held on even in death. The man sank and he tried to push himself upward with his hand on the hilt, but that just made the croc sink faster and then the tar came up to his neck and then to his lips and he screamed and screamed until the tar filled his mouth ...*

She snapped back from her imaginings and stared at the screen for a moment. She regained her bearings and brought up the next picture. In this shot the divers were working to remove tar from the disk of the shield. The next pictures showed the steam jet peel more of the tar away and the surface of the shield was uncovered gradually. There were designs cut into the metal. The next photograph and the next after that revealed more and more. At first, Mercy thought she was seeing symbols or writing, but the etchings didn't resolve into script of any kind: neither pictographs like Egyptian hieroglyphics nor the strokes used in oriental languages. The lines were wavy and seemed to wander across the surface of the shield, for that was surely what it was. The front and back revealed characteristic shield design, down to a hand grip on the back side that went all the way across the disk.

She continued paging through the pictures one after the other as the tar was removed and the shield became clearer. She paged to an image and then stopped. The shield was almost clear of tar and the underwater lights shined on its surface. The camera had a full shot of the shield at an oblique angle that emphasized all of the wavy lines on the front surface of the shield. Mercy tried to gauge its scale and mentally stepped back. It was indeed a good sized item. She remembered the size of the sword and the size of the skeleton. Then she guessed the shield's size by the diver's hand that was near it working to remove the last bits of tar. She decided that the shield was between three and four feet in diameter. It was made of the same, nearly translucent metal of which the dagger had been composed ... and what was that design on the front surface?

A cart was wheeled into the lab with a large object protected by bubble-wrap. The techs carefully moved it to the large metal work table next to the huge sword. *That bubble-wrapped thing must be the shield. Hayden will be close behind.*

Mercy paged to the next image. It was still an angled shot, but more perpendicular to the front. Mercy flipped to next shot and stopped. She moved her face closer to the screen, her eyes squinting. She touched the screen with a tracing finger and followed along one of the oval, wavy lines on the flat panel image. Mercy's breath caught in her throat and she forgot to exhale. Her eyes grew very wide and then she slowly turned her head to the metal table where the wrapped specimens lay. She stared at the bundled object that could only have been the shield. She felt almost giddy with excitement.

Hayden walked into the lab and said, "Well? Did you see the photographs I sent?"

Mercy spoke in command voice, "We have to get that thing uncovered. Now!"

# CHAPTER 15 - THE DELUGE

*"Into this wild Abyss, the womb of Nature, and perhaps her grave"*
*— John Milton, Paradise Lost*

Hayden said, "Is it what I thought it was?"

Mercy was busy examining the unwrapped shield from several feet away. She felt bursting with excitement and something else, life? *Whatever. I feel great, but hungry.* She grabbed an energy bar from a pocket and started munching. The techs had worked carefully, every hand covered by protective gloves. Everyone had understood that the objects mustn't be touched. It had taken a few minutes to get the wrappings off and the item flipped front side up, but now, Mercy could point to the beautifully ornate surface of the shield and say, "Did you think it might be a map? Then, yes. I believe you were right. At least that's what it looks like to me."

Hayden stepped closer and leaned in. His short, gray goatee nearly touched the metal as he tilted his head to look at it through the bifocal section in his glasses. "Blast these eyes of mine, can't focus close like I used to. Well anyway, the ornate etching on the shield shows an upper bulge here, a slightly narrower waist and a lower bulge here. Sounds trivial, but it's almost a jelly-bean shape.

Mercy pointed again with her finger and said, "No, I think it looks like a shoreline map. See the outline you pointed out here," her finger traced without touching, "it looks similar to an outline of the Black Sea today, except there's no Bosporus straits and the sea's not quite the right shape."

Hayden turned his head and nodded. Mercy pointed at a place on the shield design, "...and what is that?" She indicated a circle that lay across the middle of the edge of the design. "Is it a marker of some kind?"

The two of them thought in silence for a minute. Hayden moved around, and looked at it from several angles. He said, "What if it is a map of something very old? I mean, what if the place it mapped no longer exists?"

Mercy said, "It's possible. Shorelines change, sometimes by miles in just a small span of time. How long ago are you thinking?"

"Hmmm. What if the giant whose skeleton we found was a warrior in a kingdom that is long gone? The shield was his, so why not date the shield from the time of his death? Even if it was an heirloom item that had been passed down to him, it would give us a ballpark figure to work with."

She said, "So, we take a sample from his skeleton and do a carbon-14 decay analysis. That should give us an approximate date of his death. Good. But there's this that I want to run by you. I think I can already name the date of his death. Well, within a few years, anyway."

Hayden said, "Really? What theory have you come up with?"

"You ever read Ryan and Pitman's hypothesis about the 'Black Sea Deluge'?" She said.

"No. But I've heard about it. Something about the Black Sea being suddenly flooded from the Mediterranean rather than filling up gradually like we were all taught?" He looked at the sparkle in her eyes and sighed in mock frustration, "Mercy, why don't you just tell me what you've got?"

Mercy said, "Like you said, we all were taught that as the last ice age ended and the sea levels began rising world-wide, the Black Sea was gradually filled up as the Mediterranean's levels rose. Ryan and Pitman, however, thought that the event had to have been sudden rather than gradual. There were groups of marine archaeologists that found fossil evidence at around three hundred feet depth in the Black Sea that pointed to a sudden change in not only sea levels, but salinity. They detected submerged ancient shorelines and at those places below the old water line, freshwater snail shells, but above the old water line there were saltwater snail shells."

Hayden said, "Oh yes. I remember this debate now. Happened in the mid-to-late 1990's. They said that the freshwater shells below the ancient shoreline and the saltwater shells above it were evidence that the Black Sea was originally a freshwater lake, and the shells are proof of that. Further, the salt water shells above the ancient shoreline were evidence that the Black Sea was suddenly converted into a salt water body, thus the rapid flooding hypothesis."

Mercy said, "Right. But they not only found the submerged shoreline, they found man-made structures and wooden beams that had been worked with tools on the Black Sea coast of Turkey. All in three hundred feet of water. Face it Hayden, there was rapid flooding. Plus, it all happened at about the same time that the dagger handle was dated at: 5600 BC."

Hayden asked, "So what caused the sudden flooding of the Black Sea?"

"We know there were sudden flooding events around the world as the last ice age ended. Take for example the gigantic Lake Agassiz in North

America that was created by the receding glaciers. It held in place more fresh water than all lakes in the world today combined, including the Great Lakes. It was a single huge water trap that suddenly gave way when the ice dams that held it broke and released all of its water into the Hudson Bay in a single gigantic pulse. That one event caused the sea levels all over the world to rise by up to three meters.

"But for the Ryan and Pitman hypothesis, the theory goes that there was a natural dam or barrier between the Mediterranean Sea and the Black Sea at the Bosporus Straits near Istanbul. According to them, in about 5600 BC, that dam broke. It happened through earthquake or erosion or maybe it was just overflowed by rising sea levels. Then the Mediterranean Sea poured through and flooded the Black Sea, which at the time was a much smaller fresh water lake fed by the ancient Danube river. Its water level was three hundred feet lower than the Mediterranean. The theory also says that the Black Sea filled up to its present level in about ten months."

Hayden whistled. "That would have been quite some waterfall, I imagine, and worth seeing."

Mercy's voice fell lower and she spoke in awed, earnest tones. "Hayden, that waterfall might have been the most awe-inspiring thing ever witnessed on planet earth. Each day for almost a year, ten cubic miles of water would have roared over that waterfall. That's two hundred times the amount that flows over Niagara Falls every day! Imagine the sound of it. Imagine the impact. I bet it caused a near permanent cloud cover over the region for the entire time with constant salty rain. It probably generated its own weather system."

"For three hundred days, the cataract roared, and the water level in the Black Sea rose <u>by a foot a day</u>. There's never been a flood like it. The pounding rain, the rising flood waters, whole towns and cities buried under the water forever, and it didn't stop! It went on and on for month after month after month. It must have seemed like the end of the world to the people that lived there. Some people think that it was the origin of the story of the biblical flood."

Hayden said, "I believe the Bible says about the Flood, 'all the fountains of the deep burst open, and the floodgates of the sky were opened.' I can look it up if you want, but that pretty accurately describes what might have happened here."

Mercy seemed taken aback and said, "I'm a little surprised that you know the Bible, Hayden."

"Why? I have great respect for the Bible. Why is that so surprising?"

Mercy said, "Well, so many geologists," she groped for words, "I mean, so many in our profession openly deride it. I just thought ..."

"You thought I might be one of those kinds of geologists? You thought I might be the kind that would make fun of the Bible?" He smiled wryly. "I guess I would say that it's easy to mock or insult people you don't agree with. But I've never thought that insulting someone or mocking them was a good way to change their mind. Sure, as a geologist used to dealing with the structure and composition of the earth and digging into its history, I don't agree with those that claim the earth is only six thousand years old. From what I've seen, analyzed, researched and experienced, I believe that the earth is several billions of years old. But that doesn't mean I think the universe created itself. I take the main point of the Genesis story to be: something greater than man started all of this." He waved one hand as if indicating the world and everything it contained.

Mercy was stunned. She said, "But how can you as a scientist believe, or accept, the idea of the supernatural? It goes against all we're taught. We're supposed to accept only what can be measured and proven with material evidence."

"Mercy, let me ask you something. What is the definition of 'supernatural' and what is 'material evidence'? Or, asked another way; are there things that exist, but cannot be measured yet?"

"What do you mean?"

"I mean that as scientists, we know that there is a lot that we know, but there is also a lot that we don't know. At the bleeding edge of every field of science, there are vast areas of knowledge that haven't been nailed down yet. We have theories and hypotheses, but there is still much that we know that can't yet be completely proven and measured. From macro-studies in cosmology to micro-research in sub-atomics, we can't yet see, test, verify and quantify everything, yet we know that there are realities that we can't yet explain. Should we call those areas, 'supernatural' since they can't be experimentally proven yet?"

Hayden continued, "Look at your own life experience, Mercy. There are things that you know, and things that you feel that can't be proven experimentally. Are they 'supernatural' because they can't be measured and quantified? Are they any less real?"

Mercy thought of the voices that spoke to her. Were they real or a product of her mental defects? What if the answer was both? She certainly had seen evidence that the Counselor could advise her as well as affect her. That made it 'real', didn't it? But she also had some kind of brain condition that could be partly moderated with medication. That made it 'real' too, didn't it? But what if the voices were 'supernatural'? She certainly seemed to have capabilities that went way beyond normal human ranges in metabolism, strength and speed. Would some say she had supernatural abilities?

Hayden ended by saying, "There are people who will tell you that nothing exists except the material universe. I am not one of those."

Mercy said, "Hayden, this may surprise you, but I agree with you. To a point. There is so much, even in my own experience, that cannot be explained by mechanistic materialism. I just never thought of you as a man that was spiritual. I didn't think of you as a man of faith."

"Mercy, everyone has faith of some kind. In my experience, even atheists have to have faith in the non-existence of God, since no experimental evidence, no scientific method can ever prove or disprove the existence of something beyond reach of its instruments. In my view, faith isn't really an option. Faith is universal, because we will never know everything, we'll never measure and prove everything. And some things though real, may never be measurable. I choose to have faith in a creation and a Creator that is larger than any possible measuring stick." Hayden smiled and said, "Sorry to have sidetracked us, but you started this by mentioning the biblical flood."

"I know, and it is an interesting idea. The biblical flood was worldwide though. This Black Sea deluge would have been local to this region of the world."

"True. This occurrence wouldn't speak to anything but the local region. Still, it is interesting to realize that virtually every culture in the world has a deluge story in its past. That says something interesting about either all of these cultures coming from a common base with an original flood story or that there were many catastrophic floods in world history at different locations. My theory is that at the end of the last ice age, the only human beings were primitive tribal peoples who of necessity had to live near water. They settled near oceans, rivers, lakes or streams. These same bodies of water would have been severely flooded by the end of the glaciation and the melting and receding of the polar ice caps. All over the world at roughly the same time period, the people of the world that survived would be telling of the rising waters everywhere. Even the filling of the Black Sea was triggered by the rising Mediterranean brought on by the end of the ice age, whether it was a gradual filling or a sudden catastrophe."

She interrupted, "And those rising waters were how, I think, our friend here was buried under the sea in a tar pit. Perhaps when he fought the giant crocodile, the tar pit was near the shore of the fresh water lake that was to become the Black Sea. The croc might have been waiting in ambush and lunged out of the water at him as he traveled near the shore. They fought, fell into the trap of the tar pit, struggled and were finally covered over by the tar. Later, the Black Sea flooded, the water level rose by three hundred feet and the tar pit containing their remains was submerged."

She waved at the map on the shield. "And this, I would lay odds, indicates the original coast line of the Black Sea. Back then, it was a gigantic fresh water lake fed by the ancient Danube." She pointed at the circular mark. "And this is his home on the shore of this prehistoric lake. This was the warrior's home, his capital city. And we've got to go there next."

Hayden said, "Mercy, there is another ancient story about the flood that might fit in here somewhere."

Mercy said, "Oh? How?"

Hayden said, "I remember reading about an ancient Jewish scripture that was written before the time of Christ. Parts of it have been found amongst the Dead Sea Scrolls. It was called the Book of Enoch. The only complete copy is in the Ethiopian language and was preserved by the Ethiopian Orthodox Church for over two thousand years." Hayden paused.

Mercy said, "…and how does that fit into what we've discovered here?"

Hayden said, "It had a story in it about fallen angels coming to earth and impregnating human women. A similar passage in the Bible refers to these offspring as the Nephilim, which means, 'The Fallen Ones'. The Book of Enoch says that these monstrous hybrids were giants."

"Like our friend here?" She pointed at the photographs of the gigantic skeleton.

"Yes, it also said that God sent the flood, in part, to destroy these half-human giants."

He started to speak again, but the laboratory door opened. Janos Parasca and Jack Truett walked in. Janos' face held a questioning look. Jack's face had a pained look.

Mercy thought, *he must have been reamed. Jack, I am sorry. But I'm not going to be bullied by Parasca ever again.*

Parasca voice was cold. "We were told you were here with some of the retrieved artifacts. Jack and I finished our tour and our … talk. Now, tell us what we've found."

Mercy started to speak, but Hayden said, "Mercy, perhaps I could summarize for Mr. Parasca?" He caught her so off-guard that she awkwardly nodded and held her tongue.

Hayden spoke, "Mr. Parasca, this is a very fine metal-work shield. We suspect that the owner (whose remains should be here shortly) was an extremely large, perhaps eleven to twelve foot tall human who died while locked in combat with a proportionately large crocodile. The shield that you see has a design on its front surface which we were discussing as you entered the room. It appears to be a map. It might even be an outline of the ancient Black Sea. This is the same sea whose surface now is three hundred feet higher than it was at the time that the giant lived and fought the crocodile. During their battle, they became mired in a tar pit and sank to their deaths. Sometime afterward, the natural dam at the Bosporus broke between the Mediterranean Sea and the Black Sea and the entire region was flooded. The Black Sea water level rose three hundred feet, in possibly less than a year, and the tar pit was submerged. We have the sword already. Today we've brought his shield out and tomorrow, we'll bring him out. The only thing that remains is to find his home and ancestry. I'll describe how we'll use the shield in a moment, but first I have an unusual request to make."

Parasca said coldly, "Which is?"

Hayden motioned to one of the large stainless steel machines at one side of the lab. "That is our DNA analysis system. Extremely automated. We hope to obtain samples from the skeletal remains of the crocodile and the giant that we can test. From these we hope to perform database comparisons with other known samples that will help us determine ancestry profiles. We'll compare the croc to other animal samples in worldwide DNA databases. With the giant, we will compare to some existing human groupings. But there is something else I would like to request. With your permission, Mr. Parasca, I would also like to obtain some DNA samples from some of your employees. Only from volunteers of course, and these would be used as additional baseline samples. Often, comparative samples like this can aid in narrowing down ancestral groups and could aid us in tracing the giant's lineage. On this ship, we have a crew with backgrounds that span much of Europe as well as the Mediterranean and Black Sea basins. By comparing the giant's DNA to some crew samples, we may even be able to detect ancestry. It would be very good additional information to gather."

Parasca seemed interested. "Of course. Ask for volunteers if you like. I would be interested in knowing the results of the analysis as well."

Hayden motioned one of the lab workers over, introduced him and said, "Alex will be the one to take the samples."

Mercy asked, "Alex, what do you need to perform the DNA baseline tests? Can you just use a hair cutting?"

Alex said, "Not usually. We'd need the roots from a hair cutting to have the best chance of success. A cheek swab would be better. I just use a Q-tip on the inner side of the cheek. It's simple and not too intrusive. It is usually the most convenient way."

Mercy said, "Then, I volunteer. Take some of mine."

Jack spoke out impulsively. "Take mine too." He looked at Parasca and shrugged. "It will be a good example for the crew if we volunteer as well."

Parasca nodded. "Mine as well, then."

Hayden said, "Better take all of ours, Alex. Me too."

Alex seemed unsurprised and smiled. "Of course. I will get some sample kits."

* * *

Alex took the cheek swabs and one-by-one placed them in carefully labeled sample bags. Hayden gave him some instructions on obtaining some additional samples from other volunteers in the crew.

After Alex left, Hayden spoke again to Parasca. "Also, we think the map on the shield might point the way to our next possible destination."

"Why?" said Parasca.

"Because of this marking on the shield," Mercy said, pointing at the circle inscribed on the shoreline of the map. "It has to indicate something special, or it wouldn't be there. Just think of what we might find at the location indicated here. It could be anything from a fishing village to a seaport to a major city. But whatever it was, it won't be under more than three hundred feet of water."

Parasca peered at the shield, switched his gaze to the sword and his fingers twitched slightly as if restrained from reaching for it. He glanced around the laboratory and then his eyes took on a far-away look. He appeared lost in thought. They all stayed silent. Finally he asked, "What is something like this worth?"

The question caught them all off guard. Mercy looked at Hayden, then at Jack and said, disbelief shading her tone, "What? You want to know how much to sell it for? You can't do that! It's one-of-a-kind!"

Hayden said, "Truly, Mr. Parasca. It's unique. It can't be priced. It's beyond price. It's like asking what the Mona Lisa is worth. To my knowledge, there's nothing else like these artifacts, anywhere. In my opinion, they are the finest examples of the art of prehistoric metalwork in existence. In fact, I would put these items up against the work of any modern artist or craftsman. Actually though, they are so anomalous that unless we find more examples of similar artifacts, few will even believe us. In that case, then the worth of these objects falls to zero. Without proof of their authenticity, these artifacts have no value."

"So, in order for these to achieve maximum value, we must locate more of similar type. We need enough to establish their authenticity, but not enough to dilute their uniqueness." Parasca said in measured tones.

Hayden and Mercy turned and stared at each other, unsure what to say. Parasca smirked at their confusion and said, "Jack, tell them why I ask these questions."

Jack spoke as if pained to do so and said, "As Mr. Parasca has just reminded me during our tour of the ship, we are on an extremely expensive industrial ship that has been commandeered from its normal mission for one reason only: the opportunity to recover amazing historical artifacts. These items, and any more if and when they are salvaged, will belong to the company. PetroRomania will ensure their preservation in one of his private collections."

Parasca said, "I anticipate little trouble concerning their ultimate ownership as we are currently close to Romania. I have friends in the governments of all of these nearby countries and can usually take care of situations with a few well-placed 'charitable' donations. Now you say that we should go to this new location to look for more items. Why should we abandon this site? We've just begun to recover artifacts here and there may be much more to be found here yet. Besides, where is this new location? If we move into Turkish waters, it will be a more delicate operation. There are precautions that have to be taken and preparations to be made if we go there."

Mercy said, "We don't yet know where this next location is. We suspect," she pointed at the shield, "that this marking is a silhouette of the ancient shoreline of the Black Sea prior to the flood that flowed from the Mediterranean through the Bosporus. I admit we need to do some more research and matching of this map to the suspected ancient shoreline. But I believe that the map is oriented with the north towards the top of the shield, so if I'm correct, this circle is not too far from the Bosporus. It is very likely in Turkish waters."

"First, you must indulge me since I am paying for all of this." He motioned to the artifacts on the large table. "I would like a closer look." Parasca walked toward the workbench and the others moved out of his way to the other side.

Mercy experienced a strong, strange, detached sensation. She felt like she was almost bursting with energy and Janos Parasca seemed to be moving in slow motion as he seemed to take glacially slow steps to the table where the shield and sword lay. All of Mercy's voices went silent and her mind seemed almost to echo from the quiet.

The voice of the Counselor spoke in her mind.

"He must not touch them."

Mercy swooned and staggered. The energy she had been bursting with moments before seemed drained from her in an instant. *Not the Counselor! How can it be the Counselor? Not now! I didn't ask for this. It's never forced its voice on me before. Now I'll be unconscious for twenty-four hours. What will I do?*

Her vision contracted and her consciousness faded to a thread as the final drops of energy seemed to leave her. She heard an echo of the Counselor and realized she was still awake, barely. Time was still slowed and Mercy saw through her tunnel vision that Parasca took another step to the table. Suddenly, she felt the tide of energy shift and begin moving back into her, her pinpoint vision broadening back out into a full field. She saw a strange pale red thread as if made of the lightest fog snaking from the shield and into her hand. Where it touched her, she felt her energy returning.

Parasca took another agonizingly slow motion step toward the table. A slight tendril of the reddish thread seemed to be reaching toward the older man, almost beckoning him. Mercy felt her energy level rising quickly. Parasca moved closer and lowered his face until it was about a foot away from the sword as if smelling it. The red thread of energy running from the shield to Mercy's hand thickened. She felt powerful. The thread of red mist thickened and nearly touched Parasca. He turned his head to look at the shield and seemed to be gazing at his own reflection. He raised himself up to his full height again and looked down at the item. Mercy's muscles tensed. Without warning, Parasca's right hand reached toward the sword.

Jack and Hayden jumped with surprise and Hayden's face turned to outrage. Jack shouted, "No!"

Mercy was already there, however. Somehow she'd swept around the table with blinding speed and held Parasca's arms back, his fingers only fractions of an inch away and straining toward the ancient artifact. Mercy and Parasca stood transfixed. They seemed frozen in time: Parasca unbreathing and paralyzed, his eyelids drooping almost shut, and Mercy's face, teeth gritted and muscles straining to hold him back. The reddish fog of strange energy seemed to coalesce around the two of them.

Mercy growled, "Stop it! You mustn't touch it!" Parasca ignored her and strained harder against her. His face grew flushed with color and his hands trembled with exertion. At last he took in a quick, gasping breath and then he opened his eyes. Mercy surged backward and pulled him away from the table and the artifacts. He stumbled back from her and turned, glaring.

"How dare you!" he shouted. "No one … no one … keeps me from what is mine!"

Parasca's eyes were dilated. Mercy felt a wave of revulsion at the sight of them. *He's getting some kind of perverse pleasure out of this!*

She shouted back, "Keep your hands away from them! You have no idea what damage you could do to them or to yourself! Don't ever, ever touch an artifact with your bare skin!"

Parasca continued to stare at her, hate filling his eyes. They seemed almost to glow with an inner fire, then suddenly, the fire went out and his facial expression changed to something bordering on deep disappointment. The other three stared back at him in mixed horror and confusion.

"Jack, Dr. Travers, Mircea …" he paused, corrected himself with a smirk and said, "Dr. Teller … here are my instructions. One: we will stay here, recovering all possible artifacts from the current site; Two: you will analyze what is recovered, do your research and find out where this next site might be located; Three: once these tasks have been completed, I will decide where we will move the ship, and not before the way has been smoothed with the local governments; Four: I am leaving. I have other demands on my time, but will return when I deem it appropriate. Jack is in charge here in my absence." He walked to the door, leaving them standing in the lab. At the door, he stopped and turned back toward Jack and said. "If you please, see to my departure and the readiness of my helicopter." Strangely, Parasca looked down at his right hand, smiled broadly, and left.

Mercy saw Jack's face go blank and he stepped into the corridor saying he had to make some calls using the ship's cellular network. *Jack's trying to hide his humiliation. Wow, Parasca really makes his VPs grovel, doesn't he? Wonder if he makes them shine his shoes too? And Parasca, he must be psychotic. The way his facial expressions come and go suddenly like he's putting on whatever expression he thinks we expect to see.*

*Poor Jack. He's almost had to surrender his manhood to work for that madman. Just shows that men like Janos do not change, they just gain a new set of victims. But at least I'm not one of them now. Jack, why do you put up with this treatment? I don't know what to think about you now. Should I feel sorry for you, or should I feel disgust?* She softened as she caught a glance at his face out in the hall while he spoke on his cell-phone. *He's miserable. He hates this job. Oh, Jack, what have you done?* She decided she felt pity for him. Her face relaxed and her eyes turned wistful. *It would be so nice to hold you now, Jack Truett.*

Hayden looked at Mercy, turned his gaze toward Jack, and then looked back at Mercy. He started to say something to her but then smiled sardonically, shook his head and walked over to the lab table to unpack some more specimens. *Don't put your foot into it.* He told himself. *They'll either see it or they won't. Their feelings will match up or not without your help.* Hayden himself smiled wistfully as if remembering younger, exciting days. *But my, they certainly do torture themselves in the process, don't they?*

\* \* \*

Parasca kept his hands in his pockets until he was aboard his helicopter and it was airborne. He looked out the window and watched with great satisfaction as the waves went by below. His smile turned broad and genuine, like a tiger that had just caught its prey.

He knew what he would see even before he looked at his hands, but he pulled them out of his pockets slowly, enjoying the delay. First he held up his unscarred, smooth and youthful looking left hand. He studied it, pleased with it. Then he held his flawless right hand beside the left. The scars, the wrinkles and the age spots were all gone on both hands. The skin of the hand was smooth but strong. He had found the most powerful artifact yet and this time, he hadn't even touched it! Mercy had held him back, but in spite of not quite being able to reach the sword, he'd felt its power, sensed it surging up his hand, healing and smoothing the scars and without touching it, he'd seen its story too.

Mercy and Hayden were close with their guesses, but now he knew more, and began to understand why blood had such great power. The question remained though, how did Mercy fit in with all of this? And, how had she been able to hold him back like that? *What strength she had! Mercy, I thought I knew you. But now I must find out, who are you really?*

# CHAPTER 16 - FINDING THE PRIZE

*"To venture down the dark descent, and up to reascend"*
*— John Milton, Paradise Lost*

They stayed at the first site for several more weeks. The undersea mound was dismantled all the way to its base and every bone, every branch or twig, every pebble or rock that had fallen into the tar at one point in the past, was removed, cataloged, tested and screened. Carbon-14 dating on several samples showed that the contents were from about 5600 BC or earlier. The deeper into the tar mound they went, the older were the contents. It made sense. Things that were trapped in the tar sank in and down. The oldest things would be at the bottom, the newest things at the top.

The other items they found were almost entirely from plants or animals. Sadly, none were very interesting. There were Neolithic animal remains: wolves, deer, even what appeared to be a saber-tooth tiger, but there were no other human remains and no tools or tack and no weapons. The sword, the shield and the original dagger remained their only links to the ancient world of Goliath, as they had named the giant human skeleton.

Goliath's remains had been tested and his time period also verified at around 5600 BC. Next, they searched for some of his DNA. Eventually they found some that had not been completely destroyed by immersion in the tar.

Over morning coffee, Hayden told Mercy, "The techs tell me that DNA recovery from ancient specimens is very dicey. It's not at all like 'Jurassic Park' where you find some insect in amber that's tens of millions of years old and then voila, you have a baby dinosaur." Mercy laughed. Hayden continued, "Yes, the techs tell me that Crichton based his book on some scientific studies at the time that had published some truly astounding results about dinosaur DNA recovered from some bones. No one

118

suspected any problems with the research initially. Later on, though, it was shown that the DNA that was retrieved wasn't dinosaur, it was modern human DNA. In other words, the researchers had accidentally contaminated the samples they were investigating and had found their own DNA."

"DNA degrades over time and more quickly in some situations than others. Really, the oldest animal DNA ever successfully recovered is from a few hundred thousand years ago. The oldest known human DNA goes back to about seventeen thousand years ago. With Goliath here, we found a bit of intact, recoverable DNA in one of his lower, back molar teeth. The DNA shows him to be human as far as we can tell. We compared him to standard human types and couldn't find any major differences. He's ninety-nine percent human in his DNA anyway."

"Just ninety-nine percent?" Mercy asked.

"Well, there are still lots of places in the human genome that are unknown in purpose. He has a few differences in those regions, but nothing that would keep him from mating and reproducing if he were alive today."

Mercy grimaced, "Who would he mate with? A seven-foot tall female basketball player would still be like a child to him. It might be possible, but it would be mighty uncomfortable, especially to the woman."

Hayden said, "True enough. I wasn't commenting on the morality or the practicality of the arrangement, just the closeness in his genes to modern humans. Oh, and by the way," he said, with a little embarrassment in his voice, "the DNA does confirm him to be a male. Of course, the pelvic bones also attest to that. But since we're dealing with a completely anomalous giant when speaking about Goliath, I thought it best to get a second opinion from the DNA."

Mercy laughed, "What, the sword and shield weren't proof enough of his masculinity?"

Hayden smiled as well, "Just being sure, boss. By the way, that tooth and a few other pieces of evidence give us an idea of his age at the time of death. He was in his late teens, perhaps as much as twenty years old."

Mercy's eyebrows shot up. "That's all? Twenty years old, maximum?"

"Yes. His teeth are practically unworn. No signs of arthritis. He had one healed-up broken bone with signs of very strong and quick mending. No decalcification of the skeleton due to osteoporosis. He was definitely a young man."

"A young giant, you mean."

Jack walked into the lab, smiled almost shyly at Mercy, waved at Hayden and said, "So, we're through here beyond a doubt? No more big surprises? No more giants or missing links?"

Mercy said, "None, Jack. The lab team has checked and rechecked. Everything's been cataloged and filed. The only thing left is to follow the shield's map and we've told you where that leads." Mercy felt a slight shudder in the ship, but thought nothing of it. A big ship always has vibrations from one cause or another.

Jack said, "Yes, that target site you gave me is close in towards the Bosporus. It's definitely in Turkish waters, shallow waters I might add."

Mercy chuckled, "Of course they're shallow, Jack. They'd have to be for there to be ruins there. We traced back through the literature to find the theorized ancient water line and then compared it to the latest sub-sea topographic maps. It matches very closely. I don't even want to think about how an ancient shield maker could have gotten hold of a map outline this accurate and from what appears to be far overhead. In fact, it's another of those 'so close to reality' happenstances that if we don't find more evidence, no one will believe us. It will look like we cooked the data in our favor."

"What, a giant human skeleton isn't proof?"

"It's just the opposite. It will instantly be assumed that it's a hoax. There's never been a reputable find of a giant fossil human before, but there've been many hoaxes concerning giants. The only legitimate giant primates that have been found were a species of ancient ape that grew up to a standing height of three meters. That was the Gigantopithecus, and it would have weighed up to twelve hundred pounds. It probably had to walk on all fours to hold up its weight. Those creatures went extinct about three hundred thousand years ago. This fellow, however, is modern human in all but scale. Well, human if you take into account how much more massive his musculature must have been to move a body this size."

"Okay, okay," said Jack. "We'll go to the next site. Anything still need to be done here, then?"

"No. There's lots of work that can be done with what we've gathered, but nothing that needs to be done on-site. I sure hope we can get moving soon. Hayden and I have a theory how we can zero in on any remains once we get close to the site. We'd really like to get started."

"We are started. I told the captain to get us underway before I came down here just now. Didn't you feel the engines come on a minute ago?"

Mercy said, "I did, but I didn't know what the vibration was. I thought Parasca wanted to be informed and make the final decision. I thought he'd be here to okay the move."

"He was informed and he did make the decision. I've had to update him daily and I've enjoyed each and every one of those sessions immensely," he said sardonically. "He decided yesterday that we should move on to the new location." He held up his hands in protest at Mercy's disgusted expression. "He also told me that I wasn't to inform you until today. More evidence, if we needed it, that you and Parasca are letting your 'issues' get in the way just a little too much. Anyway, he has been working behind the scenes with the Turkish authorities. Suddenly, they're all sweetness and light and very welcoming to our presence in their waters. The old guy does have diplomatic skills when he wants to, there's no doubt about that."

Hayden said with a little exposed irritation, "So I suppose he's going to let us get there, wait until we've done the hard work and then show up to claim the treasure again? I'm surprised he left a few bones and the sword and shield here."

Mercy agreed silently. Jack looked like he was struggling to keep his reply under control. Finally he settled with, "Something like that, yeah. He'll come in when he thinks it's the right time. I believe he left those items so we'd have comparisons for any new finds."

Mercy said, "Speaking of new finds, here's what Hayden and I propose: once we get to the general site location in the Bosporus, we should start a magnetic sweep of the ocean floor. We lower one of the instrument pods that we have on board for our regular oil and gas exploration work and sweep it along just above the ocean floor as we sail in a coverage pattern. We've found that the shield and sword both have a characteristic magnetic signature that goes along with their metallic structure. We think we can detect metals like them through some post-processing of the magnetic sweep data. Hayden wrote a program that should detect the signature of similar metals there."

"Why do you think there'll be more items of the same kind of metal?"

"Why not assume that? The shield had this location engraved on it. Maybe there's a complex of some kind, maybe a guard post or barracks that was engulfed in the flood but still preserved under a layer of silt. There might be entire armories in there that have weapons like this. We might find remains of the furnaces where they smelted this stuff. If nothing else pays off on this expedition, modern steel companies would sell their souls for the techniques for making this alloy."

Hayden said, "Jack, that is really something to consider. We've had some time to run analyses on this 'crystal steel'. That's what we've started calling it anyway. It's an entirely new technology. It's amazing."

"What's so good about it? I remember the preliminary analysis we got on the dagger. They said it was some kind of high carbon steel."

"True, but remember that even primitive steel wasn't invented until about a thousand, maybe as early as two thousand years ago. The first references we've been able to find are from India, which shipped steel ingots to the Middle East as early as 300 AD. If we assume those dates are accurate and then assume it was actually invented hundreds of years earlier, we still have no evidence of steel before about two thousand years ago. High-carbon steel weapons first came into large scale use around 1100 AD, when European crusaders told of metal weapons that the Islamic warriors used. They called the material, 'Damascus Steel'. It was incredibly sharp and seemed to have been made by beating the Indian steel ingots thin, folding it, beating it into another thin layer, folding, beating thin and repeating over and over again. It made an edge so sharp, because it was actually many, many folded layers, each with a razor sharp edge of its own."

Hayden continued, pointing at the display cast that now held the sword and shield, "This giant weapon though, was found in the hands of an oversized human that dates to 5600 BC, and it was lodged in the skeleton of a giant animal of the same time period. That means that the sword had to pre-date both. That makes it at least seven thousand six hundred years old. So now, fast-forward back to the present. With the *Fortuna's* metallurgy and microscopy labs we've been able to uncover some extremely interesting and puzzling things about these weapons. This isn't just high carbon steel. Look at it. See how it's semitransparent? That effect is caused by a small amount of light being able to travel <u>through</u> the blade. Now, we know that iron is not transparent. We also know that carbon is transparent when in crystal form. So the reason some light makes it all the way through this metal, is that it has many, many microscopic carbon crystals in it." Hayden paused for effect and said, "That's carbon crystals as in diamonds. In fact, look at this using high enough magnification and you see that the whole structure of this thing boils down to countless layers of hollow carbon crystal tubes that are filled with iron."

Jack said, "Hollow crystal tubes? Diamonds? This sounds like something you'd see on the Discovery Channel about nanotechnology."

Mercy said, "That's what we're talking about, Jack. These are carbon nanotubes encasing threads of molecular iron. It isn't as hard as diamond, it's <u>harder</u> than diamond. The iron threads that run through the carbon crystal tubes act like reinforcing iron rebar in concrete. Then, every few molecules of thickness, the grain of the nanotubes shifts at an angle of sixty degrees and a new laminate layer of nanotubes are laid down. It all boils down to this; it's a metal that is harder than diamond but isn't brittle like diamonds. This diamond matrix doesn't have a shear plane like normal diamonds." Mercy then said, "Jack, this is beyond anything we know how to do right now. This is technology that doesn't exist today. This is indeed a steel sword, but beyond steel we can fashion."

Jack replied in disbelief, "Technology like that couldn't exist almost eight thousand years ago! We don't have it now, so how could they have it then? You're imagining things."

Mercy said, "Jack, don't play dumb. We're not imagining anything. This brand new equipment you brought in is very good. And our lab guys here are really sharp. We're not exaggerating when we say this stuff is beyond bleeding-edge. This sword," she gestured to the weapon, "is one massive crystalline structure. It is an iron-reinforced diamond. Think of its structure as diamond straws, and each straw is filled with a piece of iron rebar. Each of the straws is laid snug against the other and the whole matrix is shaped into a sword."

Jack had forgotten his disbelief and said, "Why would they fill a diamond structure with iron?  Forget <u>how</u>, just answer the question 'why', for me."

Hayden said, "I think they did it to beef up the shear strength. Diamond is the hardest natural substance known, but even diamonds can be cut. A jeweler that is skilled can make a cut in a diamond using nothing more than a sharp tap along the crystal shear plane.  But if you shape the diamond crystals into hollow tubes, fill the tubes with iron and then crosshatch the results, then you've got something like this sword and shield."

Jack said, "Crosshatch?  How's that?"

Mercy said, "Think of it as plywood, where a large sheet of wood is made from thin wood layers that are glued to each subsequent layer but turned at ninety degrees to the layer above. That makes it stronger than natural wood. This sword is made up of layers of iron-filled diamond tubes, with each new layer turned at sixty degrees to the layer below. This stuff is basically indestructible by anything short of plasma cutting torches or lasers."

Jack looked from one to the other. "This is not happening. So we're talking science fiction here?  Maybe these are unknown substances from another dimension?  I'm warning you, do <u>not</u> tell me this stuff is from the future. Or worse, don't tell me it was left by space aliens. If either one of you says such a thing, you will be fired on the spot. I mean it!"

Hayden jumped in, "Nothing like that, Jack. We just think there might have been some ancient metalworking arts that have since been forgotten. This shield and map and the sword all point to a lost culture that was destroyed in some catastrophic event, like the breaking of the dam at the Bosporus. Think about all of the losses that would happen in a gigantic flood like that. Think of the lost arts and sciences, and also remember that there were probably a lot fewer people in the world in those days. If some ancient genius had stumbled upon a way to grow crystal structures like this, he might have had no idea what was happening at the molecular level. He just knew that he'd developed a repeatable process. If he'd then been trapped in the deluge, his knowledge would have been lost with him. We're not talking about science fiction."

Mercy said, "Jack, we need to go after this next location now that the original site is depleted. If there is a chance we can recover more samples, maybe even clues on how they created these items, we've got to go for it."

"You're right," Jack said. "We're under way and will be there by tomorrow morning. Work out your plans and have them ready to go. This whole adventure needs to be wrapped up so we can get this ship back to its original task, finding oil."

Mercy said, "Jack, we could find something a lot more valuable than oil if we locate more clues on how this metal is made."

"True," Jack said. He looked at Hayden who had turned back to his computer screen, then lowered his voice a little. "Um, Mercy, do you have a minute? I need to discuss something else with you."

Mercy raised her eyebrows and said, "Sure. Now?"

"If you can. We could go to cafeteria and grab some coffee."

"All right, but can I meet you there in ten minutes?"

"Sure, see you then."

Jack left and went down the hall to the stairs. He avoided the elevators so he could get the exercise. He worked out every day in the ship's gym, but still tried to take advantage of any other way to stay in shape. He arrived in the cafeteria and saw some of the men on later shifts finishing up a late breakfast. He waved and they waved back. One of them motioned him over. It was Antonio, his sub-driver of a few weeks back.

"Hey Jack, word is we're heading out. We going back to oil work or are we still doing grave-robbing?" He laughed and the other men joined in. "I mean, we got some good practice with our undersea gear, but we aren't making any headway finding oil or gas. This is an expensive rig to use for 'Indiana Jones' stuff, isn't it?"

Jack waited for the chuckles to die down, smiled and jabbed his finger playfully at him, "What do you care, you still get paid don't you? Don't worry, you'll still be able to buy presents for your wife _and_ your girlfriend." All laughed at Jack's comeback, including Antonio.

"Anyway," Jack said, "We're moving to a new spot closer to Istanbul. Mr. Parasca's asked us to continue our work with these archaeological remains for a while. We think there might be some more to be found at this next location. For you Antonio, it'll be some more practice with your sub. I'm going to make you keep practicing with it until you get it right."

One of the other men spoke up. He was one of the two head tool pushers on the drilling platform and his English was heavy with an Eastern European accent. "But Mr. Jack, this Janos Parasca, the men do not trust him. He is wheeler-dealer Soviet-style boss-man. They say he is old secret-police-type officer. What was called in Romania? Oh, yes. Securitate. He was Securitate chief before Romanian revolution kills Ceausescu. How can we trust him? We trust you, Jack, not him." Many of the men nodded.

Jack said, "Andrei, I know how you feel, but we all work for him, me included. We have to show proper respect, even if we don't like it. I know something of his history, but I have to hope that he has changed for the better since then. Besides, we're all professionals here and we do our work well and with pride. We don't always get to choose our bosses, but we work hard, we work safely and we do it because we have integrity. We work to provide for ourselves, our families, sometimes our girlfriends," here he nodded with a smile at Antonio, "but we also work because it is our calling.

People like us don't live out on ships for months at a time because we have nothing better to do. Those of us who keep working like this are here because we can't imagine any other life. This is what we <u>want</u> to do. So don't get too concerned about the boss and all of the politics at corporate. We all should concentrate on what we need to do, what we love to do. Right?"

Andrei nodded and smiled. "Sure, boss. We work hard for you, Jack. I just ask 'cause I hear things from men."

Jack turned around to go to the coffee machine and saw Mercy already standing there by the coffee pots, a cup in hand. She'd been listening to Jack talk to the men. She offered the cup to him.

She said, "Those men respect you, Jack. I know you're trying to walk a fine line between their loyalty and Parasca's orders. I also know I couldn't do it half so well. But doesn't it grate on you sometimes?"

"It really does. I don't know how much longer I can do it. It used to not bother me so much, but the whole situation is changed now with you around." Jack grimaced. "I'm just a lot more aware of how hypocritical things sound when I know you're listening. I used to just spout the company line and go with it. Even if I knew the corporate office was telling me to say things that weren't true, I'd just shrug and think, 'What can I do about it?' Now, even when you're not around, I can hear the hollowness more strongly. The corporate B.S. seems to stand out to me more than it used to. It's like I'm hearing things with your ears almost." Jack looked down and his voice sounded discouraged, "I know you must think I'm a hypocrite."

Mercy nodded her head slightly and said, "I did for a while, but ... I know you're in a really tough spot, caught between jerks like Parasca and men who trust you like these fellows. I just think you should worry less about what Corporate says, and worry more about what these men think. Consider this, if you lose Corporate's respect, you'll just get a job somewhere else. If you lose these men's respect, they'll still be around and so will you. They'll know you've done them wrong, and you'll know they are thinking about it every time you're around."

Jack looked back up at her. "But Mercy, I can't just be irresponsible and throw a job like this away. I've got to suck it up and take whatever they send at me. It takes years to work into a position like this. I just have to get through this assignment."

"...and the next assignment after that, and the next after that? Jack, when you put up with stuff like this, people like Parasca think you're one of them. And horribly, even if you don't start out like them, piece by piece, you lose part of your soul until you <u>are</u> one of them." Mercy moved closer to Jack and put her hand on his arm. "Don't let that happen to you."

His face creased in concern, "Could you love someone that would throw their career away?"

"I couldn't love someone who _wouldn't_ throw their career away. I want someone that's married to me, not their job." She put her other hand on his other arm and moved even closer.

Jack felt his blood rising. He felt uncomfortably warm. He moved his lips to her ear and was about to whisper that they should 'go someplace more private' when he noticed how quiet the room had become.

Jack stepped back from Mercy and turned around. All of the men in the cafeteria were silent and looking at him. Most were smiling. Antonio's face lit up with a grin and he said, "So, boss, you going to just stand there, or are you going to kiss her?"

Mercy stepped past him. "The show's over boys. Back to work." Some chuckled, some shook their heads as if waking from a dream. Antonio smiled encouragingly to Jack, but averted his eyes when Mercy's gaze swept over him. Mercy walked away and the men followed her exit. Several of them sighed visibly when she left the room.

Jack sighed as well. _Oh my. She is as hypnotic as ever. So she couldn't love someone who wouldn't throw their career away? And here I thought I had to stay for her sake! I've got some serious thinking to do._

\* \* \*

The next day they arrived at the new location. In the distance, they could see the shores on either side of the Bosporus Straits, with the city of Istanbul covering the hills on both ends of the giant bridge that spanned the gap. A Turkish coast guard ship met them and after some pleasantries were exchanged that showed Parasca had prepared the way well for them, they lowered the sensing pod and began slowly sweeping back and forth.

In the control room, Mercy, Jack and Hayden watched the progress on their monitors.

Jack said, "So Hayden, the instrument package we lowered and are dragging along is sending back magnetic data. We're gathering the data as it streams in and then what?"

Hayden said, "Every so often, the data up to that point is saved in a file. Each file contains the magnetic readings complete with the latitude and longitude data from the GPS chip in the sensor array. The array measures distortions in the natural magnetic field produced by the earth. If there is something that is strongly magnetic in nature, like iron or steel, it shows up as an anomaly in the earth's magnetic field. There are actually multiple magnetic sensors in the array, arranged both vertically and horizontally, so we get more of a three-dimensional map of the magnetic distortions down there."

Mercy said, "Then, we take those files and run them through programs to filter out noise and natural effects. We remove problems caused by the ship's own distortion of the earth's magnetic field, for instance. After the filtering, we run the data through Hayden's program and look for similarities to the signature of these artifacts."

Jack said, "So what will the characteristic signature look like?"

Hayden said, "On tests we ran here in the lab, the shield and the sword both showed an interesting distortion of the earth's normal magnetic field. On a graph it looks like a sudden downward pull, similar to what a large amount of steel would do, say for a sunken metal ship. In the lab, we used even stronger magnets and found an even more pronounced reaction when at angles that were multiples of sixty degrees to the artifact. It probably has to do with the orientation of all of the nano-sized iron threads in the crystalline carbon. So, along with sensing the distortion of the earth's magnetic field, we'll be sending out strong magnetic pulses of our own and recording the reaction. Once we process the data, we should be able to spot the absorption effect that will happen at the correct angles."

Mercy said, "That will give us good locations to return to and look for more indications."

"How long will it take?" Jack asked.

"Depends on how close we were on our initial estimate from the map. It depends on how accurate the map is. It also depends on if our hunch is correct and that there is more of this metal down there somewhere. We'll be running Hayden's program against the data as we go, but there will be an increasing backlog of data built up during the day. The algorithm can't keep up with the speed at which the data is collected, though it should catch up each night when we stop and drop anchor. Hayden's written the program to send an e-mail when it finds something that might match up."

Twelve hours later, Hayden received an e-mail alert and Mercy and Jack converged on the operations room. It was evening and the ship had already stopped for the night. Hayden had the large screen display on and was rewinding through a video display.

"We also had several video cameras running down at the end of the instrument pod. I think I've just about found the place where the anomaly happened."

"Have you had a chance to look at the data yet?" Mercy said.

"Just briefly. I think it's a good possibility. I just want to make sure there's nothing else visible there that could have caused the reading."

The video looked straight down on the ocean floor. Numbers rolled by in the upper right of the screen. The scene fast-forwarded through at dizzying speed until Hayden found the latitude and longitude reading he was seeking from the data.

"Okay, we're getting in close now…there." He stopped the video.

Jack said, "I don't see anything."

Mercy said, "That's probably a good sign."

"Why?"

Hayden said, "If there were a sunken ship or a large rock outcropping visible, it might mean that we had a false-positive reading. As it is, all I see is this gently sloping mound right under the lat-long coordinates we want."

"What's next?"

Mercy said, "We turn the ship around and go back to this spot on the video. We roust the lab crew and the instrument boys, and once we're over the site, we get the package back down right above this spot. We take some more readings from various angles and then, if it looks right, we start the routine again. We'll have to get the pumps going and wash away fifty or so feet of silt and find out what's down there."

Hayden did a quick calculation. "Looks like the site is about eight kilometers from our current location and about ten kilometers from where we started. If this is pay dirt, our initial starting point was a pretty good guess. We could move the ship tonight, get the instrument readings during the night and scrub the data, and be ready to do sub-sea work by morning if you wanted to."

Mercy said, "I say go for it. The crew wants to get this job done as soon as possible anyway. I'll get on the phone and call up the captain and the team leads."

Two hours later, the ship had repositioned over the site and the instrumentation team got their package down through the moon pool once more. Since there would be no dragging of the instrument package horizontally this time, it sent out magnetic bursts all the way down to yield a series of readings. A short time later, the data was run through Hayden's algorithm and his phone buzzed at his side. He had received another e-mail alert.

"We got another bite, Mercy."

Without saying a word, Mercy seemed to wince and then called the subsea operations team lead. "We are 'Go' for in the morning. We start at 7:00 am sharp. Got it?"

She hung up, shook her head as if to clear it and said, "I'm going to go work out and then grab a few hours of sleep. See you in the morning."

Jack watched her leave, turned to Hayden and said, "Am I imagining things or was that a very abrupt departure for her?"

Hayden shrugged and said, "I agree. Looked to me like maybe she had a headache. In fact, she's been rubbing her temples off and on for the last two hours, ever since we arrived over the site. I think she just needs some sleep. I once asked her if she'd ever been checked for migraines. She almost bit my head off. I don't ask anymore."

Jack's brow furrowed. "That must be it. If she's not better in the morning, I'll check on her."

# CHAPTER 17 – LOOKING AT DEATH

*"As if ... man had not hellish foes enough besides"*
*— John Milton, Paradise Lost*

Mercy stumbled back to her room, fumbled at the lock, entered, slammed the door behind her, and slumped down to the floor with her back to the inside of the cabin door. It was late and she was tired, but that wasn't the problem. It was the voices. They had come back strong and hard. The screaming between her ears felt like it was ripping her scalp off.

*He's here. He's coming. We have to hide. There is no place to hide. There is no place where we can flee. He will drive us away or consume us! No, we will ally ourselves to him. Is there nothing we can offer him? We can compel for him. We can shape and direct the weak for him. One of them doesn't need us, he can compel by himself...*

They went on and on. A dozen voices argued back and forth, but why wasn't the medicine working? Not only were the voices overpowering her, she almost couldn't hear external sounds at all. Now, there was a low rumbling in her head that was new as well. It was almost as if a thunderstorm were sounding in the distance. Mercy got up slowly and found her medicine box in the bathroom. There was a small compartment for each day of the week and today's pill was gone. *All right, so I took the pill today like I remembered. Why isn't it working, then? I'll have to push them down with a hard workout, I guess.*

She rubbed her temples slowly, shakily donned her workout clothes, grabbed a couple of towels, sat on the edge of her bed until she felt steady, then left her cabin and trotted down the hall to the stairs. The voices kept up a running argument. Really, more like a screaming match amongst themselves about someone they all feared. She felt almost deaf. Sounds in the real world were drastically muffled by the inner ranting. She ran down the stairs two at a time for six flights and came to a landing. The sound of her feet on the stairs seemed like a distant tap … tap … tap rather than the pounding she knew she should be hearing. Opening a door to the outside deck, she trotted back to the exercise facility. She opened the door and turned on the light. Good, it was late and no one else was using it. She closed the door behind her and locked it from the inside. She dashed to one of the treadmills, stepped up on it and set it for its top speed. The motor's whine moved up in pitch as the belt ramped up. Mercy's trot turned into a run and then moved into a sprint. Her legs went faster and faster. The treadmill maxed out and she ran and ran, legs blurring. *Got to keep going until they die down or I'm starving. Oh blast! I forgot to grab something to eat in the cafeteria before I got here.*

* * *

In the control room, Hayden was paging through files of data, visually comparing the magnetometer readings to the model data they had from the lab simulations done with the sword and shield. Everything looked good. Behind him, someone cleared his throat.

Hayden turned and saw the head of the security department, Sergei. He had a concerned look on his face.

"What's wrong, Sergei?" Hayden asked.

"I think you should see something. Can you come to the security office for a moment?"

"Sure, what is it? Should we get Mercy or Jack?"

"Jack, maybe after I show you. Not Mercy. It has to do with her."

"What do you mean?"

"Easier if I show you," Sergei said.

The big security man moved to the adjoining doorway off of the control room that lead to his office and motioned Hayden inside. He closed the door and held up both his hands as if already trying to apologize for something.

"Hayden, I am going to show you something, but I don't want you to think I am some kind of voyeur. It happened like this: ten minutes ago, several of the ship's interior power sensors showed activity in one of the large rooms where all had been shut down for several hours previously. It also showed that the door to the room had been locked from the inside. We monitor these things routinely so we can adjust the power consumption needs, and also to make sure that no one is doing things with company property that they shouldn't. When the indicator showed that the area involved was the exercise room, I just did a routine check to make sure whoever was using it was okay. It's not often that the room is used at 1:00 AM in the morning. And not very often at all that anyone locks the door."

"So I remotely activated the overhead video camera for a moment to check and this is what I saw." He motioned to the computer monitor on his desk.

Hayden looked and saw Mercy running quickly on a treadmill. Another window on the computer screen showed an internet session. He looked up at Sergei questioningly. "So what's your concern? She told me she was going to work out before she left the control room."

"I was not worried until I noticed that she was running so fast. At first, I thought that the video camera wasn't working properly, so I shifted its view over to the clock on the wall there with the second hand. It showed a normal speed for the clock. Then I zoomed in on the treadmill that Mercy is using. That one is an American-made machine and very expensive, I believe. It shows she is running at sixteen miles per hour. I converted that to kilometers per hour and then looked it up on the web. She is running very, very fast and for quite some time. This is not a healthy speed for her to keep up. I am afraid she'll hurt herself."

"You're right, sixteen miles an hour seems awfully fast." He did a quick mental calculation and seemed even more concerned. "That's faster than a four-minute mile. How long has she been running like this?"

"Now, it's almost fifteen minutes. See there on the treadmill display? She's run four miles already," Sergei said.

The two men looked at each other and then back at the monitor. Hayden said, "Mercy's an Olympic-level runner? She's never said anything about this. And look at her. She's concentrating, but she doesn't look in distress. Of course, I'm no medic. Should we call the ship's doctor?"

Sergei said, "Exactly my question. I don't want to embarrass her, but this seemed possibly serious to me."

"She doesn't look strained. This is so odd. No, let's not interrupt her. I'll talk to the doctor in the morning and check with Jack. Mercy and Jack used to be close and might even be getting back together. He may already know this side of her, but my word. She is amazingly fast, isn't she? Sergei, you did the right thing letting me know. As I said, I'll speak to the doctor and Jack. Are you all right with that until the morning?"

Sergei shrugged. "If you say so, Hayden. I just want what's best for the boss-lady. She's smart and the men respect her. And of course," he seemed embarrassed to say so, "she's easy on the eyes. I don't mean any disrespect. I just don't want her to hurt herself. You understand?"

"I understand, Sergei. Don't worry. You wouldn't be alive if you didn't notice that she's 'easy on the eyes'. Well, I hope she works out the stress she was feeling. For me, I'm going to go to my cabin and get a few hours of sleep. Take care, Sergei. I'll let you know what I find out."

\* \* \*

The next morning, the sub crews were in the water and the ocean floor operations were underway before 7:00 am. Everyone on board wanted to find out what, if anything, was beneath the ocean floor, so pump lines, divers and subs were all deployed in record time. From the monitors in the control room, Mercy watched while the ocean floor silt started peeling away from the site under the force of the high pressure pumps. The operation would probably take longer than it did at the first site. Though they did have the deep in-flow current from the Mediterranean working in their favor to carry away the silt, they weren't dealing with an entirely similar situation. Last time, they'd been working to unveil a tar mound whose tip rose all the way to ocean floor. This time, they'd be going deep to reveal an earlier shoreline. They might be here for a while before they found anything.

Jack and Hayden came into the control room. They looked at Mercy with concern and Jack took a chair beside her.

"Mercy, are you feeling better today?"

Mercy said, "I'm all right." She didn't look up from the computer screen, obviously distracted.

Jack sighed in mild exasperation. "No, Mercy … could you look at me for a minute?" She looked up with lowered eyebrows and spoke with some irritation.

"Jack, I'm busy. What is it?"

"Last night you seemed to have a really bad headache. Are you feeling better? Did you take something for it? Sudden, severe headaches can be really serious. Have you ever had yourself checked?"

She relaxed a little but still seemed on guard and kept glancing back at the screen. "I'm okay. The headache is a little better. I went to the gym and did a hard workout and blew off some steam. I was able to get a little sleep. Now I'm back. Let's just leave it at that." Her gaze went indistinct as if listening to something.

Hayden said, "Mercy, we were just concerned, that's all." She showed no reaction and still seemed to be listening to a distant sound. Hayden felt a twinge of fear in his gut. He said, "Mercy? Mercy?" Her eyes came into focus and she jerked them back and looked at him.

"What? Hayden, did you say something?"

"Yes. I said we were just concerned about your headaches. Are you sure you're all right? You seem really tired and distracted. Maybe you should go take a nap. Better yet, maybe you should go see the ship's doctor."

She yawned. "I may take you up on the nap suggestion. The sub-sea work is off to a good start, but it'll take a long time to get down to depth at this rate. I don't need to see the doctor. I'll be okay once I get some sleep."

Jack said, "He might be able to give you something to help you get to sleep. Why don't you go let him check you?"

Mercy said, "What is this? Are you two double-teaming me? I'm okay, I just need some sleep." She yawned again. "I'm leaving right now for my cabin, and no, I don't need anything to help me sleep. You'll let me know if something happens?"

"Sure," Hayden said. "Get some rest."

"I can walk you to your cabin if you don't mind the company." Jack offered.

Mercy smiled sleepily. "Thank you, but no. I'll make it fine. You stay and keep him out of trouble." She motioned at Hayden. Before Jack could answer, she left.

Jack waited a minute just to make sure she wasn't coming back and said, "I still don't know what to make of that video clip you and Sergei showed me earlier. I knew she was an exercise buff, but why wouldn't she tell anyone about that kind of ability? That's spooky that she can run like that and hasn't said anything. What's the big secret? She could be doing marathons or one of those ultra-ironman runs. Plus, she's almost forty now, though she looks like she's still twenty-five. Apparently, she could make the next Olympic team if she wanted to. This is just weird."

Hayden appeared thoughtful and said, "The doctor seemed very concerned too. When I told him that she didn't seem in distress physically, he said that makes no difference. He said runners sometimes go into a euphoric state during extreme exertion and don't recognize the distress signals their bodies are sending. Extreme runners have been known to push themselves far beyond safe levels. He said people run themselves to death every year. He wants to see her and said if she won't come to him, he'll go to her."

Jack said, "That may be the only way to get Mercy checked by the doc. As far as I can remember, she's always been healthy. In fact, except for these headaches, I can't remember her being sick before. Well, I have to send a report to Parasca and then I'm going to visit the doctor myself and give him an update. I'll be back in a couple of hours. They won't be to the target depth by then, will they?"

"No, you've got plenty of time."

Jack left and Hayden turned back to his computer. He pulled up the data from yesterday. He ran it through an analysis program and then looked at the data in a spreadsheet. *This confirms the initial conclusion. The magnetic distortion effect is even stronger than what we detected in the lab with the artifacts. We may really have something here.*

The work at the site continued steadily. Every few hours, the divers and sub-operators returned to the ship and switched out with their replacements. Hayden always breathed easier after each shift of divers made it back up safely. Even though these men were experienced, industrial diving was considered one of the most dangerous jobs on earth. Divers had some of the shortest life expectancies of any profession, and that included the military.

Foot by foot, the ocean floor was uncovered. At this rate, they'd be to depth soon.

* * *

As tired as she was, she couldn't sleep. The voices kept getting louder. The medicine seemed to have only a small effect now and it was harder and harder to concentrate on work at all. She was nearly deaf to sounds around her and was grateful for the chance to get out of the control room. And, she had to use every mental trick in the book to keep from talking back to these voices. She knew it was getting bad when the conversational voices started talking to her. Most of the time, the voices were talking amongst themselves or commenting about her and her actions, but these voices tried to speak directly to her. They kept getting more insistent when she didn't respond.

Mercy got up from bed and decided to do crunches for a while. She lay on the floor and started the abs exercises. This time she didn't aim for hard and fast exertion, so she went steadily through dozens and then hundreds of forward crunches, leg lifts and obliques. She built up a good sweat and kept going until the voices started to fade. She had wondered about this effect many times. Why did strenuous exercise suppress the voices? Eventually, she had developed a theory: she believed that the point when 'runner's rush' hit, the point where endorphins started flooding her brain, was the moment when the part of her that let in the voices was temporarily disabled. It was as if the endorphins allowed her to close a door in her head, cutting the voices down to a muffled rumble. She had no idea if it were true, but she accepted it. At the very least it gave her a workable method of control during her bad episodes, as long as she could do prolonged, strenuous exercise.

After a while, she slowed down and stopped the workout. She drank several bottles of fruit juice, wolfed down four granola bars, two candy bars and an apple. She rose and went straight to a cool shower and toweled off. Naked, she fell into bed and finally slept.

* * *

Mercy stood on a broad beach, the sea breeze rustling her hair. Seagulls called to each other and the smell of the ocean drifted by. She had on a light-weight sari and wondered briefly where she had found it. She walked down to the water's edge and then parallel to it, the warm liquid lapping at her bare feet with each wave. The sound of the breakers soothed and calmed her. She felt a wonderful floating sense of wholeness and peace.

She continued walking. The currents of sounds and smells lulled her. She felt that she flowed with the ocean in its endless motions of washing forward and back. The sand stretched indefinitely in front and behind. The world became timeless and her footprints trailed off in the distance, a lazy line of relaxation that was the only signal of progress marking the passage of instants in this warm cocoon between worlds.

Then she noticed a black, spherical object half-buried in the sand at her feet. She nudged it with a toe. It seemed solid and only half dusted over with a layer of white sand. She dug her toe in further and lifted it up and out of the sand, rolling it over. It was one of her Magic 8-Balls.

A smooth, familiar delight flowed through her as if meeting a friend that never needed reintroduction. She kneeled down to pick up the black oracle.

Turning the smooth sphere and rolling it from hand to hand, she looked at the window on the bottom. Through the inky blackness, a pale shape rose as if a whale breaching, and a phrase was revealed: 'Outlook not so good'. She frowned at the answer. It wasn't in line with how she felt. She was relaxed, warm and calm…or was she? In fact, the feelings she'd had moments ago were all gone. Now she felt on edge, uncomfortable and nervous.

She looked again and the eight-ball's window into probability looked different, it was a miniature porthole with a latch. She fingered up the latch and opened the little window. The inside of the eight-ball was filled with a thick, purplish inky fluid and again the polyhedral shape rose through the liquid and revealed a phrase: "Why don't you listen?"

"That's not right," she said. "That's not one of the phrases." Irritated, she turned over the eight-ball to pour out the contents. To her horror, the liquid inside was thick and slimy. It bulged out of the hole and the ball itself felt elastic, almost spongy. She squeezed the ball and the fluid oozed downward like a thick, cold syrup. Something was in the blob of slime reaching toward the ground and she realized it was the polyhedron of messages from the inside the eight-ball. As it descended, the polyhedron seemed to twitch and wriggle. It elongated and grew legs and a tail. It became a pale, lizard-shaped creature that lay gasping on the ground as if it had spent hours of exhausting work extricating itself while hatching from an egg. The rest of the purplish fluid flowed over it like after-birth and left the shell of the eight-ball a rubbery empty husk in her hand. She dropped it and reached for the lizard.

Her hand approached and the lizard leapt and bit into her thumb. Pain lanced up her arm and she shook her hand, frantically pulling at the lizard and trying to remove it with the other hand. The lizard released its grip and she jerked it off of the bitten thumb and threw it away. Pain shot through the thumb and to her horror, it showed an instant bruise that quickly became a darker patch and then turned altogether black. Mercy trembled in terror but she couldn't look away from the injured hand. The bitten flesh twisted and shrank and smoke curled upward in wisps from her fingertips. Mercy screamed. She looked back at the lizard and saw that it had grown vastly in size, towering over her.

"Why?" she cried. The creature didn't answer but gestured at her twisted hand, which burst into flame as if it were an igniting match. Mercy collapsed to the ground in agony. The flames moved up her arm toward her shoulder. Her screams grew hysterical. The flames leapt from her shoulder and into her hair. Her face was engulfed in searing fire. She thrashed and wept. Her tears sizzled in the flames that covered her.

Through waves of heat and fire, it said to her, "Why didn't you listen?"

Mercy's eyes jerked open. She sat up in bed, gasping for breath. Deep, wrenching sobs escaped her and she hugged her arms tightly to her chest.

"What was that?" She whispered between sobs.

After a minute, the disorientation of the nightmare faded enough for her to stand and stagger to the bathroom. She splashed her face with water. *Such a vivid dream!*

She went back into her cabin and looked at her desk and found what she sought, her eight-ball. It looked normal, but for the first time ever, she felt afraid of it. She forced herself to pick it up. She turned it over and the clear window in the bottom didn't have a porthole cover. She sighed in relief, but her breath caught as something white surfaced. *It's just the fortune polyhedron.* It settled to a phrase and Mercy felt a freezing, cold wave roll from her toes, up her legs, to her chest and grab her throat. She locked in a rictus of terror and stared at the one word that appeared in the window: "Listen!" Her sight turned black and she felt herself falling.

\* \* \*

Mercy struck the floor. Her head thumped against the carpet and she woke for a second time.

"Ow! What?"

She realized she was lying beside her bed, partially tangled up in covers, one leg twisted up to the bed, the rest of her body down on the carpet level. Her head hurt. She tasted salt and her mouth hurt. She touched a finger to her lips and held it up to her eyes. In the dark of the room, she could only make out an inky smudge of liquid on her finger. *Blood. I bit my tongue. I'm bleeding.*

She shook her head, sat up and switched on the lamp by her bed. She untangled herself from the twisted sheet and covers. *Oof! I thought I had awakened, but I was dreaming that too. A dream within a dream. Weird. That is the most intense dream I think I've ever had.* She used the restroom and came back to the bedroom. She saw the desk and the eight-ball and felt a chill. *This time I'm really awake though, aren't I?* She almost pinched herself, then stopped her hand from reaching for the eight-ball. *No. I have more control of myself than that, don't I?*

Her head continued to clear and she became certain that the dreams were over for now. Looking at the clock she realized she'd been asleep for a good four hours. *It's time to get up anyway and get back to the control room.* She wanted to be there when they uncovered whatever the instruments had detected. Whatever it was, it had to be significant. Magnetic signals, like any other electromagnetic force, decreased their strength exponentially with distance. So, if these new items of crystal steel were indeed buried under fifty or more feet of silt, there was potentially a huge amount of the metal, just from the strength of the signal.

She dressed, cleaned up a little, downed several more high-calorie snacks, drank a protein shake, ate two candy bars, stuffed a half-dozen more into her small side-pack and trotted to the control room. She arrived and found Hayden there.

"Either you never left, or you sleep less than I do," she said.

"The latter," He said, turned and smiled. "Good to have you back. Besides, didn't you know that old guys like me sleep less? It's how we keep our wives happy."

She smiled, "Oh, give me a break. Don't put a picture like that in my mind. It's like imagining my parents having sex. It's a thoroughly frightening thought."

"Hmm. Just because I'm happily married, you think it's cute or disgusting. I may be sixty, but I still enjoy married life. You really should give it a try. If only there were someone you could respect that also loved you deeply. Hmmm?" Hayden looked at her with raised eyebrow. As if on cue, Jack came through the door carrying two cups of coffee.

"Where are we?" Jack asked.

Mercy looked at Hayden. *Don't push me.* He looked right back at her as if to say, "Why not?"

Hayden spoke first. "Jack, we're just minutes away, I think. The signal is getting stronger from the suspended magnetometers that we keep lowering as the silt gets cleared away. We're close."

"Good. Mercy, you feeling better?" Jack asked. He handed her one of the coffee cups.

She took the cup, grateful at his thoughtfulness. "Yes, Jack. Thanks. Mmmm. That is good." She took out a food bar and started munching.

Jack said, "Good. 'Cause the next feeling you're going to have is anger at me. I spoke with the doctor. He's coming by to check on you and those headaches. Don't argue, just talk to him." He dropped the stern attitude. "Please?"

Mercy sighed, "All right, Jack. He won't find anything though. The headaches just happen sometimes."

"If he doesn't, then okay. If he does, then you take his direction. All right?"

"All right," she said. Jack thought she sounded either resigned to her fate or was just playing along.

"Look!" Hayden said. He was pointing at one of the monitors that showed the underwater view of the excavation site.

The undersea cameras caught the image of silt billowing away from the pressurized water cannons as the current coming in from the Mediterranean carried the silt away. When the water cleared, they saw a mottled silver and black stone come into view. It was about ten feet long and four feet wide. The surface of it was streaked with veins of a shining, metallic substance and the top had a T-shaped design on it. She was confused. *A cross?* The water cannons continued clearing away the silt and uncovered the stone down to its base. Mercy felt her blood run cold as she saw the designs cut in the stone. Human faces in bas-relief, frozen forever in agony, were carved all along the outside surface of it. Mercy had an idea what this thing was. *It's a sacrificial altar, with a cross on the top surface? What does it mean?*

# CHAPTER 18 – THE BLOOD FORGE

*"Horrid king, besmeared with blood of human sacrifice, and parents' tears"*
*— John Milton, Paradise Lost*

The underwater crew moved on and forced the water cannon to clean away a larger and larger area around the altar. There was a sizable amount of rubble a few feet from its base that at first appeared to be an indistinguishable jumble, then Mercy understood what she was seeing: skeletons, bones, skulls of every size. Some were tiny, but some were adult in appearance. There were dozens of piles of remains. The silt was cleared away further and further out. No, not dozens; there were hundreds of skeletons, with no telling how many more there were still to be uncovered from the ocean bottom.

*How can there be skeletons here, and so many? It makes no sense! I know the deep layers of the Black Sea have very little oxygen, but these remains should have decayed and dissolved away under that silt. The only reason we were able to recover the bones of Goliath and the crocodile was that they'd been buried in the tar for those thousands of years.*

One of the cameras moved in closer to one of the skeletal figures. In the floodlights, Mercy saw that the skull was shiny, as if covered with metallic paint. The camera panned away and she saw that all of the skeletons, bones and skulls were coated in the same chrome-like plating.

*How on earth? Are these all statues? But why?*

Hayden broke the silence. "We need to recover some of those things if possible. They might be human remains, though I don't see how, or perhaps they're manufactured instead, like those terra cotta soldiers that were buried in the tomb of that ancient Chinese emperor. I don't understand how this happened, but if they are human remains, it looks like these things have been preserved somehow. I want to examine some in the lab. Mercy, do you agree?"

"Yes. Ask the divers to see if they can safely bring in some of them."

Hayden moved to relay the message. Mercy turned to one of the other monitors to see what they had found around the altar. It was a hideous thing, some kind of black rock with streaks of the same chrome-like coating. The terror-filled human faces carved into it made the image eerie and frightening. The camera shifted to the top surface of the altar again and Mercy sat on the edge of her seat. She saw the cross-shaped design and realized that it wasn't a coating or coloration of the stone. It was a cross-shaped depression in the top of the altar.

"Why is there a cross cut into the top of that hideous thing? If this is from the same time period as Goliath, it predates Christianity by thousands of years." she said.

Jack said, "I don't know about it being a cross. It looks more like a sword to me. In fact, it looks a lot like our little friend from the first site that was stuck in the tar. Don't you think so, Hayden?"

Hayden said, "It might be, but I have to ask: why? Why have a sword-shaped depression cut into an altar?"

Mercy looked at the monitor screen, noted the code in the lower left and spoke into the comm-line to the second sub. "Sub Two, could you move camera four in as close as it will go so I can see the surface of the altar in the highest definition? Thanks."

"Sure boss." Came the reply and after a pause, the camera zoomed in on the top of the altar. The image focused on the depression and Mercy saw that the newly-cleaned area was coated in the chrome-colored metal. It was indeed sword-shaped.

"It's crystal steel. Definitely." Hayden said.

Mercy said, "What is?"

Hayden said, "I have the magnetometers measuring this area still and the instruments show this altar, the bones, all of it is covered in crystal steel. It isn't paint. It's the same substance that the sword and shield are made of, the magnetic signature is identical. It's what led us to this spot. The whole area is streaked with the stuff and especially the altar."

Mercy said, "But what does it mean?"

Jack spoke up. "I think I know."

"What?" Hayden and Mercy said simultaneously.

"That altar is where the crystal steel sword was forged. The outline in the altar might be the same size. And it's the same metal."

"But the bones? Why all the bones, and why are they covered in the metal? Is the crystal steel what's preserving them? It's horrifying!"

Hayden said, "Perhaps we can tell something from the remains when they're brought in."

* * *

Parasca sat at the chair behind his desk in his penthouse office. He looked out the window but indistinctly, staring into the distance. He glanced at his reflection in the glass. He looked better than he had in years. *I look five, maybe ten years younger than a few weeks ago and it was that sword that did it. But the amazing part is I didn't even touch it!*

He thought back on the vision he'd seen while straining against Mercy to grab the sword. The closer his hand had approached it, the clearer the scene had become. He hadn't touched it, but images were much more distinct and more complete than any other memory he'd ever gained from an artifact.

He'd seen a tremendous crowd, thousands of men, women and children, all standing in a circular, broad plaza. The people were dressed primitively and seemed to be terribly afraid of something. Many of the children were crying and clinging to adults. None of the men were armed.

At the edges of the crowd, there were men with spears, also dressed primitively, but also obviously soldiers. They acted in concert to keep the people from escaping the plaza. In the center of the area, a large, black stone block stood on a circular island of stone, surrounded by a twenty-foot wide moat filled with flame that separated the altar's island from the rest of the plaza and the throng of people.

On the island next to the altar were two figures, one standing straight and the other hunched over the stone block. At first, Parasca couldn't judge the sizes of the figures, but then he realized that compared to the people on the other side of the moat, even the twisted person at the altar was gigantic. Bent over, with gnarled limbs and bowed legs, the creature was perhaps four or five meters tall. It seemed to be examining the surface of the altar with great care.

The second figure stood erect and regal and about three times the size of the people outside the moat. He reminded Parasca of some idealized human male shape, like a giant masterwork sculpture. He and the hunchback were speaking.

The hunchback said, "I will guide the flows, but you must hold the energy in and keep it from escaping. As they expire, their energy will be loosed. You must capture it all and keep it from dissipating. I will draw it from you as required in one flow while I also weave the flows of fire, soot and iron. Holding that much power and letting me draw it from you will sear you. Are you sure you still want to do this?"

The regal one said, "Yes. I must have weapons that can match his. He has the advantage of unlimited draw from the Creator, but we are stripped and limited to what we can eke out in this desert. He didn't think that we'd be so determined as to draw from these cattle as needed. Do it, Mulciber!"

"I will try. But when I built Pandemonium, we hadn't yet been cut off. Now I feel so weak that I can hardly move. I think we'll have enough. Four thousand of them for the essences that the sword will be built from and their life energies for the forging and one thousand more for the life energy to be stored in the sword. I think we'll have enough and to spare. But these creatures, they have their little ones with them. That troubles me. Moloch, how did we come to this?"

"You know how. It was through Michael's treachery. But don't go weak now. You've done much worse than this before. We were banished to this desolate place because of those experiments, or 'crimes' as Michael called them. That was why we were cut off and receive no life energy from the Creator. It's why we scrounge with the blood and entrails of these creatures, even though they are little more than beasts themselves. They have the life energy and their little ones have even more than the adults. Enough talk. We can do this. The dagger you made two moons ago as a test proved that the process will work. I'm ready. Start this."

Mulciber closed his eyes in resigned concentration. "Then give the signal to your guards, Moloch."

Moloch held both arms straight out from his sides and slowly lifted them until his arms were extended their full length above his head. He clasped his hands. From all directions across the plaza, his spear men gripped and leveled their weapons and stepped forward. The crowd shrank back with a moan. A compression ripple like a wave in a pond flowed through the thousands of tightly packed people. Those closest to the fire moat were forced closer by a half step. The smoke of the moat filled with burning tar bit at their eyes.

The soldiers took another step forward and another. The moan of the crowd changed to screams. The people pushed back from the spears. Empty spaces within the crowd were squeezed out. The ring of those nearest the fire staggered toward it. Shouts of terror rolled from that inner ring. With sudden realization, those closest to the fire understood what waited for them and surged back against the pressing thousands. The crowd was compressed from the outside by those trying to get away from the spears and compressed from the inside by those trying to flee the fire.

The sound of the mob changed to a rumbling mass of shouts, screams and fear. The soldiers pressed forward and the wave of retreating humanity pressed against those behind, and behind those and behind those. The surge from the outer edges overran the smaller number pressing back from the inside. The mob bulged back toward the fire and dozens toppled into the burning moat.

Fifty screams of agony lifted from the flames. Shadows writhed in the pitch. Moloch held his arms out again at his sides, fingers cupped upward and waving gently as if motioning followers to gather around. A misty reddish glow flowed from the moat and encircled his hands. The hunchback lifted his head to look upward. His face grimaced in pain. He raised one arm overhead and one arm out to the other giant. The red glow flowed across the gap between them. A wisp of fire moved from the fire moat toward his upward hand, coiling and threading into a rope of twisting hot gas that circled around in a gathering spiral.

A hundred and then two hundred more people fell into the moat, screaming at their impending deaths, cursing these two living and cruel gods. The red glow increased around the two giants, the fire spiral built larger around the hunchback's raised hand. Another thread, this one dark, streamed up and away from the fiery ring of the dying. It seemed to billow high above the flames as if carried by the rising heat, but then it flowed back down and gathered around and flowed through the fire spiral, becoming an entwined thread of deep red twisting and weaving between the orange of the flames.

More of the mob of twisting and writhing bodies fell over the edge and into the moat. Hundreds fell into the fiery pit. The red glow around the two giants increased. Moloch clenched his fists and grimaced. The orange threads of fire and the darker reddish thread were joined by a third thread of bright yellow. The threads twisted and entwined into a rope and then flowed into the depression on the top of the altar.

Mulciber was covered in sweat. His upraised hand continued to gather the colored streams of fire. They twisted and wrapped themselves into amazingly intricate weaves of heat. The yellow streams even seemed to thread through the other reddish threads to make thicker threads. Mulciber's other hand guided the finished weaving of fire into the sword-shaped depression on the top of the altar. He guided it to fill a layer, then another layer and another. He kept at it for hours. Moloch stood like a statue of glowing red flame. His arms were at his sides, bent outward at the elbow, every muscle strained against the effort to pull in and hold the life of these dying cattle. He held the pose for hour after hour. The screams of the tortured and dying never stopped.

Finally, Mulciber filled the sword depression with the final layers. Then, holding the spirals of fire, he paused in his construction. He blinked heavily at Moloch and croaked. "Almost done. The sword is forged. Now you have to do the hardest part and hold the energy for a few minutes while I prepare it for the next step. Can you do it?"

Moloch's face was contorted with effort. Every cord on his neck stood out, every muscle on his frame strained, but he did not flinch. He gave a very slight nod.

Mulciber closed his eyes again in concentration and drew a complex web of multicolored fire out of the threads circling his hand. The web floated in the air above the glowing sword and took on a cross-like shape as it was suspended above its twin. Mulciber suddenly released the spirals of fire and using both hands, he drew a huge flow of the red energy from Moloch and channeled it directly into the web above the sword. It glowed with a brilliant shine that seemed to pierce the eye. Mulciber lowered the web on to the forged sword and it sank into the cooling silvery metal. With the last ebb of energy from Moloch, Mulciber finished the top surface of the sword and molded the bull shape into its hilt and placed intricate tracings on the blade. The energies flickered out. Moloch and Mulciber leaned heavily against the altar. The only sound was the crackle from the fire. Moloch's soldiers stood near the fiery moat, their spears covered in blood. The crowd was gone, but the pit was filled and overflowed with skeletons that all shimmered with a thin coating of metallic glint.

At last Moloch spoke in a voice heavy with fatigue, yet still triumphant. He addressed Mulciber and their soldiers, "This altar and these remains are to be left inviolate as a monument to what we have done this day."

Mulciber said, "Let it also stand as a warning. Go." He waved a weary hand at the soldiers.

The soldiers back away, bowing repeatedly, eyes full of terror and awe.

Parasca came to his senses gradually. He found that he was still sitting in the chair behind his desk. *What a memory. They killed all of those people just to make the sword. I have to guess it took a similar event to make the shield. Those two beings were massive. Could one of them ... the one named Moloch ... could he have been the skeleton we found in the tar under the Black Sea? No, that skeleton was only almost four meters tall. This Moloch was five to six meters tall. But he mentioned a dagger. Is that this dagger?*

Parasca rose and walked to the cabinet and looked through the crystal doors of his display case. The dagger they'd found in the tar whip lay there. *Are you the one they made as a test?*

* * *

Mercy, Jack and Hayden sat at a table in a corner of the lab. Remains were still being sorted through, cataloged and labeled, but they still didn't know enough to solve the mysteries they'd uncovered.

Hayden said, "The crystal steel coating on the bones we've seen is no more than a microscopic layer. Very much like a thin plating of the metal. At a microscopic level, the iron-filled carbon nanotubes are only one or two layers thick. Whatever process was used to make the sword, there were a lot of dead people nearby whose bones were plated with stray bits of the metal during the forging of the sword. Also, the bone matter underneath the crystal steel is extremely charred. This caused me to think that either these bodies were burned before they were coated with the steel, or the steel was hot and charred the bones on contact. The depth of the charring causes me to lean in the direction of the first conclusion."

Mercy said, "It's awfully macabre. Why are all the bones so close to each other? Did they have the forge built near a mass burial site?"

Jack said, "Maybe it was a ritual, like those Aztec sacrificial rites where they killed thousands of people by cutting their hearts out. Maybe they carried out a mass human sacrifice before making the sword."

"Maybe." Mercy said. *Could it have something to do with why the voice told me to stop Parasca from touching the sword and shield? It said, 'He mustn't touch them.'*

"I wonder," said Hayden, "if there will be a similar site where the shield was made?"

"It would make sense that the shield went through a similar ritual, though I can't really say I'm very anxious to find another mass-murder site like this." said Jack. "Mercy, how much time should we spend here?"

Mercy was thoughtful. Her mind worked quickly and she felt very energetic, almost hyper. She spoke her thoughts out loud.

"Hayden, help me think this through. First, we may have found the place where the sword was made. We don't know the process, but with the fine layer of crystal steel we've found," she motioned at the skeletal remains, "we may have found some secondary effects of its making. Second, this site also contains the remains of hundreds, possibly thousands of humans. We don't yet know the cause of their deaths, but they may be evidence of a large ritual sacrifice of some kind. They may have died during the making of the crystal steel sword. Third, the shield may have been constructed using a similar process, but we've not found the location where it was made."

She took a deep breath and continued. "Now I'm going to posit some things about this location. First, the number of human remains here causes me to wonder about this site. The stone of the altar indicates craftsmanship as do the worked stones in the surrounding area. I will hypothesize that this site is part of a city complex because any settlement that could have spared hundreds or thousands of its inhabitants to a sacrificial ceremony must have had many multiples of that in its overall population. Second, the manufacture of the shield may have required as many sacrifices as this one did for the sword. That would indicate to me that this city must have been tens or even hundreds of thousands in population. A city that size would require a huge footprint and vast agricultural zones to keep it supplied. It would have gotten its water supply from the pre-deluge fresh waters of the Black Sea."

She continued, "Third, this city would have been only a few dozen miles from the Bosporus Strait dam. That distance would have kept all of this from being instantly washed away when it broke, but wouldn't have protected it from being very quickly covered over in rising waters. If there were indeed a massive flood that covered this area due to the natural dike being breached, that would account for the burial of this site under fifty feet of silt. Fourth, the city must have been many square miles in area, and we've uncovered only a tiny portion of it. It is true that we could take the brute force approach and just start uncovering more and more adjacent areas, but I think that will require a larger time investment than we want to make."

Hayden said, "I agree with your line of reasoning, Mercy. I think we'd be better served by noting this spot, cataloging the finds we've made here and then start searching again for the next concentration of crystal steel. At the least, we may locate the site where the shield was forged and perhaps that site will give us more insight into how the metal is produced. If on the other hand, we don't find the shield site, perhaps we'll find a cache of some kind. Perhaps well find some other weapons or tools made from the metal."

"Makes sense to me," said Jack. "The thorough investigation of this city will be the work of future archaeologists. If it is as large as you suspect, Mercy, it'll keep them busy for generations."

# CHAPTER 19 – RECOVERY

*"Which if not victory is yet revenge"*
*— John Milton, Paradise Lost*

After retrieving as much as they could from the site where the sword was made, Hayden tweaked his programs to exclude the present site and reset the plan to seek the next concentration of crystal steel. They took the ship in an interlocking grid pattern that day for several square miles but found nothing. They finally called off the search for the day.

Jack had been making some plans earlier with the ship's catering staff and at the end of day, after the anchor had been dropped, he made an announcement over the ship's intercom. "Attention, please. Jack Truett here. I know everyone on board has been working extremely hard under some truly extraordinary circumstances, and on behalf of PetroRomania, I want to thank all of you for your efforts. As a small token of the company's appreciation, I've asked our wonderful catering staff to prepare a celebratory meal tonight along with some extra-special treats after the meal. Dress up a little if you want to, at least take your mudroom boots off, Jake!" He gestured at one of the big mud engineers who shrugged his shoulders and pointed at his work boots. "We'll also have a movie night after supper with some prizes to be given away at intermission. To allow as many as possible to enjoy the evening, I'm declaring it a night-off from work for everyone that can possibly do it. Navigation and Engineering, you guys take turns to at least come and grab some food. Sorry guys, we have to have someone manning the controls even if we are at anchor. I promise you though, that I will personally deliver some coffee and desserts to you this evening."

At the party that night, the catering crew had gone all out. A full open bar was set out and tended by the Director of Catering and the Chief

Steward. Mercy and Jack stood at the bar and ordered some drinks. Mercy's pale blond hair was a bit wavy tonight and she showed subtle signs of makeup: a little eyeliner and blush, a hint of lipstick. She wore a flattering blouse with a slightly lower neckline than normal and a pair of smoothly tailored dark slacks. She wore comfortable low heeled shoes, having given up heels years ago. Compared to the jeans or khakis that they all wore on normal days aboard ship, this night she stood out like an orchid in a grain elevator. Every eye looked over at her, either boldly and unblinking or surreptitiously with an occasional side-glance. There were some looks of plain and open lust, but there were more looks that showed longing or loneliness. More than one of the men looked at her, then turned and pulled out their wallets or their phones and started showing off pictures of their families.

Jack held his drink, took a sip and said, "You look lovely tonight."

Mercy said, "Thank you. I thought I'd dress up a little more than usual. After all, it is movie night. What movie is it, by the way?"

"The Abyss," said Jack smiling.

Mercy said, "Is that the one where the drilling crew goes down in a deep submersible, gets stuck and meets aliens?"

"That's it."

Mercy frowned slightly. "I didn't care for that one. I thought they were too hard on the female lead."

"That they were."

"And the way the aliens suddenly show up at the end to save them all. That was such a 'deus ex machina' ending."

Jack looked confused. "A 'what' ending?"

"'Deus ex machina.' It means, 'the god from the machine'. The ancient Greek playwrights, at least the bad ones, would get their characters in a play into some kind of impossible mess and then using a hoist, they would lower an actor dressed like a god or goddess who would solve all of the problems and plot twists with a wave of their divine hand. This was considered very bad play writing technique, so they were warned by their betters to never resort to such a lazy way to finish a story. But that's what the director did in "The Abyss". Out of nowhere these aliens show up, save the people, calm the hurricane and solve everything. That's lazy, bad writing."

"Okay, I'll remember that. When we have problems, we fix them ourselves. No waiting on gods or aliens. Got it." Jack said. "And speaking of problems that need fixing, I need to go mingle a little with some of the crew. Some of them need to be gently scolded. I can't really blame them too much, but they haven't stopped staring at you since you walked in the door." He kissed her lightly on the cheek and walked off to do some glad handing and redirecting of the ones that wouldn't stop ogling her.

Mercy smiled at Jack's protective attitude then ordered another dark beer and took a deep drink. *That's another advantage I have, I guess, with my hyped-up metabolism. Alcohol doesn't really affect me. I guess my system processes it way too fast. A momentary little buzz is all I ever get and I've never tried to push it to the limit to see how much I would have to drink in order to get blasted. It might not even be possible. My bladder would probably burst before I could get drunk.* She took a sip. Someone stepped up to the bar beside her.

The tall, rangy man spoke to the bartender, "Do you have any Baltika beers?"

"The Russian brewery? Yes I think so. Yes, we have the gold, the Baltika 5 and the dark Baltika 6."

"Give me the dark."

Mercy turned to him and said, "I've never had any of the Baltika beers. Any good?"

He gave a slight smile and a small shrug. "Better than most of the beers I've tried in Europe." The bartender finished pouring the beer and handed it over to the man. "Some people call this style the 'Baltic Porter'. I don't care about that. I just like the way it feels going down."

Mercy said, "I like Porter beers. Very good for a slow, sipping drink. Not so good on a hot work day. By the way, I'm Mercy Teller." She held out her hand for a shake. The man took the offered hand in a firm grip and shook it.

He said, "I know who you are, Dr. Teller. I am Vasiliy Cherenko. I work in the security department."

Mercy said, "Oh yes, I think Andrei introduced us sometime that first week. How do you like working on the *Fortuna*?"

"It has its interesting points. Of course, I am not an employee of PetroRomania. I work for the company that is contracted to provide onboard security for PetroRomania's offshore fleet. Just like the catering crew and the navigation crews are contracted by their companies."

Mercy said, "Yes, and I suppose it's much the same way most of the oil and gas drilling and exploration crew is contracted to us by their companies. In fact, if you think about it, there are only about a dozen of us 'company men' on board that actually are employees of PetroRomania, myself included. An interesting thought."

Vasiliy said, "Yes, and one that security people on these ships must keep a close eye on. Where are people's true loyalties for instance? You and others of the senior management have your loyalty to PetroRomania, but what about the others?"

Mercy said, "Are you saying that we shouldn't trust each other? I think the crew functions very well together."

Vasiliy said, "Now they do, but what about when the unexpected happens? Will they still work together, or will they pull in different directions according to other loyalties? Will some of them collect and sell industrial secrets of PetroRomania? I watch for things like this. If you will excuse me, I need to visit more people and observe. Thank you for your conversation."

He stepped away, keeping to the outer edge of the milling cocktail party and observing. Mercy watched him. *He seems slightly familiar somehow. Where have I seen him before? I can't remember ...*

Mercy met and spoke to dozens of the ship's various workers. Everyone got more relaxed as the cocktail hour went on. Finally, a bell rang and the cafeteria doors were opened. The room had been redecorated and food was set out on all of the tables for the occasion. The crowd moved in and took seats over the next few minutes. Mercy sat next to Jack.

"So how did the 'correctional' conversations go with the oglers?" Mercy asked, a touch of a smile in her voice. "I doubt it did much good. Some of these macho European men consider leering an inalienable right and any woman with roughly the right shape will do as their targets. I'd hate to see what they'd do if I wore a tank top or halter top. They'd probably riot if they saw a woman in a bathing suit. These men need shore leave, Jack."

"Let's just say, they took my suggestions with good humor, but some suggested they'd stop leering at you as soon as I stopped as well," Jack said.

Caught by surprise, Mercy laughed loudly. She moved closer to Jack and looked directly in his eyes.

Jack said, "Mercy, we're both a lot different now. A lot of time has gone by and things have changed, but we still have a strong connection. I know it's there and I'm pretty sure you sense it too. Don't you?"

Mercy smiled, "I do, Jack."

Jack said, "I like the sound of those words."

"What words?"

"I do. One of these days I want to hear those words from you in a little more formal setting. No rush. No pressure. It would just be so right."

Saying nothing, she reached over and squeezed his hand. *I'd love that too, Jack. There's just too much about me that you don't know yet, though. Maybe someday ...*

After supper and desserts, a screen was lowered at one end of the hall and the movie started rolling. Fifteen minutes in, Jack felt Mercy squeeze his hand again. He leaned close to her.

"What's up?"

Mercy said, "It burns me up the way they portray strong women in movies. You can't be strong, efficient and warm at the same time, it's always cold, heartless and bitchy if you're good at your job."

"We don't have to stay. I need to deliver those desserts to the on-duty crew. Want to help me and then go for a walk?"

"Sure, but you don't think it will raise a lot of eyebrows?"

"Let it."

They rose quietly and made their way to the back of the large room. They gathered up a selection of desserts and some coffee supplies on two trays and moved to the back doors. Mercy caught Hayden's eye. He smiled happily at her as if to say, "Good for you two" and nodded. Mercy inexplicably blushed. *I'm not some teenager stealing a kiss! What is the matter with me?*

They delivered the desserts and coffee to much appreciation from the working crew. After chatting with them for a few minutes, Mercy and Jack went back to the deck, and walked, Mercy's arm through Jack's. The warm night and the breeze from the sea made for a perfect time, even if their walk was on board a huge industrial vessel and not a romantic cruise ship. They moved from the control tower and down the starboard side. Overlooking the submersibles that were docked and suspended below, they looked out over the sea.

"Jack, what are we going to find tomorrow? The sword and shield and giant skeletons all are amazing. That site we found yesterday with the altar, the one that seems to have been used to mold the sword ... that was so macabre. It felt evil. I think all the skeletons of people we found there were victims of some kind of mass human sacrifice ritual. Maybe it was done while the sword was being made. That would mean that sword in the lab, at least symbolically, has been bathed in the blood of those poor victims. That makes me feel really weird. What kind of fanatical madmen would have their people sacrificed by the hundreds for a sword?"

Jack said, "I hope I never meet those kinds of people. Perhaps we'll find the location where the shield was made. It might be very similar, with another altar. You might want to steel yourself for that. Or, maybe it will be something else."

Mercy said, "Jack, we've gone so far afield from our realms of expertise here. I'm just an amateur archeologist. Actually, I'm more of a hobbyist really. I'm not qualified to do this."

"I disagree. I think between you and Hayden, we have a pretty good knowledge of what we need. Plus we have lab people who know the metallurgy, the carbon dating and the paleo DNA side of things. I think we're doing all right."

"So far, Jack. So far," Mercy said.

"That's all anyone can do in a place like this with so many unknowns. There's no playbook for this kind of situation. We have good people, with good skills. We have great, open-minded thinkers in you and Hayden. You're the best I've ever seen at improvising and creating new plans as needed. We'll make it."

Mercy smiled at the compliment, then tipped her chin upward slightly as if listening for something. She changed her stance and stiffened. "Jack. I'm tired. I need to get some sleep before tomorrow. I think I'm going to turn in early."

"What? Aren't you feeling well? This is kind of abrupt. Did I say something wrong?"

"No nothing like that. I ... I just had a twinge ... of nausea. Maybe something at supper didn't agree with me." She saw the look of concern on his face and softened. "Jack, Jack. Don't worry. You don't have to walk on eggshells around me. I need to turn in. There's ... just a lot on my mind right now." His expression changed to discouragement. She felt sorry for him and brightened up and gave him a cajoling smile. "Jack, would you walk me back to my cabin?"

Hope lit up in his eyes. "Of course I will, my lady. This brave knight is at your service."

"Good sir, I thank you."

Arm in arm, they walked back toward the control tower and her cabin.

Behind them, near the stacks of pipe by the starboard side of the ship, Vasiliy stepped out from behind a large forklift. He watched, being careful to not be seen in case one of them were to turn back and look. The Russian pondered. *That was an interesting conversation.*

\* \* \*

The next morning after Hayden verified that his search algorithm was still correct in spite of the futile effort the day before, they resumed their grid pattern search. Within thirty minutes, the computers signaled a hit and they restarted the undersea operation to home in on and uncover the cause of the signal. The subs and divers deployed and soon the control room crew could see video of the silt billowing away from the water-pressure cannons held by the subs. Everything seemed identical to the last time when the altar had been uncovered. After a moment, the cloud of particles settled, and they could see in the floodlights at the ocean bottom a rectangular corner. It was completely different from their last find. Jack's first thought was that it was the top edge of a metal shipping container that had been buried in the silt, but it soon became clear it wasn't that. And, it was too straight and too long to be natural. This was no rock altar streaked with a thin plating of the translucent metal. This thing was large and was probably solid crystal steel from edge to edge. The underwater crews redoubled their efforts. Soon they had the entire top surface of the object uncovered. It was a large surface, with a carving of a giant, rampant bull cut into the top in deep relief.

All three of them sat motionless. Jack gave out a low whistle. "That bull, what does it remind you of?" he said to Mercy.

"Well, it's like the bull carvings on Crete from the Minoan civilization, but a more refined version than the artifacts found at the Palace at

Knossos." She continued, "I'm betting this predates the Minoans by a long shot. That civilization was wiped out by earthquakes from the Santorini volcanic eruption in about 1600 BC, I think. Besides, if this is anything like our earlier finds, then this is almost eight thousand years old. And, look at that thing. It's beautiful."

Hayden said, "I'd bet a month's salary that plate is pure crystal steel. Look at the size of it! What, two and a half meters wide by six meters long? Incredible!"

The subs continued the work and soon they saw that they were watching not the uncovering of a metal plate, but a huge, three-dimensional rectangular box. Sometime later, they saw the full extent of it: two and a half meters wide by two and half meters high by six meters long. It was gigantic.

Jack said, "It's the size of a small bus. What would something like that weigh?" he asked Hayden.

Hayden did a quick mental calculation. "No way to tell. If it's solid crystal steel, we could figure it out. But if it's hollow, there's no way to tell how heavy it is without knowing how thick the inner walls are. And of course, if there's anything inside it." Mercy and Jack turned to look at Hayden. The techs in the control room turned to look as well.

"Inside it?" Jack said.

"He's right, Jack," said Mercy. Look at the top of it, then trace down about a foot from the top edge. There's a seam that runs all the way around. I think that seam is the edge of a lid. We've found a giant lidded box, eight feet by eight feet by twenty feet. And there," she pointed to an adjacent screen that showed the other sub's video feed. "Those three features look like latches to me."

Jack's phone rang. He pulled it out and looked at the display, shook his head as if to say, 'Here we go again...' and answered, "Jack Truett here. What can I do for you Mr. Parasca?"

\* \* \*

Jack said, "I had to tell him what we'd found!"

Mercy said, "Yes, but he's acting too hastily. We shouldn't disturb the site by removing something like this. What's the hurry? There may be a lot more to find here and we've got time. We should remove more of the silt to get an idea of the extent of this find. Maybe there are ruins to be found as well. Perhaps we'll find another altar. Some of those rocky shapes near the box look like they might be worked stone. We need to thoroughly map, photograph and catalog the position of everything before we disturb the site."

Hayden said, "Jack, I agree with Mercy. We really shouldn't try to raise it to the surface. It might not be as solid as it appears. What if we tried to lift it off the ocean floor and it broke into pieces? We don't know that it can take the stress. Also, we don't know if it is attached to anything else. What if it's part of a submerged foundation or building? And think of the weight of this thing. Even if it is hollow, it could weigh many tons. It might be beyond the lift capacity of our cranes."

"You're right of course, but he's the boss. You heard me. I tried my best to talk him out of it, but he's fixated on it. Once we admitted that the cranes might have the capability to lift it, he was determined. I am sorry, but it's not something we can override at this point. We have to at least try to bring it up," Jack said.

Mercy shook her head wearily. She looked at the monitors. The mini-subs and divers were already acting on Parasca's orders that Jack had relayed and were getting cables down to the "Monolith," as they'd begun calling it. The artifact wasn't really that similar to the famous slab of black stone from the book and movie, "2001", but somehow the name seemed appropriate. This giant box of metal with its carving of a rampant bull seemed to be as much a part of some alien world as Clarke's 2001 "Monolith". Mercy squinted at the image. There seemed to be a plaque of some kind on the thing's lid, engraved below the picture of the bull. The camera wasn't close enough to make it out. But at this rate, she'd be able to examine it herself, once it was on board.

They continued watching from the control room as the heavy steel cables were threaded through rings they'd found attached to the top and bottom corners of the Monolith. Perhaps the corner rings had been purely for decorative purposes, but they also made handy lift points for the crane cables. The rings looked to be crystal steel as well and Mercy guessed that presently they'd know a little bit more about the tensile strength properties of the metal. Soon enough, the divers and submersibles had secured the cables and sent word up to the crane operators to slowly take up the slack. The cables drew taut.

"Control. We're ready for a test lift. Do we have permission to go ahead and check the load on Crane One?"

Hayden lifted his eyebrows at Mercy questioningly. She sighed, grumbled and waved her hand dramatically as if bowing to grant permission.

Hayden spoke into the comm-link. "Go ahead, Crane One. Slow and steady. Don't break anything up here or down there. And, give us a count on metric tons of lift as the load increases."

"Will do, Control. Starting lift." There was a pause. The sub-sea camera showed that all of the divers and subs had retreated from the Monolith and the attached cables. Nothing seemed to be happening. Then the count started. "One metric ton." There was a long pause. "Two."

The count slowly rose, though the sub-sea camera showed no change.

Jack said, "What did you say was the maximum weight of that thing, again?"

"It's just an outside guess. Based on the weight of a cubic foot of conventional steel being equal to approximately five hundred pounds, plus that thing's dimensions being eight by eight by twenty, if it isn't hollow, that comes to about two hundred and ninety metric tons. Give or take a few. That's my guess at its upper weight limit. I don't think it's that heavy though. For one thing, that thing is almost certainly crystal steel from its magnetic signature. Our other samples show that crystal steel is about half the weight of a similar volume of conventional steel. So that would cut its max weight in half."

Mercy said, "It won't weigh even that much. It must be hollow. Why put a lid on something solid? Why even make a giant slab of solid crystal steel eight feet thick? This is a monument, but it's also a container of some kind. Even though I still think we shouldn't be lifting it, I can't wait to see what's inside."

"… Sixty-nine metric tons … Seventy … Seventy-one …"

Clouds of silt shot out from the bottom edges of the Monolith. Crane One had found the lift weight of the object.

Mercy's eyes lit up. "It is hollow. Let's get it aboard and see what we've got."

* * *

Dmitri spoke into the phone, "Get the *Lucian* ready for departure. We leave tomorrow morning. We're going to catch the *Fortuna* and relieve Parasca of some of his burdens. Make sure we are fully stocked with weaponry and a full crew. We must go in expecting trouble. Do you understand?" He waited, seemed satisfied with the response and said, "Good."

A younger man walked into Dmitri's office without knocking. Dmitri looked up with sudden anger at the intrusion, but when he saw who had entered, his mood lightened and he waved the man in and toward a chair.

"Alexi, I didn't know you were coming. Did you just arrive?" Dmitri asked.

"Brother, let us cut through this. What are you doing? I find that two million is gone from our cash accounts and I am told by our accountant that you've hired a 'consultant'. What is going on? Only one kind of 'consultant' costs two million Euros. We can afford it, sure. But why?"

"Alexi, I didn't know you were back in Romania or I'd have told you. That pig Parasca has found something very rare and valuable and I've decided to take it from him."

"Dmitri, that is not the whole story. I know you. If you want something from someone you take it from their hide through sharp business deals, not this kind of dirty work. Not anymore. Besides, you just cost Parasca millions if I remember. Didn't you have his ship held up in court? When he got it free of your legal entanglements, it cost him millions more to repair the faulty work done by the workers you were paying off. Why go after him again?"

Dmitri looked at Alexi thoughtfully and said finally, "You remember Tresa Rodica?"

Alexi grimaced as if to say, 'not again,' but said to Dmitri, "Of course. But Dmitri you will never be free of those memories if ..."

Dmitri cut in, "Alexi! Look at this." He shoved the open dossier over to his younger brother and pointed at the attached picture. "Tresa's daughter is on board, working for Parasca. The daughter. I can't let that stand."

Alexi shook his head in resignation. "Nothing will ever be enough, will it?"

The words shook Dmitri. *Will it? Will it ever be enough?* His mind staggered under sudden grief. *How many years ago? Almost forty? Can it be that long ago? She's been gone for so long? But Tresa, I still remember!*

* * *

Dmitri Slokov and Tresa Rodica had been very close. They had been childhood friends and then best of friends and as sometimes happens, the friendship slowly turned into something deeper. *It was all so simple and pure.* It hurt Dmitri's heart to remember it. In those days, even a kiss could light a passion in him that still amazed him. He was willing to do anything for her, accomplish any task. The energy it inspired in him, just a smile from her would seem to fuel him for days.

When they neared graduation from high school, Tresa Rodica announced she would attend the technical university nearby. After all, her mother was a teacher there and Tresa could live at home and save the costs of going away to school. Money was tight for everyone and she couldn't afford some fancy university in Bucharest. Besides, children of party members got all of those spots.

Dmitri announced that because of his father's connections, he had received an offer to join the Securitate. When Tresa looked dismayed, he had hastened to add that it was well paying and dependable work. He told her someone in the Securitate could rise quickly and be respected. In a few years, he might be able to support a wife and family.

The next day, when he met Tresa, she was miserable. She had told her mother about Dmitri's ambition to enter the Securitate and Sonia Rodica had informed her daughter that the Securitate was inhabited by monsters and the "tools of the dictator". Dmitri warned her strongly that she mustn't ever repeat statements like those her mother had made and extracted her promise she would warn her mother as well.

He had begun training in the Securitate, and found it suited him well. The job fit him like a glove and he made friends with some of his fellows. His best friend, and one he shared gossip with, was Janos Parasca. He was a war orphan who had grown up on the streets of Bucharest. Through natural toughness, manic energy and slyness he'd advanced from a starving waif to a leader of street gangs. He'd been such a good organizer of his gang that he'd attracted the attention of a captain in the Bucharest police department who managed to capture Parasca at the age of seventeen. He'd made Parasca an offer: spend six years in jail or join the Securitate. Janos Parasca had joined.

One evening, Dmitri invited Janos to go with him and Tresa to get some supper at one of the few restaurants that would be open that time of night. As party members and young officers in training of the Securitate, they usually got a deep discount anywhere they went. After all, no restaurant owner wanted to chance making the Securitate angry at him or have them suddenly 'forget' to protect his restaurant from criminals.

Dmitri remembered. *I should have realized what Parasca would do the moment he first saw Tresa.*

When Tresa stepped from the bus where they waited, Dmitri caught a peripheral glimpse of Parasca's odd expression and turned to look at the other man. Parasca's eyes were wide and his mouth was open as he stared in Tresa's direction. His face flushed red. *What is the matter with him? He looks like he's choking on something,* Dmitri thought.

Parasca coughed suddenly just as Tresa stepped to Dmitri's side and hugged him. Parasca coughed for several seconds more and Dmitri was tempted to slap him on the back, but Janos suddenly stopped. He begged their pardon and bowed and waved them on as if to say 'lead the way'. Tresa laughed and holding Dmitri's arm, they walked past Parasca who began following a few steps behind them.

Dmitri dismissed Parasca's coughing fit, but then as they approached the restaurant's glass door, he caught sight of Parasca's reflected expression where he stood behind Tresa. Janos was staring at Tresa with a look of concentrated, starving desire.

They entered the eatery and were seated quickly. There weren't many choices on the menu, with all of the food shortages, but the meal was cheap for the three of them. Dmitri didn't think the bill would have been as inexpensive for other non-Securitate patrons.

Dmitri lost himself, as usual, in the company of Tresa, but still caught unguarded glimpses of Parasca that were disturbing. *I need to talk to him, to warn him off from Tresa. She's too good for a gutter-rat like him. Besides, she's already with me!* Dmitri snapped back to reality. What question had Parasca just asked her?

"Beg pardon?" Tresa asked.

"I asked about your mother. Dmitri told me that she was a scholar at the university."

"She is …" Tresa spoke warily.

"Dmitri also has told me about some of the counterrevolutionary talk that goes on behind the scenes at the university. You might want to warn your mother against associating with those types of people. You never know when someone like Dmitri is going to suddenly turn you in," Parasca said as lightly as if he'd just remarked on a sunny weather report.

Dmitri deflected the conversation while wondering what game Parasca was playing. They finished up at the restaurant and walked back to Tresa's apartment. All the way there, Janos walked behind them. Once, Dmitri turned to look back at Parasca and immediately narrowed his eyes at Janos when he realized that his friend was eyeing Tresa up and down from behind.

Parasca laughed at Dmitri's expression, shrugged and hung back while Dmitri said goodbye to Tresa. After the door closed, they turned to walk back to their barracks. Before Dmitri could say anything, Parasca spoke.

"She's quite a woman. Have you slept with her yet?" Parasca said.

"Shut your mouth! Who are you to ask such a question?"

"Someone who wants to make sure that such a woman doesn't go to waste."

"Don't talk about her like she is a piece of meat!"

"Isn't she a piece of meat?"

Dmitri turned on Parasca. "You take that back! You can't talk about her like she's a whore!"

"Why not? Isn't she? How do you know if you've never slept with her? Offer her some new shoes or a nice box of candy. You'll find out what her price is. " Parasca seemed amused at Dmitri's purpling face.

Dmitri swung his fist wildly at Parasca. Janos sidestepped and swatted Dmitri's fist away, grabbed the extended arm and jerked Dmitri forward and off his feet. Dmitri hit the sidewalk lengthwise, all of his breath shot out of him and his chin bounced off the concrete. Blood filled his mouth and his eyesight was blanked out in white pain.

Dmitri felt his face being slapped again and again. The taste of copper came to him and he rolled to his side and spat out a mouthful of thick bloody liquid. He felt himself pulled up by his collar and lifted to unsteady legs.

"Pull yourself together, Dmitri!" Parasca shouted into his face. "You think I don't know how to fight? What do you think I learned all those years growing up in the alleys of Bucharest?"

"I ... I..." Dmitri couldn't speak.

"Be a man! You've got her, then use her! If you don't, someone else will." Parasca pushed Dmitri's back to a wall. "And don't ever swing at me again." Parasca pulled a long blade knife blade from his belt and held it under Dmitri's nose. "... because the next time you do, I won't just leave you with a split lip."

Dmitri sagged and slid down the wall until he sat miserably against it. Parasca gave a mock salute and walked away.

A few days later, Dmitri was confronted by a superior officer. The man called Dmitri to his office and proceeded to question him.

"It has come to my attention that you have received word of subversive activities in the populace and have not reported it. How do you answer this charge?"

Dmitri was disoriented by the question and could only ask in reply, "What? I don't understand."

"Idiot. The question is simple. You apparently are even simpler. Have you knowledge of activities and speech that seek to discredit the Romanian Socialist Revolution?"

"I ... don't ... know anything of this..."

His captain struck him across the mouth with the back of his hand. Dmitri was so surprised and stunned he could think of nothing except the feel of his mouth bleeding and the familiar, metallic taste of the blood.

"Let me spell it out so that even a simpleton like you can understand. Some girl you know spoke subversively of the Revolution, the Protectors of the Revolution (the Securitate) and our glorious leader, Nikolai Ceausescu. I believe we were described by her as 'tools of the Dictator'. Who spoke these words to you?"

Dmitri's mind cleared suddenly in a rush of adrenaline. *The captain was asking about Tresa! What can I do? How did he know what Tresa had said? I can't admit to him that Tresa told me this! They would arrest Tresa. How can I protect her? Wait, Tresa was just saying what her mother told her! I'll tell the captain that. Then Tresa will be all right.*

Dmitri told his Captain of Sonia Rodica's comments. After much cross-examination, they accepted his story, but as punishment, they sent him to do customs duty at the opposite end of the country in Constanta. He was the lowest ranked man at the port and it was six months before he obtained a leave permit to visit Timisoara again. He had written to Tresa constantly, but had not heard from her.

On his leave, he traveled by bus and train from Constanta to Bucharest and then to Timisoara. At her mother's doorstep, he knocked and waited for her to answer the door. For months, he'd anticipated, rationalized and tried to develop excuses for what had happened. He'd finally decided he would throw himself at her feet and plead forgiveness. He continued to wait.

The door opened and Janos Parasca stood there. He appeared startled at first, but then smiled mockingly at Dmitri. "Well. You have guts to come back here, don't you? Tresa, darling. Come see who has come to visit."

When Tresa appeared, she looked older, tired and heavily made-up. Her cheeks were unnaturally rosy and her clothes were extremely provocative. She had on dark hose, a very short skirt with a slit up the thigh and a low-cut top that showed considerable cleavage. She glared at Dmitri and then her expression changed to contempt.

"You dare come back here? My mother is still in prison because of you! I was in jail for weeks until Janos got me out by pleading on my behalf. Then I find out you ratted on me to your captain, all to save your stinking skin!" She spat on him.

Dmitri tried to fumble out an explanation but he was incoherent. All he could say was, "It's not like that. They forced me to talk. I couldn't help it." He wept. *She doesn't understand! She won't believe what I say!"*

She stormed back inside, not speaking to him then, or ever again.

Dmitri turned to Janos who'd been listening the whole time. "Parasca, tell her. The captain knew what her mother had said already! I didn't tell him anything. He already knew! I never told the captain what her mother said. I never told anyone!"

Janos stepped back inside the door frame. He stood looking at Dmitri, as if trying to decide how smart he actually was. He locked eyes with Dmitri and finally spoke. "You told me," then Janos closed the door.

Dmitri sat down on the steps of the building, held his hands to his face and couldn't seem to breathe. His vision went black. *'You told me.' 'You … told … me.' I told Janos, and he told the captain. The captain took me from Tresa and locked up Tresa and her mother, Sonia. Janos got Tresa out and told her I'd betrayed her mother and herself. And he stole her from me. 'You … told … me,' he said.*

Dmitri had finally gotten up and stumbled away. He found the local Securitate office and checked in. They had no place for him to spend the night. He did find out from one of the other officers that Janos had moved in with Tresa after Dmitri had been shipped off and she'd gotten out of jail. Parasca had bragged to the other men that Tresa was his mistress.

Dmitri spent his remaining money and leave time on liquor. He never remembered where he slept during the rest of that time in Timisoara. By the dirt he found on his clothes, it must have been on the ground or in a gutter. He vaguely remembered the drunken journey back to Constanta. He never returned to Timisoara again, but he did make himself a promise. *Someday, I will take everything from him just as he took Tresa from me.*

\* \* \*

Dmitri snapped out of his reverie and looked at his younger brother, Alexi. He was the only one to whom Dmitri had ever told the whole story. He said grimly to Alexi, "No. Nothing will ever be enough."

# CHAPTER 20 – THE MONOLITH

*"This enterprise none shall partake with me"*
*— John Milton, Paradise Lost*

It hung suspended over the mid-deck of the ship, brought up from the bottom with the use of port-side cranes One and Three. After they'd used Crane One to determine the dead-lift weight of the Monolith, they'd allowed it to briefly settle back onto the ocean floor, and connected the lift cables to the two port-side cranes so that they could share the load equally. The starboard cranes were rigged to racks of steel drilling pipe that acted as counter weights over the starboard side during the lift operation. Though the ship's engines could overcome an off-center downward tilt through use of its stabilizers, the captain didn't want to take any chances. He had requested and had gotten agreement that the PetroRomania crane men be allowed to counterweight the lifting activity on the Monolith with an approximately balancing load on the other side of the ship.

The lift operation was over and the Monolith hung suspended over the midship upper deck. The area was typically used for drill pipe and casing storage, but much of that had been moved to other deck areas or used for counter weights. After the Monolith was placed down on the midship deck, the drill pipe and casing racks were carefully stacked back on the midship deck so as to balance the tons of extra weight.

Mercy spoke through her phone to the crane operators of One and Three, "Bring it down and then maneuver the suspended racks, leaving as much space as possible around the Monolith."

Mercy watched from the walkway outside the bridge, leaning out to catch as good a view as possible in the lowering light of dusk. The operation to bring up the Monolith had taken all day. The Monolith settled down to the deck as floodlights switched on and bathed the object in light.

*It looks like a casket.* She shuddered.

Crew started to gather around to look at the find. She ran down the outside steps two at a time, flight after flight and trotted to the Monolith. It rose to two feet taller than her height. She reached out her hand and stopped her fingers one inch away. *Mustn't touch yet.* She heard low murmuring voices behind and saw the crew members lining up in rows, staring at the Monolith.

Mercy walked around the giant box and looked for hinges, lock mechanisms, or what she'd thought she'd seen earlier: latches. *Ah. There they are.* She saw three outcroppings near the top of the Monolith. They looked like handholds on a rock-climbing practice course and she guessed they were about seven feet above the deck. From the corner closest to Mercy, they were spaced at three feet, ten feet and seventeen feet. *Latches or maybe hinges.*

"Someone bring me a ladder," she said.

She moved along the side, examining the Monolith. *This is definitely crystal steel. It's more opaque, though, maybe because it's so thick.*

"Dr. Teller, here is a ladder." The crowd peeled back to let through a man carrying an A-frame ladder. He opened the eight-foot object in front of her, checked it to make sure it was stable, and stepped back. Mercy pushed it closer to the Monolith and carefully climbed without touching the object. The silence of two-hundred drawn-in breaths caught her attention. *What is going to happen?* Her head came even with the top of the Monolith and she noticed the edge. It was still sharp after possibly thousands of years under the waters of the Black Sea.

Her eyes cleared the top and she looked out onto the surface of the Monolith. There was a carving covering seventy percent of the top cover: a very detailed bull rendered in profile from its left side, with lifelike proportions. She smiled faintly at the part of the carving near its back legs. *Anatomically correct too, and from the looks of it, chasing after a female in heat.* The surface of the Monolith was obviously crystal steel, but the carving of the bull seemed to have been done with an instrument that could cut into and shape the steel as if it were soft clay. *What cuts crystal steel? What's harder than the hardest substance?*

The bull carving was centered side-to-side on the lid, but the head of the bull was further from its end than the feet of the bull were from their end. Near the head of the bull, between it and the top edge was a rectangular design. She couldn't make it out from her angle, but thought it might be something important, so she climbed back down and started to lift the ladder to carry it to the end near the bull's head. The man that had brought the ladder stepped quickly forward and motioned her away.

He said, "That's okay boss. I'll carry it. You lead the way."

She let him and walked to the end closest to the head. Once in place, she climbed back to the top and looked out onto the top surface again. The bull's eye stared directly at her. In front of her was the rectangular area. It appeared to be a plaque with swirling designs inside.

She leaned as far forward as she could without touching the Monolith and studied the plaque. She tried following the swirling shapes. Could it be writing of some kind? She concentrated and felt a twinge in her head like the start of a headache. She flinched from the sudden pain, blinked her eyes heavily and opened them again. The designs seemed to be acting like some kind of optical illusion. As she stared, the shapes seemed to rotate counterclockwise. She fought the urge to move her eyes in the opposite direction, but as she resisted, the carvings inside the plaque seemed to pull at her eyes. A nagging feeling hit her of something familiar and her eyes went out of focus, came back in, went blurry again and then cleared up. She saw that the plaque had writing in it. The whole process from confusion to clarity had only taken a second.

She stared, then shouted, "What?" and turned away from the writing, quickly climbed down the ladder and marched to the stairs, ran up the flights and to the control room door. The men on the deck behind her looked at each other in bewilderment as if wondering what she was doing. A questioning murmur ran through the crew. Mercy opened the control room door, stepped inside and slammed it behind her.

"What's going on, Mercy?" Jack asked. "What's wrong?"

"Everything is wrong. That thing is a fraud!" She shouted.

Hayden's face carried a very concerned expression. "What did you see Mercy? We had a camera on you and the surface of the Monolith, but we didn't get a good picture of that plaque thing you were looking at. What is it?"

"It has writing on it. Romanian writing."

Jack said, "What? That can't be right."

"It is right and it's written in Romanian, no doubt about it."

Hayden said, "Might you be mistaken, Mercy? I don't see how it's possible …"

"It's Romanian all right. It said, 'închis până la pocăit' in Latin letters no less."

Jack said, "Latin letters? But from here it doesn't look like letters, it looks more like swirls."

Hayden said, "'închis …' as in, 'Imprisoned?' … and what was that last part of the phrase?"

"'… până la pocăit': 'Until Repentant.'" She looked at their stunned expressions. "Exactly my thoughts! This thing is a hoax. I can't believe I got so worked up about this. Romanian writing proves this thing is recent and …"

Jack said, "But Mercy, it was buried under fifty feet of silt. How would that be possible?"

Hayden said, "That's true ... and its general location was indicated on an artifact buried for almost eight thousand years. You must have misunderstood. How can it have Romanian writing on it?"

Mercy said testily, "Hayden, I didn't 'misunderstand'. I don't know how that writing got on it, but I am going to find out. If there is one thing I despise, it's being made to look the fool. You two better not be behind this in some way."

Jack laughed bitterly, "You think this is a practical joke? Come on Mercy! Give us a little credit. How would we even do it? Why would we spend the time and effort, and expense to make a massive practical joke like this? That's unfair."

Sounds from outside on the deck caught their attention. They looked through the control room window and saw a man standing on top of the Monolith, pointing at the plaque and shouting. The crowd of men yelled and motioned for him to come down. A lithe man jumped up, caught the top edge of the Monolith, pulled himself up as easily as a gymnast and swung up to the top. Mercy remembered seeing him at the party the other night. It was Vasiliy, the security guard that had ordered the Russian beer. He stepped to the end of the Monolith and leaned over to look at the plaque. He rubbed his eyes with his fists, leaned over, rubbed them again, looked, and then started laughing.

"What're they doing? We've got to get out there and stop them!" Mercy said and jumped for the door.

They burst through the doorway, Mercy first and then Jack. The two of them shouted down to the crowd below and tried to wave off the ones crowding around the Monolith, but the noise from the crowd was too great for them to be heard. More men had climbed on top of the Monolith. Mercy looked around behind her toward Jack and then, a moment later, saw Hayden coming through the doorway. At first she thought, *what took him so long?* Then she saw that he carried a bullhorn that he'd taken from its hook by the door. *Good thinking, Hayden.*

A shrill screech like a dying hawk came from the bullhorn. Hayden had used the detachable mike cord in front of the mouth of the horn to set up a nearly deafening feedback loop. The men below flinched involuntarily. "Attention! Stop where you are! You may be endangering the Monolith, its contents or even yourselves! I repeat, stop!" Hayden then repeated the warning in Greek, Romanian and German. The men halted where they were, looking about sheepishly. A few looked defiantly at Mercy, Jack and Hayden. One of the men on the lid called to them in accented English, "Why did you really bring us here? This is no ancient artifact. This plaque is hard to make out at first, but it says, how to say in English? That someone is prisoner until sorry. What does it mean? What is this thing?"

Shouts of agreement rang out. Men pointed up at them or over at the Monolith. The Russian man who'd climbed like a gymnast looked back at the plaque and seemed to confirm something to himself. Hayden squawked the horn again before he spoke.

"Men, climb down from there carefully. Be careful to not cut yourself on the edges of that thing. Some of you may be bleeding without even realizing you've cut yourselves, those edges are probably razor-sharp."

The talk of blood distracted them. The Russian found that his hands were bleeding, though he seemed not to be overly concerned. He looked slyly at the trio of bosses above, then walked to the edge, jumped off, and stuck the landing like an acrobat dismounting from a tricky maneuver. The other men milled about and mumbled.

A sudden surge of air and noise from above caught them by surprise. Mercy looked up and saw a helicopter rushing down to the helipad that sat on the top of the control tower. A minute later, a huge bruiser of a man stepped out of the receiving room and came to them where they stood near the door of the control room. Behind him came a nattily-dressed and vital-looking Janos Parasca.

"So, no one welcomes me at the helicopter landing pad? My pilot has to bring us in practically unaided. My bodyguard, Rakslav here is my only escort. So I am wondering why. But now that I see the Monolith down below, I am not wondering anymore. Jack, you have done well. Maybe if you learn to keep Mercy under control you may become good executive someday. Now, send all of these men away to their work and tell me what we have found!"

\* \* \*

Jack, Hayden and Mercy stood in the control room with Parasca. The bodyguard, Rakslav, stood outside the door, warning off those crew members that came close with small shakes of his massive head. Mercy could see him through the large windows that overlooked the deck below where the Monolith stood out in the illumination of the floodlights.

Mercy steeled herself against the rising feelings of confusion, rage and repulsion she felt about Parasca. Their last encounter had ended with her barely being able to hold him back from touching the crystal steel sword. She had been shocked at the older man's strength, especially compared to her carefully concealed abilities. Now, he had returned, well-tanned, hair freshly colored darker and looked like he had just dressed in new, tailored, very expensive clothes and, could it be possible, his face looked like he'd just received extensive Botox treatments. He looked like an active man in his early fifties rather than someone on the doorstep of seventy. *What vanity the man had!*

Jack was finishing the recap of the raising of the Monolith and the discovery of the plaque on its top. Parasca looked skeptical and said, "The writing is Romanian? I don't believe it." He walked to the window and looked down at the huge box. "It is too far, I can't make out any details. Show me pictures of it."

Hayden said, "We don't have any good photographs yet. Mercy just discovered the plaque when you arrived. As you saw, the crew was going a little crazy and we were busy trying to stop a riot." Jack seemed to have an idea and said, "I think we should move the Monolith down to the drilling deck by the moon pool. We can better control access to it from there and won't have such difficulty with a big crowd of crew around it."

Parasca nodded in agreement, "I like this idea, Jack. Dr. Teller, do you agree?"

She fought off a visceral desire to disagree with whatever Parasca approved and said, "Yes. I think it would be best if we got it out of the way down on the drilling deck. The Monolith's weight won't be an issue and the cranes are very suited to raising and lowering massive weights to and from the drill deck level. It will make things crowded down there, but we don't anticipate doing any serious drilling operations on the remainder of this trip. Yes, I agree. Hayden, could you see to it that the crane operators get it repositioned to the drilling deck?"

"Certainly, Dr. Teller," said Hayden. He took out his phone and made a call. After issuing the instructions, he continued, "We should have some pictures of the plaque soon, though. I asked one of the crane operators that will be moving the Monolith to first lower his block and tackle assembly down there. For these new cranes, there's a high-res video feed on the end of the block and tackle that allows the crane operator to see what's happening near the hook. We're patching that video feed to here so we can get a close-up of the surface of the Monolith ..." Hayden's phone buzzed with the receipt of a message. He took it off of his belt and read the text on the small screen. "... and we should be seeing the feed ... now." He pointed to the large screen.

They saw a bird's-eye view of the Monolith. The camera was being lowered by the crane operator and the image got steadily larger. They saw the bull carving on the surface and soon the plaque was visible with a small design showing at one end. The image grew clearer as the camera got closer to its target.

Mercy saw the plaque come into focus and then saw the Romanian words again. She shook her head grimly and looked over at Jack. She watched his face to see his expression when he read the message. Instead of the disgust she thought to observe, she saw confusion and bewilderment. Finally, there was the light of dawning comprehension. She just knew his next words would confirm her discovery.

Instead, Jack read the plaque out loud, "'Confined Until Penitent' ... and it's in English. This isn't Romanian. Mercy, what's going on? Why'd you say it was written in Romanian? Not that it makes any difference to it being a hoax. English, Romanian, they both prove that it can't be ancient."

Mercy said, "Jack? It **is** in Romanian. I see it right there on the screen. You think I don't know Romanian when I see it? I learned Romanian when I was in college in Timisoara and I think I can recognize it."

Jack started to protest, but Hayden interrupted, "Mercy, I see English as well. Are you sure you see Romanian words?"

Parasca said, "It is Romanian all right. I see it just like Mircea."

Mercy almost flinched at Parasca's use of her name, but was so grateful that he'd confirmed her reading that she stifled her normal anger.

Hayden cocked his head sideways and looked at the screen skeptically. He put his finger to the flat panel display and slowly dragged the digit across the screen.

"Mercy, do you see what I'm tracing with my finger? I'm slowly tracing the letters of the first word, 'Imprisoned'. Do you see me tracing the letters? If not, what do you see?"

Mercy said, "It looked like you were tracing the first letter or two, but now I don't know what you're tracing. Whatever you're outlining, it's not the Romanian letters. You're not staying lined up with the letters at all."

Hayden nodded his head as if expecting that answer. He turned to Parasca who spoke instantly. "Mircea is right. You do not trace anything I see that looks like the Romanian letters."

Hayden turned back to the screen, clicked a nearby mouse a couple of times and the printer whirred to life a short distance away. Hayden retrieved the printed sheet and held it up to look at. Mercy could see Hayden nod his head, then rotate the page a full one hundred and eighty degrees until it was upside down. He looked long and hard at it and then rotated it back to its original position. He smiled with a wistful, wonder-filled expression and handed the page to Mercy.

"Does this look right?" Hayden said. Mercy could see instantly that it showed a picture of the plaque with the Romanian words on it.

"Yes. Just as I said. Written in Romanian."

Hayden nodded and turned the printout in her hand one hundred and eighty degrees. Mercy saw that the plaque was upside down, but something was wrong with the words now. They weren't just upside down, they were all different. The letters looked wrong and ill-shaped. The strokes were looping swirls now where straight-edged letters lay before. Before Mercy could say anything, Parasca, who had been looking over her shoulder, spoke.

"What is this? Some kind of fake? A trick? What did you do to the words?"

Hayden ignored the question. "Mr. Parasca, is your bodyguard Romanian?"

"No. He is Bulgarian. Why?"

"I'd like to ask his opinion about this printout. Does he speak English?"

"Of course. He is my head of security but also escorts VIPs and visiting government officials sometimes. He has to know English. Not excellent, but good enough. You want to ask him something, maybe? Why not? Go ahead. Ask him."

Hayden took back the printout and walked to the door. He held out the paper and asked Rakslav a question, then another. He turned around and came back to the group. "He claims it says, 'Trapped until sorry.' Oh, and he says it is written in Bulgarian."

# CHAPTER 21 – BLIND SPOT

*"Dream not of other worlds, what creatures there live,*
*in what state, condition, or degree"*
*— John Milton, Paradise Lost*

Jack said, "Wait, wait. But what does it mean? The inscription, what is it saying? Someone is imprisoned, until they're really sorry? Who is it talking about? Where are they imprisoned? Is this thing a prison cell for someone? Is it the ultimate in solitary confinement?"

Hayden said, "If it is, then they've been dead a long time and it's too late for them to be sorry now. But I'm actually more curious about the nature of the writing, not so much its meaning. Or rather, that its meaning is understandable by so many yet this script is foreign to all of us."

Mercy said, "Hayden, you have a theory about this, I can tell. How can this be written in multiple languages at the same time?"

Hayden, frowned and said, "Almost everything I say at this point is speculation, but here is what we know: one, the plaque is legible to each of us; two, several of us perceive the writing in written languages that are different from the others; three, the plaque itself is inscribed in a script that is different from any of our written languages."

Jack said, "I follow you on numbers one and two, but how do you know the third: that the plaque isn't in any of our languages?"

Mercy said, "When he printed it out on paper and showed it to us upside down, the writing appeared completely different."

Hayden said, "Yes, and also when I traced the writing I saw on the screen, it didn't match what you saw on the screen."

Parasca said, "You are saying that we each see this in our own language, but the inscription is written in none of them? Let me warn you that I am skeptical of 'magic' or anything supernatural. I hope you have proof or another explanation."

Jack, Mercy and Parasca all looked at Hayden expectantly. He nodded knowingly to Mercy then said, "Perhaps it is 'magic' ..." he saw Jack and Parasca drawing in breath as if to protest, "... or perhaps it's simply a trick of the way our brains work." He continued, "Think of how we communicate with each other. With speech, before any words are spoken, our brains have to translate our thoughts into those words we want to speak, an imperfect process at best. After all, how often have you heard the expression, 'there are no words to describe ... ' But as difficult as it is, our thoughts get approximated into spoken words. Those sounds then travel through the air where they might be distorted or obscured by noise or other speech, and strike our ears as vibrations in the air. Those sound waves create signals in our auditory nerves and then are processed in the brain into new thoughts, which may or may not be equivalent to the thoughts of the one who originated the speech."

Mercy picked up the idea, "I think I see where you're headed. Written words go through a similar process, only they have an additional translation step, changing the thoughts into words and then coding those sounds into the script of individual languages. But how does that explain this?" She pointed toward the window and the Monolith outside.

Hayden said, "I will speculate that this swirling text, that only became apparent when it is inverted, bypasses the decoding and translation circuitry in the brain and skips directly from visual impressions on the eyes to thoughts in our heads. It is essentially a universal written language that is understandable by any human, anywhere, and at any time."

Jack said, "How can something 'skip' from our eyes directly into our thoughts? That sounds like the 'magic' that Parasca warned us about."

Hayden continued, "For one thing, our eyes are integral parts of our brains. The receptors on the inside back of our eyes are very specialized neurons that sense the light and send those signals through a connection of thick cords of other specialized neurons, the optic nerves, that link the brain and the eyes. In effect, our eyes are extensions of our brains themselves, not separate organs."

"Second, it's been known for a long time that our brains interpolate and fill-in the blank areas in our vision. For example, there is a large blind spot in our field of vision where the optic nerve meets the back of the eye. There are few if any light receptor cells there, and hence, the blind spot. But think about it. Did you know you had a blind spot near the center of your field of vision?"

Parasca had been listening intently and said, "No, in fact I find it hard to believe."

Mercy said, "Hayden's right. I remember reading about this. We don't realize the blind spot is there because our eyes compensate by each having a slightly different field of vision and so the two blind spots in our eyes rarely line up, and our brains compensate for the blind spots anyway by filling in the gaps with image features and colors that are similar to the areas around the blind spots."

Hayden said, "Let me stress what Mercy just said. Our brains fill in the blanks that our eyes produce. There is considerable evidence to indicate that the optical centers of the brain, when presented with inadequate information, fill in these blanks with what it expects to see. This is the principle behind some optical illusions, and why we are sometimes fooled into believing things that we know are not real."

Jack said, "I still don't see how that explains this plaque that reads in multiple languages at once. And why does everyone who reads it come back with a different translation? Parasca's bodyguard and the mob out there say it reads, 'trapped until sorry', but it looks like 'confined until penitent' to me. To Mercy it read, 'imprisoned until repentant'. Why the different meanings?"

"But are they really different meanings?" Hayden said. "If my theory is correct, the swirling characters of this written proto-language short-circuit our neural machinery and jump from optic nerve straight to thoughts. True, each one of us came up with non-identical but nearly equivalent translations, but that just proves my point. No two people ever think exactly alike. Our life experiences, our schooling, our families, our native intelligence, all go into the way we think. I believe our minds are filling in the words we believe we're seeing from the thoughts that have been put into our minds with this cross-lingual script."

Hayden mused, "There has been speculation for decades that there must be some kind of universal language or a universal grammar within the brain itself that all modern human languages are translated from and to as we communicate with others. The old story of the Tower of Babel told about an original language for all of humanity that became scattered and confused."

Mercy said, "I felt disoriented at first when I read the plaque. What's that about?"

"Yes, we couldn't read it at once, could we? It took a moment or two to focus and become understandable, didn't it?" Hayden said. "It reminds me of something … I know. Have you ever looked through a chain-link fence and at first, couldn't focus correctly because your eyes couldn't seem to decide whether to focus on the fence or what was beyond the fence? Sometimes there is a hesitation between seeing and understanding."

Hayden continued, "So that hesitation between first seeing the Monolith's script and finally understanding it was a combination of the brain's processing time and also time to do mental double takes when the eyes couldn't figure out where to focus while the writing skipped the usual translation steps and we didn't believe it and forced ourselves to repeat the process again."

Parasca scoffed. "This is scientific mumbo jumbo. You don't know what's happening here any more than the rest of us. My brain doesn't 'make up' things. I see what I see and that is that. You are asking us to distrust everything we see. Why didn't you save us time and insist it was 'magic' after all?"

Hayden said, "Mr. Parasca, I'm sorry to disagree, but our minds make up pictures every time we dream. I'm beginning to suspect in the case of this plaque, that these swirling patterns bypass our mental symbol and word circuitry and instead are understood directly by our brains as thoughts. A few moments later, our visual centers fill in what they expected to see with words in our own languages. These swirls," he pointed at the inverted paper, "are a written language that anyone from any background can read. Maybe it's because they match our mental circuits so perfectly that they skip the translation process and become thoughts. A few moments later, our brains catch up and make us think we recognize the written language that we are most comfortable with."

No one spoke for a moment as their thoughts spun furiously, but after a few seconds, they all spoke at once.

Mercy said, "... the possibilities for education ..."

Hayden said, "... it could revolutionize language studies ..."

Jack said, "... business and international relations ..."

Parasca waited until the others were finished, "I do not say that I am convinced, but something strange is going on, I do admit that. If this does turn out to be some universal written language, this discovery will be worth more than any invention in history. And ... it belongs to PetroRomania." He broke into a wide grin. Mercy thought the smile looked particularly evil.

* * *

One after the other, Hayden, Mercy and finally Jack had gone to their cabins for what remained of the night. Parasca stood outside on the deck with Rakslav at his side. The Monolith rested below down on the drilling deck a hundred feet away and under high intensity lights.

Parasca asked, "What did you find?"

Rakslav said, "I did a quick examination and got a few pictures. One of the images turned out very well."

"Did you e-mail it to the lab for analysis?"

"Not yet. I wanted to wait until I got your permission. Here is the picture." Rakslav handed the print to Parasca.

The photograph showed the plaque from a different angle, but it was still legible. Parasca was amazed at how the writing changed to become understandable.

"Send it to my technicians. Then tell them to get to work on decoding this writing. The first ones to have this solved and patented in international court will own a lock on the most profitable business ever created. We will need to control this tightly, with all uses of this script licensed through us. If only there was a spoken form of this universal language. If there were, we could also bring down the rest of the world's language barriers. For a price, of course."

Rakslav said, "Perhaps there are more clues inside the Monolith. It could contain more samples of the script. With enough samples, who knows? Perhaps your experts could figure out the key to the spoken form of this language."

Parasca turned and looked at Rakslav, shook his head slowly and chuckled. "Sometimes, even I am misled by your appearance to believe that you are all muscle and no brain. You are right, we must open it and perhaps it will provide us the answers we need. Oh ... and tell our men in the crew to get ready for action if needed. They should be armed."

"Yes, sir." said Rakslav. "I have another suggestion as well."

"What is it?"

Rakslav's voice rumbled, "Communications are still wide open between this ship and land. By this time, crew members are sending messages with rumors of strange things that have been found by the crew of the *Fortuna*. It would be unfortunate if some of these rumors came to the ears of your competitors. I would also like to check the e-mail traffic that has been going to and from the ship."

"Good thinking, but before you review the e-mail, lock down the communications lines to prevent any further traffic. It is a shame to think that our ship-to-shore communications lines are about to start experiencing some difficulties, isn't it?" Parasca looked at Rakslav meaningfully.

Rakslav said, "I will go speak to the chief security officer and see what can be done about these communications difficulties. I am afraid that we may experience an extended drop off of ship-to-shore telecomm for a while."

Parasca said, "Let us hope so."

* * *

The next morning, Mercy called a meeting in the control room to discuss plans for further analysis of the Monolith. Hayden and Jack were there. Parasca and Rakslav were speaking heatedly outside the door. Mercy decided to go ahead and start without Parasca.

Mercy started, "We need to discuss our next steps with the Monolith. The way I see it, we can take it to port and get it shipped to where it can really be analyzed, or we can carry on here, since there may be more artifacts to recover from the sea floor. I don't see that we can really do comprehensive work on the Monolith until we get it to a fully stocked laboratory. The plaque will need to be investigated thoroughly as well. This is potentially more than a Rosetta Stone discovery where we'd be able to finally understand an ancient language by comparing it to another known language. It occurred to me last night that we could be dealing not just with a proto-language. This may be the original language of humanity itself, and going further back in history than ever imagined. Before I started having problems getting to the internet last night, I was able to look up a few things. No other written language has been discovered prior to the 3000-4000 BC time period. If this plaque dates to 5600 BC, we'll be opening up a new chapter in archeology."

Parasca entered as Hayden was saying, "I've been thinking along similar lines. I sent an e-mail to a colleague late last night when I couldn't sleep to ask for some names of ancient language scholars that might be able to help. Due to the preliminary nature of what we've found so far, I've been discrete in what I said. I hope to get a reply soon, but there seemed to be some trouble with the outbound e-mail server this morning. My message got bounced back. I'll check again in a few minutes to see if it got sent out successfully."

Parasca cut in, "Unfortunately, we don't have the luxury of waiting for months of research on these items. We need to act quickly. Therefore, I am authorizing the immediate opening of the Monolith."

Jack turned to Parasca, amazement on his face. "Janos, I would advise against this. We can't do an adequate job of analyzing or safeguarding the discoveries we might make here on the ship. We need to get the Monolith to a university or museum where it can be handled properly."

Mercy said, "Absolutely! I'm stunned you would even suggest otherwise."

Hayden said, "Mr. Parasca, I would not recommend such an action. If we open the Monolith and we find something inside that is fragile or delicate, we risk breaking or destroying a priceless relic. Though Mercy and I have both participated in archaeological digs, neither of us is expert in the field. In my opinion, we run a huge risk of damaging important historical relics. Please do not do this."

Parasca walked to the door and knocked on it. A moment later, Rakslav walked in and closed the door behind him. He stood with his back to the door.

Parasca said, "I have taken all of this into account. I am confident in your diligence and competency. We have a more important problem to deal with. Tell them what you found during the night, Rakslav."

The huge man held out a sheaf of papers. "Someone in the crew has been sending details of our finds to a member of the Romanian crime syndicate. It appears from this message," he held up a paper, "that they are planning a possible intercept of the ship and may act before we reach port. I don't know how they plan on doing this, but I suspect it will be made to look like piracy. Apparently, they are planning to seize the ship and the artifacts we've found."

Mercy, Hayden and Jack were speechless. Parasca continued, "We have to take what we can and leave the ship immediately. Rakslav has detected enough communications traffic to know that we can't wait to act. We have to gather what we can and escape on my helicopter. Obviously we can't take something as large and heavy as the Monolith with us, so we need to open it and remove anything of value. We can't risk losing the finds we've already made or anything within the Monolith."

Jack said, "Sir, why don't we send for help?"

"I have. I had Rakslav shut down the communication connections so no further messages can be sent by this spy that is on-board, but before that, I contacted the corporate offices. They are sending some contract security forces that can handle high risk situations. It will be tomorrow before they can arrive, however, and we cannot assume that they will arrive before the pirates."

Hayden said, "Wait. Wait. We're only eighty kilometers from shore here. This isn't the Atlantic Ocean we're in, it's the Black Sea. In a few hours we could be into shore and seeking protection from the Turkish authorities."

"That won't work. The evidence that Rakslav has found indicates possible complicity with the local authorities. Probably some officials have been bribed by these gangs once they knew what we'd found. If we go toward shore, we'll be stopped by local authorities and then handed over to the crime bosses. Our best option now is to open the Monolith and escape with what we can. The on-board security crew will try to keep the pirates at bay until our reinforcement security forces arrive. Rakslav's security people have some standard weaponry and he brought a few additional items with him for their use."

Jack said, "Mr. Parasca, are you sure? I didn't think our security people were equipped with a more than a few light weapons and Tasers, enough to handle drunken crewmen or maybe prevent some industrial espionage. As far as I know, we don't arm them enough to deal with pirates. I'm concerned that the Romanian Syndicate may not be interested in ransoms. From what I've heard, they can be very targeted and merciless. Just a few weeks ago, there was a gang-style killing of two men near our headquarters building. These people are dangerous."

Rakslav said, "All the more reason to take you three and the artifacts off of the ship. We can't risk losing you or these items."

Jack said, "Janos, I fear for the crew, but if you think Rakslav's security people can handle this we'd better get moving. Let's get the crane operators going and see if we can open the Monolith."

Parasca said, "Get everyone to work. I want that thing open within the hour. In the meantime, I suggest you identify items that need to be removed on the helicopter, especially the sword and shield. Also, bring anything that you might need for removing and safely storing items we might find inside the Monolith."

# CHAPTER 22 – INSIDE

*"Majestic though in ruin"*
*— John Milton, Paradise Lost*

Forty-five minutes later, Mercy and Hayden finished supervising the identification and packing of the last high-priority artifacts to be sent up to Parasca's helicopter. Mercy's phone vibrated and she saw the message from Jack. *Thank goodness that internal communications are still up. Only the ship-to-shore is out.* The message said that the three latches on the Monolith had been released and the crane was in place for the raising of the lid. Mercy and Hayden jogged back to the lab and made sure that they had gloves, tools and all the instruments they might need for the artifacts they might find inside and trotted to the top of the short flight of stairs leading down to the deck of the ship.

Hayden said between huffing breaths, "Mercy. Slow down. Not everyone is an Olympic athlete like you."

Mercy froze and turned to Hayden. He was breathing heavily. She tried a self-deprecating laugh, "What are you talking about? Olympic? That's crazy."

"I'm not criticizing you. I'm glad you're so fit, but a middle-aged man like me can't keep up with a superwoman like you no matter how much exercise he gets. Let me catch my breath before we get down there."

Her expression became opaque and cagey. "Well, don't exaggerate. I'm not a superwoman. I just try to stay in shape."

Hayden said, "Mercy, you can trust me, but don't think I'm blind. I know some of what you're capable, and it's far beyond just being fit. You don't look like you're on anabolic steroids, but if there is something you'd like to tell me later, please remember I'm on your side. Besides, we all may be very glad of your … endurance … before this is over."   Hayden continued up the stairs. Mercy watched him go and then followed behind.

She felt panic. *Hayden knows! How? How much does he know? He knows I don't do steroids? So he just has suspicions. Or maybe he knows a lot. That's probably it or he wouldn't say anything. More importantly, what can I do about it now? Nothing.*

They came to the top of the stairs and onto the deck, then moved across to the drill derricks and the stairs descending down to the drill deck and the moon pool. Cables from the cranes had been attached to the rings at the corners of the lid and more had been secured to the opened latches as extra hold points. Workmen were gathered around the railing overlooking the moon pool to look down on the Monolith as it was opened. Jack watched the bustle at the moon pool through video feeds to the control room and broadcast a message throughout the ship.

"This is Jack Truett. I won't waste time with a lot of preamble here. As you can see, we are moving ahead with opening the Monolith. As soon as it is open, we'll get Dr. Teller and Dr. Travers inside to take photographs and remove any artifacts. We don't know what we'll find inside, but time is of the essence here. We have to move quickly and thoroughly. I see everyone is in their places now, so crane operators, begin lift on the lid."

The steel cables whined as they were drawn tight and stretched visibly, but the Monolith's lid did not budge. A metallic groan vibrated through the cranes overhead and the latch-side bottom edge of the monolith tilted up, a quarter-inch and then a half-inch off of the drilling deck floor.

Mercy called over her two-way, "Jack, the lid is stuck! It's not opening! The whole Monolith is lifting up on one edge. Didn't all of the latches get released?"

The Monolith's latch-side edge was an inch off the deck. Jack's voice came over the ship's speaker system, "Crane operators, stop the lift! The lid appears to be stuck ... Wait! You two men on the hinge side, step back! You're too close!"

At that moment the world seemed to come apart. Two curious workmen had stepped toward the Monolith from the side opposite the latches. With a tremendous screech of metal against metal, the stuck lid burst loose. The freed lid swung open on its hinges and continued its arc up and over. It kept swinging past the apex point and then down toward the hapless men. A look of terror froze on their faces as the gigantic steel lid swept down on them and crushed them against the side of the Monolith. A spray of blood gushed from the ends and onto the crowded workmen.

At the same time, a cloud of black mist rolled out from the inside of the Monolith. Heavier than air, it flowed over the sides and down across the floor below. Mercy felt a massive surge of energy and grabbed Hayden by his shoulders where he stood in front of her, turned and threw him back toward the stairway leading to the upper deck and the control room above.

The dark fog billowed toward her and she leapt after him, taking most of the thirty feet in a single jump.

The crew men around the Monolith were covered in the black cloud. They choked, gagged and fell to their knees, involuntarily inhaling more of the noxious gas. Hayden landed awkwardly where Mercy had thrown him, stumbled to the stairway and limped upstairs. Mercy landed on her feet and charged up behind him, coughing and gasping from the putrid mist. Everywhere on the deck, men lay choking and vomiting. To those that inhaled it, the smell was like being smothered in a million rotting bodies.

At the top of the stairs, Mercy and Hayden looked down into the Monolith. Inside it, the mist slowly cleared away and she saw that a large figure lay with arms at its sides. *It's not a chest, it's a burial container: a sarcophagus. I was right all along, it's a coffin.* The dark haze flowed away from the coffin-like box and the figure inside took shape. Compared to the sickened crewmen near the sarcophagus, Mercy saw that the remains in the box were gigantic. Even more massive than the eleven-foot giant's remains they'd found in the undersea tar mound that had contained the sword and shield, this figure was easily seventeen or eighteen feet from head to foot. An incongruous thought came to her. *It's the size of Michelangelo's "David". Only, that sculpture is the epitome of form and beauty. This is hideous.*

Hayden said, "Mummified remains? It's even larger than the skeleton we found in the tar. Huge! Oh, Lord, look at it!"

The giant was emaciated with brown, leathery skin that appeared stretched but intact. It was naked with massive bony shoulders and long arms that still displayed lean muscles beneath the jerky-like hide. The creature filled almost all of the inside length and width of the Monolith. The head of the creature consisted of tightly stretched cords of sinew and hide over a skull that was two feet wide. Black, tangled hair clung to the scalp and the lids were closed over sunken eyes. Teeth protruded through lips that stretched back into a fixed smile. Mercy's chest constricted with terror but she fought back against the feeling.

Men all around the sarcophagus were on their knees but seemed to be starting to revive from the nauseous fumes that had poured out a minute earlier. Jack's voice called through the speaker system. "Medical team, get the injured to the first aid station and check on the lid side of the Monolith. I fear we can't do anything to help those two men, but be certain. Mercy and Hayden, can you continue with your team into the Monolith?"

Mercy spoke into her two-way, "Jack, are you kidding? We have an emergency situation down there, is it really necessary? The Monolith is a burial box, it's obvious now. It's a sarcophagus. The remains inside are mummified but appear naked. I don't see any clothes, jewelry or any kind of adornment. We can't remove the mummified skeleton in there. It's too big, so what do you want us to look for?"

Hayden interrupted, "Mercy, sorry to disagree, but …"

Mercy shouted, "Jack! Who is that? Someone just went over the side of the Monolith and into it! You down there! What are you doing? Get out of there!"

In the confusion below, someone of the crew had scaled the side of the box and had gone inside. From above, Mercy couldn't see the man's face, but he looked familiar. In a moment she remembered. It was Vasiliy again: the same man who yesterday had first examined the plaque on the lid. And now he'd beaten Mercy and Hayden into the sarcophagus. Mercy clenched both fists and said to Hayden, "I think I've found our spy. He must be the one sending messages to the pirates that Parasca warned us about. I'm going down there."

Hayden was on the walkie-talkie. "Security, move in toward the Monolith. Make sure the medical team is able to get to the injured, but don't let the man inside the Monolith get away. He may try to remove something from it and we can't let that happen."

Mercy was already past Hayden and down the stairs three at a time. She crowded past the men who staggered away still trying to catch their breaths from the noxious fumes that had engulfed them moments earlier. No one seemed to have been killed except the two that had been crushed by the opening lid. *No use worrying about touching it now!* She jumped lightly and caught the upper lip of the foot-end of the Monolith and pulled herself up until she could see into the sarcophagus. It was Vasiliy all right. He was standing next to the head of the prone remains and looking at it and around it. He did not see Mercy. In comparison to the size of the thing, he looked like an infant. The forehead of the mummified creature was at the same height as his upper thigh.

Mercy pushed herself up further and swung her legs over the top edge. She flipped around and let herself down lightly and dropped into the sarcophagus between the feet of the thing. As she landed she felt the hard surface under her. She turned around and saw the man at the other end watching her.

"What are you doing in here? Trying to make off with something before the rest of the ship knows about it?" Mercy said.

"Dr. Teller, when everyone else panics, a man like me sees opportunity. I thought I would check out the find." His Russian accent was thick.

"No you didn't. We know what you're doing and who you're trying to sell us out to." Mercy shouted.

"Do you? I doubt it, but that is beside the point. I see nothing here except this giant naked corpse. I would say this person, whoever he was, was not well respected or he wouldn't have been buried without gold and jewels. In fact, given the inscription on the plaque out there, I'd guess he was a criminal."

"What do you mean?"

"Come, Doctor. 'Imprisoned until repentant'? It could only mean one thing now that we see the contents of this box. He was a condemned man and his punishment was to be buried alive! But even that would have been acceptable to me if he'd been buried with something worth salvaging." He gave a bitter, harsh bark of a laugh. "But that is of no importance now. Goodbye, Doctor."

Mercy shouted, "Wait!" but as easily as a professional gymnast, he leapt up and vaulted himself over and outside the sarcophagus. She considered chasing after him, but decided against it when she heard shouts outside. *Good. Security would stop him.* Even if he got away from them, where could he go? He would still be on the ship. Mercy was left inside with the body.

"Need some help?" Hayden said. She looked up and saw him looking over the edge. He flipped a rope ladder over the lip and climbed down it to the inside of the sarcophagus.

"Did they catch him?" Mercy said.

"No. He dodged past them and through into the passageways between all the oil and ballast storage compartments. They're after him though."

"That's bad. What if he gets a message out? We may not have even the few minutes we thought we'd have," Mercy said.

"We'd better move quickly then, hadn't we?"

They knelt down to examine the legs of the creature. Hayden looked carefully at the feet and toes. Mercy pulled out her phone and began taking pictures. *These will do until we get the better quality gear down here. At least I chased him off and kept him from looting anything.* She worked up from the feet toward the thighs, taking pictures continuously. *He … yes … it definitely was a 'He', hadn't decayed normally. His skin seemed more like tanned leather. There was still muscle definition there. How could this have happened?*

She said, "Hayden, what was that dark fog that poured out when the box was opened?"

"I'm not sure, but obviously this thing was airtight or it would have been full of water. My guess is it was noxious gases left from the decay of this thing."

"Could be, but it seemed worse than that somehow."

Hayden ignored her implication and said, "This specimen is terribly unique and the mummification is very unusual. Look how the skin tissue appears intact. The flesh and muscles seem to have shrunk somewhat from the living state, perhaps through dehydration, but otherwise the remains are amazingly preserved. The skin layer shows no brittleness. There's no cracking, tears or creases. Obviously the sarcophagus was watertight, perhaps for almost eight thousand years. This creature is better preserved than Otzi the Iceman when he was found in the snows of the Swiss Alps."

Mercy said, "But Hayden, should there be this much left of him? He doesn't look decayed and mummified as much as he looks, well, almost like jerky. That's it, look at this joint," she pointed at the huge left knee. "There are the outlines of sinews and tendons showing through the tightened skin. This doesn't look like a cadaver so much as it resembles, possibly a starvation victim? Except we see in this case, without the muscle loss. What is this, some kind of unique preservation process? Maybe he was killed and then smoked before he was put into this box."

"I suppose it's possible, but perhaps it has to do with the unusual burial. Suppose he was put into this box while still alive. Someone sealed inside an airtight and watertight container would rapidly use up the remaining oxygen, if he weren't already dead when they closed the lid. With the lack of oxygen, he'd have suffocated within a short time and died. But in a low oxygen environment, decay gets interrupted and bodies can be preserved like those mummified bodies found in peat bogs. Maybe that's what happened here. But still, he looks emaciated, not decayed. And the skin looks … moist? How does that work? There are so many mysteries here. Such a pity we don't have more time. Well, we absolutely must close this sarcophagus back up at the very least. Every second it is exposed to the air is probably doing irreparable damage to it."

She reached down and almost touched the skin on its leg, but stopped herself. She held herself very still and forced herself to pull her hand back. *I mustn't touch it with my bare skin. I could damage it permanently.* She moved past the broad ribs and arms and up to the head. She stood there for several minutes and studied it. Black tangled hair, broad forehead, wide, prominent nose, sunken cheeks, sunken eyes. *It has some beard stubble. Hmmm. How long does the beard continue growing after death, I wonder? Thick, corded neck. More of the long matted hair. This clump of hair near his hand is detached … was it pulled out?*

Hayden and Mercy exchanged glances and nodded to each other. She checked her pocket and found one of the zip lock bags she had placed there earlier. She opened one of them and Hayden used a ballpoint pen from his pocket to lift the tangle of hair up and into the bag. *Alex said hair samples needed roots attached. These should work then. The creature must have torn the hair out while dying in here. What a hideous way to die.* She sealed it and took several dozen more pictures.

Mercy held up the bag and said, "I need to get these samples to the geology lab and get DNA comparison work done. I want Alex to run the standard series and also compare to the baseline samples we collected." She took her two-way radio out and told Jack what they needed from the DNA lab and asked him to alert Alex of the sample coming his way. She climbed up the ladder and standing at the top, looked over the gathering of crewmen. She waved over one and said, "Take this to the geology lab and give it to Alex. He'll know what to do with it. He's getting instructions from Jack." She watched the man head off and down the passageway leading into the ship's lower deck. The geology lab was almost level with them on the drilling deck and almost directly underneath the control tower.

She reached for her two-way radio again to call Jack. Before she pushed the switch, she saw something move in the direction of the foot of the sarcophagus. *What was that, something shifting?*

In her mind, she thought she heard a sound as if a sleeping person were groaning in pain. It sounded remarkably like the voices she always heard. This one just seemed to be nearer. The voice seemed to indicate extreme thirst and it felt parched and choked. Mercy felt the strain in it, as if it were someone fighting to awaken from a nightmare that held them in bloody jaws. She was jolted out of her thoughts by a trembling motion.

A strong shudder shook the ship. Men shouted outside the sarcophagus. Jack's voice called over the ship's speaker system. "Fire Control Teams One and Two to the engine room. Medical Team, to the engineering deck, we have reports of explosions and casualties near the engine room control desk."

Mercy looked at Hayden. He said, "We have to get out of here. Jack will need help keeping people organized. Hopefully we can return for more study later."

She nodded and a motion in the periphery of her vision caught her eye again. She looked toward the corpse's huge right hand. The hand's knuckles stood out, each almost the size of a grown man's knee joint. The hand was in a slightly different position than she'd remembered. Now the hand lay open at the giant's side, palm up. *Must have been moved by the trembling in the ship from that explosion in engineering.*

In her mind, she heard sounds again as if a sleeper were trying desperately to awaken. She heard thoughts as of someone calling through a long dark tunnel, though the words were still garbled. She suddenly heard a mountainous voice shout, "No, anything but this!" Then she heard a low, thunderous roar like a bull in torment. *What new horror of a voice has my mind cooked up now?* She looked straight at the corpse's hand and waited, certain that the fingers would suddenly spasm to life, but the alarms continued and the shouts grew louder outside the sarcophagus. The hand only vibrated with the shuddering of the ship's hull.

Hayden said, "Mercy, we have to get out there and help Jack's men! I have a bad feeling about those fire reports."

"I know, I know. But ... this thing ... don't you feel like at any moment it will wake up?"

Hayden simply said, "You too?"

* * *

A first surge, and a second. It was like two whispers as light as two drops of water into a still lake. That meant something, but the thought evaporated back into slumber that was dry and thick. He tried to swallow but his throat felt clogged with dry splinters. He fell back into restless, nervous sleep.

Time passed and he twitched again, his sleep disturbed. A third pulse, his thoughts seemed to say, and it felt like something jabbed into his side. He drifted in uneasiness, knowing his mouth couldn't say anything, not stuffed with dry leaves like it was. His tongue was thick and parched. He felt that it would splinter into jagged shards of deadwood if he spoke. A fourth wave. "Four." Numbers. What were they? Thoughts, what are they? Nothing. He fell back into the haze of uneasy dreams.

* * *

They climbed out and onto the drilling deck then followed a group heading down passages to engineering. They stopped behind a group of men that stood to the side as three groaning figures were carried by on stretchers. The light was too dim to recognize the faces and Mercy noticed that only the emergency lights were on. Smoke trailed out of the top of the doorway ahead. She and Hayden stepped into the engineering room and into a scene from The Inferno.

Light came from only two sources: fire and the emergency lights. Patches of diesel fuel burned along the floor. A large block of twisted metal shone with a glow where licking flames still heated it past red and into orange. Smoke hung in the air and Mercy realized that the exhaust fans were out along with the rest of the electrical equipment.

An engineer carrying a toolbox shouldered past a group that was using fire extinguishers. Mercy grabbed him by the arm and said, "What happened?"

"We think someone set off a bomb on the drive shaft near the main engine. The engine and drive shaft are ruined. We're trying to see if we can salvage anything."

"Go," she said and released him. She turned to Hayden, "Let's help get these fires under control and then see what the damage assessment has turned up."

They moved to help but stopped when the ship shook as if hit by a wrecking ball from above. A growling rumble shook the floor. Mercy lurched against a wall but held herself up. Hayden went down to one knee and caught hold of a nearby pipe.

Mercy's adrenaline surged and she ran through the passages and sprang up stairways with furious energy. Clearing the stairway ahead of Hayden, she found the deck covered in smoke. A fire with a huge billowing black cloud curled away from the top of the control, office and lab tower. She bumped something with her foot and looked down on a helicopter tail rotor. Her head jerked back upward and she knew where the black smoke had come from. *Parasca's copter exploded. Oh God, the artifacts were to be loaded on it!*

She sprinted across the deck, dodged around the edges of pipe racks and almost flew up the outer stair of the control tower. Hayden stumbled behind, his mouth open in amazement. She went up the outside stair like a squirrel up a tree.

Mercy reached the stair landing just below the top and realized she couldn't go up any further with the flames shooting out like they did above her. Without thinking, she grabbed the handle of the door leading into the reception floor one deck below the landing pad. As she turned the handle, a fleeting thought shot through her mind. *It's hot!*

Before she could process the thought, she'd jerked the door open. Flames shot out at her. She gasped in agony and stumbled back against the railing, momentarily blinded by smoke and heat. She felt a moment of vertigo and she was falling. Her hands reached frantically. Her left arm bounced off something metal with a crack. Her right hand grazed something and she clutched at it and caught for a moment, then lost her grip. She dropped another foot and felt something again with her hand. She twisted toward it and clenched her fingers with every bit of strength she could muster. She grabbed and held on then opened her eyes. Her vision cleared and she saw she'd caught hold of a railing one floor down from the reception room below the helicopter landing pad. She was dangling sixty feet above the deck.

Hayden huffed up the last flight and ran to Mercy. He helped her onto the landing and they looked up at the flames shooting from the reception room. Mercy said, "All the artifacts, destroyed!"

Hayden said, "Not all, Mercy. The sword and shield won't be melted by a fire like that. If we can put the fire out, we may be able to salvage them."

Thunder rumbled overhead. For the first time in hours, Mercy noticed the sky and she looked upward. The afternoon was ending and the evening was coming on. There was a solid ceiling of dark clouds overhead. Mercy saw a brightening in the clouds and then another closer by. There was lightning in those storm clouds. She turned back to Hayden.

She grabbed a fire extinguisher from the wall near the door. "Hayden, get some help and ..." A series of explosions hit the ship, one after another. From their position on the stairs of the control tower, they saw smoke billow from the front right side of the ship, then a second explosion near that but further back on the right side. The explosions walked back along the ship, one after the other, all the way to the back and then on the left side they came toward the front. Mercy and Hayden looked at each other with dread. She shouted, "The lifeboats!"

Then the rain started falling.

# CHAPTER 23 – AWAKENING

*"Awake, arise or be forever fallen"*
*— John Milton, Paradise Lost*

Hours later, with the drenching rain still falling outside, the exhausted group leaders gathered in the control room. Jack called on the ship's engineer who said, "First, the engine room, we have the fires put out and the injured down in sick bay. We had three hull leaks from the explosion there but they've been patched and welded shut. That's the good news. The bad news is that the saboteur got away, two more men died down there, and we can't repair the main engine or the drive shaft until we get to port: the damage is too severe. Second, the lifeboat fires are out except for one and that one we have contained. With this rain, it'll be out shortly. All the boats are total losses. We were able to salvage three inflatables from storage cabinets near the lifeboats, but the rest were destroyed in the explosions or fires that followed. We found four more bodies near the lifeboats. Third, the helicopter is completely gone. The landing pad is destroyed and unusable. The refueling pump there exploded and burned for a long time until we were able to get to a cutoff valve at one of the lower levels. The reception area fire was just put out."

Mercy said, "How many dead total?"

"Eight that we know of, could be more. The supervisors are trying to get a count but there are men still missing."

Hayden asked, "Power was out for a few minutes, but now is back in some places. Do we still have power because one of the generator motors is working? Can we use that power to move the ship?"

The engineer said, "One diesel generator is still good and another is repairable. We may be able to get it fixed and restarted, but that won't be for hours. I don't have a definite time yet, but men are working on it right now. The other diesels are ruined and a lot of the electrical switching system is burned up. We have limited power, mainly to drilling operations and the laboratories, but we still won't be able to get anywhere with the main drive shaft destroyed. We need to get to dry dock. I would have asked to send one of the launches out to Constanta to return with some tugs to haul us in for repairs, but all of the launches are destroyed."

"Could we use maneuvering thrusters to get to Constanta? They're electrical aren't they? It would be slow, but we could at least get under way."

"No, it would take days or weeks to get to port on just thrusters."

"We can't send an SOS out. The telecomm system was destroyed by the same blast that got the helicopter. Some of our electrical systems are down, the lifeboats are destroyed and with them their radios."

"Great design we have here on this ship. With limited power, many of our safety systems are useless. Of course, in an emergency, the power will always be on, won't it?" Jack said, his voice almost dripping with sarcasm. Then he suddenly sighed and looked at the stricken faces of the engineers and said, "Sorry guys. That was out of line. I know you're doing everything possible. I was letting my frustration show though."

The lead engineer nodded at Jack's apology.

* * *

The next thing he felt was an electric surge of energy. It hit him hard and made his muscles spasm and twitch. A feeble thought seemed to float through gelid murk to the surface of his mind. *That was the fifth one. Five. Five of what?* His thoughts seemed to move glacially slow. *Five.* Some part of him seemed to be counting something. More important was the pain. *Why do I feel so much pain?* His arms burned as if they were being held over flames. His thoughts grew a trifle clearer. *I'm asleep. This is a dream.* He was paralyzed, but not so much that he couldn't feel the stabbing pain as if from millions of needles piercing his entire body. The pain seemed to double as more oxygen-starved cells twitched into half-life. The pain doubled again. *I have to awaken from this.* He tried to open his eyes, but just that slight, infinitesimal movement of his eyelids felt like flaming daggers gouging into the sockets, slicing through his eyeballs. He tried to scream, but his mouth wouldn't open. It felt like his jaws were locked closed and not even the slightest gap could open between his teeth. He tried to inhale a gasp of breath, but his chest felt bound by immovable bands and his throat was collapsed.

Another jolt hit him and his fingers on both hands balled into fists. Agonizing pain shot up his arms through atrophied muscles. *Six*, something inside him counted. Real fear surged into him and his mind leapt nearly to full consciousness. *I'm trapped and blind. I can't breathe or open my eyes. I'm being suffocated alive. My muscles are cramped and screaming for air and water. I can't move except for spasms. What is happening, can I get free? That surge of energy, was it a death draft? What is wrong with me? Why can't I see? What's wrong with my eyes?*

He heard a rumbling, thunderous sound and a moment later the countless stabbing needles leapt back to the front of his mind. Something was pelting his skin and redoubling his agony. The renewed pain lasted only for an instant and was replaced by a surge of numbness and then wetness. His skin felt wet. His hands were moist and drops ran down his face. His skin soaked up all the water it could hold and cried for more. The taut skin on his face relaxed a trifle. His clenched jaws opened two millimeters and water trickled into his mouth and onto his petrified tongue. The pain subsided as his starved tissues replenished themselves. The rain washed over him in a drenching flow. He opened his mouth further and his wooden tongue relaxed enough to swallow a gulp and then another. He spat the remainder of the water from his mouth and gasped in great lungfuls of air.

He opened his eyes and the agony returned. His sight was almost nonexistent and the slightest light stabbed into him. He lowered his rasping lids back almost closed, but still open enough to allow some of the rain in between the lids and onto his eyes. After a few minutes, he blinked repeatedly until genuine tears of his own mixed with the rain. His vision started to clear.

He tried lifting his arm and the bulk of it was almost too much for his weakened state. He slowly, achingly, pulled his hand up to his face. He touched the skin of his face and would have recoiled from the feel of it if his weakened muscles would have allowed him to recoil. He lowered his arm back to his side. His face had felt coarse and knotted as if made from smoked meat. *What had happened to him?* He couldn't remember. *Rest*, he thought. *Drink in the water. Gather your strength.* He closed his eyes again and willed his thoughts into a once-familiar pattern. *Search them out.* He thought. *There is prey nearby and some have already died.*

He felt more energy pour into him. *Seven. Eight. Nine. More dead. Just what he needed.* There was a pause of a few seconds, then he felt strength and life flowing into him in greater and greater amounts. *Ten. Eleven. Twelve.* He counted. And smiled.

\* \* \*

Mercy gritted her teeth and shook her head over the bodies covered in the tarp. *At least twelve dead now.* Rain ran in rivulets down her forehead and over her face. She looked up again, trying to search the darkness. *Would the ones that had done this be coming soon with a ship and boarding party? We're stuck here like fish in a barrel with all of our launches and lifeboats destroyed. Sure, we could put a few dozen men in the inflatables we have left, but they would be easy prey. Anyone that would do this to us wouldn't hesitate to kill helpless crewmen in life rafts.*

Mercy said, "It must have been that security officer Vasiliy that set the explosives and killed these men. They both have knife wounds and probably bled out pretty quickly from the way it looks. He must have killed them and then set the explosives. Nice and tidy. Now we have no way off this deathtrap of a ship."

"There are some inflatable life rafts left and we can gather the life jackets that weren't destroyed. We could put some men in the life rafts and when they got to shore, they could send help to us," said one of the crew.

"It's possible, I suppose, but you can't row from here to shore quickly. The fellow that did this must be working for someone that wants what we've got. He didn't try to sink us, just immobilize us and keep us from escaping. He could have put those explosives on the inside hull, sunk the ship and killed us all, but he used the demolitions to immobilize us and keep us here. Why? He wants us stuck here until reinforcements arrive, I think. Maybe he saw that we were preparing to leave the ship with some of the artifacts on the chopper. Has anyone found any emergency flares that might have survived the fires and explosions? Mightn't there be something in the lab that could be used to create a flare? I'm sure there are other ships that are close enough to see one."

"Dr. Teller, we searched and haven't found any usable flares yet. I think word must have been sent to the mainland about the artifacts we found. Now others know about the sword and shield. They probably know about the giant skeleton we found. They must know about the coffin, the magic writing and maybe even the huge mummy we found inside. Someone wants what we've found."

"...and they're willing to kill us for it," said Janos Parasca. The huge shape of Rakslav moved up beside Parasca as menacing as an attack dog.

Mercy spun at Parasca's voice and said, "What do you know about it? Is that killer some 'friend' of yours? Maybe you met him during your time in the Romanian Securitate?"

Several of the Romanian crew turned and looked at Parasca coldly and questioningly. He bristled, visibly calmed himself and said, "You men get back to your jobs or assist with the damage team. This conversation is none of your affair." He waited while the crew members walked away, noting their sullen expressions. He turned back to Mercy. "I'm here to find out what has been happening. These are more dead men?" He pointed at the tarp. "How? And never mind about my time in the previous regime. Those days are far behind us. They were dark for all of us."

Mercy leaned in closely and almost spat her words. "For some of us the dark days never ended. What did you do to my mother?"

Parasca snarled, "You don't know what you are talking about. I interrogated her to find out what she had done and who she had been working with. Don't call her your mother. I knew your real mother. The man and woman that practically kidnapped you from Romania as a baby weren't your parents. You should be quiet about things you don't understand."

"I will not be quiet! And I'll not be intimidated by you anymore! You and your thugs in the Securitate must have thought you were brave, terrorizing a widow like her! She probably rescued me from a miserable life of neglect and starvation in some hellish Romanian orphanage. I'm glad she 'practically kidnapped' me. What would I have had in Romania? Nothing!" She stopped. Her eyes got bigger and she looked as if a memory had just returned. She spoke slowly. "Did you say you knew my real mother?"

"I will not discuss it further. Get control of yourself, *Mircea,*" he said with a sneer. "You have a job to do now. What happened to these men?"

Fuming, she said, "At first we thought they'd been killed by the explosions at the launches since we found them nearby. But a close look showed that they'd been stabbed and their throats cut. But you know something more about this don't you? You said someone is willing to kill us for what we have. Why?"

Rakslav moved to step between Mercy and his boss, but Parasca motioned him back and said, "I will tell you this. You don't rise to my station without awakening the notice of competitors. There are some that are very envious of my achievements and they would only be too glad to take over a venture like this. They obviously managed to place a spy or two on board. Now they have tipped their hand with this sabotage and murder." Parasca motioned to his bodyguard to move closer to listen.

"Rakslav, it is time to break out some of your equipment and organize the security team. See to it."

The big man nodded and trotted away.

Mercy stared at Parasca. "So you had him bring weapons on board? But why should the ship's security team follow him?"

Parasca said, "He is the head of all of PetroRomania Security. His second job is being my bodyguard."

"You think you've got the angles covered, don't you?"

"I do. I am going back to the control room. Since we cannot leave with the helicopter and these boats are destroyed, we need to get ready for the attack that may be coming at any moment. I fear we'll have more dead on our hands than these before we get to safety," he turned and walked back toward the bridge.

Mercy called after him. "These dead men are on your hands, you mean!" She saw him slow, and stop to listen, his back toward her, "This is your company and your ship. This is your responsibility. The rest of us recommended against this wild chase after artifacts! You were the one who had to have them. You were the one who had to see the sarcophagus opened! You were the one who wouldn't hear of waiting until we got to shore to proper facilities! This is your doing! These men's blood is on your hands and nobody else's, Janos Parasca. You coward! Come back here! Just remember the killer is still on board! He's still here, you monster! If there's any justice, he'll kill you first!"

Parasca's fists clenched, but he walked on without turning. Mercy felt triumphant.

Mercy needed to go back to the bridge herself, but she took the other way around. She wanted to check the other launch cradles to see if anything else could be salvaged. She found Jack at one of them and told him about the dead men.

"Jack, the saboteur isn't going anywhere. He's disabled us and must be waiting for us to make a move of some kind. But we can't contact anyone with all of the telecomm down. We can't get to shore either ..." She had turned to go back to the control room but then caught herself and faced instead toward the stairway leading down toward the port side of the ship. She narrowed her eyes in consideration and then spoke to Jack.

"I need to check on something. You head back to the control room and I'll meet you there in a few minutes."

"Mercy, what're you thinking? That look on your face ..."

"...forget it Jack. Something just occurred to me. I'll tell you all about it in the control room. You go ahead. I'll see you soon."

Over his objections, she headed down the stairs. Jack felt uneasy about her behavior, but didn't try to stop her. He walked back to the control room. Once there, he updated Hayden and said that Mercy would be back soon. He asked Hayden about Parasca.

Hayden said, "Haven't seen him since he left to find Mercy. I thought you would have seen him."

Jack said, "I didn't, but maybe Mercy saw him. She looked very angry. I wish I'd never brought the two of them back together again. I should have refused Parasca's order to hire her, but how was I to know that they had this long, poisonous relationship dating back for twenty years?"

Mercy walked into the control room. She looked around as if ensuring her audience and said, "Good, he's not here. Listen. The submersibles are both still usable. I checked, and they have full electric charges. Whoever set the explosives didn't think about disabling the submersibles. We might be able to use them to get to shore. I say we put someone in one and send them off for help. We might even be able to put any surviving artifacts in there and get them to shore."

Hayden said, "Well, that might be a last resort to investigate, but I seriously doubt one of them holds a charge large enough to get to shore.

We're at least eighty kilometers from Varna right now. More than that from Constanta. Probably wouldn't even get you half way there."

Mercy said, "Come on Jack. Hayden. You can't seriously intend to sit here and wait to be hit by pirates. They could take prisoners or murder the crew, and I don't intend to wait around to be raped."

Jack said, "Whoa, Mercy. Slow down. We're not going to let that happen to you or anyone. But you can't be serious about just heading off in the submersible."

"Well, if I have to take a submersible or swim to shore, I will. I won't be trapped."

Hayden said, "Mercy, don't do anything hasty. Besides, you're the only one that could even think of swimming to shore. No one can do what you do."

She looked at him. *Please don't tell Jack.* She thought.

Hayden said, "Mercy, Jack knows everything I know. I've already told him. You probably <u>could</u> swim eighty kilometers to shore, but you're the only one that could make it."

Mercy leaned in closer to Hayden. Jack moved in closer to hear. She whispered, "Hayden, okay, you're right. I'm strong and fast. Very fast. You don't know how fast. You have no idea. I've been working and training for years. But I <u>will</u> swim to shore before I'm raped. I won't be forced. I won't."

Jack cleared his throat. "Mercy, you need to be honest with us. And … I'll level with you too. Let me tell you what Hayden and I saw. We were shown some security surveillance footage taken of you a couple of nights ago in the ship's gym. We were informed by the head of security. Now why don't you tell us what's up with you? How can you run like that? Why haven't you ever told anyone?"

"You've had security spying on me?" Her face contorted into a snarl.

Hayden said, "No Mercy, we didn't. Sergei was worried about you and came to us. He didn't know what to do."

She said, "There's no time for this now. I'll tell you the whole story, but not now. We have to move quickly. We don't know how long we've got before the pirates arrive."

They still looked skeptical. Mercy sighed. "All right, here's the short version. I'm really strong and really fast and I don't know why. I've never told anyone because it's truly freaky how strong and fast I am. I scare myself sometimes, but I think I'm just an outlier."

"A what?" said Jack.

Hayden said, "You mean an outlier, like in statistics?"

"Yes. I think I'm just at the far end of the normal distribution on strength and speed. If you had a bell curve of the strength and speed of normal people, I'd be at the far right edge with the strongest and fastest of all people. Normal people can lift X. I can lift ten times X. Normal people can run as fast as Y, but I can run four times Y. I just happened to be the one born with the right genetics to do these things. I'm not magic, I'm just rare. I'm way out at the far end of the bell curve in speed and strength. I'm an outlier."

Hayden and Jack looked at her skeptically and with arms folded across their chests.

Hayden said, "Mercy, no one was spying on you. It was triggered by you working out after hours. The security guard got concerned when he saw on the video just how fast you were running and for how long. He thought you might be hurting yourself with exertion. We saw it and frankly didn't know what to make of it. You're obviously a world-class athlete and probably capable of winning Olympic gold medals. So, why are you here? What's the big secret?"

She could tell this wasn't going anywhere fast. She sighed. "I wasn't always stronger and faster than others my age. I didn't start getting that way until I was about sixteen. When it started my parents thought I was just going through a terribly clumsy stage. I learned to hide my ability as I started to understand just how different I was. I became frightened and because of some other symptoms that developed at the same time, I feared I'd be institutionalized. So, I was very careful about revealing my ... handicaps."

Mercy continued, "So the bottom line is: if I need to, I can swim to shore. I don't tire easily. And if I find Vasiliy, I'm pretty sure I can take him. I've trained long and hard and am very good at self-defense. I can take almost anyone." She walked to the window and looked out at the soaked deck below. The rain had lessened to a sprinkle. She looked out toward the east for a moment then spun around to them.

"There's a ship out there, and it's coming closer!" Mercy said.

# CHAPTER 24 – SIEGE

*"Rather than be less, cared not to be at all"*
*— John Milton, Paradise Lost*

Dmitri looked out the control room window of his tanker ship, the *Lucian*. A half-mile away, the *Fortuna* sat, wisps of smoke still trailing upward. He looked through binoculars and said, "Vasya has done his work. The lifeboats on this side are all destroyed."

The captain said, "…and the *Fortuna* is adrift. The anchor is up and the ship is not under power. Radar shows it is slowly drifting to the east. Only limited lighting is on, so the main power must be out. They must be operating on a backup generator."

Dmitri turned to a man dressed for combat and said, "Nicolae, repeat to me again the plan for taking the *Fortuna*."

The man said, "Sir, first, we get the assault teams on those launches and ready to go. Second, we bring the ship alongside and pretend we are here to render aid to the *Fortuna*. The first member of each assault team will be dressed as a ship's officer so they can get aboard without arousing suspicion. Once our people are on board, there may be resistance and the teams are ready to deal with it by any means necessary. Those that don't resist, will be herded together to be held as captives. The teams have been instructed to take care and not harm Dr. Mircea Teller and Janos Parasca. They must be kept safe. The squad leaders all have photographs of the two. Dr. Teller is to be treated as an honored guest. Mr. Parasca is to be chained and put under strict guard. The rest of the mission is to secure and transfer any artifacts that can be moved to this ship."

Dmitri said, "Correct. Contact your men and confirm that they are ready."

"Yes, sir." He spoke into a walkie-talkie, then spoke to Dmitri again,

"All is ready, sir."

Dmitri waved his hand forward and at the signal, Nicolae left the bridge. The ship moved toward the *Fortuna* and once it was fifty meters away, the captain spoke through external speakers that were loud enough to carry across the water in between the two ships.

"*Fortuna*. Can you respond? Do you require assistance? Please respond." The captain repeated his message several times.

In the control room, Dmitri said, "With their power limited, telecomm out and their launches destroyed, they have no radios. They may try to raise us on battery-operated ones or they may use portable bullhorns to reply. Either way, we will approach to 'render aid' no matter what they respond." Through his binoculars, Dmitri saw a crew member of the *Fortuna* step out of the bridge and onto a ladder platform with a bullhorn.

"*Lucian*, are we glad to see you! Our drive shaft is broken and we have no operational powered launches. We've suffered multiple casualties and need medical assistance. Can you send over some engineering and medical personnel to assist? Also, can you offer us a tow? If you can get us closer to Constanta so that tugboats can bring us in the rest of the way, it will greatly lessen our time to get repairs done." The crew member repeated his message.

Dmitri instructed the captain and he responded through the external speaker system, "Message acknowledged, *Fortuna*. We will send launches with personnel to assist. We will also reposition in front to ready for towing operations. Please prepare your ship for towing as best you can. Please acknowledge."

Dmitri had the captain send a command and two of the ship's launches began lowering to the surface of the water. Once down, they moved toward the *Fortuna* while Dmitri's tanker moved in front of the *Fortuna*. Towing lines were thrown and fished out by the *Fortuna* crew, and soon larger and stronger lines were brought in and connected so that the massive bulk and tonnage of the *Fortuna* could be pulled by the *Lucian*.

At the same time that the towing preparations were under way, Nicolae led the assault team on one launch and his lieutenant, Constantin, lead the other. Their boats quickly crossed the distance between the two ships. Nicolae and Constantin and their assault teams and boarding parties stayed out of sight below the deck. The boats drew close to the *Fortuna* and Nicolae saw that rope ladders had been lowered down to them. Nicolae motioned to a man in a white crew uniform.

"You know the next steps, Dragos, right?" Nicolae asked.

Dragos nodded and walked to the rope ladder. He stepped quickly up the ladder and then ducked through the hatch above.

Nicolae knew that Constantin was sending Petru, an identically uniformed man up the rope ladder dangling above his launch. *So far, so good,* thought Nicolae. He looked upward through a small window above his head and watched the hatch opening in the side of the *Fortuna*. He waited for what he knew was coming next: there were two possibilities. If all went <u>very</u> well, there would be nothing but a signal from above to bring the assault team up. If that didn't happen, then the next sound should be gunshots. There was a brief moment as if everyone were holding their breath at once, then shots rang out from both hatches above.

Dragos stuck his head out of the hatch above and waved to the launch below. Nicolae motioned to his men and they began swarming up the rope ladder.

From the second hatch, there was more gunfire and every few seconds, there were more shots. Nicolae looked out a side porthole and saw two of Constantin's men on the second launch begin climbing up the rope ladder. More gunfire sounded above them and suddenly a body fell past, tumbling and splashing into the water below. It was Petru, the uniformed man who had entered the hatch moments before.

Nicolae saw a huge man step to the open hatchway and look down on the boarders swarming up the ladder below. The nearest man was five meters below. The boarder looked up, saw the man looming above from the open hatchway, stopped climbing and, holding the ladder with one hand, he reached for the machine gun on his shoulder. The big man in the hatchway calmly shot him from above. The boarder lost his grip on the rope ladder and fell, striking the man below him. The two of them fell to the deck of the launch with such force that the boat rocked. They lay unmoving. Constantin shouted and he and his men opened fire at the big man above, but he had ducked back into the doorway.

Constantin and his men continued firing for another minute and then stopped. No answering fire came. He sent three men running for the rope ladder to try again, and held the other men back with their guns ready to fire again at the hatch. First one man, then the next, then the third were moving up the rope ladder. Constantin sent a fourth out to get ready to climb up the ladder. Constantin looked up through the small window above his head when he saw an apple-sized object fly out of the hatch. It arced outward and away from the *Fortuna* and bounced on the deck of the launch and rolled to the base of the rope ladder. His eyes widened and he realized it was a grenade.

The explosion blew the three men off the ladder, shredded the fourth man at the base of the ladder and threw the first two men's bodies off the deck and into the water where they floated face down. Their blood seeped into the water. Constantin shook his head and tried to get his wits back. His world had gone silent and muffled. *I've been deafened by the explosion.* Yet, somehow in spite of his deafness, his ears were still ringing. Constantin felt the prow of his launch dip forward. He looked out and saw that the grenade blast had sheared off the front of the launch and the boat was taking on water … a lot of water. The boat continued to dip forward.

"Abandon ship!" he yelled, though he heard his own voice's sound not at all. He staggered on the tilting deck and waved the remaining men after him. He felt thuds that might be explosions above. Constantin felt the jolt of a hammer blow to his left shoulder. *I've been shot. The boat's sinking and we're taking fire from above.* His left arm was useless, but he waved his men to jump and he threw as many lifejackets into the water as he could. One of his men took a bullet to the neck and rolled lifeless into the sea. Constantin was the last off the launch and he and his men gathered on the far side of the boat to gain some shelter, but it was obvious it would sink within minutes. He and his men began swimming toward the other launch. Nicolae might need some reinforcements and Constantin wanted to put a clip full of bullets into the big man that had killed his men and sunk his boat.

\* \* \*

On the bridge of the *Lucian*, Dmitri cursed and barked a command, "Get that chopper up and put those snipers to work. Then launch the second wave of boarders!"

The captain echoed the commands. Seconds later there were sounds of an engine starting and rising in volume and pitch. Marksmen ran to the chopper and climbed in and it lifted up from the tanker. Once the chopper hovered some distance off the side of the ship where the rope ladders hung, the marksmen laid down a continuous fire shield over the boarding hatches and the top of the ship, firing at anyone or anything on the *Fortuna* that might be hostile.

\* \* \*

High-powered rifle rounds punched through the outer skin of the *Fortuna* or ricocheted off the metal walls of the passageway. Rakslav moved further back from the hatch area. *I can't hold this place any longer.* He trotted back to the first intersection of the side passage with the main corridor that ran almost the length of the ship. He removed a disk-like object from his backpack, and held it close to the main corridor wall, four inches above the floor, just around the corner from the external hatch passageway. The disk's magnets snapped it to the metal wall. Rakslav pulled a thin, nearly transparent line out of the disk and across the opening of the passageway and attached its magnet to the opposite wall. He pushed a button on the mine to arm it, grabbed his backpack and trotted a little further down the main corridor. *Let's see how they like this welcome.*

\* \* \*

The second wave of boarding launches approached and this time, with the covering fire of the snipers, the boarders climbed up the rope ladder. Andrei was the first man up and at the top he tossed a grenade into the hatch. The explosion blasted toward the interior of the ship and shot debris out above the heads of the boarders on the rope ladder. As soon as the blast sounded, Andrei dove into the hatch firing his machine gun blindly ahead. There were a few badly damaged bodies nearby, but there was no sign of the big man that had destroyed the launch with the grenade earlier. Andrei stepped forward, sweeping the area ahead with his gun while his men came up the ladder and into the hatch behind him. Once they were all up the ladder, he motioned them forward and they moved inward around the bodies and past the bullet-riddled walls. Wisps of smoke drifted past and he lead them down the passage toward the main hall just ahead.

Andrei held up a hand and motioned for a stop just before they moved into the intersection. With gestures, he instructed the men where to move and station themselves once he gave the signal. He had just finished with his instructions when he caught movement in his peripheral vision and a thump sounded just over his head. Andrei twisted around, trying to see what had hit above his head and he heard the clatter of something striking the floor down the passage behind the men.

The man at the back of the group shouted, "Grenade!" and several of the men surged forward in sudden panic toward the passage's intersection with the main hallway.

*No! Don't run! Drop and cover!* But it was too late to shout. A man ran past him and Andrei saw the man trip over something that seemed no thicker than a spider web. *A trip wire!*

An explosion rang out from the trip-wire activated anti-personnel mine mounted on the wall at the intersection. The man who tripped the wire and stumbled into the intersection seemed to shatter. A hail of metal tore through him like he was tissue paper. Bloody chunks of him flew away from the blast and a red mist seemed to hang in the air. Then there was a second explosion that lifted Andrei off his feet and threw him into the bloody intersection and against the far wall. The grenade that had landed on the floor behind his men had just gone off.

Andrei crunched into the wall and was immediately pounded from behind as more bodies slammed into him. He slid down under the press of bodies on top of him. His head rang with the concussion of the two nearby explosions, but he thought he dimly heard the sound of machine gun fire and felt the thud of bullets striking those on top of him. His consciousness was fading, but still he thought, *how many traps does this ship have?*

* * *

Rakslav relaxed his trigger finger. Smoked coiled from the barrel of his machine gun and he studied the mess at the intersection. He'd been close enough to the corner that he could bounce the grenade into the hall, but still far enough away that he could duck into a recessed doorway to escape damage from the magnetic trip-wire mine.

He stepped forward and nudged the bodies with a foot. *These are gone. Let's see if any around the corner survived.* He grabbed a body, lifted it as easily as a doll and held it in front of him as he stepped into the intersection facing the passage leading back to the hatch. It was strewn with bodies and bloody splatters dripped from the walls. *No one left. Good.* He dropped the body and turned back. He heard a groan of pain from the pile where he'd taken the body he'd used as a shield.

He raised his gun to fire but heard a voice and held back. A man's blood streaked face turned to look at him. The rest of his body was still covered with dead men. The voice spoke weakly, "So, kill me."

Rakslav stepped back into the main hallway and crouched by the bloody face. He pointed the gun at the man's face and said, "Why should I? You're as good as dead already. You'll be gone in a few minutes. Why waste a bullet?"

"It hurts." Andrei groaned. "If I give you information, will you kill me then? That'd be worth a bullet, wouldn't it?"

"I suppose it depends on the information." Rakslav said. He paused and considered. "Talk, then. Who's the boss of this operation? Is it Dmitri?"

The weakened voice said, "Yes. Dmitri Slokov. He sent us to board and take the *Fortuna*."

"Why?" Rakslav said.

"He wanted Parasca and a woman that's on the ship. He also told us to grab artifacts."

"What were you going to do with Parasca and the woman?"

"Parasca was to be taken prisoner. The woman was to be well treated."

"Why? What's special about the woman?"

"Don't know. We were given pictures. She's a tall blond woman. A real looker."

*Dr. Teller. You got that right.* Rakslav shrugged. He said, "How did you happen to be nearby in your ship? How'd you know we were in trouble?"

"Dmitri has a man or two on your ship. One of them we call 'the Russian'. He was supposed to set explosives and disable the *Fortuna*. We were waiting to move in and board. But then you wiped us out." Andrei gasped at knives of pain through his chest. He choked the next words out. "I'm all busted up. Feels like I've got broken arms and legs. My ribs are crushed. My chest is bubbling. That was worth a bullet, wasn't it?"

Rakslav nodded. "Yes, that was worth it," and he shot Andrei in the head.

* * *

The building surge of life energy mounted higher. Dozens of deaths had sent their charge of vitality through him. He felt electrified. Then came the additional souls freed by the two rattling explosions. Then there was a pause and more bursts of energy flowed into him. His thoughts moved more quickly. *Ah, the sweet taste of the dying. It's the one good thing about this filthy prison of a world.* He felt ready to burst.

Mulciber had once described the process to him. "The death of a human being is not like a flame being quenched. It is more like contained energy being released in a moment. It is like a lightning bolt. The life force, the soul of a single human creature, is normally enough to keep the body going for a few decades. But the actual power contained in one human soul is almost unimaginable. At the moment of death, all the remaining life is released from its container at once. The soul burns through the barrier between this plane and the next and that break in the planar barrier causes a small splash of the life energy to be reflected back into this plane. That is what we feel, Moloch, when they die. We receive a small backwash of the energy of the soul's passage to the next plane. The size of the backwash also depends on how old the soul is. The older a soul is, the weaker the backwash. But with children, now that is different. The young souls of children burn brightly. And infants, they burn brightest of all. With enough of those deaths, we could even be as powerful as we were before."

Andrei's death came and though Moloch did not know who Andrei had been, or how he had died, Moloch gasped as he felt that one final draft. It invigorated him and coursed through him and he opened his eyes. His flesh was full again and his muscles rippled. He rose from the sarcophagus.

* * *

Jack shouted, "That chopper is firing on us!" From the control room, they could see the muzzle flashes from the helicopter. It hung suspended about two hundred feet above the Black Sea and one hundred yards from the side of the ship. One of the windows into the control room shattered. *We're being shot at!* "On the floor! Everyone get down!"

Mercy shouted, "We're such idiots! We're being boarded. They may have a tanker, but they're still pirates. We thought they were helping us!" She slapped herself on the forehead. "They'll be after the artifacts! The only ones we were able to salvage from the helicopter were the sword and shield and they were taken back down to the geology lab. I'm going down there."

Hayden said, "I'm with Mercy."

Jack said, "Don't go! Those things aren't worth getting killed for. Let them take it all."

"Not a chance, Jack. Those artifacts are the only proof we have that we're not crazy. I'm going."

"We all go then. We're dead in the water here and most power is still out. We have no control and now we're under tow by the pirates. I'm going with you and we'll try to protect what we found."

They started for the outside staircase but were greeted by a barrage of shots. They were moving and that drew the fire of the marksmen from the chopper. They threw themselves back and closed the door. Several shots pierced the control room door.

Hayden said, "Down the inner stairwell, then," and they opened a closet-like door that lead to a spiraling staircase.

Mercy felt another deep rumble within the ship. The lights in the stair well flickered and went out. *They must have gotten the generator.* Emergency lighting flickered on. *That will have to be enough.* They ran down the stairs several flights. With nothing but emergency lights running, Mercy and Hayden removed flashlights from their belts and turned them on. They stopped at a door and opened it into a long hallway. Two loud explosions sounded from down the hallway followed by a popping sound that she could only guess was gunfire. She felt her heart jump with adrenaline after each sound, but looked down the corridor in each direction. *No one in sight at the moment, but that might not last for long. We better keep moving, but I've got to stop pretty soon and eat what I brought in my pockets. If only I'd brought some more with me.*

They turned down the short hallway and ran to the geology lab. Mercy started to run her security card through the scanner and then realized the electronic door lock might be out along with the power. Almost as if he'd read her mind, Hayden stepped forward, pulled a large key chain out of his pocket and physically unlocked the door. She nodded at him thankfully. The three of them dashed in under the dim emergency lighting. The sword and shield lay on the large table and showed some soot discoloration, but appeared otherwise undamaged. Hayden moved toward the table.

Hayden said, "We need to wrap them up again and get them out of here. I'll get started."

Jack said, "Question. Where do we go with them, then?"

Mercy pulled an energy bar out of a pocket, tore it open and ate it in three quick bites. She took out another and unwrapped it just as quickly. She said, "There aren't many good choices, but I suggest we try to get to the mini-subs. If we can get to them, we can put two of us in one sub and the other of us with the artifacts in the other sub. If we can get submerged before we're seen, we can get far enough away, then surface and maybe use the sub radios to call for help. The subs should also have emergency beacons we can use to call for help." She took three more quick bites and the bar was gone. Hayden and Jack were staring at her.

"What?" she asked.

Jack said, "Did you bring enough to share with the whole class?"

Mercy smiled and said, "Can I help it if you two didn't think ahead?"

Hayden had finished taping up the remaining protective covering for the sword and shield and said, "Oh. I had forgotten completely about this." He motioned at a stack of paper reports on the desk next to the DNA sequencing system. "Alex must have finished the analysis on that hair sample from the mummy in the sarcophagus before the power went out completely. He may have compared it to the ones he'd done earlier on our baseline samples. I need to read this..." Hayden stopped talking suddenly. There had been a knock at the door.

\* \* \*

Constantin climbed in through the outside hatch, assisted by his remaining men. They were the last ones inside and brought up the rear of the assault team. Somewhere ahead of them and to the front was Nicolae's team, led by the Russian.

There were so many rumors about the man, so many stories. They usually said he had been KGB and then had gone freelance after the fall of the Soviet Union, but Constantin didn't think so. The Russian was only in his early forties. He was too young to be KGB. The Soviet Union had fallen over twenty years ago and you don't get to be a KGB killer in your early twenties. It takes more training than that. No, Constantin thought that the Russian had to have been a Russian mafia assassin or maybe Russian Special Forces, or maybe both.

Up ahead, the column started moving again. Constantin heard a voice shouting commands as they got closer to the front. "You four move aft and down to the engine room and secure it. You four go to the moon pool and secure it. Report back via channel eight when you've completed your task, or if you run into trouble. There has been heavy resistance along the main starboard hallway. We lost an entire assault team there to a couple of grenades, so be careful. You four head to the geology lab and check for any artifacts that might be there. Remember to report back immediately if you spot Janos Parasca or Dr. Teller."

Constantin pulled a laminated card out of his vest pocket. It had a map of the interior of the ship. Circled on it were the locations he'd just heard listed. He found the geology lab on the map and led his squad at a trot to the stern of the ship down a corridor that ran parallel to the main hallway. The other teams had gone down different paths so this one was all theirs at the moment.

They made a turn to the right and trotted past pipes, racks and storage lockers. They stopped as they came up to the main corridor. *It's here that we'll run into trouble, if there is any.*

Constantin moved to the corner, back to the wall and moved his head out into the hall for a brief instant. No one was visible toward the fore of the ship. He moved to the opposite side of the passageway and repeated the motion. No one was looking in the other direction either. He waved his team forward and they jogged across and closer to the geology lab which was now only a few doors away.

They moved up and beside the door and listened. There were voices speaking on the other side. Constantin looked at the door and quietly tried to turn the handle. *It's locked. How do we get in now? We could blow the door with explosives, but that might damage any artifacts. We need a key ... or...*

Constantin stepped to the door and knocked. *Maybe they'll still think we're 'rendering aid' and won't realize we're here to take the ship.* He knocked again and heard steps coming toward the door. He chuckled softly, raised his machine gun and pointed it at the door.

* * *

The knock at the door repeated. She turned to Hayden and lifted a questioning eyebrow. Hayden folded the DNA report and stuck it in an inner pocket of his work coveralls.

"I don't know, Mercy. Maybe it's someone who needs help. We did kind of leave the men in the control room behind. Or, maybe some of them came to help out." Mercy turned the handle to look out.

The door slammed inward and into Mercy's shoulder as soon as it was cracked open. Mercy stumbled back, wincing. A man dressed in military-style uniform forced his way in. His men moved in and forced Mercy, Hayden and Jack backward with their raised weapons. The leader looked at a laminated card and then straight into her eyes. "Dr. Mircea Teller. You will please accompany us. We have come to rescue you from Janos Parasca."

# CHAPTER 25 – DEMON

*"Immortal hate, and the courage never to submit or yield."*
— *John Milton, Paradise Lost*

Moloch stood in the sarcophagus, held up his arms to the sky and took deep breaths. He tilted his head back and closed his eyes. A deep rumbling laugh rolled out of him and grew into a shout and finally a battle cry that shook the deck under his feet. He stepped out of the coffin that had held him for more than seventy-five centuries and looked about. *What is this place?* He turned in a full circle, seeing the sea on all sides. *Is this a keep built on a small island? Where am I?*

A group of men ran out of a stairwell and onto the drilling deck on the opposite side of the sarcophagus from where he stood. They were looking behind them as if they'd fled from something and had not noticed him looming above the deck of the ship. He studied them. *What is this clothing they wear? Form-fitting and elaborate, but how is it made? And what are they doing? They seem to be fleeing from something, what, I wonder? They appear to have no weapons, no blades or spears and no bows. If they are pursued, they will be overcome quickly without weapons.*

A sharp, cracking sound rang out from the stairs they had exited and one of the men fell back, his face covered in blood. Moloch felt the surge of a death-draft at very close range. The energy swelled in him. *The man has been slain. How? And what caused that snapping sound?* The remaining men at the top of the stairs pointed some short, metal objects down the stairs and more sharp claps of sound rang out. Another of the men fell backward, blood soaking through the chest and onto his strange garments. Moloch felt another death-draft. *Were they struck by arrows? Yet I see no arrow shafts. What is killing them? It is not the power, I would feel it.*

Moloch stepped softly nearer to one of the men to observe from around a stack of metal pipes. *He points the metal object as if aiming. Strange. I need to learn what they are doing and what they know.*

There was a surge of movement from the stairs below and half a dozen men ran upward, holding more of the bent metal objects. The same small thunderclaps rang from the objects. Men who stood above and on the stairs, fell bleeding or dying. All those that had hidden nearest him were down on the deck or dying. Moloch savored the taste of their life's energy. *From each death there is a small amount of power to be gained, but most of it escapes.*

Moloch took two steps forward covering all of the distance between himself and the attackers. He seized two of the men by their heads, completely engulfing them down to the shoulders in his gigantic hands. He squeezed slowly. Caught in sudden terror, the men's screams were muffled by Moloch's huge hands. *Prolonged pain is the first way to intensify the release of their life energy.*

Moloch lifted them slowly above the deck, their necks stretching. They thrashed wildly with their arms and kicked their legs. *Fear is the second way to multiply the effect of their dying.*

Moloch squeezed his fingers around the men's heads. The muffled screams grew doubly frantic, hoarse and desperate. Then with a sudden clenching of his hands, their skulls cracked and caved in. Blood squirted between the giant's fingers. *And at the moment of greatest terror and pain, sudden death at your own hand was the most effective way to multiply the power.*

Two drafts of energy, one up each of his arms, seized him in streaks of lancing fire. Each was many times the intensity of the previous death drafts, multiplied first by the pain, then by the terror and then by the contact with him. *More like this and I'll be ready to command again.*

The other soldiers turned at the sound of the struggle. At first, they didn't understand what was happening in the darkness, but as Moloch had lifted his victims above the deck, they'd finally made out the twisting, writhing forms of their comrades and heard the crackling of the their skulls being crushed. One of the remaining men screamed and turned to run. One fell to his knees, numbly staring at the towering form in the darkness. Two others raised pistols and fired into the giant form of Moloch.

Moloch flinched at the bite of the bullets. They slammed into him with surprising force and made him snarl in pain. He surged forward and grabbed the men by their outstretched arms as they continued firing at him and into his hands. Gritting his teeth at the pain, he swung his arms and slammed his captives into the nearest walls with such force that one of the men's arm tore completely away from his shoulder. The rest of the man slumped to the deck, blood pumping from the ghastly wound. The other man was smashed into the wall and seemed to flatten into it, half of the bones in his body broken into shards and splinters. He slid to the floor and lay unmoving. In a fury of pain, Moloch grabbed the prone man by the shoulder and pulled him up into the air and close to Moloch's face. The man's eyes rolled back in his head and he fainted. In disgust, Moloch threw the insensate body far over the side and into the dark sea.

With the deck clear, Moloch retreated back to the side of the sarcophagus. He felt at his hands and the wounds in his chest and legs. *This is far worse than arrow wounds. It feels similar, but like the shafts broke off and the arrowheads are still inside the flesh. Curse these animals! What have they been up to since I was trapped?*

With the word 'trapped' still ringing in his mind, Moloch suddenly remembered it all.

\* \* \*

Moloch had been sleeping in the harem that night. He'd roused momentarily when Chalara had slipped out, but had immediately started drifting back to sleep. She was heavy with child and had been getting increasingly uncomfortable. No doubt she'd left to relieve herself or stretch away some of her aches.

A shadow of a smile crossed his face. Chalara was the only one of his wives that had borne him a living son. The others, well, it was hard on them no doubt. His size for one thing, made relations difficult if not injurious to these women that were as tiny to him as their children were to them. But even if they were limber and pliable enough (and many weren't), most did not conceive. Of those few who conceived, most miscarried quickly. Some, miscarried later and often suffered or died in the experience. Of the few that had conceived and succeeded in carrying a child to term, eight of the infants had been born dead. Often the sorry babes were monstrous and could not have survived anyway. Of the remaining two, one survived for two days before dying and the mother died of some strange bleeding disease that took her in hours. The remaining, surviving woman was Chalara and she had presented him with his half-human son, Melekan.

Years later and with her son Melekan a full sixteen years old, Chalara was pregnant again. Amazing. Out of all the women on this forsaken rock, she was the only one brave enough and hardy enough to deliver a living child to him. Now, she was almost ready to give him another, though this one would be a female. He could sense the potential in the tiny infant's mind to one day control the power. He lost his train of thought and his mind swirled away in drowsiness. He breathed deeply and faded into a dream where he hunted a pride of the giant long-toothed cats. He ran after the great felines, determined to bring one down with only his hands. A hunting horn sounded in his dreams with a jolting call. The hunt seemed to vanish around him.

He heard a rumble, then shouts and screams. He was disoriented and opened his eyes. The memory of the dream vanished from his mind. Women near him in the harem were crying out and screaming. A huge rumbling roar filled his ears and blocks of stone fell from the ceiling and came down on some of the women. A giant weight slammed into his head. He grimaced in agony and his mind blinked out in pain and blackness.

The next he knew, he was being pulled to his feet. Groggy, he tried to push away the grasping hands, but without success. He opened one eye. The other was strangely unwilling to open and he blinked heavily at the dust billowing around. He coughed and his chest felt as if pierced by a thousand knives. *My ribs must be broken. What is happening?*

Blood ran down his forehead and into his one good eye. From there it flowed down his cheek and past the corner of his mouth. He spit out the blood. He tried opening his eye again. In front of him stood one of the Cloud Guards, one of Michael's men! *What is he doing here?*

The Guard said, "Say nothing, rebel. You are done with your cruelty. Lord Michael has come to deal with you at last." Moloch wanted to shout or fight, but he felt too hazy and numb. *Am I still asleep?* Another of the Guard came over and the two of them grabbed him and lifted Moloch by his elbows and pulled him forward, dragging him with his face hanging downward, feet trailing behind.

Finally, his wits came back to him. He started to struggle, but he was still oddly weak. Where was his strength? He closed his eye and reached for the power and there was nothing. He felt nothing! It was like the day they'd been overthrown, defeated by Lucifer's treachery. He was cut off from the very energy he'd killed for, built a kingdom to obtain and protect, harvested to build cities and cast down enemies. He couldn't reach the power. He shouted in rage. He cursed.

The Guards dragging him stopped and stood him up, still holding his arms. He opened his good eye and cursed again.

A figure as large as himself stood before him. Michael wore a breastplate over a shining white tunic. A helmet covered the top of his head and glossy hair flowed from under it and down to his shoulders. Gigantic wings stood out from his back. He held a sword in one hand and a shield in the other. At his right and left sides there were rows of Guards like the two that held Moloch. Over to one side sat a large rectangular metallic box on an area of flattened rubble. Arrayed behind the Guards were the monstrous cherubim: sphinx-like creatures with the faces of bearded men, the bodies of lions and wings three times larger than Michael's. Moloch spit at Michael.

Michael ignored the insult and spoke. "You were banished from Heaven because of your pride, rebellion and support of the monstrous experiments of Mulciber. Your sentence here was intended to compel you to realize the folly of your ways and to force repentance. Instead, you furthered your evil practices and amplified them. You've enslaved these poor children and twisted them to your desires. You lie with their females and sire monstrous children on them. You've encouraged them to worship you as a god and taught them the abomination of human sacrifice. But now," he motioned with his sword pointing off into the distance, "I've finally been commanded to deal with you." Michael paused and smiled at Moloch. "This will be so satisfying. I never believed this exile would reform you and the others. The other Archons hoped for the best, but I knew you'd not change. Not after all those ages that you, Mulciber and the others listened to Lucifer."

Moloch said each word as if it were covered in poison. "Such bravery, mighty General. I'm naked, unarmored, unarmed and cannot touch the power. It takes you and your entire host," Moloch motioned with his head at the array of Guards, "to capture me? Cowards. You know that you could never beat me alone. You do realize that the Guard talk about you when you're not there to hear, don't you? They know. They know you fear me."

Michael moved even closer to Moloch and spoke in a low voice that rose in volume with each word. "A great flood is coming and nothing you have built will survive it," he ended with a shout. He swept his sword back over the remains of the harem and the palace grounds as if indicating them as part of his prophecy.

Moloch surged forward, but his guards held him tightly.

"You've even conspired with Mulciber to circumvent your limitations here and to steal the life's energy from these pitiful creatures. You even kill their infants. No perversity is too extreme for you or your brother in evil, Mulciber!"

Michael stepped aside and motioned. Two Guards stepped forward carrying a limp form, heavily wrapped in chains. Michael sheathed his sword and took the chains in one hand. He held the chained form suspended and moved it in front of Moloch and shook the hapless captive in Moloch's face. Michael laughed.

Moloch screamed mentally. *It is Mulciber!* Moloch jumped forward again, tearing free from the two Guards that had held him. He lunged to reach Mulciber, but Michael moved between them and slammed his shield into Moloch. It staggered him. Michael dropped Mulciber to the rubble.

"Yes, we have Mulciber too!" He motioned at the silent form on the ground. "The great architect and builder of Pandemonium and inventor of the crystalline steel lies chained with his own creation." Michael stepped forward and grabbed Moloch by the neck with a mailed fist. "The Creator gives you an entire planet on which to reach repentance, but instead, you and Mulciber experiment with the hapless children here, learning to wring energy from their death pains, fashioning dark weapons in mockery of the true spirit weapons of the heavenly realm. We know that from their life's blood, Mulciber extracted the essences to make first a dagger, then your unholy sword and shield."

Michael slammed Moloch in the gut with the edge of his shield and he fell back against one of the Guard. "Are the chains we made frustrating Mulciber, do you think? Of course, we didn't have to make these chains from the blood of humans. When one has access to the Creator's energy, as all do who are not exiled, the trivial power you soak up from these creatures is not needed. All you had to do to have access to the power again was to repent and be forgiven."

Moloch cursed Michael, "Forgiven for what? Wanting to be recognized for my skills in command? Heaven's army should have been mine, not yours! It was a travesty that I was passed over for you! I am the elder of the two of us. You aren't as skilled a tactician or as skilled a fighter as I, yet you are promoted and I am banished to earth, until I beg for forgiveness! Where is the heavenly justice in that?"

Moloch continued shouting, "And Mulciber is the premier craftsman of this or any age, he should have been raised to design the heavenly city! Why was he passed over? Because he took the power and essence from a few dying human animals to fashion a dagger made in a new way, created particle by particle? Only Mulciber of all of us could have developed such a process, yet he was exiled with me because he made use of the power of a few dozen human lives. Weak! You're cowards! You're too afraid to harvest a few cattle?"

Michael said, "They aren't cattle. They are self-aware and have a better understanding of good and evil than you do. And don't feel sorry for Mulciber. He is about to receive his own punishment. Save your pity for yourself. You've been sentenced and I've come to administer the sentence." Michael drew his sword from its scabbard again. Moloch crouched and tried to leap in spite of the guards holding him. They held him firmly and without further warning, Michael swung his sword and struck Moloch on the temple with the flat of the blade.

Moloch fell to his knees, nearly senseless. *These bodies are so weak! Curse this form and curse this exile.* The wind seemed to howl in his ears and then resolved into a cry, a woman's scream. Moloch heard Michael's voice as if from a far, distant place.

"It appears that one of your concubines has escaped the destruction of your hovel. She won't escape the flood, though. If she drowns, it will be a mercy no doubt. She seems to be large with one of your foul get. Perhaps I should slay her? No. I am told plainly, she is not to be killed. But I will rid us of her spying at the least. There. She'll have to survive the rising sea and only the Creator knows if she will live. Now take him and lay him inside." Moloch felt a dim sense of being lifted and then a moment later, he was lying on a cool surface.

Michael's voice seemed even more distant and spoke again. "For your rebellion, you were sentenced to exile on this world. Now you've

211

compounded your crime and enslaved and abused these children beloved of the Creator, but you are not to be released from your exile. You will continue to be held to this earth, only now with much greater restriction and smaller chance of harming the humans. Until the end, you will lie here trapped and covered in the waters of the sea. Never will you be released from the physical form that cages you. Perhaps this will cause even you to come to true penitence." Michael paused again as if waiting for Moloch to speak again, but Moloch could not or would not. Michael's voice seemed to hint of a smile. "Seal him up now. Close the lid …"

There was a resounding clang of metal and all other sounds suddenly stopped for Moloch. He shook his head to clear it, but nothing changed. All was dark. *Where am I?* He felt around where he lay on his back. *I must be inside the box I saw.* He tried to rise and could not, the lid was tightly shut. The darkness seemed to close in around him, gaining a thickness and coldness he would not have thought possible. *How long will they leave me in here? Hours? Days?*

Moloch shouted and cursed. It seemed the only thing he could do, but hours later, his curses changed to pleading. Days later, the pleading changed to weeping. Months later, there were only the sounds of madness in the dark.

* * *

Moloch ground his teeth at the memory but looked around and tried to take in the ship, the dead men, the weapons and the confusing array of metal all around. *What is this place and what is its purpose? I must have been in there for ages.* He looked back at the sarcophagus and shuddered. *But why am I free now? What has happened, and where is Michael? He told me, 'Until the end, you will lie here trapped ...' So why am I free now? Is this 'the end' of which he spoke? Or has something happened that wasn't planned. If so, how would that have been possible? If I hadn't been cut off from the power I'd still have access to the Counselor. I'd know what had happened. That line of thought is fruitless though. I might as well wish our rebellion hadn't been betrayed by Lucifer.*

He was pulled back from his thoughts by the grinding pain in his hands and chest. *This body feels pain and injury just like the humans feel. The difference is that I can't die. The humans used to call me 'the undying one'. They never realized that it only meant I'd never be free of this trap.* Examining the wounds, he determined that whatever had hit his hands, the projectiles must have passed completely through leaving nothing behind. The wounds in his chest and legs on the other hand, seemed to be worse and he felt some type of fragments beneath the surface of his flesh.

He stepped away from the stairway and behind a large rack of steel pipe. He held his bleeding hands over his chest wounds and concentrated. A nimbus of red light surrounded his head. Threads of lacy white fire crackled

212

and flowed down his neck and shoulders and to his arms. When they reached his hands, the lightning traces seemed attracted to the wound sites and flowed into them. His muscles clenched and spasmed as the agony of healing struck him. *Mulciber once told me that the power flows to the site of the wound, then causes the flesh to speed up its normal mending by many times, but that the pain of healing was also multiplied many times.*

The first visible effect of the energy flow into the wounds was that the blood stopped pulsing from the punctures in his hands. He was saving his legs and chest for the next step. Moloch directed the energy flow by imagining the clotting of the blood in the vessels then picturing the rebuilding and reuniting of the flesh in his hands. Seconds later, the wounds in his hands scabbed over, then a minute later, the scabs fell away. The wounds were covered over with new flesh, pink and tender. He flexed his hands to loosen the stiffness and panted from the energy he had expended. *Healing has always drained great amounts of power. With as little energy as I have, I need to find more power sources quickly.*

He turned his mind to the fragments embedded deep in the wounds in his chest. He could not get them out without resorting to the power, but this would require directing it in a much different way. While most healing required supplying extra energy to the tissues to accelerate its natural healing ability, moving lifeless objects took a much different kind of directed energy. Moving inanimate matter like the fragments under skin used the power in a strange and arcane way.

*Mulciber told me about it. "Every object in creation occupies a very specific location. Everything is some-where, some-when and moving at some-speed in some-direction. The hardest thing of all to change is the some-when of a thing or creature. The Creator has done this, I saw it happen once and only once vast ages ago. The Creator made a seed of the power and changed its 'some-when' to a great distance back along the arrow of time, and as soon as it was gone from our sight, this Universe appeared around us. Only the Creator could have done this. The power required to change a some-when is incalculable."*

*"If you want something to be at a different place, however, you could do it in one of two ways. The hard way is to try to directly change its 'some-where'. It's possible, though very costly with the power, to force an object to suddenly shift from one location to another. It first requires the use of the power to gain the object's truth: all that can be known about it, including its true location. Lifeless things take the least power to gain their truth, but more power is required for living things without free will. For the living with free will, it takes enough power to overcome their minds and compel the truth that not even they themselves know. Then, expending even more power, the thing is forced to the new location by overcoming and overpowering its old location with the new. The thing or creature instantly shifts to the new 'some-where'. This is complicated and uses tremendous power. I used this technique once to move a small object, but that was before we were cut off from the power of the Creator. This method is only practical for the Creator or one of his empowered agents."*

*Mulciber also said, "The least costly way to change something's location is to change its 'some-speed' and 'some-direction'. No power need be used to gain the truth of the thing. One only needs to give a push or a pull to it, in the direction you want it to move. The harder the push, the faster it moves in the direction of the push. Just remember that all objects in creation are anchored to every other object and the greater the thing is, the stronger the anchor. The push or pull you give must overcome the anchoring and the amount of the push depends on the amount of the power you use."*

Moloch had already used large amounts of power to heal his hands, but he still had work to do on the wounds in his legs and chest. He concentrated and directed the power again and this time, the crackling light lanced into the other wounds, but not to stop the bleeding, yet. First, like grasping fingers, the threads of power reached in, cutting through the damaged flesh, seeking those things which should not be there. One by one, accompanied by gouts of blood, the bullets ground past the shredded meat of his body and fell to the steel deck at his feet. At last, he directed some of the last bits of his remaining power to the wounds to stanch the blood flow, reknit the tissue, scab it over and then complete the cycle of healing to reveal the new, raw flesh.

Moloch was near to complete exhaustion. *I must gain more power. I have to start the sacrifices soon. I have to find some humans.* He began climbing up and out of the drilling floor to the upper deck above.

# CHAPTER 26 – COMMAND WORD

*"What can be worse than to dwell here, driven out from bliss, condemned?"*
*— John Milton, Paradise Lost*

The emergency lighting glowed dimly. Constantin said, "Dr. Teller, you will not be harmed. Come with us. I have instructions to treat you as an honored guest."

Mercy heard a voice and felt terror when she recognized the Counselor speaking to her inwardly. "You must not leave the ship with these men. In a short while, a moment will come when you can overpower them. Seize that moment." She felt suddenly very weak, but almost as quickly started to feel some energy returning.

*What is happening? The Counselor spoke to me again like it did earlier so I'd stop Parasca from touching the artifacts. Why does it speak to me now? I could collapse unconscious! In fact, why aren't I in a coma already? By this time I should be snoring. But I didn't go unconscious that last time either. Could it be the artifacts themselves?* Mercy tried to stall the man and said, "I can't go with you and leave my colleagues here. I don't know who you are. You're not wearing anything that identifies your country or jurisdiction. You're pirates for all I know."

"We're not pirates. We work for a corporation that has an interest in what Mr. Parasca has been doing here. I was to find you and bring you safely to our ship. I have no instructions concerning your colleagues. If they don't resist us, they will remain here unharmed. If they do resist, we will kill them."

"You didn't come here just to 'save' me." Mercy said.

"No. We will also take these specimens and artifacts with us." Constantin said, motioning to the sword and shield. "Gentlemen," he indicated Jack and Hayden, "please step away from those items and move to the far wall. Make no sudden moves." He motioned to the other three

215

men in his squad to move in and take the items.

Hayden and Jack backed away from the table and Constantin's squad members moved forward.

*Instead of lapsing into a coma, I already feel energized again. What is happening?* Mercy stepped toward Constantin and said, "You can't take those things. You don't know how to handle them or protect them."

Constantin said, "You will do that for us since you're coming with us. Tell me if and when the men do something wrong with the artifacts. Otherwise, be silent."

Two of the squad members shouldered their weapons. One of them picked up the bubble-wrapped shield and another took the sword. The third kept his gun leveled at Jack and Hayden. Constantin motioned them to leave the room first.

"We go back to our ship now. Stefan, you take the point. Grig and Karl, follow Stefan with the artifacts. I will follow with Dr. Teller."

As Stefan stepped past Constantin and Mercy to lead the others into the hallway, Mercy saw her opportunity and moved with blinding speed. The world around her seemed to slow down. She grabbed the short muzzle of Stefan's gun and twisted it up toward the ceiling. With her other hand, she seized his trigger arm by the wrist, twisting and squeezing. The bones in his wrist splintered with sickening crackling sounds. She tore the gun free from him and with the same upward motion, she slammed the side of the machine gun into his jaw. Before he could cry out from the pain of the broken wrist, he was collapsing unconscious to the floor.

Mercy spun toward Constantin. He seemed to move in slow motion, as if his body were caught in syrup. Mercy took in the entire scene in a moment: Stefan was folding to the floor, his face contorted, his mouth filling with blood. A single broken tooth from Stefan's mouth seemed to float lazily down to the floor, feather-like. Constantin's eyebrows were raising and he was turning his gun towards Mercy. Grig and Karl were caught in mid-step, their mouths just starting to open in surprise. Constantin only completed half of his motion to aim his gun at Mercy when she hit him across the temple with the butt of the machine gun she'd taken from Stefan. His eyes rolled upward and his knees buckled.

Mercy held the gun in her left hand, crouched, put her right hand to the floor and did a spin-kick. Grig's leg broke at the knee and bent sideways at a horrifying angle. Grig held the huge shield in both hands but twisted as he fell into Karl. The shield slammed into Karl and knocked him off balance and the wrapped sword that Karl had held tumbled in a slow end-over-end above their heads. As the two of them collapsed into a heap, Mercy vaulted back to her feet, leaned over Karl and slammed her right fist into his left cheek, shattering his jaw.

Mercy stood over the four-man squad. Only Grig was still conscious and she took care of that quickly with a kick. She looked up and saw Jack and Hayden staring wide-eyed.

She smiled, shrugged her shoulders and said, "Oh well."

Jack said, "There's a lot we still don't know about you, isn't there?"

She said, "You don't want to know everything, believe me. We'd better move. Grab their guns and ammo, would you?"

They tied up and gagged the pirates with duct tape from the supply cabinet. After searching the squad that had come for them, Hayden and Jack pocketed their extra magazines of bullets and each of them slung a captured machine gun by its strap over a shoulder. Hayden had Jack duct-tape the shield to his back with a long strip that wrapped all the way around him and the shield. Jack almost agreed to have the sword taped the same way to his back, but decided it might trip him so he just carried the awkward thing. Mercy carried a machine gun and the squad leader's pistol. She felt almost giddy with energy.

"Where to?" asked Jack.

Hayden said, "By now, we're under tow by the pirates. We have little or no power and only emergency lights," he lifted his chin toward the single light in the lab, "the launches and lifeboats are destroyed and it's no use going back to the control room. We could try to get to the mini-subs and cast off from there ... at least we'd be away from the ship. But Mercy, why did they say they were here to rescue you from Janos Parasca? I know he's not your favorite person, but what was that about?"

Mercy said, "I don't know, but I'm guessing they are from a 'competitor' of his. When he and I were arguing by the destroyed launches earlier this evening, he as much as told me that any pirates would be from a rival of his. I'm not surprised. A man like him probably has more enemies than friends. I wonder ..."

Jack said, "What?"

Mercy thought about the battered and tied-up men back in the lab and said, "... those pirates, or soldiers or whatever they were ... I wonder if the enemy of my enemy might have been my friend?"

Jack said, "Too late now. I say we get to those mini-subs. We have the most important artifacts. Let Janos and his 'competitor' fight over the scraps!"

Hayden said, "Jack, he's still our boss. He's our employer. Should we really leave him to pirates?"

Mercy said, "Well, I'm turning in my resignation effective immediately. How about you, Jack?"

Jack said, "Absolutely. The next word I communicate to Parasca will be, 'I quit'." Jack smiled sardonically, "This company seems to be having stability problems and I have the feeling that it's about to go through some radical downsizing and restructuring. Don't you agree, Hayden?"

With a slight grin, Hayden said, "Well, when you put it that way, I see your point. I'm with you two."

"Good." Mercy said, "Let's get to the mini-subs. They're our only way out of here."

* * *

Mercy, Jack and Hayden stopped at the bottom of the stairs. Dead bodies lay at the foot of the stairs and were scattered all along the way leading upward. Silhouetted in the opening to the night sky above was a pair of legs, jutting out over the top row of steps.

Jack said, "What happened here?"

Hayden said, "A fire fight, it looks like. These bodies are riddled with bullets. I don't think we should go up there."

Mercy said, "It's quiet now. I think we should chance it, go up and try to make it across the deck to the ladders going down to the mini-subs. I don't want to try to make it through the passageways down here anymore. We almost got caught trying to get to the connecting passages to the subs. I don't want to dodge any more of those squads down here. We need to cut across the deck to the ladders."

Jack said, "All right. Let me take a look on deck and see if we have a welcoming committee waiting for us. I'll see what we've got to deal with anyway."

Mercy started to protest, but she saw a warning look from Jack as if to say, "You can't do it all yourself" and so she backed off. Jack crept up the stairs heading toward the dead legs suspended above him and lifted his eyes barely above the level of the final stair. He looked in all directions and then crept back down the stairs to Mercy and Hayden.

He spoke in a low voice. "It looks clear. Twenty feet in front of the stairs are racks of pipe stacked around. If we move to the right immediately as we come out of the stairwell, we can walk between stacks of the pipe and at least have some cover from anyone looking down from the control room tower. Through the pipe racks, we can get to the opposite side and then go down the ladders to the mini-subs."

They nodded and followed Jack up the stairs. As they got to the top, Jack rose quickly and trotted to the right toward the row between the racks of pipe. Hayden followed behind and Mercy brought up the rear. As she trotted behind him, she thought of the sarcophagus, undoubtedly with its lid still open. She shook her head. *Too bad we couldn't retrieve that mummy. What a sensation that would have caused if we could have taken it with us.* Jack reached the end of the rack and turned down the eight-foot wide passage running between the stacks, Mercy and Hayden right behind. They paused. The only light was a few reflections around one end of the stacked pipes from the emergency lights back by the stairway.

Mercy whispered, "Let's wait a minute for our eyes to adjust to the darkness." She squinted down the row between the racks. It looked like something large blocked their way a short distance ahead. *A large forklift, perhaps? No, that's too big for a forklift.*

Hayden said, "Jack, I think we'll have to try another way. There's something blocking the row between these racks of pipe."

Jack said, "What is it? Maybe we can squeeze around it ..."

Mercy said, "It might just be a loader, but if it's not, if it's a stack of pipe that collapsed, we shouldn't go near it. These pipe racks are dangerous: they'd crush us in a second if we were caught underneath."

Hayden said, "Well, my night vision is not improving that much. Let's see what it is anyway."

Hayden reached into his pocket and pulled out his phone. Pushing the button on it, the screen lit up. He turned the light in the direction of the passage between the pipes. Something large was in the way and it seemed to take up almost all of the space between the racks. Hayden couldn't make out what he was seeing. It was a large, curved shape with a coarse surface that reflected dully in the phone's light.

Hayden gasped, Jack whispered, "What?" and Mercy felt her skin crawl. The thing shifted, moved, and seemed to uncurl. Mercy felt rooted to the spot. A large head lifted up and she saw black eyes glaring at them. The thing rose and stood, towering above them, rising higher and higher until it reached its full height.

Hayden said under his breath, "Impossible."

The giant looked down at them and the corners of its cracked lips twisted upward with a smile.

\* \* \*

Jack lifted his gun and pointed at the gigantic creature. He struggled to speak until finally he rasped at the other two, "Get behind me!"

Moloch narrowed its eyes at Jack and waited as if weighing its options.

Hayden said, "Mercy, what happened to this thing? How did it revive?"

Mercy laughed harshly, "How did it revive? How should I know? It should be dead from a hundred causes: suffocation, dehydration, starvation, decay; arthritis by itself should have destroyed all its joints by now. It should have died seventy-five centuries ago!"

Jack said, "If it takes one step toward us, I'm shooting!"

Mercy said, "Jack, it's as big as an elephant. It probably weighs two or three tons. You might bleed it with that gun some before it killed us, but we'll still end up dead if you pull that trigger."

Jack said, "Not if I shot out an eye or two. If it's him or us, I choose us!"

The giant tilted its head as if it had been listening to them. It lifted an arm corded with muscle and pointed it at Jack. With a motion it signaled Jack with a brush-off gesture as if to say, 'put aside the gun'. Jack thought he understood it, but shook his head. Instead of putting the gun aside, he raised it and pointed the gun at the giant's face.

The giant glared at him, narrowed his eyes and spoke a single multi-syllabic word.

The long, low series of sounds rolled out of the creature's mouth. Unrecognizable at first, they seemed to fill Jack's head with sound, echoing and swelling. He felt himself slow and stop, his arms unable to move the gun, his finger frozen over the trigger. His heartbeat thudded slower and slower. His mind ground down to a sluggish pace, seeming to circle as if stuck on something. He couldn't think or consider anything else but the word the giant had spoken. His thoughts felt as if they fell downward to the meaning of the word, and once landing at the bottom of the maelstrom, were stuck there. "HOLD" the giant seemed to have said, and Jack could not move.

\* \* \*

Mercy waited, tensing for Jack to shoot the giant. Even after the creature had spoken something, Mercy still thought that Jack would fire the gun, but nothing happened. A second later, Mercy finally made out what the creature's mumbled word meant: "Halt" or maybe it had said, "Hold" she couldn't quite decide. Still Jack didn't shoot. *What's the matter with him?*

She chanced a look over at the other two. "Jack, Hayden, let's get out of here." Neither of them moved, turned or even looked like they'd heard her. *What's with them? Are they that terrified?*

Mercy reached out and shook Jack by the shoulder. He felt rigid and hard as stone. Every muscle seemed to be taut and stretched. Mercy felt fear trickle into the pit of her stomach. She reached over to Hayden, but immediately saw something was horribly wrong and didn't touch him. He was in the middle of a step with one foot barely touching down by its heel, its toes pointed upward and ahead. The fear in her turned into a thudding heartbeat. *Hayden's paralyzed! Jack too. But why not me?* She looked up at the monster. It stared at her with a curiously surprised expression.

It spoke again. The words seemed muffled and jumbled, but the more she heard, the clearer it sounded and the more easily she made out what it was saying.

A deep, rumbling voice came from it. "Have you come to welcome me, child? To be here at my return?"

Mercy said, "What did you do to my friends? Are they dead?"

"No. Of what use are they dead except as a temporary taste of power?

They yielded to the word I spoke to them."

"What word? Why wasn't I affected?"

"Obviously you are different."

"I don't know what you mean," Mercy said cautiously.

Moloch replied, "Your companions are normal humans. You are not."

Mercy scoffed, "Tell me something I don't know. Release my friends. Whatever you're doing to them, let them go."

"I won't. They were about to use those strange weapons. They cannot kill me, but they can still cause very painful wounds. I won't release them. I run low on energy and cannot afford to waste it on constantly healing myself."

"How did you paralyze them?"

"You really do not know? You are truly a child. I spoke a word of power at them. It goes through the mind and penetrates the will, lodging in the center of movement, locking all motion until the power dissipates or the counter word is spoken. They are too weak to fight it off and their will is too soft to resist it. Of course, only a few have wills strong enough."

"How could a word do all of that?"

"Everything that is done starts as a thought. Words are just spoken thoughts. Some words carry thoughts better than others, and some words cut straight through the mind to the will."

"But that didn't sound like English. I didn't recognize it at first. It sounded like a foreign language."

"All language is foreign to the mind, except the language of the mind."

"What does that mean?"

"Come with me and find out."

"Oh, no. I'm not going anywhere with you. I'm no idiot. I've seen movies. Never go somewhere alone when there are monsters around. And don't ever listen to the siren's song that wants to mislead you."

"Your mouth is full of senseless chatter. I haven't hurt you, though your friends were about to hurt me. What have I done to make you fear me? Tell me, how did I get here? How long was I confined? Where is my palace? When Michael took me, he had me trapped near the harem wing of my palace."

"I know nothing of your palace or your harem. You were brought up from the sea bottom by us and this ship. We were looking for things made of the metal from your coffin. When we opened it, we found you. Now you answer a question: why did the coffin have a plaque on it that said, 'Confined until repentant'? And why was it readable in any language?"

The creature laughed sadly and said, "That sounds like something Michael would write about me. He was my chief rival. When Mulciber and I ..." He stopped talking. "No, that is a story for another time." He took a step forward. "Come, child. We have much work to do. I need you to interpret for me all that I find surrounding me. You are made of stronger stuff than these cattle. You will serve me and teach me of this world that I find myself in."

"Think again, 'Monstro'. I'm not going with you. I and my friends are leaving here as soon as we can. You can just stay here until the heavy artillery is brought up. You may think you're something special, but to me you're just tall. You won't last ten minutes when gunships start pounding you from above. Good luck!"

The giant shook his head in disgust, then moved with speed so great, she only saw his movements as a blur. He reached out and grabbed one of the stacked steel drilling pipes, swung it up above his head as if it were no heavier than a baseball bat and smashed it into the deck three feet in front of Jack. The force of it punched through the steel flooring and tore a furrow in the deck at Jack's feet. The entire ship rang as if it were a giant bell.

She staggered back. The sound of the blow had been so powerful, she was deafened to the world except for a whistling, ringing tone in her ears. And of course, the voices. Quieter just moments before, they became loud in just an instant. The Executioner, the Torturer, all of them were there, shouting, talking, yelling, crying at once for her to run, to flee, to throw herself into the sea. She sagged to her knees, holding her hands over her ears. She felt like sobbing. *Not this too!*

Her distress was obvious. She felt the inner voices continue rising in her. They felt overpowering.

The giant's face changed to one of annoyance. She saw his mouth move as he spoke two short, two syllable words. Though she could not hear the words with the ringing in her head and the cacophony of voices, she was somehow sure that these were the same kind of words that she'd heard him say minutes before as he'd paralyzed Jack and Hayden.

Then her world changed forever. The voices went completely and totally silent.

* * *

As the ringing in her ears faded away, she realized for the first time in her adult life, that there were no sounds in her head, not even a murmur far in the background. She was astounded. *How is this possible? Where'd they go? How long before they come back?*

She cried out, babbling almost incoherently "How did you do that? Can you teach me? Please tell me how! I'd do anything to learn that ..."

"They are the unbodied. They cannot resist the power words. I can teach you, but only if you help me."

"How ...? How do you know I can learn?"

"I said you are different from these cattle. They are only useful as slaves or food. Come, no more of this. We will kill these two and take their energy after all. You are not strong enough yet to learn all I must teach you, so you'll have to feed on them. ... And you still must explain this ship and this world to me. I have slept too long and need a guide."

"Kill them? Are you insane? These are my friends!"

"It is inefficient, I know, but if you are touching the creature when it dies, you receive more of the energy of its soul passing through the barrier between this plane and the next. We could get more through torture but we don't have time. The best method of all is a willing sacrifice, but I haven't any fanatical followers here. Yet."

Moloch took another step toward Jack.

Mercy raised her machine gun and shouted, "Back off! I may not be able to kill you, but you're going to be miserable without your eyes for a while! Get back!"

Moloch stood his ground. His face clouded with anger. He still held the bent steel tubing in one hand but did not raise it.

"You are upsetting me." It's voice was low and venomous. "You aren't immune from all command words, child. Some don't act on the mind. Some act on the inanimate." He spoke two words.

In a blur of movement, Mercy sighted along the gun, determined to fire before Moloch could reach her, but she felt a gigantic force jerk the gun from her hands. It flew free, untouched by her, the giant's hands or any visible force. Up and away high above and over the side of the ship, it rose and then fell out into the sea. Her eyes met his and she steeled herself to leap forward. She had to get her paralyzed friends out of harm's way.

Gunfire suddenly erupted behind the giant. He flinched and turned toward the muzzle flashes. Moloch held one arm in front of its face and lifted the pipe with the other. Mercy saw a crowd of the invading gunmen on the other side at the far end of the corridor between the racks of pipe. They were firing at Moloch and suddenly she knew what she had to do.

As Moloch was occupied with his attackers, she ran forward in front of her friends and spinning, turned her back on the giant. She grabbed Jack and Hayden by the back collars of their coveralls and dragged them down the corridor, away from the fire fight behind them. *Got to get to some place safer.* As she pulled them behind her, the sounds of gunfire overwhelmed the thud of the wrapped sword as it fell from Jack's grasp to the deck. She paused for a moment at the top of the stairs, lifted Hayden over one shoulder and Jack over the other. She huffed down the stairs, to the bottom landing and then set them down again, shifting and dragging them once more by their coveralls down the hallway.

A few minutes later, she lurched into the lab again. Dragging Hayden and Jack in, she shut the door behind them. She did a double-take at the soldiers she'd left lying on the floor earlier, and bothered by their presence, walked over to them and hauled them one at a time to a small meeting room off to the side. *There. I won't have to look at them now.* She wiped sweat off her forehead with one sleeve and sank to the floor beside Hayden and Jack, trying to catch her breath. She heard a weak voice and looked over at Jack.

"Hey," he whispered, "Why didn't you tell me you were a super hero?"

# CHAPTER 27 – FOLLOWERS

*"Yet from those flames no light; but rather darkness visible"*
*— John Milton, Paradise Lost*

Moloch killed the last of his attackers as slowly as was possible without tools, stretching the arms of his victims slowly until each dislocated from the shoulders, then stretching their legs from their hip sockets. The trick was to cause as much pain and terror as possible without letting the victim die or lose consciousness. He crushed the bones of a sobbing man's hands into paste and continued with cracking and snapping every bone in each arm and leg without breaking the skin. The man gasped, begged, screamed, sobbed and shrieked, but Moloch continued relentlessly, building the charge of the man's life force to its maximum. When he knew the man was at his maximum pain and terror, he took the man by the head and twisted it completely around, shattering the man's spine and severing the spinal cord.

*Ah. That's more like it. That's what it should feel like to feed.* With remembered ease now, he removed the lodged bullets from his legs, arms, chest and face and then healed the wounds over. Since he'd been able to spend the proper time dispatching this last victim, he had some remaining energy after the healing was over. *Tortured, they give up ten times the energy of a normal death. I have to get established and get a regular supply of these creatures. The paltry energy I start each day with is just a little more than I need to exist. If I am to use any of the power that is mine by right, I will need their lives to supply me with energy. Curse the Creator and how he stripped us and exiled us here without access to the power!*

Moloch dropped the corpse and stepped away from it. He bent over and picked up the pipe he'd employed as a weapon. Though bent, it still looked usable. He hefted it and looked at the crushed bodies all around. He looked back in the direction where the woman had stood by her paralyzed friends. They were gone. Nothing but a cylindrical object lay on the deck where they'd stood. Moloch grunted in frustration.

*I have to get her back. She is one of our blood, I am certain. She has the right smell and also has the mind of one of ours. Besides, who but one of our blood would have suffered from the nipping of the unbodied? They know when a creature can hear them and can't keep them out, so they centered their attention on her. Those with our blood always attract the attention of the unbodied, but the untaught lack the skill with the power and cannot rid themselves of the parasites.   I had to teach Melekan how to make the unbodied flee him, too.*

*Shortly after our exile had started on earth, we learned of the nuisance of the unbodied. Of course, we'd known of the lesser chaotic spirits, but they had never troubled any of those of the higher ranks before. It was not until much later and after one of our number had sired a half-human child and it had gone mad that Mulciber puzzled it out: 'All of us that were cast down into exile were cut off from the Creator's power. Those of us from the highest rank, the Archons, were imprisoned on earth in physical form. The lower ranks of the expelled were confined here without physical form. Just as we do, they do as well: receiving only enough strength of power to exist. They do not receive enough to thrive or strike back, so the unbodied need to feed on the humans as we do. The difference is: they take power from the humans not through death, pain and torture as we do, but through draining without killing. Also, the humans cannot hear the voices of the unbodied clearly as those of our blood can, but the unbodied can touch the humans through manipulating their emotions and appetites. They nag at them, mislead them, outsmart them, tempt them, and trick them into error. The more they cause the humans to taint themselves, the more power they leech from their victims. Every act of selfishness, of arrogant pride, of lust that a human commits, causes it to lose a bit of its life energy as if it were aging prematurely and the unbodied are there to lick it up.'*

*'And, since they have no physical form in which to store the life power, the unbodied must use it as quickly as they take it in. Of course, there is the rare instance when they have drained some hapless human down to almost nothing and then succeed in possessing the human for a time. Then they have a body in which to store the power, but it is a tenuous hold even at that. The human victims often die during the process and one word of power is all it takes to dislodge them from the human they have possessed.'*

*'Still, the unbodied will ignore any number of humans if they can attach themselves to one of our blood.   The humans that have a mix of our blood have much stronger life energy than any normal human. They sometimes look strikingly different as well, perhaps much larger than their human brethren. They often have Archon characteristics that set them apart, giving them greater strength or speed than normal humans. They sometimes stumble into ways to use the power even without being taught. They sometimes grasp how to look into other minds and they <u>always</u> hear the unbodied and their babblings.'*

*'With those of the mixed human and Archon blood that are untaught and vulnerable, the unbodied can gain small amounts of the power just by tormenting the victim with their insane voices. Every bit of anguish suffered causes one of our blood to lose power to the unbodied. Unless the victim learns to resist, the unbodied may eventually drive them mad. Madness is like a conduit to the power, a flooded river overflowing its*

*banks'. Moloch remembered Mulciber looking at him intently, 'That is what happened to the crazed half-human child. He went mad because we did not realize he was affected by the voices of the unbodied so severely. Once he had been driven mad, the unbodied seized him and tried to take over the wild flow of power. As you remember, the surge killed the half-human and leveled an entire human settlement.'*

Moloch thought about Mercy. *She may already be precariously close to the edge of madness. Perhaps I can still convince her to ally with me if I teach her how to fight off the unbodied. Of course, if she goes completely mad, and falls even momentarily under the control of the unbodied, she could destroy herself, this vessel and everything all the way down to the floor of this sea.*

He walked to where they'd stood paralyzed and stopped to examine the cylindrical package that had been dropped as the woman fled with her companions. *What is it? I sense power inside this wrapping* ... He stooped and picked up the object and felt surges of undirected power wash over him. *By the Abyss! What is this thing?* He examined the wrapping and decided it could be torn away from whatever was inside. Slowly at first, but gaining in speed, he ripped the covering away. Inside was a sword. *Not a sword. My sword! Melekan was carrying you when I was captured, and I thought you were lost! With you, I can do almost anything!* He took the hilt of it and placed his left over the top of his right and cradled it against his chest.

In that moment, with the sword in hand, Moloch felt threads of energy reaching from it into him. No word of command was necessary with this item. It took only a mental easing: an embrace of the power stored in the sword. He almost heard the ages-distant screams of terror and agony that had built the weapon layer by layer. Still holding the sword, he relaxed his arms and let them hang by his sides, the sword in his right. He closed his eyes in complete surrender and felt himself fill with renewed energy. He smiled and remembered the Blood Forge and the making of the sword and shield. It had taken the blood of thousands of tortured humans, all sacrificed in one massive orgy of death.

After its making, Moloch had held the sword for years, testing it in battle dozens of times and using the sword in countless executions, but the sword was more than a weapon, it was a container for the power. For all of the time of their exile on earth, he and Mulciber had lamented the limitations of their bodies. Beings like himself and Mulciber originally transcended physical form, but part of the punishment he and the other fallen had received was to be doomed to containment in these envelopes of flesh. One result of that was to be limited in the usage of the power. These frail forms could only hold so much life energy and each day, just like the cursed humans, they only received enough new energy to survive through until the next day.

*Mulciber told me, "The Creator's power permeates everything, available to be drawn upon, but the amount of the power that a being can draw depends on its nature. Each being's nature limits in some way the amount of the power and the use to which it can be put. Those of the lower forms are unaware of the power and draw only that which they need for their meager existence. They do not know or care about all that could be done with the power if they were able to draw on it and direct it. Those of us that transcend the lower forms are aware of it and able to draw vast amounts of it. We can put it to use in ways that are almost unlimited. The more creative of us can even fashion new uses. But our exile here ended that.'*

Moloch wondered. *Where is Mulciber now? Was he imprisoned as I was?* Mulciber had painstakingly worked, experimented and finally created a structure made out of the tiniest particles, and like a living creature, it could store the power. Until then, only living beings, whether purely physical or immaterial, could store and use the power. The structure that Mulciber fashioned, though not alive, had to be built from the very substance of something that was alive. At the moment of the structure's creation and the living creature's death, Mulciber had succeeded twice: first, in drawing its building blocks from the living and second, in trapping the echo of life energy of the dying.

Moloch had finally sent the sword and shield with his son Melekan when he'd traveled to visit Mulciber at Varnach. Though he had created them, Mulciber had wanted to examine them both in deeper ways to study them more carefully and to understand better the limitations of what he and Moloch had created. While Melekan was en route to Mulciber, Moloch had been captured by Michael and his horde and then entombed. Moloch shuddered with the remembrance. *I must not let Michael locate me again. My physical form might survive, but my mind surely could not withstand that living death again.*

Moloch brought his thoughts back to the present and with sword in hand, he walked cautiously down the corridor of pipe racks and stepped to the top of the stairs that went down into the lower levels of the ship. He moved carefully, picking his steps. When he got to the bottom, he towered above the opening to the deck below. *She said this thing I stand upon is a ship, though I never knew such a vessel when I was here before. I'll never be able to fit in these passages below deck. I might be able to crawl on my belly for a while, but I'd not get anywhere. I'll never be able to move freely down there.*

*I'll have to compel obedience and get some of them to act for me. I'll need to gather a group of followers. I must find out about this ship, determine how many people are on board and capture and compel them. Then I will send some of them after the woman. If she destroys some of them, so much the better. I'll get the life boost from their deaths and cause her anguish at the same time. She's too soft to realize that she needs their deaths. She'll be one of those that can't accept the necessity of it. I'll have to change her mind.*

\* \* \*

228

Mercy helped Hayden back to his feet and over to a chair. The numbness and stiffness were finally wearing off, but Hayden was shaky still. Jack was recovering more quickly. Hayden patted himself absently and withdrew some papers from his pocket, seemed to realize what they were and started looking at them. He spread them out on the table next to him.

Jack said, "Hayden, what happened to us? I felt rooted in place. Every part of me was immobile but I could still hear what was going on. I could see too, but only in the direction my eyes were already looking. I couldn't even move my eyes!"

Hayden swallowed and slumped back into his chair, his hands on the papers. "You're right, but it wasn't total paralysis. My heart slowed down, but it still beat. I believe my breathing slowed down as well, but didn't stop. I'm trying to puzzle through it. I remember hearing the giant speak a word. I think it said, 'HALT' and then time seemed to slow down for me. That much I remember. But the word seemed almost to bounce around in my head, like it was moving from place to place in my mind, switching things off and slowing things down. Maybe that's what a computer feels like when it is infected with a virus. That one word overpowered all my voluntary actions. Amazing."

Jack said, "But why didn't it affect Mercy? She kept going and got us out of there, thankfully."

Hayden said, "Mercy, the giant seemed to be suggesting that he wasn't surprised by your lack of paralysis, like he expected it."

Jack said, "I remember now. He talked about how certain kinds of words went straight to the nerve center of the brain ... but he didn't expect Mercy to be affected."

Hayden agreed, "... words of power, he called them."

Jack said, "He talked about killing us to get our energy, like he was some kind of giant vampire."

Hayden said, "... and he said something about ways to get more life energy from us through torture ... or even through fanatical followers offering themselves as sacrifices."

Jack said, "I wish I could remember more ..."

Mercy said, "It'll come back to you. You two need to rest. I've locked and blocked the door. Hopefully you can get a nap at least. Both of you are running on fumes."

Hayden looked at her with concern. "Mercy, what was that the monster said about you hearing voices? Do you really hear voices sometimes?"

Mercy looked at them helplessly, moved to one of the chairs and sat wearily. *Haven't I told them enough lies? I can't lie about this anymore.*

She hung her head, her voice clouded with emotion and said, "Yes. But not just sometimes. All the time since I was a teenager. I hear them all the time. My head is filled with voices. I can mostly damp it down with medication, but I hadn't been able to get to my cabin today to take my dose. The voices came on me with a vengeance just now when we were out there. It almost drove me to my knees, then the monster said a couple of words and the voices went silent. They haven't come back. I keep waiting for a whisper or two to start in the back of my head, first the screaming and the weeping voices, followed by the murderous and sadistic ones, then all the rest. Hundreds, maybe thousands of voices are constantly shouting in my head." She raised her head and looked at Jack. Tears welled up in her eyes. "Did you know I'm a severe schizophrenic? I have to take anti-psychotic drugs. I'm a mad woman." The tears overflowed and fell down her cheeks. Her voice fell to a whisper, "I never told you. I couldn't."

Jack came to her and knelt in front of her. He reached up his right hand and gently lifted her chin with his thumb and forefinger. Tears ran onto his hand. He looked at her in silence for a moment and said softly and slowly, "I don't care about that."

She looked at him, tears flowing. Tragedy was etched on her face, but her eyebrows arched slowly, disbelievingly.

"Why not?" she asked, a distant note of hope against all odds creeping into her whisper.

Jack said, "Because I don't believe it."

She looked at him in confusion and started to say with an edge of despair, "No, it's true! I do hear ..."

He took her hands and squeezed them gently. "Mercy, I believe you hear the voices and have to take the drugs. I just don't believe you're crazy. I believe there are doctors that diagnosed you like you say. But don't you remember what that thing said? I do. It said, 'Obviously you are different. Your companions are normal humans. You are not.' That much I remember clearly."

Mercy said bitterly, "Different. Different as in insane."

Jack spoke gently, "No, Mercy. Different as in a step above. He didn't expect us to resist him and he didn't expect you to need to resist. He tried to recruit you. You told him to get lost, but he tried to get you to join him."

"I don't know why he said those things. It was horrible." Mercy said.

Hayden cleared his throat. Mercy realized it had been some time since he had said anything and looked at him. He had paper reports spread across the table in from of him. He locked eyes with her.

"I know why he said it," Hayden said, his face expressionless.

"Why?" Jack said.

"DNA."

* * *

"What's that supposed to mean?" said Jack. He looked over at Mercy. She had a frightened look on her face.

Hayden said, "You remember when Alex took cheek swabs so he could run DNA comparison to the Goliath bones we found at the first site? Alex also got samples from a dozen more of our crew. He ran the tests and did all the compares. These are the results."

Mercy said, "... and?"

"In all the confusion of the last twenty-four hours, I'd forgotten about the sample we also collected from the sarcophagus. Remember that, Mercy?"

"Sure, we were inside next to the mummy, at least that's what we called it at the time, and we picked up some of its hair and put it in a sample bag and sent it on to Alex for testing."

Hayden said, "The results from that analysis are here too."

Jack said, "Hayden, get on with it. You're killing us. What does it say?"

Hayden said, "I'll start with Goliath and that monster out there on deck. No huge surprise here, but they are related. Close blood relations ... probably father and son. Their patrilineal DNA matches completely, but their mitochondrial DNA from the mother's side doesn't match at all, so they can't be full brothers. They could be half-brothers through their father, but with the size difference, my guess is the big one out there is the father and Goliath was his son.

Mercy murmured, "Interesting. I had wondered ..."

"The next thing is a little more shocking. They only have a ninety-nine percent overlap with human DNA."

Jack said, "Well, isn't that pretty close? Considering some of the obvious differences there are between us and them ... like the gigantism, for instance?"

Hayden said, "It's more than that, Jack. Even Gorillas and Chimpanzees are very close genetically to humans, but they're still not human. Those two giants aren't human either, though they are close enough that they can interbreed with humans."

Mercy said, "Wait. How can you tell that? I didn't know that could be determined from DNA samples."

Hayden said, "You're right. It usually can't be, but in this case, well you'll understand when I get there."

Hayden continued, "I'm going to call that thing out there the Monster for ease of reference. The mitochondrial DNA tells us a lot here. Goliath and the Monster are related through their male line but had different mothers. They could be father-son, grandfather-son, uncle-nephew, but not full brothers with the same mother. Got it?" They nodded.

"There were other samples taken though. A lot of us and members of the crew volunteered samples. Those are in here too. I'll skip past the details about what tribes and ethnic groups we all came from and jump to this." Hayden stepped closer and took one of her hands in his. Jack saw what was happening, stepped behind and put a hand on her shoulder. Mercy swallowed heavily.

"You <u>are</u> something different and you aren't quite human. Almost, but not quite. You're more than ninety-nine percent human, but still, not quite. And, you're related to them. Somewhere back down the line, you and Goliath share a common female ancestor. The mitochondrial DNA proves the female relation. And just to add strangeness to this mix, no other humans tested were related to that common female ancestor that you and Goliath share. Furthermore, the maternal DNA you share is from a woman that is one hundred percent human. Your non-human side comes from the paternal side and you and Goliath seem to have a similar paternal line."

"So here is my hypothesis: I believe that Monster out there is probably the father of Goliath whose bones we found in the tar pit. Neither Goliath or the Monster are human. Nearly so, but not quite. Goliath is more human than the Monster and you and Goliath have a common female ancestor. I think she was Goliath's mother. That would be your three-hundred-generations-removed-grandmother. If I'm correct, your common male ancestor was likely that Monster. So that probably makes him your three-hundred-and-one-generations-removed-grandfather. Which explains why you're not quite human, but more so than them. It also possibly explains why we were paralyzed and you weren't. You're one of them. We're not."

\* \* \*

Mercy spoke before Jack could get a word out. "Jack, don't say it. I just know you're going to say something lame like, 'that doesn't matter.' Don't say it. It does matter. In fact," her voice changed to a stronger tone, "Maybe I'm relieved this has happened. It finally gives me some reasons and a framework for what has been happening to me all my life."

She stood up and paced back and forth. A feverish gleam shined from her eyes and her mouth was set in a grim line. "I've heard these hellish voices all my adult life. I never knew why, but now I know that I'm related to monsters and giants. I've had this freakish strength and endurance and I never knew why, but maybe it's due to the same thing. I have the appetite of a horse and eat ten thousand calories a day just to maintain weight. I just thought I was a freak, but now maybe I know what it's all about. I'm not entirely human."

Hayden stood up and walked to her. He gently took her arm and walked her to one corner of the lab. He turned back and saw Jack looking with raised eyebrows as if to say, "What's up?" Hayden lifted a hand and motioned to Jack in a gesture that meant, "Don't worry, I'll take care of this."

Hayden spoke softly to her and said, "There's one other thing you need to know. The DNA analysis showed something else. Janos Parasca shares the same maternal DNA as you and Goliath."

Her eyes flared wider. She whispered, "What?"

Hayden continued, "I pulled you aside because I thought you might not want me to blurt this out in front of Jack. You can tell him your own way in your own time if you decide to do so."

She protested, "But you said no one else tested showed that maternal DNA."

Hayden said, "I said, 'no other human tested', not 'anyone else tested'." He waited and saw in her eyes when the truth sunk in.

She said, "So he's not completely human either?"

"That's right, but the other thing is this: your paternal DNA matches Janos'. I'm certain he is your biological father."

She hissed, "No!"

Hayden said, "It's true. He is your father, and both through him and through your mother, you are related to Goliath and the Monster. Maybe it was the convergence of the male and female lines that made you so unique."

She hung her head, clenched her fists until her arms trembled and whispered repeatedly, "No!" She squeezed her eyes shut and turned her back to him.

Hayden started to reach out to her, but thought better of it and left her standing there to go back to Jack. He sat down across from Jack but held out a hand to stop his questions. He only said, "She'll tell you what she wants you to know."

Jack looked helplessly over at Mercy. She stood facing the opposite wall and leaning into it with one hand. Her other hand was clenched, the fingers blanched pale from the strain.

Jack shook his head slowly, sadly. *I wish I could help her.*

Hayden put a hand to his chin thoughtfully. *Mercy and Parasca are both descended from those things and Parasca is her father too. How horrible. But what did the Monster say about gaining energy if it had killed us? He implied that both he and Mercy would gain energy by our deaths, so he can sense that Mercy is a similar being to himself. He said something and caused the voices in Mercy's head to stop too. He called the voices the 'unbodied', meaning that he believed them to be immaterial creatures. And the energy he used on us, it can stop Mercy's voices and move objects by power of will. It can paralyze people. What else can it do? He said something about getting a small amount of energy by killing us, more through pain and torture, and the most energy of all by what ... something about willing sacrificial victims? That's it. He said he didn't have any fanatical followers yet that would willingly sacrifice themselves for him. That's a chilling thought, and something I don't want to be around to see.*

* * *

The Russian stepped over a row of bloody, uniformed bodies. *This will not do, I only have so many men.* He turned to one of his officers still standing from Dmitri's forces.

"I don't want any more ammunition wasted. Any unarmed crew members should just be rounded up and confined. The ship's security force is the group on-board that is still dangerous. That creature on the deck is something else entirely. It seems to be enraged by our gunfire but not seriously hurt while we, on the other hand, have lost over a dozen men to it. Leave it alone for now. Obviously it wasn't dead when we recovered it in that coffin, only unconscious. If it had been dead, Dmitri would have wanted it retrieved for his collection, but alive, it's just a menace. We can't deal with it until heavier weapons are brought to bear."

"In the meantime, we need to get the artifacts that can be retrieved and get off the ship before Dmitri has it scuttled in deeper water. What happened to that team that went to the geology lab?"

The officer said, "They never returned, sir. Perhaps they were taken by the ship's security officers."

"Position the men in barricades at the hallways approaching the geology lab and keep them in position until I return. Make sure, though, that they are ready to leave as soon as I return. Looks like I'll have to take care of this myself."

\* \* \*

Parasca motioned to Rakslav to come up past the rest of their men to speak with him.

"How many were hurt in that last fire fight?" Parasca asked.

"Two dead, three injured. I think we killed four of the pirates and wounded two or three more, but they're more wary now. They hold most of the starboard side and are consolidating their positions. Good thing our men are well trained."

"We can't afford to lose men at even this rate. There are more of them than us. I've decided, we can't take the ship back with the numbers they've brought against us. We can't even hold what we've got. The artifacts that survived the helicopter crash were taken to the geology lab, if I remember correctly. We'll need to get what we can and leave."

Rakslav looked skeptical and said, "And how will we leave?"

Parasca said, "In the mini-subs, of course."

# CHAPTER 28 – PRIEST OF DARKNESS

*"Whose waves of torrent fire inflame with rage"*
*— John Milton, Paradise Lost*

Parasca followed behind the huge figure of Rakslav as they worked their way through the below deck passages. The dim emergency lights seemed to have lost some of their brightness from a few hours earlier. Parasca thought, *the batteries are draining.* Rakslav held up one arm for a halt. One of the men came back to Rakslav and whispered to him.

"What is it?" Parasca asked.

"Our scout says the way to the geology lab is inaccessible from this side. The pirates have thrown up barricades at both approaches and have posted defenders behind them. Unless we want to launch a frontal assault, I can't think of a way to get there from this side."

"Well, think some more! Figure it out! Get us there. We've got to get those artifacts. The crystal steel in the sword or the shield is worth a hundred times the value of this ship," Parasca said.

Rakslav thought for a few seconds. "If I remember the layout, isn't there a stairway down from the control tower that leads almost directly to the lab? Yes, that is correct. Sir, we need to go up to the deck and into the control tower. If we can get to the stairs there, we may be able to get down to the lab."

Parasca nodded and said, "All right. Up to the deck and to the control tower. Make it quick. I want to get those artifacts and then get out of here. As long as we have either the sword or the shield, we can get away and still make a profit on this venture. Even if these pirates get the other artifact, they won't realize what they have. I'll get this new steel to market before they even have a clue."

Parasca followed as Rakslav lead the way back and to the stairs. They found dozens of dead bodies along the way, some of the pirates and some of their own men. There were a few of the PetroRomania company men as well, but it seemed that most of those had avoided these fire fights. Parasca scowled. *Those cowards. My own employees and they run away and hide. If the pirates try to ransom them I won't pay for a single one. They can all die as far as I'm concerned.*

Rakslav stepped up the stairs quickly but carefully, avoiding even more bodies on the way. Some of the bodies were in very bad shape.

Janos Parasca grunted in distaste and muttered. "What has been going on here? Have explosives been used up here on deck? These things look like they were ground up in the gears of a machine. Huh! That one is missing its head entirely, and there's only half a body there!"

Parasca heard the sounds of one of the men behind him vomiting. Rakslav stopped and turned to make sure the man was recovering. Parasca frowned, disgusted by the man's weakness and hissed at him, "Pull yourself together! You act like you've never seen a corpse, you fool!" He turned back to Rakslav and growled, "What are you waiting for? Keep moving!"

Rakslav stepped onto the deck, advancing cautiously with gun at the ready. He scanned the deck, noticing another ten or twelve bodies strewn about, several collapsed in heaps near the racks of pipe. Each body lay in a pool of blood. There was no sound except the wind.

He studied the path to the control tower about a hundred feet away. Several racks of pipe lay between them and the tower. Rakslav noticed that some of the pipe lay strewn about the deck, though nothing indicated the cause of the misplacement. Their group would have to weave their way past two corpses and past the rack of pipe beyond it. Then it was twenty feet to the lower door to the control tower. Since there were two bodies by the lower door, it might be too dangerous there. If they needed to, they could go up the outer stairway to one of the higher levels and back down through the inner stairway.

Rakslav stepped out and Parasca and the others followed close behind. They reached the rack of pipe and stopped when Rakslav gave a signal. Several of the men were muttering and pointing at a uniformed body that was cleanly sliced through in a bloody diagonal running from the left shoulder down to the right hip. Parasca glared at the men. Rakslav made a signal for silence and stepped to the edge of the rack. He motioned that the way was clear and then moved toward the door to the tower now clearly in sight.

Without warning, a huge shape reared up from the other side of the rack of pipes. At first, Rakslav thought it was a piece of heavy machinery, but then noticed the silhouette shape of head and shoulders. A fear like an icy chill flowed through his body and he knew somehow that he must run away or be lost. Before he could act, the thing lifted an arm holding a sword and pointed it at them. A short series of sounds came from the monster and

Rakslav felt a mental stretching and tearing like a sheet being ripped apart. His mind reeled in blinding pain. His thoughts felt disordered and disconnected and he thought he heard a distant echo of a voice saying, "Come closer". With horror, he felt his legs move and realized he was walking toward the monster. *Wait! I don't want to move closer to that thing!*

Rakslav heard a voice nearby shouting, "Shoot it! What are you doing? Stop! Shoot that thing!" Rakslav knew the voice was Parasca's, but he had somehow lost command of his body. He neither stopped nor obeyed Parasca's command to fire.

He walked to the feet of the monster and heard the whispering voice speak again and say, "Kneel". Helpless to do anything differently, he went down on one knee and bent his head forward. In his peripheral vision, he saw that the other men of their group were kneeling beside him in front of the monster.

From behind them, Parasca shouted, "Get up, you cowards! Help me fight it." None of them answered. Rakslav wanted to answer, but his mouth would not obey. He and all the others knelt silently.

The creature in front of them spoke. It was a rumbling, almost musical sound. Confusing at first, Rakslav soon understood what the creature was saying.

"Another of our blood. How interesting. Come here, little man. I know what you are. You think because my compulsion worked on them, but not you, that you can escape? I sense what kind of man you are. You're not like the woman. She wouldn't have the stomach to do what was necessary. You, on the other hand, won't allow a few little inconveniences to get in your way, will you?" The monster's voice turned angry. "Now, none of that!"

Rakslav heard a cry of fear. It sounded like Parasca's voice, but Rakslav could not see. He still knelt and could not lift or turn his head to look for Parasca. He heard an insistent whisper in his head echoing, repeating, "Kneel ... Kneel ... Kneel ..." The next moment, he heard Parasca shouting and the sound seemed to come from above Rakslav's head. The insistent whisper said, "Rise and look up ... Rise and look up ..."

Rakslav felt his muscles move as he stood and tilted his head upward. It was like someone were pulling strings and lifting his arms and legs. He could feel his limbs, but they were under the control of someone else.

Janos Parasca shouted, "Put me down! What are you doing?"

Rakslav saw Janos Parasca suspended in midair above them and a meter from the tip of the giant's outstretched sword. Parasca's gun hung in the air between him and the giant. The gun suddenly crumpled into a fist-sized ball of compressed metal and dropped to the deck. The giant growled, "What am I doing? I've taken your weapon and now I'm holding you above the deck of this ship, aren't I?" The giant swirled the tip of the sword and

Parasca rotated in midair like a goose on a spit. "Why am I doing this? To show you that you can't stop me. Consider it your first lesson." A chilling smile crossed the monster's face.

* * *

The floor looked a long way down: three meters beneath his feet. It was far enough that he'd likely sprain or break a leg if he fell. Parasca felt a wave of pain and nausea wash through him. A headache pulsed behind his temples and it felt like something were prodding his brain.

The monster spoke again, "Now that I have enough energy to see into you, I am certain that you are one of our Blood ... distantly ... hmmm, you don't seem to be bothered by the voices like the woman. You must have erected a primitive barrier of your own, or the voices just seem natural to you. I grant you are clever since you must be self-taught, but any barrier you have wasn't enough to keep me out." Parasca felt memories come to mind unbidden as if something were rifling through scenes in his life. "My, aren't you the glutton! You've been torturing your fellows for years and stealing their energy, though you didn't understand what was happening. You only knew that you loved the feel of watching and experiencing their deaths ... and feeding on them." More memories flashed through his mind like pages in a book: the finding of the original crystal steel dagger, the skeletons in the tar, the location of the sarcophagus, the pirates and the firefights. The monster muttered something under his breath, "...that dagger must have been Mulciber's original test, the dagger I gave to Chalara ..." Finally the images of the past stopped running by.

The monster motioned at Parasca and his slow rotation in mid-air stopped with him directly facing upward. The monster leaned over and locked eyes with him. Parasca felt he had never seen a more terrifying sight than those sunken eyes.

The monster said, "You are a man used to commanding others, but also a man of appetites. You've never understood those appetites, but have learned to use some of them to your advantage. You have been a man who used, dominated or killed others, so what I say next will not be hard for you to grasp." The creature considered him and continued, "You have a choice before you now. You may choose to die with your men right now. If that is what you choose, I will torture each of you to death in front of your fellows. Your drawn out dying will feed me with your life energy."

Parasca's heart pounded in his chest. He felt the kind of helpless terror that most often comes in the form of nightmares, from dreams where one is pursued, trapped, paralyzed and helpless before a vast darkness of monstrous power.

"You are afraid. Good. It may help you make the sensible choice." The monster continued, "Your other choice is to be my servant. You will do everything that I command, as soon as I command it. You will never question my commands. You will stop acting for your own purposes and act only for mine. Your thoughts will center on how to serve me best and to anticipate my next commands. In becoming my servant, I will allow you to command others." The monster waved his sword to indicate the kneeling men. "These men will be yours to use in serving me. They will be yours to command, but only as they can aid you in carrying out my commands."

The giant moved a hand upward and Parasca's body lifted and rotated, then lowered to the deck. His feet touched down lightly and he was able to stand. His arms felt bound to his sides. Parasca looked down and saw faint, glowing lines of red wrapped around him from his feet, up his legs and around his arms. He was bound tightly.

"Before you choose between serving me and dying, I will show you this." The creature looked over the line of kneeling men, chose the one next to Rakslav and motioned with his left hand. The man stood up and turned around, his back to the monster, his unblinking eyes facing Parasca. Parasca recognized the man. He was the head of the *Fortuna*'s security force, Sergei. The man lifted his arms and held them straight out parallel to the floor in a "T" position.

The creature held out the softly glowing sword and touched it carefully to Sergei's outstretched right arm. The point of the sword nicked the cuff at the end of the sleeve, slicing through the fabric of the man's coveralls like a razor through tissue. The sword moved quickly along the arm, parting the cloth as it went, across Sergei's back, up to the collar and then along the other arm to the cuff at the end. The sliced fabric parted at the top of the coverall and slumped down where it hung suspended by the belt cinching the man's waist, which was quickly cut. Beneath the coveralls, Sergei wore a tank top undershirt and boxers. The sword sliced them away in a moment, revealing the muscular chest and torso of the ship's head of security. He still held his arms out, rigidly parallel to the deck of the ship.

The sword tip moved to Sergei's right shoulder, just beside his neck. At first, Parasca thought, *he will take Sergei's head off*, but then he saw the sword point begin slicing and peeling a line over the shoulder and down the arm to the elbow. As the sword moved, a strip of skin an inch wide curled away as the strip of bloody flesh grew longer and longer. Red, raw meat was revealed as the strip of skin peeled away from the arm. Blood oozed from the flesh, rolling down in rivulets and dripping from the gash. The sword moved all the way down the arm to the back of Sergei's hand and finally to the tip of his middle finger. The sword point moved back up to the shoulder and began peeling a new strip of skin off of Sergei's arm. *The monster is flaying the man!*

No sign of pain showed in Sergei's paralyzed face. His eyes did not move from side to side and his muscles did not flinch as he was skinned alive. Only one thing indicated his torture: the tears that flowed from his unblinking eyes.

Parasca also noticed something else that he imagined was linked to the man's pain: Sergei's body seemed to be shining with an inner reddish light that built in intensity as his skin was peeled away, strip after strip. Sergei's body was covered in blood and it pooled on the deck. The sword moved faster and faster, slicing away the man's skin in wider and wider strips. The glow around Sergei's body shone brighter. Strangely, Parasca felt his own teeth chattering, his own body almost vibrating with the dying man's agony.

Finally, the monster said, "Place your hand on his chest."

Parasca obeyed and put his right hand on the bloody chest of the paralyzed man. The giant's sword peeled one final strip of skin from Sergei's side and drew back. Parasca looked at Sergei's sunken red eyes, now tearless. Parasca's hand spasmed as if by electricity where he pressed it to Sergei's bloody chest.

The monster pulled the sword back and placed the point left of center on Sergei's back and with one smooth motion, thrust it through the body. The point of the glowing sword erupted through the front of Sergei's chest and slid out only inches away from Parasca's outstretched hand. Parasca felt his hand ball into a cramped fist where it touched Sergei, as if paralyzed by high voltage. All of the man's torture and pain of the last few minutes shot into him at once, turning Parasca's body into a twisting, writhing arc of torment. Parasca's face was paralyzed into a mask of surprise, pain and pleasure that seemed to go on and on.

All at once, it ended and Parasca slumped to the deck, as did Sergei. After a long moment, Parasca roused, and found himself lying in a spreading pool of Sergei's blood, staring into the prone, flayed man's still, blank face. Parasca rose to his feet, calm, steady and poised. He felt like he could do anything. He looked up at the monster.

It spoke, "That is what you've been trying to feel all these years: the total agony of your victim and the full burst of its life energy. Now make your choice. Will you and your remaining men die as this one did, becoming food for me, or will you serve me and join me in drinking the life of our victims? What will you be, prey or hunter?"

Parasca said, "Hunter."

* * *

Parasca said, "Master, I sent the men to collect the surviving crew members. Many of them are gathered in engineering, but I instructed the men to bring them to the moon pool at the center of the ship, where you rose from the sarcophagus. We can reach it from here and there is room for you there as well. Below deck in engineering, you would not be able to stand. At the moon pool there will be room for all of the rest of the crew and us as well." Parasca pointed out the location of the moon pool midship. "There is a problem, though. These men," Parasca pointed at some of the strewn bodies lying on the deck, "are pirates that are trying to seize the ship. My men and I were fighting them when we came up here ... and found you. The pirates have already taken us in tow. There are too many pirates on board for my men to deal with. We need your help to kill them or drive them off the ship."

Moloch nodded, but put the point of his sword under Parasca's chin and lifted, tilting his head upward and exposing the man's neck. Moloch said, "I know what you are trying to do."

Parasca asked, his voice almost trembling, "Master?"

"I will give you this warning once. Do not try to deceive me by shading or hiding the truth from me. I can see that you know parts of the truth that you are not telling me, and you are keeping them from me intentionally." Moloch pushed the point of the sword into Parasca's neck enough to prick and draw a drop of blood.

Moloch looked at him grimly, "I had ruled your people for many years from the time we were exiled to the time I was entombed in this." He motioned to the sarcophagus. "Under our direction you refined the power of speech and gained in intelligence. You learned to grow food, tame animals and begin to feed yourselves. We taught you warfare, structure and hierarchy."

"I know your minds and how you think. You can't hide from me, but I can see that you are attempting to conceal something from me. This is your single warning. Tell me now and I will spare you."

Parasca felt the prick of the sword point and the blood drops trickling down his neck. He felt real fear and fumbled for words, "Master, I ... I ... don't know what I did to anger you. I told you of the men and the crew. I warned you about the pirates and how we need to fight them. What did I do?"

Moloch said, "You said that you and your men came up on deck and found me. As you said that, I sensed that you thought something different from what you said. I sensed that your words clashed with the path your thoughts were on at the time. In other words, I knew you were lying or concealing something. You will tell me now what you concealed, and why."

Parasca stumbled over his words. "We were coming up on deck and going to the tower. We needed to get to the stairs leading down so we could get to the laboratory and retrieve something..."

Moloch interrupted, "<u>That</u> is what you are concealing. What were you going to retrieve and why don't you want to tell me about it?"

"It ... it is an ... artifact ... like a shield. Made from the same metal as the sword ... your sword ... the one you are holding. I wanted to get it back. Then I was going to ... leave the ship with it." Parasca closed his eyes. "I didn't tell you because I thought you might not know about it..."

"... so you could keep it for yourself." Moloch finished and prodded him with the point of the sword, then pulled it back. Moloch leaned down to Parasca's still upturned face. "That shield is mine as well. You know where it is and you'll get it back for me. First, though ..."

Moloch reached out with his huge left hand and slapped Parasca lightly.

Parasca felt the bones in his left cheek shatter. His head whipped to the right and he felt his neck twist and strain almost to the breaking point. His legs seemed to turn to water and gave way. He fell insensible to the deck, spitting blood from smashed lips. Every tooth on the left side of his mouth was broken and felt like shards of broken glass on his lacerated tongue. His head spun and he felt himself lifted up. He looked through dazed eyes and saw the deck some distance below. *How did I get so far away from the deck? I can't reach it ... I need to lie down ...*

He felt himself turning over, his gaze upward into the night sky. He was lowered onto something hard and cold and then saw Moloch's face directly overhead, occluding the stars.

"I can't spend much time training you and I have too much to do to waste time on disciplining you. You will learn quickly or I'll dispose of you. Do you understand?" Moloch spoke coldly.

"Yes. Yes." Parasca mumbled through smashed lips.

Moloch growled in frustration, put a hand to Parasca's ruined face and spoke a word. Parasca convulsed and writhed like an insect in a fire, then lay breathing heavily, gasping great lungfuls of air. The pain in his cheek was gone, but he still felt the shards of broken teeth in his mouth. He turned his head, spit them out and realized he was not on a flat surface. He was lying crossways on top of a rack of pipes. The broken teeth clattered down through the piping and rattled to a stop on the deck. Reflexively, Parasca probed with his tongue and realized first, there were no missing teeth. Second, he realized his jaw was again whole and undamaged.

Moloch seized him again and set him down on the deck. Moloch said, "I healed you just now because you may be useful to me, if you learn this lesson. You will not conceal anything from me, ever. I will know if you do. You will volunteer any information to me that you think I might want to know. If you tell me too much, I will stop you. You will attempt in every possible way to anticipate what I want done, not waiting until I ask. If you do all these things, I will reward you. If you do not, I will torture you to death without a second thought. Do you understand me?"

Parasca said simply, "Yes. I will go get the shield for you."

Moloch said, "Good. You are learning. Go, but return with it, immediately. I will know if you try to escape, so do not think to elude me. You will not live if you make another mistake. Bring the shield to me at the moon pool."

# CHAPTER 29 – CHILD OF DARKNESS

*"Confounded, though immortal"*
— *John Milton, Paradise Lost*

Mercy leaned against the wall, her forehead held in her right hand. *I <u>cannot</u> face them right now. I can't bear Hayden's pity and Jack's disappointment. And, they know Parasca's my father. Of <u>course</u> he is. That's the most sadistic possible outcome, so, of course, that would be my life. I wonder. Does that make me a crazy, half-breed freak as well as the daughter of a war criminal and murderer? My birth mother killed herself in prison after she had me. What did he say about her? '…like your real mother, you've grown up to be a flawless Romanian beauty.' I wouldn't be surprised if Parasca had raped her and that's my real story. I'm the child of rape and suicide. No wonder I'm insane. Oh, God. How can I bear this?*

*But … at least the voices are silent … how did the monster do that? The voices are gone. I can't deny that. All my life I've wished for this, and now they're gone. I can't believe it. How <u>did</u> he do it? When he said those words they didn't sound like anything I'd ever heard, but it seemed that it meant something like, 'Stay Back'. No, that's not quite right, though almost. 'Move Away'? No. Definitely not. Hmmm. 'Get Out'? Hmmm. Yes. That's it. 'Get Out'. From where? Get out of me?*

She paused, took a deep breath and concentrated on the feeling of her breath going in and out slowly. She felt some calm return. The frantic thoughts subsided. Gently, she tried listening for where the voices used to be. *It's crazy. How can I listen for voices that don't actually make sounds? What sound does a silent voice make, and from where does it sound?* She took another deep breath and calmed herself again. She tried to picture what had happened to her and an image seemed to snap in place. *It was like a domed stadium and the voices were a crowd inside the dome with me, all screaming and calling to me. The monster seems to have forced the crowd out and closed the doors. They can't get back in, at least for now.*

She focused on the picture in her mind and took slow, deep breaths. She imagined herself inside a massive room. Columns ringed the outside of the circular chamber and a vaulted, arching roof soared overhead. She pictured herself turning slowly, gazing at the structure, studying its lines. At one end, between two columns, stood the closed double doors that she knew had been there. *This is how they got in. They came into my mind here and they never left until a few minutes ago. Perhaps the medicine pushed them back some, maybe it even pushed them out of the room, but it never closed the doors. The voices just called to me through the open doors. I can't hear them now, because the doors are shut. How long will they stay shut, I wonder?*

She pictured herself walking to the doors. There was a huge cross bar that held them closed. She touched it and felt a vibration in it, almost like a heartbeat. *Somehow I know this is all true in some very real sense, and all this is a model that I can understand and use. I'd wager anything that if I lift this bar and open these doors, the voices will return. The words the monster spoke somehow sent the voices out and then closed the doors and nothing can open the doors from the outside as long as the bar is in place.*

She noticed the floor below the bar and bent down. There was something like sawdust on the floor at the base of the doors. She studied the bar across the double doors. It was made of wood. She ran her hand along the beam and looked at her fingers. They were smudged with a fine powder. It was sawdust. She looked at the bar and saw several flakes of dust separate from the bar and float to the ground. *The bar is coming apart slowly. When it all turns to dust, the doors can be opened from the outside. I can't let that happen. I have to figure out how to keep the voices out.*

*I wonder if the Counselor is shut out, too? The monster called the voices the 'unbodied'. Are they like ghosts? Evil spirits? The Counselor wasn't an evil spirit, though. Relentless, but not evil. Just talking to the Counselor used to knock me out cold for a day, but maybe that was just the cost of speaking to it? The monster talked about how doing anything required the use of power and he couldn't afford to waste the energy. Perhaps it took power out of me to talk to the Counselor. Maybe I didn't have enough energy to reach the Counselor without going unconscious.*

*So what's different now? All of these deaths on the ship? The monster said that if it killed Jack and Hayden we'd absorb more energy. I was feeling more and more energized the more people died aboard the ship. And the monster didn't revive until all those deaths started happening one after the other. What am I, some kind of energy vampire? And that monster, too? Hayden says I'm genetically related to it, so what is it, the head vampire? Am I its great-great-great-grand-daughter? And what does that make my father, Parasca? He's also been looking crazy-eyed since the deaths started. Maybe he's drinking this up like me and the monster.*

*No, this has gone too far. It's nuts. I don't believe in this kind of nonsense. Evil spirits. Giants. Life-Energy. Undead creatures brought back to life after thousands of years. Magical writing. Telekinesis. Paralyzing with a word. It's all unbelievable. But ...*

*true, isn't it?*

*I have __not__ imagined the voices that have been speaking to me since I was a teenager. It __has__ been more than a day since I took my last dose. I should be a basket case by now, and I almost was until he silenced the voices. I did not __imagine__ my physical and mental abilities. I didn't make this up. I am freakishly strong and fast. I can't deny it. Now I've seen all of these other things: the paralysis and the moving of things at a distance, and I have witnesses who also saw it all too.*

*I've got to stop fooling myself. This stuff is real. It's as real as anything else I know to be real. There __is__ more than just the material universe. There are things that are beyond what we ... what __I__ know. Whether I call it the supernatural or not makes no difference. I wanted so badly for there to be only that which could be tested and measured, but there is more and much of it is terrifying. It sounds like Hayden was right about this stuff.*

Her mind went back to that image of the dome. She saw again the decaying beam of wood holding the doors shut. *That won't hold much longer. I've got to figure out some way to keep them out. What can I do?*

She lifted her head, took a deep breath and said, "Jack ... Hayden ... could I bounce some thoughts off of you?"

* * *

She finished telling them what had happened and what she'd thought. She told of the image she'd built in her mind, of the voices and the bar keeping the door shut. Mercy paced up and down the length of the lab as she spoke.

Hayden said, "The bar, the chamber, the columns, of course they are all metaphors. They are the ways you picture the structure of your mind and its protection from those things, the voices. They are metaphors, but not only metaphors. I think they're real as well."

Jack said, "Hayden, it's just a way for her to imagine what's been happening. How can it be real?"

"Mercy has this image of her mind being a domed stadium with barred doors that keep the crazed voices out. I say, if it works to help her understand what is happening, then end of discussion. Don't talk to me about what's real and what isn't. There's a lot going on right now that, two weeks ago, I would have sworn was impossible. Now, I know it is possible. That's enough for me."

Mercy said, "Hayden, I need to figure this out. How can I replicate what the monster did? The spell it cast, or whatever it did is wearing off. That bar is deteriorating and will collapse soon and the voices will come back with a vengeance."

Jack said, "So, the words it said were, 'Get Out'? Is that it?"

Mercy stopped pacing to consider and said, "I think so." She stood beside the lab table, a few feet from the wrapped shield. Her mind seemed to be practically fizzing with thoughts. She had difficulty concentrating.

"You don't know?"

She shook her head, trying to think clearly. "That's just the thing, it's like a foreign language and yet I was able to pick up the meaning without the sounds making any sense at all." Mercy said. She clenched her fist tightly. *Wow! I feel so energized. Did I really pick up all this extra energy by people dying? I wonder what I could do with this? Would I be even faster if I were running? Would I be even stronger than I normally am? One thing is certain, I am starving!* Mercy reached into her pocket to get an energy bar, but they were all gone. *Blast it!*

Jack said, "That sounds familiar, doesn't it? It's like that engraving on the sarcophagus. You know: the phrase that was written in some kind of universal language. Maybe the monster used a universal spoken tongue and that's how we understood it."

Hayden jumped up. "Jack, I think you're right. The creature spoke and we all understood instinctively, without the sounds being what we expected to hear. It's like the sounds bypassed the translation circuits in our brains and jumped straight to the interpretation center. But it's more than that, I think. Those words it spoke went directly to the control centers of our brains. It overrode our wills and we froze in place, except for Mercy. It didn't work against her because maybe she doesn't have quite the same mental wiring that we have. Good thing for us that you have that one percent different DNA, isn't it?"

Hayden continued, "None of us understand the workings of our brains, Jack. I once read that the human brain is the most complex structure in the universe. It's too complicated to understand. By that I mean, the brain is too complicated for even the brain itself to understand. But, that doesn't stop us from using our brains. Just like we can use a car without understanding everything about how a car works. And who really understands computers or cell phones? Very few people alive could understand everything that a computer or phone does and how it does it, yet we use them every day."

Mercy moved to a counter in the lab and looked down the row of canisters. *I was right! They have a candy jar in here and it's almost full!* She walked three steps and took the jar, turned and upended it next to the wrapped shield on the table. Packages of chocolates and candy bars tumbled out. Mercy took a large chocolate bar, unwrapped it and wolfed it down. Another followed quickly.

Hayden smiled at Mercy, nodded as if he understood and said, "Remember, we use computers through metaphors too, just as we use our brains. We call the picture on the computer's screen a desktop. It's not really, of course. It's just a picture that reminds us of the top of a desk with manila folders and documents. The only reason it works is because we've learned to make sense of it that way. We don't care that what's really happening behind the scenes is that electrons are moving about in ridiculously complicated ways, but still we can get lots of good use of it, exactly because we can use metaphors and symbols to represent the work and the activities we want to accomplish."

"I think we use our minds in some of the same ways, without understanding how it does what it does. For instance, no child is born knowing a language, but through years of practice and repetition, children learn to read and write and speak because we can use symbols and sounds and metaphors. Of course, our thoughts don't actually run on those symbols and sounds that make up our languages...unless..."

Mercy was halfway through the pile of candy. She paused and said to Hayden, "Where are you headed with this train of thought?" She downed another candy bar.

Hayden burst out laughing. "Listen to what you just said! 'Where are you headed' and 'train of thought'? Those are perfect examples. One sentence: two different metaphors for what is going on in my brain. If someone is 'headed' somewhere, it means that one is going in a certain direction. The metaphor is 'headed', as in which direction one's head is pointing. But of course, you weren't referring to a physical direction. You were referring to a *mental* direction for a 'train of thought'."

"Of course, a train is a type of transport vehicle that connects wheeled containers in a sequence and moves them to a destination. A train of thought is a metaphor for a sequence of thoughts, and in this case, the sequence of thoughts is 'headed' in a direction that you don't grasp yet." Hayden sighed with slight exasperation. "'Grasp' is another metaphor for holding something in one's hand. Our language is so full of metaphors, not because we're lazy, but because it's the way we work and it's the best way we've found to communicate and function…"

Mercy interrupted. "Hayden! Get back to the point. What were you going to say about our thoughts not really running in the languages that we use?"

Hayden chuckled sheepishly. "Sorry. I was going to say that maybe our brains are computers in other senses as well. Computers have built in languages called 'machine language'. It's an incredibly detailed set of minute instructions: very complicated, but a computer's 'machine language' is what really makes it work. Everything else: the math, the logic, the user interface, the sound, the graphics of a computer; all happen because they are built up out of that machine language that runs deep inside the computer."

"My point is this, maybe there is a 'machine language' for our brains. In fact, there would almost have to be. We don't know yet what it is, but maybe it's like a basic, universal grammar built into the gray matter in our skulls that is what really makes us work and think the way we do."

Jack said, "Hayden. And this means …?"

Hayden said, "It means, the monster spoke commands that paralyzed us. He spoke commands that chased away Mercy's voices. Maybe what he spoke is our brain's machine language. We couldn't disobey those commands any more than a computer could disobey instructions in its machine language."

Mercy said, "Okay, I can see that might be part of an answer. But what about the metaphor stuff you were going on about before?" She was three-quarters through the candy. She slowed down her eating as she started getting that "refueled" feeling and a sense of peacefulness spread over her. Her mind was quiet. Really quiet.

Hayden said, "Some anthropologists believe that there was once an original single language. Perhaps it was very primitive, built of only a few pieces combined in a lot of different ways. If so, I think, in the millennia since that monster and his kind must have ruled humans like slaves, people lost the original language. People forgot it, or modified it, or added words and eventually, no one knew any of it anymore. Maybe a few 'magicians' stumbled upon words occasionally that seemed to carry power to force people to obey them. Maybe hypnotists have learned to put to sleep layers of the mind that would normally interfere and instead, can send commands more directly into the language of thought. Regardless of all that, normal languages developed that are extremely high in metaphors. Why?"

"Because they're easy to understand?" Jack asked.

"Yes, but why are languages heavy in metaphors easier to understand? Maybe it's because they're just one step above the mental machine language. Our brains were built to remember and learn and repeat stories. Stories run on metaphors. I think Mercy might be able to control those voices by using metaphors. If she could learn to control her thoughts in that way, she might be able to at least keep the voices away by herself. Unless one of us learns the language that the monster used, it might be a way ... Mercy, what are you doing?" Hayden stopped talking and starred directly at her where she stood at the lab table.

Mercy's hand was poised in the air six inches above the wrapped shield. She spoke in a quiet voice. "I didn't notice it before. How could I not have noticed it?" She lowered her hand towards the shield and stopped three inches above. "It gets stronger the nearer I get. Maybe I was too weak before…"

Jack stepped closer. "Mercy what is it? Is there something wrong?"

Mercy said, "No, Jack. Nothing is wrong …" She closed her eyes as if drinking in her surroundings. She moved her hand all the way to the bubble wrap around the shield. "Oh, my."

Hayden said calmly, "Mercy. Tell us what you feel."

Jack stood by Mercy, not touching her, but his eyes showed that he wanted to reach for her.

Mercy laid her hand firmly on the shield and opened her eyes. "It may look like a shield, but it's more like a container. I see what looks like a hurricane of energy swirling around inside it, trapped. This close, though, I can feel it pulling at me almost like a magnet. And there seems to be a reddish thread of some kind, trailing from it and into my hand. There's only one thing to do, you know." She looked at Jack then Hayden, challenge in her eyes.

"What?" said Jack.

"We have to open it."

\* \* \*

Mercy tore at the wrapping, almost desperately.

Hayden said, "Wait Mercy! Stop! Think about this first. How do you know this is the right thing to do? What if this is a trap of some kind? If it really is a hurricane of energy, as you say, how do you know you won't be overwhelmed by it? If it is that powerful, it might even kill you. Please wait!"

Jack said, "He's right, Mercy. A lot of bad stuff has been happening. Luck isn't exactly running our way right now. Maybe you should wait until we know more, until we can tell if it's the right thing to do."

*The right thing to do... I can always tell the right thing to do if I'm willing to pay the price. Now it looks like I can afford the price that I never could before. Maybe I can ask the Counselor. Maybe I can even ask more than one question ...*

Mercy said, "Hayden. Jack. There's something else I need to tell you. There's another voice I sometimes hear, but only when I ask for it, and it might cost me a lot..."

\* \* \*

After Mercy had finished explaining about the Counselor's voice, she said, "...so you see, if we have to know what the right thing to do is, I can ask the Counselor."

Hayden said, "Aren't you forgetting something, Mercy? If this Counselor is one of those voices, they're shut out right now, correct? They're still being held back from your mind. They're still shut out, aren't they?"

Mercy said, "Yes. They're still shut out, but that won't hold for much longer."

Hayden said, "So you shouldn't be able to speak to the Counselor either, will you? If it's one of those insane voices: the 'unbodied' as the monster called them, then it can't speak to you, can it? If it's the same as the others, it can't reach you until your mind is accessible again."

Jack said, "Mercy, don't open yourself up to those demons again. Just skip the shield for now. We'll think of something else."

Mercy said, "There's no time, Jack. I probably don't have more than five minutes anyway before my defenses go down. That monster didn't give me a lasting defense. He probably wanted me dependent on him, so I've nothing to lose. Besides, I've always felt that the Counselor was different than the other voices somehow."

She reached over and took hold of Hayden's shoulder. "I'm going to try. If something bad happens, and I lose control, knock me out, or disable me." She turned to Jack and hugged him fiercely.

She kissed him and said, "I'll need to lay down when I reach out to the Counselor. If not I may just collapse in a heap. Also, if I don't have enough energy to do this, I might be unconscious for a long time."

# CHAPTER 30 – THRONE ROOM

*"For so I created them free and free they must remain"*
*— John Milton, Paradise Lost*

Closing her eyes, she calmed herself and breathed deeply. She thought absurdly of the Magic 8-Balls that she had clung to since she was a teenager and realized for the first time that they were surrogates and poor substitutes for the Counselor. *First, before I reach to the Counselor, I've got to put away childish things. This is a new reality for me, but it is real.* She mentally pictured herself back in her childhood home, in her bedroom. She lifted the lid on the large toy box by her bed and held the Magic 8-Ball over the opening. *'Goodbye'* she said and laid it amongst old dolls and games. She shut the lid of the toy box and turned her back on it.

Her adopted father stood in the doorway. She ran to him and hugged him. He smiled at her and said, "Mercy, you're almost ready. I'm so glad. You've been through a lot, I know. I need to introduce you to someone, but we have a few moments. I know you have questions. Ask me and I will answer what I can."

"Father, is this my imagination, a dream or is this ... the afterlife? I don't know what to believe," she asked.

"Mercy, you know that you're more than human. You've found out that much I know. For those like yourself, sometimes you can view another plane of existence. That plane is where I am now. You're 'seeing' into it as best you can. Your mind shapes what it sees here into things it can understand. In this place, your mind has some control over what you see. You saw that just moments ago when you created this childhood room out of memories. This isn't a dream. As for the afterlife question, I'll let you decide for yourself what and where this place is."

"What is that giant monster? How did he get trapped in that

sarcophagus and how can I fight such a creature?"

"Moloch is a powerful being gone bad. Ages ago, he and others became frustrated with the Creator and ... let's just say they tried to do some things their own way. They were stopped, captured and exiled to earth thousands of years ago. They were supposed to stew for a while, reconsider their deeds, repent and then be accepted back. Instead, they went wild on earth, and corrupted its primitive people. Moloch was captured again and this time kept in that sarcophagus for more than seven thousand years in solitary confinement. Even that punishment didn't change his attitude. He's even worse now. As for how you can fight the creature, you should meet the Counselor." The image of her childhood room had transformed into a palace. She looked at him as if to say, 'Did you change this?' He shook his head and stepped into a huge hallway and led her toward a throne room. He whispered to her, "In this reality, the most powerful mind wins." He didn't explain further. The throne room was the largest structure she had ever seen. She followed him toward the three thrones towering at the end of the room.

As they walked, Mercy looked around. At first, she thought the throne room was a vast empty space, but gradually, she began to notice more and more detail. She heard the sound of water and saw that there were fountains in the throne room. Actually, there were dozens, if not hundreds of pools and fountains. The sound of water everywhere was almost like laughter. She heard the murmuring of voices and almost panicked, thinking her hallucinations had returned, but then realized that there were people in the room with her and father. *Why didn't I notice them earlier?*

There <u>were</u> people, many people. Amazingly, there were throngs of people. There was a huge crowd gathered in front of the thrones. They seemed to be listening, but Mercy could not make out to whom or what they were listening. There were also other things besides people. Some were smaller and some larger, even much larger. Some were the size of Moloch and some seemed to be almost the size of buildings and only partially visible, as if only a part of them were in this room and the other part remained somewhere else.

A huge creature strode past Mercy and her father as it walked toward the rear of the throne room. Its body was the size of a large bus and it had wings folded back against its sides. Its face turned to look at them as it drew close and it nodded its giant head slowly as if in recognition of her. Its face was manlike but at least six feet from chin to forehead. It had long dark hair that was caught up behind it in a complex braid and a dark beard that was woven in long locks and cut off square two feet below its chin. It walked on four massive legs that ended in lion-like paws. The wings remained folded against the immense body. It lashed a thirty-foot long tail side-to-side as it walked by.

Mercy was afraid to turn around to look at its receding form and whispered sidelong to her father, "What is that, a sphinx?"

Her father said, "I believe that is one of the captains of Michael's Cherubim. They are monstrously strong and capable fighters."

"Did you say, Cherubim? As in a cherub? The kind of little angel you see with Cupid holding a little bow and arrow on a Valentine's day card?"

"Real Cherubim are not like that. They are more like the one you just saw, though there are variations in form sometimes to match function." Her father said. "You should see it with its wings spread, it's an awesome sight. It's as big as a large airplane back on earth."

They continued their walk to the front of the room. The crowd in front of the thrones was dense, but when they came closer, either it parted to let them through, or it wasn't as crowded as she had thought. The center throne and the left throne were vacant. The throne on her right had an occupant that was shrouded in a mist or fog. Or perhaps the occupant wore a diaphanous garment. In any case, Mercy couldn't make out any details of the appearance of that third occupant. Mercy's adopted father bowed low and said, "Counselor, this is my adopted daughter. You sent for her and she seeks your guidance."

A voice came from the misty figure on the throne. "Thank you. Mercy, step closer and sit by me. This conversation is for the two of us, child." Mercy's father withdrew and Mercy noticed that a chair had appeared next to the Counselor's throne. Mercy sat on it and looked at the Counselor. The swirling mist surrounding the being seemed more clothes than fog, but also came up over the head so that the face was obscured as if in gauze. The Counselor spoke with a low contralto voice. Mercy thought, *Is the Counselor female?*

"Always before, you held so little power that to speak with you nearly extinguished your life's candle. Now, you hold much more power, though this is by accident. You have absorbed some of the death drafts of other humans as the rebel Moloch killed them. Also, you have been near two artifacts of great power, either one of which could bring great devastation to your world. Because of the way Mulciber constructed these, as twisted imitations of the Creator's handiwork, the sword and shield leak power. A being of angelic descent such as yourself would be attracted and energized by such devices."

Mercy's mouth gaped open. The Counselor stopped speaking and then said, "Go ahead child. What is your question?"

"I am of angelic descent?"

"It is true. There are not many on earth at any time that have that distinction. A few dozen at most. The line has never been very robust and even when viable offspring were produced they were very often infertile. It was never intended that crossbreeds exist between humans and angels or demons. It was a travesty wrought through the misuse of free will by the rebels like Moloch and Mulciber."

"Then I am some kind of monster, a half-breed? Am I something that lives on the life energy of other people? What is to become of me?"

"You are of utmost worth, my child. The infant has no say in its parentage. If any folly is to be repaid, it owed by the parent, not the child. You are a rare treasure. Because of a convergence of bloodlines between your parents, you have massive potential, but the first thing you must know is, a death of a mortal creature is a precious thing and the power that you might absorb from it accidentally is not to be accepted except in the case of willing sacrifice. I know that you absorbed the illicit power you hold in innocence, so first, we must take care of that problem. Hold out your hand."

Mercy held out her right hand and the Counselor's hand emerged from its shrouding mist, smooth and ageless. The Counselor took Mercy's hand and lifted their joined hands together. Mists of red flowed upward out of Mercy, changed color to pink, then became white. The white mist seemed to be drawn toward the three thrones and was swiftly absorbed by them. Mercy felt herself weaken considerably.

"The energy from the transitions of these souls is not to be used as a substitute for the Creator's power, and so I have helped you release it to its proper domain. Moloch and Mulciber have created an abominable system that allows them to absorb and store the power parasitically. When they rebelled against the creator, they were cut off from the energy that flows like life-giving water," she gestured to the fountains and pools in the throne room. "To make up for this, once on earth, they set about corrupting the creatures there and using their deaths as a substitute. They set themselves up as gods in the eyes of those early people and instituted sacrifices to add to their power. Moloch and Mulciber even required the deaths of infants in the sacrificial fires because they knew that babes shine brightest with life energy. It was a plan of pure evil."

The Counselor's voice seemed to grow distant. Mercy felt faint and her vision turned into a narrow tunnel at the end of which sat the Counselor. The Counselor took both of Mercy's hands and said, 'I know you weaken, but you can hold on for a few moments. I will give you access to a small portion of the Creator's power. Not too much. You aren't strong enough yet. Too much and you would burn up like a cinder."

The Counselor continued to hold one of Mercy's hands, but with the other, the being reached up as if plucking something gently from the air. In the Counselor's hand, Mercy could see what seemed to be a butterfly. The Counselor held the small creature and said, "This will establish a link between you, wherever you are, and a small source of the Creator's power." Mercy saw that a faint blue thread like a spider's silk seemed to trail away from the butterfly and into a small pool of water that lay nearby. Mercy realized this was one of the many pools and fountains throughout the throne room and that hers was smaller than most, but close by.

"This should be enough for the task you have at hand," said the Counselor. The butterfly hopped gracefully to Mercy's outstretched arm and into her palm. Mercy seemed unable to look away from the tiny creature. It briefly circled her palm and then seemed to melt into her hand leaving nothing behind but the thread of blue.

Mercy felt energized again and vibrantly alive. She sat up straight and looked at the Counselor.

"You said I have a task at hand," Mercy said.

The Counselor said, "Yes. You have work to perform, but first you will go through a very difficult time. It is necessary, for there are things you must learn and quickly. During that time you will have doubts and will be tempted to take the wrong path. You will feel alone and abandoned. I warn you now to prepare you. Do you understand what I am telling you?"

"Yes…" Mercy said nervously.

"You must not falter. You will be told truths mixed with lies. You must discern the difference and not believe the lies."

Mercy asked shakily, "You said that I would have a task?"

"Your task is to recapture Moloch. He must not be allowed to run rampant again on the earth. His escape from confinement there is already disrupting and causing changes to many plans that have been long waiting for the proper moment to be executed."

She stared at the form of the Counselor and said in disbelief, "How can I recapture Moloch? He's too powerful! He will crush me in moments. You'd best send someone else or at least send additional help. Didn't you know that Moloch would escape? Were you caught by surprise?"

A sound almost like a slight laugh came from the Counselor. "We did know that this was a possibility, child. In fact you played some small part in opening his tomb and releasing him, did you not? Would you have us override the free thoughts and actions of many, including yourself? There are nearly infinite possibilities that reality can follow. Not all realms are alike, but on earth, choices of beings like yourself are allowed to influence the course of Reality's river. What has happened was not the most likely path, but then humans often make surprising choices."

"I am afraid you send me to a quick death if I face Moloch alone. He is too powerful for me."

"I would not send you if the task would be hopeless, but I did not say the task would be easy either. You will be hurt. You will likely suffer greatly. But you also have the chance to succeed and be transformed for the better by this trial. Child, remember, his power is that of the parasite. He must constantly replenish his power and his options are limited. You however, have a link to the creator's power now, though not enough to destroy him. In fact it must be limited so it will not destroy you. Remember this: as you gain the ability, the capacity to draw more will grow with you. The power you have is not intended to destroy him, but it may be enough to recapture him. It depends on you."

Mercy shook her head, "May be enough? Capture Moloch? I don't know how I can succeed." She lifted her head and looked into the mists where a face would be if the Counselor would show one. She looked for an answer, and waited for the being to say something, anything. Its form sat, immovable. Mercy felt herself rally. She steeled herself and then replied.

"But then, knowing how to succeed may come to me yet. It's my task, and I'll do it." Mercy said determinedly.

"You are learning, child. Good. Return now," said the Counselor.

The throne room faded. The mists surrounding the Counselor swirled around Mercy. Mercy closed her eyes and thought, *I didn't say goodbye to Father* ...

* * *

Mercy opened her eyes. Jack said, "Good, you changed your mind. You're not going to try to talk to that other voice."

Mercy stood energetically and bounced on her toes. She smiled broadly. "What do you mean?"

"You only closed your eyes for a second. What's come over you? Do you still hear the voices?" Jack asked.

"Only a second? Things move more quickly over there I guess. No, I spoke with the Counselor and the voices are still gone." She closed her eyes and concentrated. The dome she had imagined as her mind seemed different, now made of some kind of bluish shimmering metal, including the doors. The decaying barrier that had kept out the unbodied was locked and bound with the same metal. Bluish energy seemed to crackle through the barrier, the same color she had seen in the throne room while speaking to the Counselor.

She said, "I understand a lot more now. I've got some work to do before leaving the ship, but you two should leave now. Take whatever you can salvage except for the shield. Get to the mini-subs and get away. I'll follow behind. If nothing else, I can swim to shore."

"And what will you accomplish by staying behind while we run away? What do you intend to do with the shield? And remember, the monster has the sword." Hayden said.

Mercy said, "I have to figure out a way to recapture Moloch. Get him back in that sarcophagus if I can. I think I'll try to use the shield as a defense against him. Perhaps I can corner him and then get him back in that coffin."

"If that's your plan, you'll need help. Hayden and I can operate those cranes. Even if you get him back in, you'll need help to get that lid closed on him."

Mercy nodded and moved toward the door. Instead of following, Jack stepped to Hayden. He put his hand on Hayden's shoulder and asked, "Could Mercy and I have a minute?"

Hayden raised an eyebrow hopefully and smiled slightly. "Sure, Jack." He leaned in closely and whispered, "Clear the air with her. You've got a great woman there. Don't lose her."

Jack smiled and said quietly, "I know. I'm going to try. Thanks."

Hayden stepped away to the far side of the room, pulled out a chair at one of the work tables, sat down, took out the DNA report and started re-reading it. Jack turned to Mercy. She stood with her arms crossed over her breasts and one eyebrow raised.

She said, "What was that about?"

"I need to talk to you for a moment."

"This really isn't the time to talk."

He said, "It may be our last chance to talk. There's crazy stuff happening out there. People are being killed. We may not make it."

"Then we need to move now. We can talk later."

"Mercy, there may not be a later. We need to talk now while we still have the chance."

"About what?"

He moved to Mercy and held out his hands, palms up. She hesitated and finally uncrossed her arms, but didn't take either of his hands.

Jack took a deep breath and dove in. "Did you break off our engagement, because of the voices ... because you thought you were schizophrenic?"

Mercy inhaled sharply and her eyes grew large with pain. "That was a long time ago. I was young and scared. I didn't handle it well ... and I was terrified. I couldn't tell you. I didn't know how to tell you but I shouldn't have treated you like that. I can't tell you how sorry I still am."

"Don't apologize. If that's why you called it off, I think I finally understand. You heard those 'unbodied' voices the monster talked about. You knew that wasn't normal. You thought you were insane. But the voices really do exist. They're not a sign of sickness. It's not your fault. You really couldn't have done anything differently."

"I could have done a lot differently, Jack. I didn't tell you everything about 'the Counselor'. Before we broke up, I asked the Counselor whether I should marry you. It told me yes, but I was too afraid. I thought I'd get you killed or kill you myself in some schizo fit. I almost killed my adopted mom once before I came to my senses. Do you understand? The Counselor told me to marry you way back then, but I couldn't. I didn't listen to it. I should have listened, but I didn't. I could've done things a lot differently."

"Well, I could've too."

"No, Jack. We broke up because of me, not you."

"I could've given you more space. I could've given you more time. I just wanted you so badly, I didn't want to wait. I pressured you and you jumped the other direction."

They went silent for a moment. Mercy blinked, swallowed heavily, sighed and said, "If we're getting it all out in the open, Jack ... why didn't you stand up to Parasca? Why did you let him walk all over you?"

"No mystery there. I didn't want to lose my job."

"Was that really it, though? You could've gotten other jobs. You didn't have to work for him."

"What else? I spent a lot of time working my way up to that level. I didn't really have that much contact with Parasca. I just had myself to care for, and I guess I figured I could live with the occasional brow-beating. It's been different since you've been here." He ended with wry look.

"Why's it been different?" Mercy prodded.

"I used to just bite my tongue, take any tongue lashings and keep going. I'd tell myself it was worth it in the end. With you watching, I realized it's not like that. When you're around, it feels like I'm knuckling under to a bully. Like I let someone kick sand in my face over and over. I don't know what to think. How'd I become such a doormat?"

"You're not a doormat. You still have the respect of the crew, but I think you should expect others to respect you as well. It might have something to do with when we broke up," she said.

"What do you mean?" He said.

"Back when we met and fell in love, you used to be a lot more brash and assertive. What happened?"

"I grew up? I matured a little?"

"Some maybe, but when I broke off our relationship, maybe you lost some of your edge. Maybe you accept too much punishment. Maybe you don't fight back like you should. Maybe you're not man enough anymore."

Jack's eyes blazed. "What? Man enough for what? What are you saying?"

Mercy winced, realizing too late she'd said something she didn't mean. "That was harsh. I'm sorry, Jack. That was a stupid thing to say. You know how impulsively I act sometimes. I should have said, maybe I burned you so bad that you go too far out of your way to accommodate people now. You let people take advantage of you."

Jack studied her carefully, questioningly. He said, "Mercy, I defer to management, but I lead my teams. I don't know how else to say it. Executives in this business and most others are not kind and gentle people.

They expect a lot – and are sometimes outrageously unreasonable about it. They've been successful mainly by pushing themselves and others to work their tails off. Most of the time, you show deference or you're out. It's pretty simple."

"Then maybe this isn't your line of work anymore."

"I've been thinking a lot about that too."

Mercy reached out and touched his arm. "Just think about it Jack. Do what you think is right, not what you think your bosses want you to do. Don't become like them. You're too smart for that. You're too good for that. And Jack ... I'm sorry about what I did to you. I shouldn't have broken up with you."

Jack moved her hand down to his. He took her other hand as well, hesitated a moment, nodded to himself as if finally certain of something and said, "... and you're right. I've let them lead me by the nose long enough." He turned to the other side of the room and said, "Hayden, we need to get going. We've got a lot to do and Mercy can't do it by herself."

Hayden stood up from the table and said, "You got it."

Jack stepped up to Mercy and held his nose six inches from hers. "Every superhero needs sidekicks. You were unlucky and got us." He smiled.

She hugged him and said, "Let's do it then. First I need to wrestle this shield under some kind of control."

* * *

She stepped to the counter holding the shield and tore its wrapping off. She took it in her grip and held it up. The energy in it seemed to writhe like an evil snake in her hand, but she concentrated, using her new ability to understand the artifact and imagined herself looking into its surface.

She saw all at once the bloody massacre and creation of the shield, saw the life forces and even the atomic elements themselves of the victims being used to forge the structure of the shield. She saw that those death energies were stored in it like a vast battery of pain and agony. It occurred to her that the only way to end the torture of these long dead victims might be to drain the energy of the shield. Perhaps she could goad Moloch into helping her drain much of its death energy.

She looked up at Hayden and Jack. "This thing is filthy with the blood of victims. I don't think these poor souls will ever rest as long as this thing exists. It needs to be destroyed. Maybe that monster can be of some use after all. Let's go."

* * *

The fire blazed upward above the top edge of the box. Parasca looked up at Moloch looming over the flames that leapt out of the sarcophagus. A smile was fixed upon the huge face. Black smoke billowed overhead as if the entire ship were on fire. Moloch held the hose that had served minutes ago to fill the sarcophagus with oil to a depth of twelve inches. He dropped the hose and rubbed his hands in the smoke as if washing them. His face turned to Parasca below him.

"Do you have them ready?" Moloch said over the roaring and crackling of the oil-fire.

"Yes, Lord." Parasca beckoned to Rakslav. "Take that first one over to Lord Moloch!"

Rakslav nodded, but his face was immobile. There was no look of comprehension in the man's eyes and only a blank expression on his face. He bent over and pulled up to standing position a man that was blindfolded and whose hands were tied behind his back. He wore a dirty white uniform that was so soiled it looked like it was well on its way from white to gray to black. He was the first in a line of more than two dozen people that were similarly tied up and blindfolded. The man's face was bruised and he began shouting.

The captive said, "What are you doing now? Where are you taking me? Take this blindfold off! Do you hear me?"

Rakslav said nothing, but dragged the man nearer to Moloch. There they stopped while the man continued shouting.

"Stop this! What have I done to anyone? Just let me get back to the kitchen!"

Parasca said, "Take the blindfold from him. He needs to see what happens next."

Rakslav pulled off the cloth. The man glared at him first, then noticed that he was in a different place than from before the blindfold was placed over his eyes. His eyes widened as he looked at the drilling equipment in front of him, then heard the crackling and roaring of the fire pouring from the sarcophagus beside him and turned to his right to gape at it. A column of black smoke rose as far as he could see into the sky. He tilted his head back and caught sight with his peripheral vision of a gigantic looming figure even further to his right. He spun, then stumbled back, gasping.

"A monster! What is it...?" He choked through a windpipe that had almost constricted closed. Then, he flinched back, hunching his shoulders and raising his hands instinctively as if to ward off an attacking animal.

Moloch's gigantic hand reached down from above the hapless cook and grabbed him around the waist, the fingers closing vice-like, digging into the flesh of his belly and breaking the lower set of ribs like sticks. The man kicked and twisted and the pain shot through him like lances of molten metal. He screamed and the giant's hand lifted him higher and higher above the deck, then above the giant's own head. The giant spoke.

"Your life now serves one greater than yourself. I take from you all that you were and are. From now on, you are remembered no more."

The monster moved its arm with the twisting, kicking human and held him in the smoke over the fire. The cook gasped and choked, and tried to cough out the filthy, tar-filled smoke. His body tried to double-over from the lack of air, but he couldn't move with the giant's hand clamped around his middle. Suddenly, he felt the iron grip release and he felt a tiny moment without pain. Then he realized he was falling and screamed in terror. In midair, his body rotated until his face was pointed downward. He fell, engulfed in the hot, oily smoke, then for an instant, the smoke ended and the blast of a furnace hit him.

There below him was the sarcophagus filled with fire and its searing strength grabbed him and pulled him down. He shrieked in such final, all-encompassing fear, that all thought, all memory, all language left him in a moment. The cook struck the oil, felt his bones snap and his body roast as he tumbled over and over in the flames. He rolled and thrashed in the oil, trying to scream, trying to cry, but the fire and oil filled his mouth and peeled the skin from his head. A last, strange thought came to him of all the creatures that he had cooked. *Had they felt like this when they died?* With that, his mind blanked, his heart stopped, all nerves seized, and he died. He convulsed into a shrunken, twisted curl. His blackened, still reflexively twitching form snapped into fragments. The pieces of the cook floated in the burning oil.

Moloch pulled in the thread of red light that floated up from the fire and savored it like a sip at a wine tasting. He turned to Parasca again. "Bring the next one."

# CHAPTER 31 – CAPTURE

*"Who overcomes by force, hath overcome but half his foe"*
*— John Milton, Paradise Lost*

Listening at the door, Mercy said, "Sounds like people in the hallway. I'll lead with the shield. Stay behind me, we've got to get up top as quickly as we can." Mercy concentrated on the shield and felt its wild energies surging and pulsing. She visualized them pulling in and forming a barrier in front of her. The shield seemed to obey instantly. She opened her eyes and saw a reddish glow surrounding the shield and swirling around it. *Wow. That was easy.*

Holding the shield in front, she shoved the door open and dashed into the hallway. She heard a shout, "Fire!" and a hail of bullets rained on her. A very few of the wild shots missed and embedded themselves in the floor, ceiling or walls of the corridor. All other projectiles were drawn to the shield, some even curving out of their path to strike it and then bounced away harmlessly. She charged forward, shield in front and time slowed down again, and this time, it seemed to have stopped almost entirely. Her sight narrowed to a tunnel straight ahead.

She ran head down crouched behind the shield and felt and heard the seemingly slow-moving bullets pinging away. Then she felt the first impacts with bodies as they slammed into the shield, and thudded away. Mercy shoved forward like a snowplow, clearing the path. A dozen or more bodies were thrown aside, stepped over or walked on before she reached a clear place in the corridor. She turned back and saw the slow-motion aftermath of her passage: bodies still caroming off of walls or ceilings or collapsing to the floor. Her eyesight broadened and time resumed its natural speed. She heard a set of footsteps racing away along the corridor. *I guess one of them got away.* The hallway went silent.

263

Mercy yelled to Jack and Hayden, "Come on out. It's over out here."

Jack ran into the corridor thinking he had been following right behind her, but he staggered to a stop when he saw how far ahead she was and the carnage she'd left behind. Every body seemed to be crushed or unconscious. Mercy realized that more than half of these pirates were dead. She'd mowed them down with such force that they'd been killed as easily as if they'd been run over by a train. She moved her thoughts through the shield. *It's only used a little of its power shielding me from those bullets. Good. Plenty left.*

Mercy windmilled her arm for Jack and Hayden to follow and raced down the corridor toward the passage up topside. She paused at the top of the stairs and was appalled by the gore and shattered corpses strewn all around. *We've got to get across this butcher's yard, but where is the monster? I've got to take the fight to it. I can't get sidetracked.*

Mercy stepped out to the deck. The racks of steel pipe lined up in rows between her and the moon pool where the sarcophagus lay. Voices came up from there and a column of black smoke rose from it. A scream of agony scraped across her ears. *The monster is down there killing people.* She took another step toward the moon pool, her senses alive and heard a slight scraping sound. From the periphery of her vision, she saw something move to her left with lightning speed. She started to pull the shield across and between her and the threat, but felt a simultaneous stab of pain in her side. *I've been shot!*

She completed the swing of the shield and more bullets crashed into it or were deflected away. She fought the pain just below her left ribcage, trying to ignore it. *This could be bad. Practically a gut shot. No telling what organs I just lost.* She gritted her teeth, concentrated on the shield, felt time slow down again and this time her tunnel-vision was rimmed in red. In a haze of agony, she charged toward the machine gun fire. *Come to Mama, you bloodsucker!*

The Russian knew he'd shot Mercy. He'd seen her flinch as the bullet went in her side. Unfortunately, she'd blocked all the other shots by swinging that bloody shield into cover position. *I've never seen anyone move that fast. I've got to kill her quickly before she recovers.* He fired short bursts of three bullets each and moved to another position two meters away. Then she charged and his blood went cold. *She moves so fast, I can hardly see her!* He struggled to pull his gun up to re-aim in time, but all he saw was the crystal steel shield. It smashed into the barrel of the gun as his finger pulled the trigger. The gun backfired and exploded in his right hand. Hot shrapnel tore into his chest and through his leg. Mercy continued barreling forward and he crunched into the shield, bounced off it and into a rack of steel pipe. The Russian slid to the floor and lay still.

Mercy stopped, puffing with exertion and pain, her eyesight blurring.

Her attacker was out of the fight, but he looked familiar. It was that same Russian again. *The one I drank a beer with. This guy is everywhere. Not so tough now, though.* Sudden, slicing pain grabbed her and she doubled over. *I'm going into shock.* Jack and Hayden ran up to her and Hayden tried to check her wound. She flinched. "Don't!" she hissed.

"Mercy, that has to be looked at now. You've taken a bad wound that is only going to get worse."

The words ground out of her like broken glass, but her head momentarily cleared. *I can think again.* "Later. Right now I've got to take care of that monster. There are voices and screams coming from the moon pool. You two get up into the cranes and I'll get to the drill floor. Make sure you engage the emergency generators for the cranes or they won't have any power. Get the cranes in position to close the lid on the sarcophagus." Hayden and Jack didn't argue and headed to the cranes. Mercy started walking carefully to the moon pool opening. A figure with hands raised stepped out from around a rack of pipe. It was Parasca.

"Mercy, I'm so glad you're all right. The carnage up here has been awful. I think the pirates are almost under control, though. I saw what you did with that one," he motioned at the still form of the Russian as he walked toward her. "That was very expertly done."

She backed away from him a few steps. Every movement was agony. She gritted her teeth in pain and continued moving away from him in the direction of the opening. *What game was he playing now?* "That was the spy that started all of this trouble. He was the one that climbed onto the sarcophagus to read the inscription, and also was in the sarcophagus looking for treasure when I went into it. He got away and probably set off the explosives that took out our engines. He's done now," she said.

Parasca said, "Good. Good. You've grown so capable since I knew you before. I know you're ready for great new things in my organization after we get away from this wreck. The metal in that shield for instance, my engineers will get it into production quickly and we'll have a new multibillion dollar industry in super strong and light steel within the year. I could use someone like you to head up that new division."

She couldn't believe her ears and said, "You snake! What are you talking about? I know the real process it took to create this steel and I won't be a part of something so evil and bloody."

Parasca stared at her fixedly, his voice suddenly low. "What do you know about the steel?"

"I know that when I touched it, I felt and saw the horrible sacrificial rites and the hundreds of people being killed when the shield was forged. Are your engineers going to set up conveyor belts to carry people into a furnace so they can make this evil metal?" She raised the shield in emphasis.

He said, "So you saw it too." He paused, "It may be 'evil metal' as you say, but you seem to have no qualms about using it. You're not so pure, Mircea."

She suddenly had no words with which to reply to this person. *How could anyone be so evil?* At last she said, "There's more than one monster on this ship."

"True." He said. "There's Moloch, there's me and there's … you. Of course, you understand now that Moloch ruled here over seven thousand years ago. He left only a few descendants, and since I've spoken with Moloch, I know that I am one of them. Since you're my daughter, you are too." He smiled at her appalled expression. "Oh, I see that you're not completely shocked by that, so you must have suspected. But still, some surprises remain. I never told you, did I, that your mother, Tresa Rodica was my mistress for years? Of course, in Romania in those days, Ceausescu had outlawed contraceptives and abortion, so she got pregnant several times. I knew the black market and was able to get abortions for her anyway. The last time, though, she was very defiant and wouldn't go to the abortionist until I forced her. That time, she was unlucky enough to get caught when the abortion doctor was arrested in a raid and before he could perform the procedure. The abortionist was executed, Tresa was jailed, and you were born in the prison hospital and then taken away to an orphanage. I could have gotten her released, but I didn't. I thought it might be good for her to develop some humility in jail, so I let her rot there for a while. Unfortunately, she was weak and killed herself. I had no interest in a baby and lost track of you when you were eventually adopted. Years later, when you returned to Romania with your adopted mother, I learned that you were my daughter when I researched her in preparation for her interrogation. That is why I forced you to stay in Romania. I wanted you nearby if you ever showed promise. But then, the revolution happened and Ceausescu fell. I lost track of you again in all of the mess after the regime change. But now … well … we have a chance to start over, don't we?"

She took another step backward. "No, we do not. There is no starting over. You think to win me to your side with this horrible story? What is wrong with you? You seduce her, then drive my birth mother into despair until she commits suicide and yet you think I'll run to you and say, 'Yes, Daddy. Whatever you want?' You are sick and pathetic. I'll never have anything to do with you."

Mercy felt her arms grabbed from behind and pinned to her sides. The pressure on her wound sent waves of nausea coursing through her. She twisted her head to the side and saw the giant Moloch behind her, where he had climbed up from the moon pool at her back. One gigantic hand tore the shield from her grasp and the other hand pinned her arms agonizingly to her waist.

Moloch said, "That's enough child. Time to learn your lessons and become one of mine." She screamed and struggled uselessly against his grasp.

Parasca said, "You'll obey him eventually, and me. Daughter."

* * *

In the darkness and relative quiet up on the deck of the ship, the Russian awoke in agony. *It feels like every bone in my body is broken.* He took inventory, sensing each limb's condition. He was only able to open one eye. The other one was swollen shut. One of his hands was broken along with the attached arm, probably with multiple fractures. His legs felt bloody and bruised, but he couldn't tell if he had any breaks in his legs. He had several broken ribs and one or more had broken through the skin. He tried taking a slow deep breath. There was agony in his chest, but no gurgling. *Lucky I didn't get a punctured lung. I'll have to see how my legs hold up.*

He slowly rolled onto his front and pulled one leg up under him and then the other. They ached horribly from the shrapnel and probably blood loss, but there were no broken bones. He pushed himself up with his one good hand and stood shakily. One ankle was sprained. *I won't be running any races today, but I can still get to Engineering, I bet. I've got one more surprise up my sleeve, Parasca. How will you get to port, with a scuttled ship?*

The Russian pulled out a small transmitter from his pocket. It looked intact. He thumbed it on and saw it light up. Static crackled from it and he pressed the transmit button. "This is Vasiliy. Dmitri, are you there? This is a highest priority message. Disengage your towing chain or you will be sunk. The *Fortuna* is foundering and will sink soon. Acknowledge." The Russian released the transmit button and switched the device to 'receive' and waited.

His transceiver sounded, "Acknowledged. We see the *Fortuna* is taking on water. We will disengage the tow line. Do you require extraction?"

"Not yet." He answered. "I have one more thing to do first. Wait for my call before sending help. Out." He turned the receiver off and dragged himself to the hatch leading down to engineering. He patted the pack on his shoulder and felt through the cloth for the contents he knew were still there. *There's the detonator and plastic explosive. That's enough to finish it all and send this hell-ship to the bottom.*

# CHAPTER 32 – ELEMENTAL TRIAL

*"Farewell happy fields, where joy forever dwells: hail, horrors, hail."*
— *John Milton, Paradise Lost*

Mercy's head ached and she felt the stab of pain in her side where she'd been shot by the Russian. *What was his name? Oh yes, he told me at the party. It was Vasiliy. He was the one that had a taste for Russian beer. I have to remember. He was the spy, probably set the explosives too.* She winced and opened her eyes. *What is that smell?* She saw that she lay on the floor of the drilling deck, chained in place. *This is very bad.* A drill bit, attached to steel pipe, was suspended above her. *Why am I here?*

A low voice spoke from near her. She turned her head and saw that the monster was squatting down on his haunches, his head inclined toward her. He took a large bite of charred meat. Mercy's mind screamed. *It's a human thigh he's eating!* Her eyes rolled wildly and she saw piles of charred and burned bodies. She heard a deep rumbling laugh and turned back to the monster.

Its language flowed into her ears and slid into her consciousness with full understanding. "You have started coming into your power, but you have little control yet. I sense you've walled away the voices of the 'unbodied' using a clumsy but effective technique. Your training under me will be much better but I don't have time to waste on niceties and gentleness. We have to get this ship to shore and I need to have you and the other assist me and help me understand what I face in this changed land. I've been trapped a long time and these humans have not been idle in my absence. They have weapons and machines that I do not yet understand. We must get to cover and gather in followers before I can begin to regain my standing here on earth."

Moloch stopped as if surprised, then said, "I sense that you have a direct power thread to the Creator. You did not have this when we first met. Before anything else, you will tell me, how did you get this thread?"

Mercy decided she had nothing to lose by telling the creature what she knew. She said, "I had a vision. I was in a throne room. A figure in a cloak sat on one of three thrones. It gave me the thread to use against you."

Moloch laughed. "This thread cannot channel enough power to defeat me. Why should one of The Three give you such a paltry gift?"

*It told me it wouldn't be enough but said it would help me.* She said to the monster, "I won't tell you."

Moloch said, "But you have already told me. 'It told me it wouldn't be enough.' I can hear what you are thinking. Still, if you have a power conduit to the creator … perhaps I can tap into it. Perhaps if the power comes through you and then into me, the Creator will not halt the flow … as long as you live. If you give me your power willingly, it will be easier for you. Regardless, willing or otherwise, you could be a source of power for me. I tire of drinking the power from these dying animals. It takes too long. It is like trying to drink an ocean a sip at a time. Your connection though small, is still so much greater than what I can get from human sacrifices. What a stupid thing for the Creator to do, give you a conduit and then send you to me. As long as I keep you alive, I can use your power."

Mercy said, "I won't let you. I'll kill myself first."

Moloch said, "You little fool. It won't get to that." He reached over and grabbed the chain at her feet and dragged her to him. She saw that the chain that wrapped around her was from the supplies used in drilling. Moloch must have found it when he climbed down from the deck above. Moloch pulled her closer and placed the palm of his enormous hand over her face. She felt his fingers tighten around her head. She was in blackness.

She heard Moloch's voice, "…there is the thread of power…how long has it been since I had a conduit like this? Since before our rebellion…the one where Lucifer sold us out … I can't find a way to tap into it…maybe if I force her to use some of the power, I'll find a way to absorb it."

Mercy felt a tremendous pressure in her mind almost like she was being forced down and squashed flat into a corner. She felt the huge presence of Moloch's mind pressing against her, forcing her down.

In a slow, chanting voice, Moloch said, "Yield to me. Give in. You know you cannot fight for long. You are hurt and helpless. You are chained and bound. You have no choices and no options. You have to give in sooner or later. Give in and I will control you. Your mind and body are mine and you can't stop me."

Mercy strained against the chains but they didn't give at all. She felt Moloch's mind pressing harder and harder against her. She imagined her consciousness curling into a little ball. Soon, Moloch would fill her entire mind and she would only be able to whimper helplessly from her tiny corner. She couldn't stop him. She tried to scream but couldn't.

Moloch said, "It's hopeless. The Creator sent you to me without the training or strength to succeed. They knew you would fail. They wanted you to fail. They hoped you would fail. They sent you as distraction to me, probably so that Michael and his forces could descend on me without warning. You've been used as a decoy. Give in and I'll let you help me. You'll be easier for me to manage if you aren't a mindless ruin. If you don't surrender, I will force you to submit and destroy your mind in the process."

Mercy grunted with the pain in her side and in her mind. She felt that any second, her mind would rupture and break. She tried fighting back, but how could she? Thoughts of despair ran through her. She was about to have her mind raped. She'd be as used and degraded as any whore had ever been with the only difference being that she would be taken mentally rather than physically. But wasn't that just as bad? How could she face anyone again? How could she face Jack, knowing she'd been forced to obey and follow Moloch?

Mercy thought, *I won't be forced! Ever! All of my life people have told me that I must give in to the culture, or to the organization, or to the institution. I've always been told to give up my needs and subordinate myself to others. I've given in to that idea too many times before.* She shouted in her mind, *Not this time though. I won't be forced! You can not make me submit!*

She hissed, "You. Can't. Force. Me."

Moloch looked at her in surprise. "I can force you, but I would rather not destroy your mind. I want you to serve me willingly because it will be so much easier." He tilted his head and looked at her as if with new eyes. "Your hair is even lighter, but you look like, what was her name? She was the only human woman that ever brought one of my children to term. What was her name? Oh, yes. Chalara. She was called Chalara and you resemble her, though you are taller and much stronger. Perhaps you'd be more successful in bearing me children than even she."

Mercy felt a wave of nausea sweep over her. *The monster did plan on raping her and impregnating her!* She felt as if her brain was filled with steam to the point of exploding. She screamed at the monster. "I will not submit to you! You'll have to kill me!"

In answer, Moloch glared at her and redoubled his mental pressure. She felt the massive weight of his mind descending on her, crushing her. She groaned. The weight of his thoughts pressed, squeezed and flattened her mind, but she pushed back. It didn't feel as before. She shoved back mentally and felt a slight shift. She shouted back mentally. *I won't give in!* The monster's mind seemed to flinch away from her by a small amount. She pictured herself, staggered under a giant sphere of rock, but pushing and lifting. The boulder gave way a half inch, then an inch. She imagined that she lifted and pressed and slowly extended her arms, stretching and extending her muscles to the limit. Finally, she saw herself standing erect, arms straight up, holding above her a massive globe that dwarfed her. She gasped with the effort and set herself firmly. At last, she hurled the gargantuan weight away. The sensation of weight fled. She drew in a breath suddenly and opened her eyes.

Moloch's eyes widened as he realized Mercy had thrown him back. He snarled with rage and moved closer to her. He reached out his right hand and extended his index finger. He moved the tip of the gigantic finger to within an inch of her bullet wound. He spoke softly and with great menace.

"Your injury needs tending. The missile has penetrated your vitals. You will die in slow agony without aid. Or ... I could heal you."

Mercy shuddered. The wound throbbed with waves of pain that worsened by the minute. "I don't want your help," she gasped.

Moloch said, "I know, you would rather die, but I need you alive. So now you need to learn how to use your power to heal yourself. The power you can reach through the Creator's channel can be used for many things. One is healing, but it is very difficult to learn and to use unless someone guides you. Another use of the power is pain. That is much, much easier to learn." Moloch moved his index finger the final inch separating it from Mercy's wound. At contact, a reddish glow seemed to flood into the bleeding site.

Mercy felt a sudden jolt as Moloch touched her wound. She cried out in agony as the pain doubled and then doubled again. She arched and strained against the chains that bound her. She writhed and twisted, but she couldn't get away from him. Involuntary tears streaked her face from beneath clenched eyelids. Suddenly the pain lessened and returned to the throbbing pulse of injury, though Mercy felt the monster's finger still touching the wound. The thought made her want to gag.

Moloch said, "That was a tiny use of power by me to multiply the pain that your body was already feeling. I did it by imagining seizing the life energy and then shaping it into a dagger. I imagined it stabbing into you, and then I made it so by willing it to be so. It is the will that activates the power. That is why you have been able to intermittently and unpredictably use the power, because your will is very strong, and you stumble into it correctly every now and again. It takes no more power to lessen pain and gain relief. I will teach you that now." Again, a reddish glow flowed into her side.

She spoke feebly, "I don't want your help ..."

Mercy felt a fluid surge of coolness originating from the wound entry point and penetrating into it like a trickle of cold water. The coolness spread into her and halved the pain, then halved it again, and again. The pain receded from her mind as if it were a distant memory. Only a small remnant remained as if to remind her that something needed attention. She breathed more slowly and sighed with relief. Her muscles began to relax and she realized how wound up she had been. She exhaled a long and slow breath, savoring the feeling, then the pain came roaring back, full-force. Her throat clenched, as did all her muscles. She gasped again.

"You just felt the soothing of the pain and then the return of it as I stopped the flow of power into the wound. The lessening of the pain was not due to healing, but due to temporarily masking it. I see you understand." Moloch took her head in both hands and said, "I can follow your thoughts. Now imagine your wound, then picture it swollen and bleeding. Ignore the pain. Good, you had it for an instant then let it slip. Now picture it again, in detail. Picture the pellet lodged in your entrails. Idiot! You lost it. There you have it, excellent. First you must remove the pellet, then, healing comes after that. The pain will be intense, so you must first mask the pain as I just taught you with soothing, smoothing sensations."

Mercy dropped her mental picture of the wound and concentrated on soothing the pain. Her thoughts were so scattered and impaired, she kept grasping at images of peacefulness but they slipped away when she felt the throbbing renew in her side. She tried again but lost the images. The pain was too intense. Moloch shook her like a rag.

"Concentrate! If you cannot ignore pain, you will never be of use to yourself or me. Do you think you are the first to experience agony? Ignore it. Use that stubbornness of yours! Think of the pain as a surging river, and you are but a small stone at the bottom of the riverbed. The river rages, but the water flows over and past you. There is no magic or use of power that will give you control over your own mind. Only self-mastery and discipline can give you that. Control your thoughts, you fool. Let the pain flow over but not through you."

Mercy tried again though she felt herself sagging. The pain was so all-encompassing. She tried to focus but could barely keep afloat in the sea of torment. It was like all those years that she'd heard the voices calling to her and mocking her. All her life they'd tried to control her, and she'd thought they were figments of her imagination. But she hadn't been crazy. They really were there. They'd turned out to be demented spirits that sought to torture her and mislead her. But finally she'd learned to master them. Because of her bloodline, she'd been able to turn her thoughts into action and to block out those foul voices. There really was power in thought. Suddenly she knew what to do.

*So let the feelings come. Don't try to stop the pain, but don't cling to it either. Let it go. Not in an act of surrender, but of will. Sink under it like a stone drifting to the bottom of a river. There. The pain rages above, but cannot reach this part of me. I am still. Now I can sense the blue thread again, and I can reach it.* She imagined herself grasping the slender cord of energy and pictured a soothing flow of cool water washing her wound. She tried to seize it, but it evaded her and slipped through her mental grasp. She calmed herself and fell back on what Moloch had said about the will being the way to control the power. She willed herself to picture a stream of cool, soothing water and then saw it washing the wound in her side. The pain seemed to lessen further and the sharp, stabbing edges of her agony seemed to blunt.

From somewhere, Moloch's deep voice said, "You have it. Now the wound. Extract the missile. Your thoughts must be built with care. Move the missile by imagining that you are pushing it slowly back out through the path of the wound."

* * *

The Russian stepped over the final group of bodies and toward the stern drive shaft. *I can't afford to waste any more bullets. I hope that is the last of the crew I have to deal with.* He discarded the empty then inserted another ammunition clip. The drive shaft was already shattered by the earlier explosives he'd triggered, but this time he needed to place the C4 on the outer wall right next to the thrust block that was used to cushion the propeller from the drive shaft and engine. A hole here would sink the ship quickly. He got to work attaching the explosive and setting the timer. *Ten minutes should be enough for me to get back up and out.*

He tripped the timer and started the countdown. He turned and headed back up the stairs, cursing his injuries. *How did that woman get so fast and so strong? Ever since I saw her do in that lackey of the Chevreau's in Dallas, I keep asking that. I've never been beaten like that before. What is her secret?*

The Russian looked at his watch and keyed his transmitter. "Dmitri, this is Vasiliy. I am ready for pick-up. The ship's hull will be breached in less than ten minutes. Repeat, I am ready for pick-up. Requesting retrieval. Over."

* * *

Mercy was deep in her trance. Distantly, the pain surged again, but she felt calm and untouched at the bottom of that river of agony. She understood instinctively that this time the monster was telling her the truth. At least, it told her part of the truth, so she pushed slowly against the bullet, back along the exit wound. It was so hard, much harder than she thought it should be. She felt it move while the pain roared far away. In the distance she sensed somehow that her tortured flesh spasmed and blood gushed from the wound, but she ignored the pain and pushed harder, redoubling her efforts. The bullet moved further out, a millimeter at a time. *I have to picture everything, each moment, each split-second. I have to concentrate and not let my mind wander. I am pushing the bullet, atom by atom, out of the wound. I feel the blood flow past, but I will not stop. My flesh shrinks back but I will not relent.*

A few moments later, Mercy felt the bullet slip from the wound, bouncing and clattering to the deck. Blood gushed from her side. She felt a distant roaring sound and her heart labored to keep up with her falling blood pressure.

Moloch's voice thundered through her mind. He sounded energized and triumphal. "Now pour power into the wound itself. Imagine it whole again and open your mind to as much of the power as you can. The body knows how to heal itself, and that is what you want at work now, but much faster. The more power you release to it, the more quickly it will heal, but don't drop your concentration! The pain will return as strongly as the healing is quick. Stay at the bottom of the river!"

She opened her mind, imagining herself as a waterfall over which the power poured in torrents. In the thunderous passage, it tore at her, peeling away her consciousness as if by the erosion of ages, molding her into a new shape, a new path. Distantly she knew her body was engulfed in agony and healing at the same time, but it seemed not to matter so much now. That moment in time seemed to hang and stutter to a stop for her. That moment of pain and change stood still in her as she felt herself poised, ready to either tumble over the falls into darkness, or to hold solid like the cliff that releases the river. She held.

Mercy had felt time slow down for her before, but this was different. She felt that time had virtually stopped for her and she opened her eyes. Her body was healing rapidly. That at least was not held back by the sensation of slow time. Moloch crouched over her prone form, and *what was that?* The blue thread that she clung to, that she was channeling into the wound with her right hand, Moloch held a thread of blue as well, but it came out of her left hand and into him. *He was siphoning off most of the power for himself and leaving her with only the minimum needed to perform the self-healing. No wonder it had felt harder than it ought. Moloch was stealing more power from her than she was using. No wonder he wanted her alive. He couldn't reach the creator's power any longer and wanted to keep her around so he could feed off her like a leech.*

Time sped up again and flowed normally. Moloch smiled with a sated expression as one who had eaten their fill. Mercy felt weak from the pain that was now dissipating and from the energy she'd consumed in the healing.

Moloch said, "I was right. Through you, I can draw power." Moloch motioned with his hand as if releasing something. The blue thread connecting him to Mercy vanished. Moloch turned to Parasca who lead another sacrificial victim. "Enough. I won't need to consume more slaves as long as she is here. Put that one back with the others. I can use them as soldiers when we get to shore."

Before Janos Parasca could follow Moloch's directions, a deep, wrenching crash sounded from deep within the doomed ship.

# CHAPTER 33 – SACRIFICE

*"Swallowed up and lost in the wide womb of uncreated night"*
*— John Milton, Paradise Lost*

A sudden rumble shuddered through the ship and the deck heaved upward. Mercy, still chained, was thrown upward and then crashed back to the drilling deck floor, the wind knocked out of her. Even Moloch smashed against the drill rig tower and was staggered and seemed dazed. The deck of the ship plunged down and then toward the stern. Moloch crashed against the drill machinery, striking his head and sliding limply with the tipping of the deck. He seemed unconscious or dazed. Parasca and the crewman crashed in a heap into a wall. The crewman lay, broken. Parasca moaned.

Mercy struggled with her chains but couldn't budge them. She strained her head and saw Moloch lying unconscious about thirty feet away, his face covered in blood and a wide gash visible on his forehead. She frantically wrenched at her bonds but they were too tight. She growled and cursed in frustration. *This is my chance! If I don't get away while he's unconscious, I don't get away at all!* She twisted and rolled as she strained. *Nothing!*

A voice hissed at her from five feet away. "Mercy. Lay still. I'll get you loose."

She twisted toward the sound of the whisper and with a crazed desperation said, "Hayden! Thank God!" She saw what he carried and almost wept with joy. "Bolt cutters! You wonderful man! How did you ..?" He was at her side in an instant and went to work on the chains, snipping them again and again. They fell away and she tried to disentangle herself.

Hayden helped her get loose and to her feet. He said, "I saw what was happening and realized the rest of our plan would be for nothing unless we got you loose from those chains. I warned Jack to be ready while I found these." He motioned to the bolt cutters.

A voice like thunder roared, "Stop!" Moloch had opened his eyes and rose up on hands and knees, blood streaming from the wound on his head.

Hayden said to Mercy, "I'll delay him. The shield is over there. You're the only one that can stop him." He pointed to the crystal steel artifact leaning six meters away against a wall and then squeezed her hand. His face seemed brighter somehow and he smiled at her wistfully then darted away.

Mercy shouted, "Wait! Hayden, don't!" From a corner of her panic-filled mind, she saw Hayden rush at the monster as if to club it with the bolt cutters. He trailed a thin blue glowing line that ran back to her hand where he had squeezed it. *He's going to get himself killed! Hayden!*

Moloch rose to his feet and stared with hate at Mercy. He seemed to have momentarily lost track of Hayden and failed to notice the man until Hayden swung the bolt cutters with all his strength and struck the monster full on the left knee cap. Moloch gasped in pain and bellowed like a bull in the ring. Hayden reared back to hit again, but Moloch swept out his left arm and struck Hayden, knocking him flying into a metal bulkhead. He crashed into the wall, and then slid limply to the floor, leaving a bloody streak on the wall where his head had struck.

Mercy screamed in anguish for Hayden, knowing he had done this for her, just to buy her some time. Before she could do anything further, she saw the blue thread connecting her to Hayden suddenly blaze into a thick, solid bar of light. She felt a surge of energy that dwarfed anything she'd experienced before. She flexed her fists and felt herself crackling with power.

She slowly raised her eyes to glare at Moloch. A single tear of sorrow from each eye rolled down her dirty cheeks, leaving twin streaks behind. Her grim whisper hissed out, "You killed him!" Moloch's face showed concern for the first time and he seemed to blink hard against the blazing blue beam that connected Mercy to Hayden. The blue energy held for one more second, but finally blinked out with a last brilliant flash as Mercy absorbed the last of the flow of power from Hayden's still form.

Moloch staggered back, one arm across his eyes. Momentarily blinded, he backed away until he was stopped by the side of the sarcophagus which still glowed from the sacrificial fire inside.

Parasca, on the platform on the other side of the sarcophagus, shouted, "Lord Moloch! What is wrong?"

Moloch waved in the direction of Parasca's voice and shouted, "Be silent, fool!" He rubbed at his eyes in an attempt to restore them to function.

Mercy darted to the shield and grasped it in her left hand. Without stopping to think, she seized the release mechanism for the drill bit in her right hand and pulled it. It fell to the floor. The bit was attached to an eight foot length of steel pipe like the head of a giant club. She grabbed the pipe and lifted it as easily as a child would a twig. Every muscle felt shot through with lightning. She shouted in rage and ran at Moloch with her shield up and mace-like club of pipe and drill-bit ready to strike.

With Moloch's sight still clearing from the flash of light that had transferred Hayden's life energy to Mercy, she knew time was short. At the end of her dash, she planted her feet and raised her shield then swung the pipe with all her strength in a side-arm swipe at the monster's left knee. The side of the drill bit impacted the tree-trunk thick joint and the bit's diamond coated cutting surfaces sliced deep. Flesh tore away in chunks and dark blood gushed from the wound. The monster's knee joint bent inward but didn't break. Mercy bit her lip in frustration and cursed inwardly. *Harder! Break his knee and he'll be helpless!*

Mercy reared back to strike again, but Moloch roared in pain and struck down with a pile driver blow to crush Mercy. She held the shield up and his fist hit the crystal steel instead of her. Mercy felt energy flow from the shield as it absorbed most of the giant's blow. The rest of the force of Moloch's strike drove through her arm and into her body. She grunted with effort, rocked back on her heels but kept her balance, then struck again.

Mercy swung the giant mace, but missed as Moloch slid to the side and grabbed the sword. His arm swung back and brought the sword directly at Mercy in a wicked sideswipe. With only a split second to prepare, Mercy angled her shield toward the blow. The sword hit the shield with a flash of sparks and a red flare of released energy. Mercy felt the shield absorb most of the blow, but also heard a faint crack as if something had broken loose. In her hyper-fast state she noticed two small, sparkling shards angle away from the impact. A piece of crystal steel seemed to have broken away from the sword or the shield or both. Mercy shuddered with the effort of standing against the monster, even with the shield. *The shield won't last forever against another crystal steel artifact. If we keep up this fight for very long, these two relics will destroy each other.*

Before she could think, the monster struck at her again with an overhand blow but she got the shield up, barely in time. Moving unbelievably fast, he struck again and again, trying to drive her into the floor. She bent lower with the effort and gasped with exertion. She went down on one knee and still the blows rained down. Shards from the shield and the sword fell like broken glass to the steel deck.

*Does it all end here? After all we've gone through, am I going to die like this? I can't let it happen.*

She screamed in frustration and swung the pipe, trying to hit Moloch's leg. In mid-swing, he corrected and brought the sword in to parry the improvised club. The sword sliced through the steel pipe like it was made of wax. The end with the drill bit clattered to the floor. Mercy now held a seven foot pipe with an angled cut at the end nearest the giant.

She saw her chance and ran forward inside the monster's reach and leapt. Her strengthened leg muscles propelled her into a vertical leap that lifted her eight feet above the floor. Her arm reared back to strike and when she was within reach, she stabbed the steel pipe into the chest of the giant. Following through with every ounce of energy in her, she drove the pipe entirely through the monster.

She dropped to the floor, landed on her feet and saw Moloch staggering backward. The steel pipe that penetrated his chest protruded two feet from his front and back. The monster clutched at it, gasping for breath. Cords stood out on his neck. He stumbled backward until his feet stopped against the smoking sarcophagus. Moloch coughed and a gout of dark blood gushed from his mouth, down his chest and over the steel pipe that protruded from him. He tried to grab the tube to pull it out, but his grasping claw-like hands slipped and slid on the blood-coated steel.

He managed to croak, "You can't kill me like this! I can't be killed. It's part of my curse that I'm locked into this form until the end of time." Blood flowed from his mouth. He gasped again and coughed weakly.

She ran at him, swinging her arm back and slamming the shield edge-on into his bloody right knee. Streamers of red life-energy fountained from the shield as it sliced into Moloch. She heard the joint snap and saw it bend at a horrifying inward angle. Moloch's mouth opened in an agonized, nearly silent scream that sounded like someone in the last throes of strangulation. He dropped the sword, the shattered knee buckled completely and he fell backward into the flaming sarcophagus.

*Jack, don't fail me now.* She looked up and saw one of the cranes moving. *Hurry!* She heard a distant click and darted to one side without thinking. Bullets stitched across the deck where she'd been standing. She ran around the edge of the sarcophagus and then darted a quick look back around the corner. Parasca held a machine gun and shouted.

"Stay back, Mercy! I <u>will</u> shoot you. We need him. He's the only one that can teach us what we need to know to use our power." Parasca said.

Mercy shouted, "… and then what, Janos? Help him eat more people? Be the priests that preside over his human sacrifices? You haven't thought this through!"

"It's not a matter of thinking. He can't be killed. In minutes, he'll be back and will have healed himself from what you've done to him. He'll just keep coming and coming. We can't fight him. We have to help him!"

She looked up and saw that the crane had stopped moving. She hoped Jack was ready for this. She looked for and found the cable hanging down from the crane and lowering toward her. *Another thirty seconds … I need to buy time.*

She shouted at Parasca, "You can't trust him. We're like bugs to a creature like him. He's lived thousands of years, and sees human beings as nothing but livestock. He'll use us and dispose of us like tissue paper. I'm not going to serve something like that!" The end of the cable came within reach and she grabbed the hook at the end of it and hooked it into the side ring attached to this end of the lid of the sarcophagus. She waved toward the crane overhead. The cable began to tighten.

Parasca's voice grew louder. *He's moving in. No more time.* He shouted, "We have no choice! Mircea, think. He will win eventually. There's nothing that can stop a creature like him. We can only hope to help him and be useful to him. We're the only two of his blood. He needs us. You've already learned how to use some of the power. He needs you too!  Give up this folly!" Parasca said.

He stepped around the edge of the sarcophagus, his gun leveled, expecting to find Mercy. Instead, he saw the lid slowly rising from where it had rested beside the monster's coffin. Mercy was nowhere to be seen. Then Parasca saw a form in his peripheral vision jumping down from the edge of the sarcophagus above. He was slammed to the deck.

Mercy kicked the gun away from Parasca and stood over him, fists clenched. She spoke with years of scorn in her voice. "Don't give in to him, _Father!_  Look at yourself. Serving a living demon. I knew you were a criminal and a murderer even, but feeding others to a monster like him is too much even for you!"

Parasca glared, stood up and then said with a snarl, "I should have had you killed in that jail where your slut of a mother gave birth to you!"

Mercy rocked back as if slapped and Parasca used the moment to pull the ancient stone knife, the first of all of his artifacts, from his pocket. He lunged forward and Mercy, caught by surprise, pulled back only partially. The dagger caught her in the upper right arm. Horrible pain shot through her. She looked at the dripping stone blade as Parasca pulled it out to stab again. She felt drained, almost as if half of the energy Hayden had died to give her were stolen in that one instant. The stone knife was surrounded in a red, pulsating halo. A sudden surge of red energy ran from it and up Parasca's raised arm. He suddenly stood almost unmoving, shuddering and transfixed as if locked in ecstatic agony. Mercy brought the shield around with blinding speed and slammed it into the side of Parasca's head. He crumpled to the deck, the glowing stone knife skittering to a stop against the sarcophagus.

*The sarcophagus! What am I doing?*

She looked up and saw the lid suspended almost vertically above her. Jack may have been ready to close the lid, but then she saw the giant figure rise up from the flaming sarcophagus. Moloch threw aside the steel pipe. His chest wound was sealed. His knee looked to be whole as well. He stood silhouetted in the tongues of fire, unfazed.

He said, "I've withstood the flames of Hell itself. You thought this would hurt me?"

* * *

Parasca felt himself being carried. *Moloch has picked me up.* He opened his eyes and saw Rakslav's large face above him. Parasca cursed and struggled. "Put me down, fool! The woman! Stop the woman!"

Rakslav stopped and set Parasca's feet on the tilting deck. "I had to get you away from there, sir. I had been in a fog for hours, but I suddenly snapped out of it and realized you'd been hurt." They were on the upper deck outside of the moon pool. *He must have carried me out. Idiot!*

Over the groans of the dying ship, the roar of engines sounded above them. A collapsible ladder rolled out of the helicopter hovering overhead and down to the deck near a scattered pile of corpses. A searchlight from the helicopter played over Parasca and Rakslav. Dmitri Slokov descended the ladder, stepped to the deck seven meters away and pointed a pistol at them.

Dmitri shouted, "Janos! What has happened to you, my old enemy?"

Parasca squinted in the blinding light and shouted, "Dmitri? What are you doing? If you've come to mock me, save it for later. Help us off this ship before it's too late."

Dmitri's laughter rolled out. "Help you? After all I've done to ruin your plans? Not a chance. Though if you tell me what you've done with Dr. Teller, I'll let you go down with your ship. How would that be?"

"Dr. Teller? What do you want with her?"

"You know exactly why I want her! I know who she is! You don't think I found out from some of your own records that my people hacked? I know that she's Tresa's daughter!"

"Is that all you care about, you fool? What if she is that whore's daughter? It won't do you any good. Tresa's still dead. Besides, Mircea's probably busy being killed right now, I imagine."

Dmitri shouted, "What? You're lying! She's not dead."

Parasca called back, "Stop this nonsense! There's a monster back there at the moon pool. We have to get away before he finishes off Mircea."

"You're worse than you ever were! She's your daughter and you leave her to die back there?" Dmitri shouted.

There was a rattle of gunfire. Dmitri turned in the direction of the noise. Parasca ducked involuntarily and glanced sidelong to see a shadowy figure that seemed to be firing bursts into the air to get their attention. The searchlight beam shifted away from Parasca and Rakslav and toward the man staggering out of the stairwell leading up from engineering. He hobbled toward the dangling ladder.

Dmitri said, "Ah, Vasya. I hoped you'd make it. You've done such a fine job destroying Janos' schemes."

Rakslav shook his head in shocked recognition, roared and ran at the Russian. Vasiliy stopped before grasping the rungs of the ladder, raised his gun and fired, but not quickly enough. Rakslav dove behind a stack of pipes as the bullets ricocheted off the deck where Rakslav had been a moment before. Vasiliy, blood running from cuts in his face, turned to anticipate Rakslav's movements. A piece of debris sailed from where Rakslav had been and struck the Russian in the chest. He gasped for breath and lost his grip on the machine gun. It clattered to the deck.

Rakslav came out from the stack of pipe, running across the rubble-strewn deck as quickly as Parasca had ever seen him move. Vasiliy dropped to his knees, grasping for the fallen gun. Rakslav closed just as Vasiliy got hold of the weapon. Rakslav charged into the injured man like a football linebacker and the two of them crashed together, rolling across the deck. Vasiliy lost his momentary grip on the gun and it tumbled and came to rest only three meters from Parasca.

Parasca smiled an evil grin and dove for the gun. Dmitri spun and brought the pistol to bear on Parasca. He fired once and the bullet ricocheted off the deck. His second shot hit Parasca in the shoulder. Janos grunted from the impact but lifted the machine gun toward Dmitri. Dmitri turned and ran for the ladder. Parasca changed his aim and sighted along the barrel at the helicopter.

Rakslav grappled with the Russian, trying to hold on to the wiry man. The Russian twisted and delivered a powerful punch into Rakslav's gut, but the larger man absorbed it without even a grunt of acknowledgment. Rakslav sensed rather than saw that the Russian was injured by the way he favored his ribs and one arm, so he mercilessly took his enemy in a bear hug and squeezed the already cracked ribs. The Russian writhed, but Rakslav bore down, straining mightily against Vasiliy's kicks and blows. A rib cracked, then another. Vasiliy gasped and then another cracked and then a fourth snapped. He went slack in Rakslav's arms and the large man relaxed the bear hug, slid his hands up, grabbed the man by the neck and twisted sharply. The Russian's head turned in a complete circle as his spinal cord snapped and the neck vertebrae shattered. Rakslav dropped the limp form to the deck and turned back to Parasca.

Parasca pulled the trigger and bullets stitched across the front of the helicopter. The windshield shattered and the slugs bounced through the interior of the cab. Four bullets struck the pilot, one in the head and he slumped over, his pulped face leering out the side window. Dmitri stared in horror as the helicopter veered downward toward him. He leapt away as the aircraft smashed into the deck.

The force of the crash swept pipe, equipment and bodies overboard. Burning wreckage slid off the sloping deck of the ship and into the Black Sea. Parasca stood alone and laughed. Everyone was gone but him. He winced at the pain in his shoulder, but turned away and toward the side of the ship where the mini-subs were attached.

* * *

Mercy shouted, more loudly than ever before in her life, "Jack! Close the lid!" She looked at the sword laying on the deck and then the crude stone knife. She ignored the sword, bent and picked up the stone knife and leapt to the top edge of the sarcophagus.

Moloch stood and spoke, anger clouding his face, "He was right. You can't beat me. I can't be killed. Your only choice is to serve me."

"Wrong," she said. "There's always another choice."

She heard a deep metallic groan and saw the lid complete its arc and begin to swing downward. It started to fall slowly at first, then gained momentum and fell faster. It slammed into Moloch's shoulder and staggered him. He roared and tried to brace himself, pushing back against the tons of crystal steel in the lid. The weight of it pressed him back and down. He thundered, "No! Not this way!" The muscles in his shoulders and arms knotted like corded cables. He pushed back and stopped the descent of the lid. His face grimaced with the supreme effort.

Mercy's vision seemed to clear completely. She saw massive looping bands of red and blue flowing across and through her field of vision. A red nimbus surrounded Moloch, and Mercy realized it was all of the remaining death energy he had absorbed from his sacrificial victims, plus the remains of the Creator's energy he stole from her while she was healing herself. She also saw that the red nimbus was shrinking.

*He's weakening!*

She ran along the edge of the sarcophagus closest to the straining monster. He turned his head toward her as if pleading and whispered between gritted teeth, "Not this way. Not again."

She held her arm out to her full reach and stabbed the ancient stone blade into his side. She pulled downward and opened a vertical gash in his side fully six feet long. Black blood gushed from him and the stone knife flared into a reddish nova glare. The energy shot from the knife, into her hand and up her arm.

Mercy was paralyzed and saw in a moment all of the ancient evil of the monster's life. There were human deaths by the thousands, even millions. She was flooded with visions of treachery and debasement beyond belief. She saw the monster raping human women that seemed no larger to him than tiny children would seem to normal men. She saw him leading armies of monstrous beings into battles that left worlds in ruin. She saw him bathing in blood a thousand times and drinking from the skulls of enemies. She saw him finally defeated decisively by an equally giant luminous being that commanded an even larger army of creatures like those she had seen in the vision she'd had of the Counselor's throne room.

She opened her eyes and looked in terror at the stone knife in her paralyzed hand. She saw the thing drawing the life from the monster and pumping it into her, engulfing her in foulness and the knowledge of every evil Moloch had ever performed. She knew she had to get loose from this or she would be destroyed. Then Moloch swooned above her.

The dagger was torn from her grasp, and with nowhere to send the energy it was drawing, it blazed even brighter. Mercy's muscles were locked into immobility and she tumbled from the sarcophagus and to the deck below. She lay, face up, and saw the stone knife in Moloch's side glaring above like the mouth of a furnace. The knife exploded in a cloud of stone fragments, with the blast gouging a bloody hole in Moloch's side. Moloch fell to his knees in the fire, his arms trembling under the weight of the lid of the sarcophagus. He screamed like a lost soul.

"Not in here! No! The darkness! Help me!"

Then the lid slammed and latched shut. Mercy thought she could hear a distant shrieking. She shuddered.

Still in shock and barely able to move from where she lay, Mercy lifted her head slightly and then lowered it back to the deck. She felt dizzy and her vision seemed to rotate around her. It came to her that the ship's tilt was getting steeper. *I have to get up. Got to get away. The ship is sinking.* She tried again to move, but felt as weak as a baby. *I'm done. I can't do it.* She lay for another minute, feeling the tilt of the ship continue growing more acute. She heard a screech of metal on metal. She opened her eyes again and saw the sarcophagus slide across the tilted deck and crash into one of the drill derricks, knocking it over to lean crazily against the edge of the top deck above. *I guess I'm going down with the ship. If they ever look, they'll find my bones right next to Moloch's sarcophagus. How strange is that?* She closed her eyes and another minute went by.

Jack's voice came at her from above. "Mercy! We've got to get away. The ship's sinking!" She opened her eyes and smiled. He stood over her panting from exertion.

She spoke through a haze of exhaustion. "I can't move. I'm done, Jack. Go on. Get off the ship."

"Not without you." He grabbed her and tried to help her stand but quickly saw that she couldn't hold herself up at all. He shifted his approach and held her up until he could get his shoulder down and then crouched and draped her across his shoulders in a fireman's carry. He turned to look at the corridor leading into the ship. Following that passageway would take him to the stairs and up to the deck, but it was blocked by the sarcophagus.

He looked around, his heart racing. "How do we get out of here?" The wreckage seemed to block every way out of the drilling floor. He thought for a moment of going down through the moon pool, but quickly remembered that the moon pool's hydraulic doors to the ocean below were closed. Without power, there was no way to open them. Besides, he didn't know how he could get Mercy through that way, weakened as she was. He had to get her up and over the deck to the submersible.

He looked again and noticed the twisted drilling derrick leaning against the lip of the deck above. The tilt of the ship almost made the derrick's lean horizontal. Jack swallowed heavily and decided. He'd have to carry her over the leaning derrick and to the deck above. He'd have to step along the metal lattice of the derrick. One slip and they'd fall.

He shifted his grip on Mercy so that his right arm pinned her leg to his side and used his right hand to hold onto her arm that hung down his chest. That left his left arm free. *I might need that arm free to steady us or to grab for support.*

He stepped up to the fallen derrick and stepped onto the metal frame. The lattice work was made of steel beams that were four inches wide: no wider than the boots he wore. From where she lay across his shoulders, Mercy groaned. The ship shuddered and he heard cracks and shrieks of tearing metal. He took a deep breath and stepped out. He took a step and then another and realized he wasn't moving quickly enough. *I've got to go for it. If I'm too careful, we'll drown as the ship sinks. If I trip and fall, we'll die from broken necks. I've got to just run for it.*

Jack took a deep breath to steel himself and felt the derrick suddenly shift beneath them. He crouched and caught hold of it with his free hand and waited. It stopped moving, but he felt the ship tilt further. His eyes looked through the frame of the derrick and saw something glint below. Out of reach, tumbled into a mass of twisted steel below, he saw the edge of the shield. Next to it was the pommel of the sword. He shook his head. *No way. I can't get them out and Mercy too. It's now or never.* He lunged forward and staggered from beam to beam until finally they cleared the lip of the upper deck. Jack jumped from the derrick frame to the deck.

Without even a pause for a breath, he ran up the inclined deck with Mercy still across his shoulders. At the side of the ship, he saw the stairs leading downward to the submersibles. One of the subs was gone. *Must have been someone else of the crew still alive. Good.* He heard crashing sounds from behind and knew some of the steel pipe racks had torn loose. He staggered down the steps and to the submersible. He unsnapped the upper hatch on the little ship and opened it. Then he laid Mercy down on the top of the sub and grabbed her legs. He lowered her head first into the hatch and gently lay her on the inside floor of the little ship's control room.

Jack unfastened the outer manual releases and locks holding the sub in place and it began sliding slowly away from the ship. Jack jumped onto the external ladder, clambered to the hatch and frantically climbed inside, closing the hatch behind him as he stood on the inner ladder. He barely avoided Mercy's prone form on the floor and darted to the controls. That was the moment when the sensation of free-fall hit him. The submersible fell from the side of the ship and for a long, suspended moment, Jack wondered if it would clear the side of the tilting ship.

With a splash, the sub hit the water. Jack held onto the control panel to keep himself from being thrown from the pilot's chair. He heard Mercy groan and winced. *She's being tossed around like a rag doll.* He flipped on the power switches and started the electric motor. *Please have a full charge!* He moved the joystick forward and the ship's drive pushed them through the water.

Jack looked at the rear video screen. He frowned and checked the instruments. They were moving too slowly. The *Fortuna* was sinking and he did not want them to get pulled down with it. He heard another moan and looked behind at Mercy. He couldn't leave the controls right now. She'd have to fend for herself.

Her tremulous voice spoke hesitatingly, "Jack? Where are we?"

He said, "We're in the submersible. We've got to get away from the *Fortuna* before it sinks."

"How did I get here?"

"I carried you." He pushed the joystick all the way forward. The electric motors shot up in frequency. The speed reading climbed upward, but not as quickly as he wanted.

She seemed to think that over for a while. Then she spoke deliberately, "I feel awful … and weak … and banged up."

"Mercy, I can't talk right now. I can't seem to get this thing going fast enough."

She spoke as if from a deep sleep. "Go deeper. It'll go faster that way."

Jack hit himself on the forehead with his palm and pushed in the depth control. "I'm an idiot. I should have remembered that."

The small sub dove and was quickly submerged. It cut smoothly through the water and away from the dark mass behind. They heard distant rumblings like thunder beyond the horizon and knew the *Fortuna* had submerged. After a while, Jack turned the sub to the north toward the shore.

Mercy climbed painfully to her feet and sat gingerly in the co-pilot's chair. Jack glanced at her and shook his head in wonder.

She saw him looking and said, "What?"

"I was just wondering how you could look so good after what you've gone through."

She smiled and lowered her eyes. She frowned and sighed. She felt almost unbearably sad. "Hayden's gone."

Jack looked at her again and said, "I know, I saw. Poor Hayden. He was supposed to climb up into the other crane and the two of us were supposed to lift the lid. He wasn't supposed to get within reach of that monster."

Mercy said, "He did it to save me, really to save all of us. I think he remembered what the monster had said about 'willing sacrifices' yielding more energy. I heard the same thing from the Counselor, but I never dreamed he'd do that ..."

Jack said, "You're saying he committed suicide?"

"No, just that he came to get me free from Moloch. I think he also gambled that if he were killed, it might give a boost to me. He was right, and it was just enough for me to stand up to Moloch a little longer."

Jack reached his hand to hers and took it gently in his. "Mercy, you're really banged up."

"Don't worry about me," she said. "I always heal fast."

"Must still hurt like crazy though," he said. "I just want you all well for the pictures."

"What pictures?" She said and looked him directly in the eyes. "What are you talking about? Do you think the media is already onto this disaster? Surely no one knows yet."

"I'm not talking about the media. I'm talking about our own photographer."

"I don't get it. What photographer?"

Jack gazed into her eyes. He paused and said, "Let's just say, that if you heal quickly ... without bruises all over your hands ... it will be more photogenic when I put a ring on your left hand's third finger."

Mercy looked down at her hand, blushed and said, "Oh."

Jack waited. She seemed to be struggling to find words. *Don't say anything. Just let her say whatever she's going to say. If she refuses again, then she refuses. You've waited for years already. You can wait a few more seconds.*

Mercy opened her mouth as if to speak, but she closed her mouth. Again, she opened her mouth and struggled to find words and ended by closing her lips again, silently. She clenched her eyes shut and finally whispered in a voice catching with emotion, "You know, and you still want me?"

Jack thought of explanations, rationalizations, arguments and pleadings. They all raced through his mind, but he knew none of it would do. None of it was needed. He didn't need to argue or to convince Mercy. All he needed was a single, truthful word. He chuckled inwardly. It was his word of power.

"Yes." He let the word rest in the air and remained silent.

She seemed to listen to the word, to test it, to weigh it. At last, she sighed visibly then nodded her head again and again. She looked into his eyes and smiled through tear-filled eyes.

"Well, Jack Truett ... I think I'll let you put the ring on me. But, on one condition."

"What's that?" he said.

"No long engagement this time."

He smiled. "I think I can handle that," and he leaned over and kissed her. She kissed back urgently. They kissed for a long, long time.

\* \* \*

A figure swam through the waves away from the sinking ship. In times past, he'd considered himself to be a large, powerful man, but no longer. Now he knew his limits and his true priorities. He knew that first, he had to survive. Next, he had to eliminate enemies and third, he had to somehow free his new master. Survival was the key now, and so he swam like a possessed man, completely focused on his target. He must reach his goal before it was too late and he dared not waste even the time it would take to stop and look. He kept on swimming.

He reached out his right arm for another stroke and felt his hand strike something hard and cold. He grabbed on and lifted his head out of the water to look. He held on to a rung in a giant chain. Before he could even think, the chain link he held jerked and started rising from the water. He grabbed more tightly and let it carry him upward, the water sluicing from him as he rose. As his legs cleared the sea, he placed first one, then the other of his feet in the link of chain below as if on a ladder step. The chain carried him upward and completely out of the water and he let it lift him above the surface until he could see the wreck of the *Fortuna* slumping into the churning water. Above him, he saw the large port through which the chain on which he rode was being pulled. He studied it and calculated the speed with which he approached it. He looked back down the chain toward the water.

*The opening's too little. I can't fit through that. Have to time this well.* He circled his arms around the large chain, linked his hands and relaxed his grip. He slid downward along the chain and splashed back into the sea. He let the chain rise through his encircling arms and braced his legs. A minute later, he felt something massive hit his feet below the surface and he flexed and stood up on the anchor as it cleared the water. He lowered himself into a squat on the huge metal weight and held on. The anchor carried him up and then jerked to a stop with his head just short of the anchor's chain opening. Above him, he heard a voice shout in Romanian, "Anchor up!" A few seconds later a klaxon sounded from somewhere above.

He felt the tanker back away, its engines thrown into reverse. Rakslav looked over his shoulder and saw the *Fortuna*. Strange thoughts ran through his head. *Hundreds of millions of dollars. Hundreds of people. All lost.* Bodies floated in the water, a few moving, most seemingly dead. The ship itself seemed mortally wounded as if the last people leaving it had stolen its ability to continue living. It wallowed, rolled suddenly as if releasing its grip on the world above and sank into the sea. Great gouts of water and fountains of bubbles shot from below and splashed back down to the surface of the water as in the last gasps of a prehistoric monster of the deep. He watched it until the frothing lessened to a simmer and the tanker turned and cut through the water again.

Rakslav held onto his place on the anchor. He needed to find a place to lay low for a while and develop a plan to carry out his master's wishes. He knew that if he could get aboard, a ship as big as this would have many places in which to hide. And plan. *I must return.* He rode the anchor as the tanker ship sailed away from the *Fortuna*'s grave.

* * *

One arm had been broken and possibly a leg, but Dmitri held grimly to a life preserver he'd found in the flotsam. He had no idea how he'd survived the crash of the helicopter. One moment he'd been jumping away from the crashing chopper and the next, he felt himself tumbling into pipes and debris. He'd blacked out until he'd suddenly splashed into the sea. By the time he'd floundered around and found the life preserver, the *Lucian* was already lifting anchor. He'd screamed for help, but no one aboard had heard him and it was sailing away minutes later. He cursed the *Lucian* for leaving him behind, but then caught sight of lights further away. Other ships were approaching to investigate. Good. After he was back in Bucharest, he'd have the captain of the *Lucian* brought to him. Maybe he'd eat the man's liver for breakfast. And then he'd see about Parasca. But what if the man had died in the same crash that had swept him from the deck? *Then, I suppose I'll just have to take his company. Small recompense for all he's done!*

* * *

The submersible moved through the dark, inky blackness of the water, tracing along the path of the bubbles rising from below. The headlight lanced downward, scanning. Finally, at about 270 meters, the light revealed the dark body of a sunken ship lying on its side. The submersible moved along above the ship and the light illuminated the word, *Fortuna*. The small ship moved past and toward midship. The light moved on until it came to rest on the drilling derrick, now broken and bent and laying parallel to the sea floor. The submersible swung away from the ship and down and scanned the deck of the ship now laying perpendicular to the sea floor.

The submersible pointed downward and scanned along the sea bed, skipping over and past twisted metal and racks of spilled pipe and stopped at a large box shaped object. The pilot took a reading and recorded the sub's position, then pointed the lights down again and scanned the sea bed. Something reflected the headlights and the pilot stopped.

There in the silt lay a metal object, a little less than two meters long with a shorter cross piece near one end. The pilot reached to a different control and took hold of it. On the outside of the sub, a remote tool sprang to life, its pincer jaws opening and closing as if from unused muscles after a long sleep. The sub moved closer to the silt-covered floor and the mechanical limb reached out and grasped the object. The pilot locked the control tightly in place and shifted back to the directional controls. The sub began to rise toward the surface, the shining sword clasped tightly in its mechanical grasp.

The light from the inside of the submersible illuminated the face of the sub operator. Parasca smiled and moved the submersible upward and away from the sarcophagus and the wreck of the *Fortuna*.

# CHAPTER 34 – EPILOGUE: DEATH AND BIRTH

*"O how fallen!"*
*— John Milton, Paradise Lost*

5600 BC

The small boat pitched and rolled but finally righted itself as it lifted up and over the giant wave. Chalara lay trembling in the bottom of the boat, wracked by weeping that would not let up.

"Mother! Can you hear me?"

Chalara did not answer. Her gigantic son tried again and again to get her to respond.

Finally, Chalara screamed at him, "Let me die! My Lord is defeated and his fortress is swallowed by the sea. Let me die!"

"Mother, stop it! What happened? How do you know that father has been defeated?"

After Chalara had finally composed herself, she told her son of all that she had seen, of the winged enemies that came down from the sky and of the armored and winged being as tall as the King. She told of the King being held as a prisoner. She told him of the shattered and crushed bodies of her sister wives in the rubble of the broken walls. She told him that Mulciber had also been a prisoner. She told how the leader of his enemies had struck down the King. She told him of the sea surging in and flooding the fortress. She told him of the winged enemies flying away without the giant rectangular chest. Finally, she finished her story and Melekan sat there in the pitching boat, stunned and beyond words. At last he was able to speak again.

"But, I've just returned with his sword and shield. Lord Mulciber wanted to study them further, but when he had examined them, he sent me back. I came to return them to father! How could this have happened?"

Hot tears of frustration ran from his eyes. He screamed at the storm and shook his fist at the clouds.

"Why have you done this to my father? Why? And he a son of heaven!" He screamed a cry of rage into the wind, straining his muscles into corded, trembling fury. Finally, his anger subsided and he slumped to the bench beside his mother.

One of the sailors called out to the giant, "Lord Melekan, where should we go? The fortress is lost beneath the waves. Should we turn back for Varnach?"

"Yes, go back. Lord Mulciber may be gone, but his Keep may have survived. I must see if anyone was spared from this disaster. Perhaps some of my wives still live."

"Yes, Lord." And then the sailor turned to his fellows on the small sailing ship, "Return to Varnach!"

Chalara's voice barely carried to him over the noise of the storm, "All is lost, Melekan. The King is gone and his kingdom with him. What is left for me?"

His voice carried through the wind to her, "I am still alive, and you carry father's child. You still have much to do. Besides, they cannot have killed father. They must have taken him prisoner instead."

She sat up. Rain streamed down her face. "You are right! He must still live. He will return and bring me back to him. I will yet present him with his second child." The baby kicked again from within her.

The storm continued all that day and the next, turning into a steady downpour. The wind lessened, but the rain continued falling. The sailors bailed the small ship constantly to keep it from being swamped. The wind blew out of the southwest and so their return trip was at least made easier by the direction of the gale. On the third day, one of the sailors spoke again to Chalara and her son.

"My Lord and Lady, we are drawing near to the shore below Varnach, but things are not right. There is much debris in the water, driftwood and even great uprooted trees. The torrential rains have caused great flooding and the waters are continually rising. We just passed a small sandy island that I know from the past. I have spent many an afternoon resting and fishing from that same sandbar and rested under its trees. I almost did not recognize the island as we passed it by. Nothing remains of it but a few tall trees and large boulders with distinctive shapes that still rise from the water. The rest of the island is buried under the waves. The water must already have risen more than a man's height above the former shore. This is a horrible thing, but I think the world is being swallowed up in water."

Chalara spoke up, "Whether it is or not, you will take us to the nearest approach to Varnach. I remember there was a river that ran down from the heights near there. Take us to the river. It will still be there, even if the waters have risen."

"But Great Lady, that river was not navigable. I could never take a boat up that approach."

"I know, but we will at least have a landmark that will guide us to Varnach. There was a road that ran near the river. We will take the road as best we can. Your job is to get us to the mouth of the river and land us."

"Mother," Melekan said, "I need to speak with you about one other thing. You told me of father's capture and that his brother Mulciber was bound in chains. You know that I brought him the great sword and shield and that Mulciber had been studying them. I must tell you that before I left, my father's brother took me aside and charged me to hurry back to you. Not to father, but to you."

"My uncle seemed very agitated and disturbed. He told me that I must take the sword and shield and find you. He said that a feeling of dread told him that he must not wait to tell me and I mustn't tarry. He said he did not understand why he had these strong feelings, but he knew that he must obey them," Melekan said.

Chalara said, "Your uncle had the gift of listening for the call of the gods. You should listen as well, for I've heard your father speak of the blood of the sons of heaven. Power lies in it, and not just in your youthful strength. Alas, his strength did not save him from those demons that came for him. Perhaps if he'd had this sword and shield, they would not have captured him. When my husband returns we shall give him these weapons. I only wish he was here to take them from us now."

The ship sailed the rest of that day and finally stopped near the mouth of a river that was a raging torrent of flood waters. They were forced to anchor a safe distance away from the river while still putting in as close up to the shore as possible. The sailors brought the ship in slowly to avoid the many submerged trees, rocks and other hazards. In the downpour, Chalara could see a hazy path that lead up out of the water, ran along beside the river and uphill off into the distance.

The sailor saw the direction of her gaze and said, "My Lady, you see the path beside the river that leads up toward Varnach. In times past, I could dock nearby at the pier that probably lies somewhere in the water below us. Now however, you see what we must do. We will keep the ship here, leaving enough crew to hold the ship safely. I and the others will accompany you and the Lord Melekan to Varnach."

"How do you know this is the right place if all of the landmarks are covered in water?"

"In part my Lady, by the smell of pitch. There is a large pool of tar that lies a short distance uphill near the river. Its distinctive smell has always served as a confirmation to travelers that they were on the right road to Varnach. If we are close enough to smell the pitch, then we are on the right track."

The sailors swam to the bank and Melekan stepped down into the water and waded ashore, carrying his mother in his arms. Her discomfort was getting greater by the hour and she knew that the birth could be upon her at any moment. Once on shore, the sailors fashioned a litter and carried her between the four of them. It was a welcome relief to get off of her feet. Chalara held tightly to her dagger, the gift of the King to her on the birth of Melekan, also made by his brother Mulciber. In her other hand, she took the nose-ring of the queen of Katal from her robe and clutched it to her breast, then put it on her wrist. Her husband's victory there would grant her strength as well. Though he was gone, his new daughter would carry the knowledge and the worship of Moloch, the warrior, the god with the strength of the mighty bull. She would raise this daughter to be a priestess of Moloch, her father. *She will make sure that the sacrificial fires never die. The fires will feed Moloch forever.*

They moved up the path and it often ran dangerously close to the swollen river. The waters came out of the banks and sometimes covered the road ahead, but drenched in the continuous downpour and already soaked to their skins with no chance to dry out, they simply waded into it. After some time of slow going, they stopped for a short rest. The smell of pitch was pervasive. They must be very close to the pit of tar. The warm air and constant rainfall would have made her sleepy if it hadn't been pounding on her so maddeningly. To make matters worse, she was definitely starting to feel the first regular, rhythmic contractions that presaged the birth of the child. She called Melekan to her side.

"My time has come. Find me a place that has a little shelter. The baby is about to be born."

Melekan looked about helplessly. There were no hills or boulders in this river's basin. Instead he found a large tree near the river's swollen bank that provided some shelter and spread his large sodden cloak in the branches. His mother's bearers arranged her litter under the cloak that Melekan had set as a roof of sorts. They tried to make her comfortable, but there was only so much they could do in the rain.

"What do you need from us, mother? We have no midwife, but we will help as we can."

"There is nothing for it now. It may yet be hours before the baby comes, still, you could prepare two lengths of twine. When the baby comes, we'll need to tie off and cut the cord. Also, see if you can find some wood that is still dry enough for a fire."

Melekan set the men to work on Chalara's requests. Soon she set her dagger next to the cords and lay waiting. First one and then another man returned without firewood, saying that everything they could find was sodden. Melekan muttered a curse and got up.

"I'll see if I can turn over a fallen tree and get something dry enough for a fire," he said and went ahead to look, sword in hand and shield strapped to his back. Drenching rain streamed from his face as he marched up the road. Chalara stayed behind, resting under the hastily improvised shelter. The four sailors squatted down beside her litter under the cloak.

The rain drummed down on the cloak and dripped through in streams. Chalara twisted as another contraction hit her. The pain went on and on. She breathed in short gasps and tried to blank her mind. The midwives had always said to ride the pains as a leaf on the wind, but this felt more like a leaf caught in a thunderstorm. *I don't remember it being this bad last time, and the baby isn't nearly as big as Melekan was! Of course I was much younger then.*

Finally the pains subsided and Chalara took long deep breaths and tried to ready herself for the next wave.

The men were looking at each other with worried expressions. Obviously they were concerned about what would happen next. None of them had ever helped at a birth and had no idea what would be required of them. Both of the men at the foot of Chalara's litter turned and faced toward the river as they talked in low tones.

One of the men stopped in mid-sentence and pointed at something in the water. He shouted and began to stand. His face turned toward Chalara and she saw the look of terror in his eyes and in his gaping mouth. Then a monstrous reptile lunged from the water at the river's edge and caught the man in its jaws, biting him in half at her feet. The head of the monster was fully as long as a man was tall and from what Chalara could see, the rest of its body was at least another six times that length. The other men jumped up and turned to flee. The monster surged forward at an amazing speed for a creature of such great size and grabbed the nearest of Chalara's bearers between its snapping, foot-long teeth. Chalara saw the hapless man's face clearly in that frozen moment: his wide eyes, lifted eyebrows, and lips thrust forward almost as if to whistle. She heard the crunching sound as the jaws crushed the man's rib cage. His eyes bulged and crossed. The monster wrenched sideways and then back, breaking the already dead man's spine, then lifted its head and swallowed the man whole. It turned back and grabbed the first of its kills and swallowed first the top half and then the bottom half of that man. The remaining two men ran screaming away into the drenched forest and away from the monster. Chalara's breath came in short, panting gasps as the next contraction hit her. The crocodile turned its head sideways, one eye fixed upon her and it seemed to smile, showing her its rows of fangs. Chalara screamed in helpless rage at the creature.

Suddenly, Melekan came roaring back, swinging the crystal sword, the shield on his left arm. He stabbed at the creature and it roared. Its tail lashed out and splintered a small tree. Melekan slashed at its side with the sword and opened up a large wound, but the monster ignored it. The croc's jaws snapped at Melekan's right leg. Some of the teeth sliced into his calf, but, bleeding freely, he still managed to jump back before the monster could crush the leg.

Chalara tried to crawl away but had no strength. Labor pains pressed down on her ferociously. It took all of her strength just to hold on and ready herself. She focused so completely on her breathing and the baby that she lost track of the battle that raged between her son and the monster.

The rain drenched them and blinded Melekan, but they fought, back and forth, Melekan slashing and stabbing with the great shining blade, the monster snapping its jaws and sweeping its tail across at the giant while trying to knock him from his feet. The fight moved twenty yards upstream, away from her, but Chalara could still see and hear the two slashing, snarling and snapping.

Melekan leapt back to avoid the gaping jaws that would have crushed both of his legs, stumbled and sank into the ground up to one knee. He shouted a curse and struggled to pull his leg back out of the ooze that had trapped him. He planted his other foot onto seemingly solid ground and it too gave way in a black, stinking, porridge of tar. The smell of pitch was suddenly overpoweringly strong. The bottom edge of the shield got stuck in the tar.

The monster crocodile lunged after Melekan. Unable to block the giant reptile with his shield, its teeth sank into his hip. Melekan stabbed with the sword and slid the blade in between its jaws and his skin, shearing away a dozen of its teeth in a shower of bone fragments. The monster roared and pulled back, its eyes red with fury and pain. Now mired up to both knees in the tar, Melekan was unable to dodge as the monster dove at him and latched onto his left upper arm above the shield. The monster rolled to one side and Melekan felt his arm snap. He screamed in pain and rage and bringing the sword point from above, stabbed through the creature's skull and down through its mouth and jaw. The beast thrashed and mired the two of them deeper and deeper into the tar. Melekan sank up to his waist in the pitch. The beast twisted in its death throes and pushed them both further into the tar. Blood gushing from multiple wounds, Melekan twisted and shouted toward Chalara, "Mother!" Using his one good hand, he reached toward her and grabbed at sodden branches that broke in his grasp.

Melekan tried to wedge himself up and out of the tar but sank up to his shoulders. In spite of his broken left arm, he held onto the shield with his left hand and tried to lift up with his right by pushing on the sword that was wedged in the beast's skull. Even if he pushed the beast further down, he hoped to push himself up and out. Instead he sank up to his neck in the black tar. The giant crocodile's tail finally sank completely under and a hideous sucking and slurping sound bubbled out from around it. Melekan screamed, "Mother!" and was swallowed in the thick tar.

Chalara screamed in the double agony of death and birth. *My son! Melekan!*

The birth pains were far worse than any she'd felt before. She felt her water break. The rain poured down on the forest around her and her screams were swallowed up in the watery sloshing and splashing of the continuous flooding. Chalara screamed again and again in loss and pain. Her son was dead ... the baby was coming ... and there was no one to help her. She held onto her dagger. She'd have to do this all by herself.

*The stories of Mercy Teller and Chalara will continue in <u>Darkness Visible</u>, planned for summer of 2014*

# ABOUT THE AUTHOR

John Grasham was born in Texas, grew up in the Los Angeles, California area, returned to Texas to finish high school and got a B.A. in Music from Abilene Christian University. He spent years working in Dallas, Anchorage Alaska, Houston, did time as a road-warrior consultant criss-crossing North America and now lives again in the Dallas area. He's been writing fiction since he was a teenager and creating stories to tell his kids and grandkids since they were old enough to sit in his lap.

www.ingramcontent.com/pod-product-compliance
Lightning Source LLC
Chambersburg PA
CBHW061541170626
46811CB00001B/49

* 9 7 8 0 9 8 9 8 7 0 7 0 2 *